Mourning Wood

Other Books by Daniel Paisner

Fiction

Obit

Nonfiction

The Ball: Mark McGwire's 70th Home Run Ball and the Marketing of the American Dream
Horizontal Hold: The Making and Breaking of a Network Television Pilot
Heartlands: An American Odyssey
The Imperfect Mirror: Inside Stories of Television Newswomen

Collaborations

The Price of Their Blood: Profiles in Spirit (with Jesse Brown)
Say What you Mean and Mean What you Say! (with Judge Glenda Hatchett)
Winners Make It Happen (with Leonard H. Lavin)
Last Man Down (with Richard Picciotto)
A Dozen Ways to Sunday (with Montel Williams)
The Hill (with Ed Hommer)
I'm Not Done Yet! (with Edward I. Koch)
You Have to Stand for Something or You'll Fall for Anything (with Star Jones)
Pataki: Where I Come From (with George Pataki)
Book (with Whoopi Goldberg)
True Beauty (with Emme)
Mountain, Get Out of My Way (with Montel Williams)
One Man Tango (with Anthony Quinn)
Citizen Koch: An Autobiography (with Edward I. Koch)
Exposing Myself (with Geraldo Rivera)
First Father, First Daughter (with Maureen Reagan)
Theo and Me: Growing Up Okay (with Malcolm-Jamal Warner)
America is My Neighborhood (with Willard Scott)

Mourning Wood

A Novel

Daniel Paisner

Volt Press
Chicago and Los Angeles

This novel is a work of fiction. Names, characters, places, and incidents either are the product of the author's imagination or are used fictitiously. Any resemblance to actual events, locales, or persons, living or dead, is entirely coincidental.

08 07 06 05 04   5 4 3 2 1

Library of Congress Cataloging-in-Publication Data

Paisner, Daniel.
  Mourning Wood : a novel / Daniel Paisner.
      p. cm.
  ISBN 1-56625-209-1
  1. Absence and presumption of death—Fiction. 2. Obituaries—Authorship—Fiction. 3. Biography—Authorship—Fiction. 4. Identity (Psychology)—Fiction. 5. Amusement parks—Fiction. 6. Actors—Fiction. 7. Maine—Fiction. I. Title.

  PS3566.A38M68 2003
  813'.54—dc21

                              2003013240

Volt Press
A division of Bonus Books
875 North Michigan Avenue
Suite 1416
Chicago, Illinois 60611

Printed in the United States of America

For Hana

The world is too much with us; late and soon,
Getting and spending, we lay waste our powers:
Little we see in Nature that is ours;
We have given our hearts away, a sordid boon!
This Sea that bares her bosom to the moon;
The winds that will be howling at all hours,
And are up-gathered now like sleeping flowers;
For this, for everything, we are out of tune;
It moves us not.--Great God! I'd rather be
A Pagan suckled in a creed outworn;
So might I, standing on this pleasant lea,
Have glimpses that would make me less forlorn;
Have sight of Proteus rising from the sea;
Or hear old Triton blow his wreathed horn.

--William Wordsworth

Contents

Fall

Winter

Spring

Fall

"Am I not a man? And, is not a man stupid?
I'm a man, so I married. Wife, children,
house, everything . . . the full catastrophe!"

--Zorba the Greek

Here

Here, now, the snaking two-lane road along Maine's rocky coast seems covered with a custom length of satiny black tarpaulin. The sky has turned quickly from not-too-bad to an ominous dark gray (there's even some fiery orange to it), and Terence Wood guesses the rest of his day has turned with it. Guy on the radio confirms this. Rog' at Large tells Wood and whomever else is listening to hunker down, lock it up right and tight, there's a full-blown, full-throttle storm warning in effect for the entire area. Get set, get warm, get toasty. (This is Rog' talking.) Get rockin' ready.

Wood—a hulking, tortured, celebrated presence, he fills the car like a deployed airbag—doesn't register the warnings. He hears them, but he's not listening. He's driving, in no particular hurry, to one of his cabins to decompress, read a couple scripts, bathe himself in Wild Turkey, avoid the phone, and it doesn't occur to him to cut his destination short until the storm does its business. It's not a prospect. There's another cabin in

New Hampshire; he'd have to double back a couple hours, but it's inland, in the mountains, and he's already called ahead and had a caretaker lay in supplies at the house in Maine, so there's no sense even thinking about it.

He's just driving, moving forward, not really thinking beyond basic traffic safety, but even that doesn't merit all that much attention. Passing scenery, passing thoughts barely enter one segment of his tortured brain before exiting another, as in a breezeway.

Already, the rain has started to fall sure and constant, like a good shower at a better hotel, the temperature dropped to where the water hugs the asphalt like a protective coating. Oh, it is nowhere near cold enough for ice, but the road is suddenly slick, and Terence Wood, even with his shift-on-the-fly four-wheel drive, even with the way he handles a car, is suddenly unsure. (There was that Le Mans movie he made, couple years back, did his own driving; nobody cared enough to go see it, but there it was.) He coasts through a still-fresh puddle, chassis-deep, and he instinctively stomps on his wet brakes to check that they are still working. They are, far as he can tell, but he pulls his black Pathfinder onto an insignificant tumor of road, which juts over the swelling sea like a diving board, and he stops there a moment, waiting for the hard rain to pass, making sure.

Car phone. The machine rings like a malfunction. He has to remind himself to answer it. Oh, yeah, this damn thing. Right. The radio mutes when Wood picks up the handset. His agent, out in Los Angeles. Something about a meeting at Paramount. The life of Vince Lombardi, the dead football coach. They want him for Lombardi, Wood learns through weather interference.

"What?" the agent mock-asks when Wood wonders about the part, "they want you for Bart Starr?" Then, in a swallowed aside, to no one else: "He's sixty years old, my famous friend, he thinks he can still play fucking Bart Starr." (Actually, he's sixty-five.)

Last week, they wanted Wood for Bear Bryant in something else. Something else, but the same thing.

"Looks sweet, Terry," his agent is saying. He hates it when they call him Terry. He hates it when they remind him he has a car phone. He hates it when they use words like sweet, or tasty, to talk about a deal. It's like fruit, the movies, to these people.

"Send it to me," Terence Wood says back, flat.

"You've had it two weeks."

"Send it to me again." Wood returns the handset to its sleek cradle and stares out across the swelling sea below. The phone makes an otherworldly beep to sound the end of the transmission, and Wood is still not enough used to the noise to keep from wondering about it. First he thinks there's another call, then he remembers. Oh. Right. That. There are all these noises, so many noises, there's no chance he could keep them all straight. He inventories his noises: the sick groan of his Hewlett Packard plain paper fax machine, the cartoon trombone of his Ungo Box car alarm, the steady bleat of the Polar heart rate monitor he wears strapped to his chest, even driving, even though his doctors say his heart's fine. There. What else? Oh. Right. There's this annoying chime thing going on—sometimes, when it wants—with his multi-function Timex Ironman watch.

And, always, there is the blather of the Mmes. Wood—Elaine, Anita, Petra—the women to whom he was once (and, in the case of his Pet, technically still) married. He puts the three women at the top of his list.

The phone, on speaker now, retreats to static. He's somehow knocked it loose trying to figure the thing back to its cradle, and the slip fills the car with a discordant hiss. Wood is not sure he minds the noise. It focuses him, but he doesn't move to right it, not right away. Right away what he does is nothing. Right away he just sits there, the rain patting down on the tinted glass of his windshield, now fogged with his breath and the weather, and he lets the static from his phone duel it out with the sky.

Looks sweet.

He lapses from dead ahead into all over the place, then he sets himself straight again. There. This is where Terence Wood is right now, what he's doing, and he's determined that the white noise remind him of his place. Perfect, he thinks. If his life were a movie, and it might as well be a fucking movie, the static and the rain would swirl into some ponderous New Age background music, and Wood's squinted reflection in the rectangle of rearview mirror would dissolve into a kind of static of its own. Instead what it does is glare back at him—empty, uncertain, tired—so he rewrites the scene in his head to conform with the one in the car. Here's the way it is, adjusted: Terence Wood's entire world, his very being, is inside this car, entombed in the cab of a Japanese import, and he is being kept here by everything going on outside. To him, now, the cellular phone is conspiring to keep him here, and it rings as both signal and testimony of his confinement.

He leans away from the mirror, pinch-rubs at the bridge of his nose, considers. Log of shit, he thinks. Spend enough time with these people and you start to think like them. And so, unlike them, he refashions his screen from the rectangle of tinted windshield—movie theater dimensions, just about—and this time he gets the big picture version. This time his point of view is through the glass across the horizon like he is at a drive-in, the world stretched out before him, for his amusement, just. The sky is darker than it was a few beats before, and Wood can't figure whether what's approaching will be like something out of a disaster movie, or nothing at all. The disaster movie part he gets from the weather and from too many years-ago break-fasts with Irwin Allen. (Remember, there was that story of the Hyatt Hotel fire, but it never got out of development.) The nothing at all he gets from everything else.

Wood cranks the defroster, adjusts the phone. He returns the machine to its cradle in time for it to ring again. It's like the rest of the world has been waiting for Terence Wood to plug himself back in, and now that he has, it wants him. He lets his own air leak from his pressed lips—an exaggerated actor's sigh. He also lets the phone ring, and ring, and ring, and with each pass, he tells himself he is getting more and more used to this new sound. It rings seven times, eight. It doesn't matter who it is. It's always someone.

═══

Here, in what passes for the *Record-Transcript* news-room, what passes for Axel Pimletz manages four column inches about a retired Brockton man—the self-celebrated "Prince of Mini Golf"—whose widow claimed he had played miniature golf courses in all fifty states, on four continents, and even once in Switzerland in the long shadows of the Matterhorn. Pimletz takes her at her word that there even is a miniature golf course in Switzerland in the long shadows of the Matterhorn. He's got nothing else to go on.

Earlier, he filed another four column inches in memory of a Fenway Park usher, somebody Gundersen, whose seating career dated to the Red Sox's glory, and who once, moonlighting, fetched a couple hot dogs for a bulging Babe Ruth during the slugger's last regular season game at Braves Field. The Babe, the story grows, never reimbursed the usher for his eats, although he did tip his cap in gratitude, which was something. Gundersen, who came to be known as Old Gundy as he himself took on in years at Fenway, wound up with a once-in-a-lifetime story for his twenty cents, which was something again. Pimletz gets to the twenty cents because hot dogs, he's told, were ten cents at Braves Field in 1935. He does the math himself. The research he leaves alone.

Pimletz, writing, rests his elbows on the arms of his ancient oak swivel chair, his wrists snapping up and down at his keyboard with each new thought. Sometimes, the entire chair snaps up and down with the same motion, the wheeze on the recline signaling his progress. When he gets going good, like he did late yesterday, reworking a wire service job on the Illinois woman who started the country's first temporary secretary agency (Steno Gals), Pimletz's fingers can flit across these keys like he is at a piano and knows how to play it, like the music is a part of him. Mostly, though, he just gets going, and he needs the empty clatter of his keys and the slow wheeze from his chair to remind himself he has something to do.

This last has become a theme for the recently fortied Pimletz—or, at least, a continuing concern. He needs something to do. He needs to feel like something, someone. He wants to matter. In fact, he wants to matter so much he tricks himself into believing he does. Sometimes, with no one on the other end, he'll even sandwich the phone between his ear and shoulder, for appearances. He is so hungry for some urgent business even the charade of urgent business will do.

The afternoon edition of the *Boston Record-Transcript*, still warm, lays halved at the corner of Pimletz's messed desk, a front-page editorial on the presumptive Republican presidential nominee for 2000 who is sort of waffling on the abortion issue riding the paper's curl. Next to it, in full view, a boxed photo of a young mother jogging along the Charles, her infant daughter in push, helmeted in a canopied runner's stroller, underneath the headline A BREAK IN THE ACTION—which may or may not have had anything to do with the mother-helmeted-daughter-jogging picture at the time it was committed to newsprint, which, in turn, may or may not have had anything to do with George Jr.'s waffling.

Lately, Pimletz has been thinking in song titles, and, as long he's on it, he wonders if maybe there's a way to make some money from the habit. "Waffling on Abortion." He's useless when it comes to lyrics (and most else), but he imagines there's a market for the kind of satire he spots in the paper every day and sets to music. Well, it's not music exactly, it's just song titles, but you've got to start somewhere, right? He's not even sure it's satire, but still. That guy on PBS, from Washington, stands by the piano in his bow-tie and sings his made-up political songs? It can't be he writes all of them himself. It can't be he's so overflowing with creativity that the stuff just bubbles forth. Probably he could use a good song title to get him started. "Waffling on Abortion." First it's this; then it's that; then it's something else. Waffle, waffle, waffle. Dee diddle dee dum. Or, something. "Tax This." "Put Away the Lox Spread, 'Cause Daddy's Got a Job." He's got a few of them filed away.

Pimletz means to take today's paper with him on his way to the Men's, but he forgets about it until he is nearly there, and, by this time, it is too late. By this time, he has already troubled the out-in-the-hall receptionist from her second application of shocking pink nail polish for the also-shocking *Record-Transcript* newsstand newspaperweight, the length and heft of which suggest one of those supermarket check-out line dividers, which has here been cutely and blatantly enlisted as a bathroom key chain, and he does not now wish to reinforce his mission by doubling back to collect any reading matter, still warm or no. Last thing he needs is to advertise his intentions, the time on his hands.

Instead, Pimletz moves forward, fits the key into the Men's lock, leans into the door, and heads for the middle stall, where he fists a couple coarse toilet paper squares and wipes down the chipped black seat. Another last thing he needs: a wet seat misted with whoknowswhat?

Sitting, his mind someplace else (or, more accurately, on nothing much at all), Pimletz finally notices his pants resting sadly in a small, clear puddle. Actually, it is just a section of pant doing this sad resting, and the garment is bunched now around Pimletz's ankles to where he cannot even guess at the corresponding, in-use location of the puddled piece, but the effect on his already sagged spirits is as if both trouser legs (and crotch! and seat!) had been soaked through. His impulse is to lift himself from the puddle, but this does not happen easily. His weight, squatting, is mostly thrown down and also forward, his legs held together at the bunched-up ankles, and Pimletz has to kind of tilt back onto his ass cheeks and pivot in a tight ball, kicking out his held-together legs to dry tile. For a moment, frozen in this awkward motion, he gets a picture of himself, and he is reduced by what he must look like. Worse, he soon notices the couple coarse toilet paper squares he fisted in preparation for this seating were the last to be had, at least in this stall, and he curses himself for this too-predictable turn. "Fuck you, Axel," he says, out loud, his voice reverberating off the also-chipped green tile walls, to where the small, empty room fairly echoes with his despair.

And so, in desperation, Pimletz considers his next move. First, he fits his gaze into the narrow opening by the stall's door hinges. He wants to make certain there is no one else about to see what he is about to do. What he is about to do is slide his pants back up around his waist, unbelted, and scamper to the adjacent stall to hunt for some toilet paper. This is his plan, and after he determines the Men's is otherwise empty, he pulls his pants up slowly, stops to notice the darkened wet spot which now alights at the back of his left thigh, and pinches his belt ends loosely together with his right hand. He peers out the stall door and makes for the safety of the one next to it, to his left, facing out. He does his scampering in a strange, low crouch, fearful of soiling his Looms, and hopeful the Groucho-like gait will somehow leave his ass cheeks sufficiently apart, or together, to keep his clothes sufficiently clean. This last is an afterthought to the scrambling Pimletz, but he puts it foremost. He tries to adjust himself accordingly, but he is not practiced enough at this, nor quick enough in a crisis, to know which way accordingly might be.

His plan works smoothly enough, except that the next stall turns up as empty as the one just abandoned, at least as far as coarse toilet paper squares are concerned. Pimletz, realizing, slams at the metal half-wall in frustration.

Stymied, he cranes his neck to the room's up-high windows, on the sills of which he seems to recall there sometimes being toilet paper packages, stacked. Today, though, there is nothing. He leans his head out the stall door and reminds himself there has been no overnight paper towel delivery, no storage area he might have overlooked, no sudden shift in bathroom maintenance strategy, nothing to magically replace the ridiculous hot-air dryers he has suffered for the almost-twenty years the newspaper has suffered him. The only paper product in Pimletz's limited view is yesterday's *Record-Transcript*, which rests haphazardly, and perhaps also magically, around this third toilet's stained porcelain base, most of it soaking in a sister to the clear puddle which had moments earlier claimed the back of his left pant thigh.

Pimletz stoops for the day-old paper—his salvation!—and it comes up heavier than he's used to, weighted by the water. Some of the paper is dry enough toward its middle, and Pimletz fumbles through the center tabloid pages as he drops his pants and backs himself onto the toilet. He's deep into the Classifieds ("Deep into Classified," now there's a song title), past Real Estate, approaching Weather. He's going by feel here, and not by content; he doesn't notice Weather turn to Around Town, doesn't realize he's torn a dry enough page from Obituaries and squared it to withstand a poke from his finger. It's not until he turns back and sees a picture of the bicycling Roxbury teenager, Allison Detcliff, sent off by Pimletz's own wooden prose after she was hit by an appliance store delivery truck driven by a guy blew two-point-something on his breathalizer, that he realizes what he's done, what he's doing: adding insult to insult, wiping himself not close to clean with what he does for a living.

Finished, he lets his mind return to its earlier wanderings. He doesn't know what he's got to think about, wonders where people come up with things to occupy their attentions. With Pimletz, it's like he has to be entertained, distracted, coaxed. He needs an agenda. He needs the diversion from the radio or television, something to read or to look at, else he just lapses into a dead zone.

Axel Pimletz—forty-three, never married, freshly bathed—is the kind of guy who reads the fine print on the backs of ticket stubs and the suggested "other uses" recipes on the sides of cereal boxes. Books you can pretty much forget; he's a whatever-is-lying-around kind of reader, whatever's on top. He's got no hobbies, no interests, no outside talents. His days are stuffed with too many minutes and not enough to fill the time. His mind, on its own, simply idles.

Squatting, Pimletz jump-starts himself with suggested topics. There's the upcoming presidential election to figure, but Pimletz does not know what to make of that whole business. His own paper says Bush should stand up for what he believes, whatever he believes, instead of treating the nomination like an entitlement, but it seems to Pimletz a man should do whatever he can to get whatever he wants. He believes this rule applies to the general human condition, as well as to politics. There's the economy, but that's a little too much for him. There's yesterday's terrorist bombing of that U.S. base in Dhahran, Saudi Arabia, but he hasn't yet read the still-warm newspaper left behind on a corner of his messed desk in the newsroom, so he doesn't know what to think about this, either.

His mother. There's always his mother. He's supposed to help rearrange her furniture one night this week. Thursday, he thinks. She's always rearranging her furniture. She doesn't have the patience or the resources to move, so she just moves things around. It's the very apartment Pimletz grew up in, and it hasn't ever looked the same more than three months running. His mother has a word for what she's got: *schpilkas*, which she tells her Axel is Yiddish for ants in her pants. Pimletz wonders what the Yiddish is for the opposite. Ants not in his pants.

From his mother, he somehow shifts onto the printer from Everett, the stamp collector from Beacon Hill, the Somerville lady known throughout her neighborhood for the elaborate Halloween decorations and spook effects she pulled every year. Ah. This is what Pimletz can think about, his fallen subjects. Morrison Gelb. Natick. Colon cancer. Eighty-six years old. (Song title: "Eighty-sixed at Eighty-Six!") Leaves eleven grandchildren and a third-generation doll wig business. It never would have occurred to Pimletz that three generations of the same family could pulse to the making of Barbie's hair, but to Morrison Gelb it was everything.

Pimletz sits in this way for a long time, wondering at other people's choices, other people's lives. He sits in this way long enough for his feet to turn to pins and needles. The dead numbness he likes—he even encourages it sometimes, with his not moving—but the pins and needles he can do without. They're like a test, he thinks, a summons. He wills himself still, afraid to move, waiting for the pins and needles to disappear. When they pass, finally, he stands to leave. He looks at his hands, his fingertips rubbed black with yesterday's wet newsprint. He reaches them to his nose, smells nothing but his primary hand smells.

Next he looks down at his shorts, which he is about to restore to their on position, and he notices his Groucho Marx impression was not nearly as successful as he had hoped. The pitiful ordeal of these last moments has left its mark, and still another last thing Pimletz wants is to sit around for the rest of the day in a pair of streaked underpants. He tugs at the already-started hole underneath the fraying label and rips at the fabric, which comes loose like he is tearing at an individually wrapped slice of cheese. This is the connection he makes. He's ripping at his shorts, thinking of processed cheese. He pulls the material from its elastic band and lets it drop to the floor beneath his legs. Then he steps through the left-behind waistband, which he stretches over his pants and shoes, and stuffs what remains of his sorry-smelling garment into the already-crowded waste bin fitted into the green tile wall. He does this without a thought.

===

Wood moves slowly—thirty, thirty-five, nothing crazy. He's trying to figure where he is, doesn't recognize the dark landscape in his headlights. Visibility basically sucks, plus he can't get his wipers going fast enough to do anything worthwhile with the hard rain, and his defroster hasn't managed much more than a few clear portholes. He pinches some cuff from his sweater into his right palm and wipes at the window with the trapped piece at the wrist. He steers with his left. He wishes he were home, dry, in bed, unconscious.

Here's what Vince Lombardi would do, now, driving: crack his window, let the cool, wet air help with the defrosting, slap himself awake. What would Lombardi care if he gets a little wet? Probably, he'd mutter something inspirational ("a quitter never wins, a winner never quits") and, inspired, plod on. Probably, he'd switch his wipers to intermittent to make the game more exciting, maybe even step down a touch on the gas, see what this baby can do in the slick.

Here's what Terence Wood does: he puddles his car into another one of these scenic lookout tumors, switches off the ignition, and leans back against his driver seat until it's in full recline. Then he looks up at his felted roof and wonders at the other side. Not the rain, but everything else. He wonders what buttons are being pushed on his behalf, what decisions are being made for him. He wonders at the disasters combusting at the other end of his car phone, plugged in. He wonders what he is doing, where he is going, why he bothers. Now that he gets his mind on it, there is nothing left for him to do, see, no more places to go, movies to make, substances to abuse. Consider: he's met everyone there is to meet—princes, Lakers, artists, first ladies, short track speed skaters, moguls. Models. Too many models. Lately, he meets a model and it doesn't even occur to him to take her home. This is true. It simply doesn't strike him. How can this be? When did this happen? Plumbing still works, it's not that, but it rarely dawns on him to open the spigots.

Now there's a solid blue-collar metaphor. He's got metaphors on the brain. Transitions. Symbolism. Some nit convinced Wood he could make some quick cash scribbling his life story—all of "veteran" Hollywood trades in this particular commodity—only now that he's pledged to do so, he can't quite get to it. His loose pages are like overworked writing class assignments. He doesn't know that he has anything to say. Publisher wants a laundry list of his conquests with locker room commentary, and, for this piece of gutless chauvinism, Wood will collect just over three million dollars, plus paperback and foreign. He's already spent the million he received on signing, so there is some incentive for him to get it over with, but even this inducement hasn't been enough to see him through. Either there's too much to tell, or not enough, or maybe Wood just doesn't have the stomach for the ordeal. True, there are enough compelling reasons to keep him from the writing, not the least of which is how dispiriting it has been to look over his shoulder at the life he has led, or is still attempting. He tries to remember when it was, precisely, he worked his way through all the people there were to fuck, where it was he lost his interest. He hasn't lost his appreciation for women, just his appetite, but this is bad enough.

Another new thing, also unsettling, is what's happened to his career, past four or five years, longer if he can be completely honest about it. Nothing, that's what's happened. Used to be he saw every script in town. Used to be he was right for everything, and if he wasn't right it didn't matter. They'd convince themselves he was right for it, or they'd make it right for him. Now all he's right for is dead football coaches. Once in a while, his agent entertains an idea for a sitcom, usually as somebody's grandfather, swaddled in domestic bliss and canned laughter, but these entertainments rarely live beyond a couple meetings and never beyond a development deal. Lately, he's even done voice-overs (he's the voice of the villain in an upcoming Disney project), and a Pizza Hut commercial.

When he really works, it's usually for the money, just. Like with this latest piece of shit, this live-action *Archie* comic book movie. *Everything's Archie*. What fuck talked him into that? Five million, plus points, to play Mr. Weatherbee, a fucking high school principal. Three scenes, three weeks, five million. The thing with Terence Wood is he's tied up in divorce nonsense with wife number three, and her lawyers are looking to skin him. Even without the ugliness of this latest divorce, he burns money like fuel, so he let his agent and the money convince him this *Archie* role would be like Brando's cameo in *Superman* or Nicholson's turn in *Batman*, even though it played out to be neither and, in some ways, a parody of each. Producers had him wearing this ridiculous monocle, said to look at the comic book, the guy always wore a monocle. Plus, they had him on crutches the entire time on the set because it was decided this Weatherbee character would be suffering from gout, which Wood has since learned is common only to high school principals of the comic book variety. In two of the three scenes, the writers had it fixed where he had his crutches kicked out from under him and was made to spin on his good heel and shake his sticks at the movie's madcap teens like an irascible codger, his monocle dangling from a cord around his neck like Harold Lloyd. *Why, you crazy kids. . . .*

The movie disappeared like something with Don Knotts in it, which Wood and the producers might have seen coming because, in fact, he was, in a small bit as the father of one of the story's principal teens, Jughead Jones. The preproduction hype was giant, but the finished product was a load. The critics who even bothered with the movie were all over it, and mostly what they were all over was Wood, mostly for just taking part. The fat guy with the thumbs up and down in

Chicago said that for the first time in Terence Wood's fabled and sometimes brilliant career, the actor appeared irreversibly lost and without tether. His words. It has only been a few months, and Wood is not entirely sure what the words mean in this context, but he guesses they will stay with him, always. He makes noise about not reading his notices, good or bad, but this one caught up with him on the car radio, where in addition to confirming Wood's own low opinion of himself and his life and his latest exertion, he also learned that the fat guy with the thumbs up and down seems to have found yet another outlet for his commentary, and that the only way he, Wood, will ever see his points is in video.

Wood, irreversibly lost and without tether, turns the key onto battery and reaches for the volume on the radio. He wants to distract himself from himself. He's lost a half-dozen stations since he started out, partly to the weather, but mostly to the long drive, in and out of range. He's anxious for some noise to clear his head. Anything. He hits the scan button and pulls the nearest signals through the other side of the Pathfinder's felted roof. Michael Bolton. The 1910 Fruitgum Company. Weather. Rog' at Large, with concert happenings. Dionne Warwick. Talk radio: a listener wanting to know if it's safe to travel to Israel, you know, after what just happened in Saudi Arabia, if there's any way to really know what's going on in the Middle East. Garth Brooks. Wagner. The Doors. Up-to-the-minute stock reports. Hendrix. Some caller wanting to know about replacing radiator fluid. June Carter Cash. Clapton singing about his kid. Garth Brooks again, or still.

He locks back onto Hendrix—"Purple Haze"—and, right away, he is transported to 1967, summer, around Monterey. Before or after, he can't remember, but the same time, place. The memories are like one long day. He sees himself sitting with Hendrix at the Mamas and the Papas' place in Bel-Air, this kick-ass mansion, and Brian Jones is there, Sharon Tate, Steve McQueen, some guy from the Monkees, and they're passing around a couple joints, dipping sliced apples into a shared jar of peanut butter, tabbing at some concoction called Owsley Purple, listening, probably, to the Beach Boys. Maybe *Sgt. Pepper's*, although maybe it was too soon for *Sgt. Pepper's*. Everyone is on the floor. (Fuck the furniture: everyone was always on the floor.) There's a pool out back, but it's limned with algae and no one's in it. Peter Lawford is droning on about RFK, Mama Cass is splayed beneath a length of couch like a big-game throw rug, and John Phillips is nursing a bottle of Crown Royal. Someone's watching the television news with the sound turned off.

The scene unfolds for Wood like he is still in its middle. He is trying to convince Brian Jones that the monsoon season in Vietnam is like a symbol for America's involvement in the war. It is all so amazingly clear to him, he doesn't get why no one sees it this way. "We're like a fucking storm, man," is how he puts things, "but all we do is water damage." He remembers this like it was on video.

"Yeah," a convinced Brian Jones manages. "Absolutely. A fucking storm."

Hendrix, here, on the radio, brings it all back—"'s'cuse me, while I kiss the sky"—and it doesn't take

Wood more than a couple riffs to realize he has peopled his flashback with the dead and gone. More, the dead are still relevant, now that he thinks about it. Well, maybe not relevant, he weighs, underneath a mounting haze of his own, but at least they're not redundant. They still matter, somewhere, to someone. Most of them, anyway. Sharon Tate. Peter Lawford. McQueen. Every one of them dead except for Papa John, and that guy from the Monkees, and me, maybe Glen Campbell was there too, and we might as well have checked out with the rest of them. No tether to those who haven't mattered since.

The images resonate, and Wood gets to wondering what Hendrix's life would have been like had he lived, and he pictures a sixty-year-old guy with a gut (and, perhaps, a still-wide bandanna), guesting on *Will and Grace*, running the Chicago Marathon with Oprah, picking up his guitar for the first time in fifteen years. Or, he's got Hendrix sitting across the desk from Larry King on CNN, plugging a boxed CD retrospective, which includes, inexplicably, a medley of Cole Porter songs. Maybe he's playing Atlantic City, or campaigning for Bill Bradley, or hawking Pepsi ("you've got the right one baby, uh-huh"), or laughing it up with Jay Leno. Maybe he's writing his memoirs.

Wood steps out of the car. It is still raining, hard, but the air inside the Pathfinder has become oppressive. He needs to escape it before it chokes him. Standing, he rolls his neck to the dark clouds, and the rain hits him full and cold. He drinks it in. He is out of the car only a few beats before he is soaked through his clothes, his long mane of thinning gray hair pressed slick against his round head. "Excuse me," he says, loud, nearly chanting, "while I kiss the sky." It doesn't sound at all like singing.

He struggles onto the hood of the car and manages to stand. The thin metal pops and sags with his weight, and when he is sure enough of his footing, he reaches out with both arms. He means to take it all in: the heavens, the rain, the choppy waters below. It's a fucking monsoon, he thinks, but he defies it. He's taken Hendrix at his word, he wants to embrace whatever epiphany he's made for himself, hug it close enough so that it will never slip away again, not ever. He wants to defy Petra and her lawyers by not being on the other end of their phone calls. He wants to kiss the sky. He's left the radio on and his nearly chanting nearly coincides with Hendrix's. He reaches back to the vinyl roof and is surprised to feel the vibrations through his hand. The music pulses through him. It is as if in reaching back to the roof of the car, he is also reaching back over a quarter of a century to touch whatever it was he once had, whatever it was could still touch him. Or has. Or will.

══

"Hey, Axel," Hamlin tries, hounding, "how'd'ja like my new headband?"

Pimletz is at his desk, leaned close enough to his display terminal for the receding hairs on his head to nearly respond to the static. He is lost in a game he sometimes plays to fill the time. About the only thing he is good at is finding ways to fill the time. He inches closer to the screen to determine the precise point of static exchange, and he tries to imagine his hairs responding to the pull. He's worked on this. When he does it with his forearms, he can actually see his hairs start to rise, and he is sometimes able to lock the exchange in mid-motion, in a static-electric freeze-frame.

The greeting breaks Pimletz's concentration. He pulls away from the screen, looks up, and sees the guy next to him, Hamlin, back from a smoke or the Men's with a ridiculous white band stretched against his too-thick hair. He looks like John McEnroe used to look, Pimletz considers, back when he used to pitch tantrums instead of financial services. Thick, curly hair, belted like a bale of wheat. Of course, Hamlin only looks this way up top, now, with the headband. Rest of him is fat around the neck and middle. Only exercise he gets is in his fingers, from the way he works his phones and his keyboard. Truly, the guy gets more done in a day than Pimletz can manage in a month, and what eats at Pimletz is the way Hamlin rarely leaves his desk to accomplish it. It's all right there. Hamlin can work the phones like no one else in the *Record-Transcript* newsroom, no one is close, and the kicker is when he finally bangs out his stories, it's like he's taking dictation. The words just burst from what he knows. Zip. Splat. Done.

The thing between Pimletz and Hamlin has been going on six or seven years, and what it is has been mostly Hamlin's doing. What it has been mostly is Hamlin riding Pimletz about anything he can find, whenever he can find it. Guy's never wanted for ammunition. Sometimes the riding is about Pimletz's failure to escape the obit desk after twenty years, his inability with women, his inertia. Sometimes it's about a foot in Pimletz's mouth regarding a colleague or some other newsroom transgression. (Once, Pimletz was goofed into calling an already-humiliated Mike Dukakis for a comment on the accidental drug overdose of his wife, Kitty; Hamlin got a good ride out of that one.) Mostly, it is just a calling to embarrassing attention Pimletz's occasional lapses in judgment, some of which have passed into lore.

Today's ammo is just about nuclear, and it is stretched across Hamlin's creased brow. "So?" he tries again. "I'm waiting."

"For what?" Pimletz doesn't know, yet. Two and two have never been easy for him.

Hamlin points to his silly headband, and, with his in-shape fingers, highlights the block-lettered PIM from the Chinese laundry Pimletz sometimes uses. Pimletz finally makes the connection, quick on his feet or no. What's not to connect? He gets an eyeful of what used to be the waistband to his underwear, stretched now and advertising his shame—PIM—and he shrinks from it. Jesus, Pimletz thinks. Fuck me dead and out the door. I'm just a humiliated piece of shit.

In a beat, he credits Hamlin with puzzling together the whole sorry bathroom episode from a few moments earlier, working backward from this thin piece of evidence. Then he thinks, wait, I'm being paranoid, right? This is paranoid. It could be anything, this PIM. How does a guy like Hamlin make the leap from something like that to me? Where does that come from? Not even

Hamlin's mind works like that. No way he knows about before. Then he thinks if he pretends not to get it Hamlin'll go away; it's never fun for him unless he gets Pimletz going.

"What?" Pimletz says, trying to salvage what there had been of his dignity. He means to play it calm and interested.

"Don't give me what," Hamlin says.

"No, really, what?"

"This," Hamlin says, playing at exasperated. "This." He slips his finger under the waistband, lets it snap back against his thick hair. The noise is not what he was looking for, so he tries it again. "This is what."

Pimletz pretends to consider Hamlin's fashion statement. "Okay," he says, "fine, it's you."

"Oh, come on, Axel," Hamlin says, mischievous, not giving up. "You gonna sit there and tell me you don't know what I'm talking about?"

"You haven't said anything. You're not talking about anything. What are you talking about?"

"Why don't you tell me?"

"Tell you what?"

"Again with the what?"

"Again with the what."

"You have nothing to say to me?"

"What do you want me to say to you? I don't know what you're talking about. What else do you want me to say to you? I'm missing something, right?"

"Fuck, yeah, you're missing something," Hamlin says. He lifts the band from his head and places it on the desk in front of Pimletz. "This. You're missing this." Then, "Tell me this isn't yours." He's got a smile on his face only Pimletz recognizes. "Claim it, and I leave you alone."

Pimletz examines the band. He holds to his plan. "Still don't know what you're talking about," he says, returning the evidence. "Where'd you get this?"

Hamlin takes the waistband, then he takes the step or two between himself and Pimletz. "In the trash, where you left it," he says.

"So now you're going through the trash?"

"Nothing to go through. It was just there, right on top, hanging out." Hamlin starts to twirl the band around his index finger like a lariat.

"Hamlin."

"Tell you what, Axel," Hamlin says. "Let me see your shorts." He stops with the twirling and makes a sudden reach for Pimletz's belt, the kind of locker room antic that doesn't usually happen in the *Record-Transcript* newsroom. "You got any on, I leave you alone."

Pimletz hadn't figured on this. "Don't be an asshole," he says, squirming away.

"Just lift your shorts."

"Enough," Pimletz says. He thinks about slapping his hands against the desk in a show of firmness, but he doesn't have this in him.

"Enough what?"

"Enough," Pimletz says, broken. "It's mine. Okay. It's mine. That what you wanted?"

Hamlin pulls at the elastic garment like a rubber band, snaps it at his prey. It lands softly on Pimletz's humiliated, piece-of-shit head and, for a moment, dangles in front of his face like a wild For Sale tag in a hat store. "No, Axel," Hamlin says, gesturing to the landed waistband in that same moment, "that's what I wanted."

===

The rain is bucketing down on Terence Wood, still on the hood of his parked car, still locked on the way things used to be. Hendrix has passed onto Smashing Pumpkins, and Springsteen, and news on the hour. Keith Richards, solo. The Presidents of the United States: she's in your head, she might be dead. Wood no longer hears the music or feels the bass thumping through his car. He's lapsed into his own meditation, and, in his head, the storm has become mere color, detail. It's there, but it doesn't bother him. If he were wearing his trademark baseball cap (plain, gray, corduroy), the water would be pouring from the bill in rivers thick enough to fill one shot glass before he could down another, but the rain does not touch him in any way more direct than as stage direction. *Camera pulls back to reveal WOOD, sitting on car, weathering the hard rain like a soldier. Camera pans to WOOD's P.O.V., across the dark horizon, into nothingness.*

The dirt beneath Wood's Pathfinder has been quagmired by the downpour. The front tires, pulled into a just-started ditch about three feet from the rusted metal rail rimming the lookout parking area, have been all but swallowed by the pool of muddy water that has, in turn, essentially filled where the just-started ditch used to be. The front bumper is kissing a section of metal railing with the message "Get to Know Us!" spray painted onto its crenelated surface, the bright graffiti mixing with the rusted grunge in a breath of inner city along Maine's rocky coast.

Wood emerges from his meditation long enough to fix on the graffiti—he saw it when he pulled up and he is pulled back to it—and, on impulse, he slides down the sloped hood for a closer look, with an exaggerated adult, "Wheee!" The momentum from his slide is more than he expected, and he is nearly thrown from the lookout's edge before he catches himself. He lands in a tributary to the puddle surrounding his tires, filling his essentially new Adidas Torsion Response Class running shoes with a cold, wet muck he cannot, at first, place. Oh, yeah, that, he realizes. Mud. Of course.

Wood pulls close, balances against the rusted railing, but it comes loose with his full weight. It doesn't snap away suddenly or dangerously, but he has targeted a section of railing that has been rotted by neglect and by the elements, and it refuses to support his leaning. It leans itself, with him. If there were sound effects, the railing would bend away from Wood with the creek of a door in a haunted house.

He stands and kicks at the still-fastened end of the railing with his muddy Adidas. It breaks free with his second try, and, with a third kick (and the same bluster that went into its spray painting), he sends the loose section over the edge of the seaside crag from which the wheee-d! Terence Wood, only moments earlier, had rescued himself and from which he is now not quite so protected as he earlier had been, even though earlier there had only been this rusted-through section of railing charged with his safekeeping. Still, he feels exposed, vulnerable, where earlier he didn't know to consider either. He imagines the descending flight of the kicked piece of metal, catching air through its ridges, slapped by the harsh winds against the rocky hillside, alternately floating and hurtling down the couple hundred feet to the stormy sea below. He figures how long it will take to reach the water—thirty-two feet per second, per second, he remembers—then he waits it out, listens.

When he hears nothing and tires, he backpedals to the driver door and fumbles with the handle. He pulls the door open. The car rocks with the heavy, powerful motion. It rocks, too, when he returns himself—also heavily, powerfully—to the driver's seat. There is sudden give to the wet earth, and the car shifts uncertainly with this new burden. Again, with sound effects, he guesses he'd be hearing the avalanche crunch of moving rock and wet soil, the coming loose of ground beneath his treads, his own difficult breathing, amplified. Wood's drenched clothes flash cold against his back when he leans against them, and he sits up straight, away from the leather seat.

Suddenly, Wood is thrown to the dash with a lurch. Actually, it is not all that sudden, and he is not quite thrown. It isn't even much of a lurch, but the effect is the same. It happens, really, in a strange, slow motion, like an action sequence drawn out for special effect, but it is very definitely a change in position. The weight of the Pathfinder, and Wood's within it, is too much for the wet, giving ground, and, as he bends forward to free his cold, clinging shirt from his back, the car shifts with him, makes a new place for itself on the changing terrain with an overstated inhale. There. Better. It doesn't occur to Wood he might be in any danger, not at first, and when it finally does, he doesn't move too swiftly to save himself. He's afraid to upset the uneasy balance the vehicle has just now achieved, and so he slithers himself tentatively along the leather seat—there, okay, just a bit more—pushes up and out against the slammed door, and reminds himself of the DeLorean he still keeps in one of his garages, somewhere.

He steps from the cab and into the mud, and the car lurches again with the shift. This time, it pitches to its passenger side at an even sharper angle, and the driver door is slammed shut by this new perspective. Without its hulking, tortured, celebrated presence of a driver, the car settles into its new space and is still.

Wood gets a thought. He doesn't know where it comes from, but his head is like a lit pinball machine with the idea. There is no ignoring it and no thinking it through. It is something to do, and the only thing to do, both. And so, also on impulse, he slogs to the rear of the car and begins to push. It's a struggle, at first, to claim his footing, to get a grip against the slick of rain on the back bumper, but he manages a kind of traction. He is giddy with what he's doing, drunk, and he doesn't stop to think. He is caught up in it, transported. He puts his full weight into the effort, but the car doesn't move. He does this again. He pulls a muscle in the small of his back (his diagnosis) and straightens himself to ease the pain.

Okay. He needs a strategy. He doesn't mean to think too much about this, but it appears now he must. Think, he coaches himself. Think: all four tires are encased in a thick of mud, the parking brake is on, and these are likely inhibiting his progress. Wood, realizing, returns to the cab, lifts the slammed driver door, unlocks the brake, and throws the car into neutral. He lets the door return itself to its foundation.

He figures the way to move this baby is with an easy rocking motion to help the treads get a new hold. He's seen this done, on location in Santa Fe, when a sprinkler valve burst and flooded a sound truck into place. One of the grips, who had a towing business as a sideline, suggested this course, so Wood retreats to the rear and presses his weight against the back bumper, like he is testing the shocks, like he was shown. The Pathfinder bounces to his considerable shifting weight, up and down, and soon it gets going side to side as well. Up and down. Side to side. Up and down. From a distance, it looks like a car full of sweaty, his-and-her teens parked on some Inspiration Point. There's another not-quite lurch, slow-motion sudden, and he strains to help it along, but the tires are bogged in the mud and not going anywhere.

He'll have to gun it, he determines, already having put more thought into this act than it comfortably should have required. Oh, he hasn't yet thought it through to its other end, but it's coming. He once again races to the driver door and lifts it open. This time, he climbs in and braces his left arm against the heavy door to keep it from shutting. With his right hand, he turns the key, puts the car into gear. His ass is half on the driver seat, half off. His left leg is anchored in the mud outside his door, ready to spring him clear, his right stretched under the dash. He stomps on the gas pedal, thinking of Lombardi, thinking, "Get to Know Us!"

The Pathfinder, gunned, responds to Wood's loose plan like a bad idea. The tires spin wildly, like the car is on blocks. The clean roar of engine is exhilarating, and it rubs against the laboring tire noises to where Terence Wood almost forgets what he's doing, why. Actually, now that he's on it, he's got no idea why. Why not is as far as he's gotten. Why the fuck not?

He gives up on the gas. He'll have to try something else. A board. Yes, that's what he needs, a block of wood, something flat and hard to wedge beneath his tires. He searches the car. About the only flat, hard surface he can find is his leather briefcase, which contains what there so far is of his memoirs. There isn't much, mostly fits and starts, some notes, one full chapter about his first wife, Elaine, a book he's supposed to be reading called *Writing Well*, a long memo from his publisher.

Wood steps out of the car and around to the front passenger side. He crouches. He burrows a space in the mud just ahead of the tire and fits his briefcase into it, like a ramp. Then he walks back to the driver door and resumes his position, one foot in, one foot out. He's ready to go either way. He guns it again. The tires spin wildly again. Nothing. He gives it another try. He doesn't know what he's doing, but he's deep into it now, can't redirect himself. This is what he's doing. This. Here. Now.

Finally, one of the tires catches traction, and then another, and before Wood can out-think himself, the car moves forward. It kicks out from under him, although this too happens in slow motion, and in this long unfolding he has time to step his right leg and half-ass from the car and with his right hand on the wheel point the machine to the new opening in the metal railing. It all happens in an instant, but it is an instant protracted, drawn out in Terence Wood's head to where he can hear his own heartbeat, bury his past, conceive his future.

In the next moment, on normal speed, he imagines his two tons of metal and leather and state-of-the-art Bose sound system careening to the choppy sea. He gets a clear picture in his head. Then he cuts to a memory of his son, Norman, sending one of his miniature Matchbox racers down the spiral staircase up at one of the cabins (possibly New Hampshire), watching it bound, and shatter, and separate at the fittings, and then he cuts back to the present, big as life, his black Pathfinder spinning front over rear, plunging, thirty-two feet per second, per second, thundering down the couple hundred feet to the water, losing its rear axle against a stone promontory along the sea wall below. He wants desperately to hear the explosion, or splash, something, to give emphasis to what he has just done. He braces for the impact.

Wood on Down

Axel Pimletz is so infrequently at his best in the morning he couldn't place it if it stared back at him after a
shave. Still, usually, it takes him a couple hours to at
least reach his norm. Even he will concede this. Most
mornings, it is all Pimletz can do to peel himself from
bed, stumble into the shower, curse the clogged drain
that leaves him wading by the time he is through, towel
off, find some outfit that isn't too hideous or too like
what he wore the previous day, reach into the fridge for
the bowl of cereal he poured and milked the night
before (he likes his Frosted Flakes sogged, substantial-
ly), and depart on his walk from the mouth of Storrow
Drive, through Back Bay, across the Common, past the
blink of theater and red light districts, and on to the
dilapidated *Record-Transcript* building. When he
arrives, he is still not there. Not necessarily. Not yet.

On this morning, it takes longer than usual for
Pimletz to achieve speed. There are reasons. First,
he'd forgotten to replenish his Flakes—yesterday,

after work—something that had been on the internal To Do list he is always misplacing, so he must leave the house hungry, and without roar. Second, he can't find a reasonable-looking tie with enough brown in it to suggest anything at all of his too-brown slacks and less-brown sports coat, the miscalculations in style to which he'd earlier committed. Third, it's raining, hard, second day running, and Pimletz's feeble umbrella proves far more efficient at inverting itself against the accompanying hard wind than at keeping him dry.

Fourth, and most troubling, he gets to his desk and discovers no one has died. Well, not no one, exactly, but no one good. Better, no one good enough for the *Record-Transcript*. Think of it: not a single newsworthy human being has perished in the hours since yesterday's routine. This happens, sometimes, but it is never a welcome thing, at least not where Pimletz and his already brittle sense of self-worth are concerned. It stops him dead, leaves him wondering what he's doing, what he's done, what's expected. This very public not having anything to do strips him of all identity and purpose, or any semblance he's been able to manage of either, and, for a moment, he allows himself to wonder if anyone would notice if he slipped out the back door and took up thumb wrestling. When he is faced with nothing to do and an entire working day in which not to do it, it is too much for him. He can't bear it. In truth, Pimletz would rather have something not to do than nothing to do at all, so he looks to pull some poor soul from the paid death notices, some belovedwife-lovingmotheradoredgrandmothercherishedfriend, and set up her passing for the complete treatment. Something not to do.

Yes. Here. Sylvia Fleishmann. Arlington. Died in her sleep on the night of her one hundredth birthday after a brief illness. Mourned, for eight dollars an agate line, by her temple sisterhood, the B'nai B'rith, her adoring grandchildren, and an organization seeking a cure for juvenile diabetes. Four ads. Not bad. One for each quarter-century—Pimletz does the math again—and one of them for pretty decent money. Normally, according to the newspaper's archaic guidelines for full-blown obituary consideration (a dedicated career; noted service or contribution to the community; historic, unusual, or otherwise celebrated accomplishments), the Sylvia Fleishmanns of greater Boston would be passed over by the Axel Pimletzes, even with their four paid death notices, but her fleeting status as a centenarian combines with her fortuitous timing and vaults her into consideration. If it's good enough for Willard Scott, it's good enough for the *Record-Transcript*. Plus, there's no one else.

Okay, so the lady is only worth a couple column inches, one hundred years or no. Pimletz, on hold with a spokesperson from Arlington Pines, the nursing home where Sylvia Fleishmann did her passing, works his lead in his head. He does this without thinking. Something about a finish line, oddly. A race, a finish line. All the time in the world, and this is what he comes up with. He fixes on the hackneyed image, likes the picture he gets of a noble old lady breaking the tape at the end of a long ordeal, maybe in a wheelchair, maybe with a walker, fists punched out or high in last-gasped exultation. Twenty years cranking the same obits for the same people, give or take, and now it has come to this. It's like a *New Yorker* cartoon, the way Pimletz figures it. As he labors to transform this picture of a dead woman he has never seen and knows nothing real about into his own flat prose, he reminds himself why he has never moved from his place of indistinction at the newspaper: he writes like a greeting card. That, and he's got the instincts of plankton.

"Any hobbies?" Pimletz tries, when the Arlington Pines person returns. If he had a dollar for every time he's asked the same of countless family members or nursing home spokesfolks, he'd have enough, say, to reupholster the salvaged armchair in his living room.

"Like what?" he gets back.

"Like, did she have any hobbies? Special interests? What kinds of things did she enjoy?" These follow-ups, too, are part of the drill, and they tumble from Pimletz's chapped lips as if they know the way.

"Well, most of our clients are involved in our crafts program," the woman on the other end reports, cheerfully. "We have a very talented local artist, comes in two times a week. That the kind of thing you're looking for? I believe Mrs. Fleishmann was active in that."

"How active is active?"

Pimletz gets an ear about Sylvia Fleishmann's fondness for crazy-colored pot holders—she liked to spell crazy with a *K*, the spokesperson tells. Recently, Sylvia Fleishmann fashioned a reasonable likeness of the South Fork ranch from the television show *Dallas* out of popsicle sticks and Lincoln Logs, with pápier mâché landscaping. Also recently, she had been helping to restore some of the antique quilts donated or otherwise discarded to the Pines by some of the other clients and their families.

He decides to go with the quilts and, going, loses the piece at the top about the finish line. Somehow, staring back at him in dull green letters from the dusty screen of his video display terminal, the notion of poor Sylvia Fleishmann, done up like Granny in *The Beverly Hillbillies*, breaking some badly metaphored tape of life and then dropping dead in front of a viewing stand of up-next Arlington Pines clients, seems to Pimletz not the way to go. He knows this much. He plays it straight, clean: cause of death, the quilts, lifelong interests, funeral arrangements, surviving family. Maybe he can get Volpe to dress it up with a picture; the woman at the nursing home said this Sylvia Fleishmann was stunning. Her word. Said they've got a shot of her posed next to the popsicle stick ranch, taken for the nursing home newsletter, shouldn't be any trouble to pinch it for a couple hours.

Pimletz slugs his copy—"OBIT.SF"—and sends it off to be digested by the *Record-Transcript*'s computer system. That's the way it registers for the once-again-resting Pimletz, like he's feeding the institution that in turn feeds him. True, all he's got to dispense are crumbs, but this is how it translates.

It's been about a dozen years since management finally acknowledged the technological revolutions of the computer age, nearly all of which remain a mystery to Pimletz, who goes through his motions, still, as if for the first time. He consults his user's guide and punches out the appropriate commands on his keyboard, but he's got no real idea what happens to his copy when it leaves his screen. It disappears, for him. He knows it winds up on Volpe's screen, and at the copy desk, and, eventually, enchantedly, in the newspaper, toward the back of the Metro section, where it looks vaguely familiar, like a distant cousin to what he'd first written, but he doesn't know where it goes in between.

When he started out, whenever the hell that was, he'd bang out his stories on a manual typewriter on special "six-plicate" paper. What Pimletz misses most about those days is the way he'd finish a take, pull it from the carriage with grand importance like everyone else, rip the sheets from their perforated tabs, and crumple the fallen carbons, ink-side down. He'd pile up this great mound of fallen carbon balls. After the last take, he'd spread out his six-sheets and start collating, happy for the chance to attach some overwrought public significance to what he'd just done. Then he'd hold up his hands like a surgeon after a scrub and march significantly to the Men's to see about the carbon stains on his fingers.

Now all that's left for him to do is beam his copy across the newsroom—zip!—with no hard proof he's done anything at all, no smudge on his hands, no way to remind Hamlin and the rest of his abutting, and occasionally onlooking, colleagues that he does, in fact, have a role at the newspaper and that he does, also occasionally, play at it. Now, for appearances, he's developed this flowery final key stroke (a poke, really), which he displays every time he logs off his computer, or feeds his copy to the hungry newspaper, or punctuates an uncommon lead, and which he hopes signals similar heat and relevance to the rest of the newsroom, even though he knows it is not the same and that it probably does not. Now, for Pimletz, it's his word against theirs, and the only time he gets to hold up his hands like a surgeon after a scrub is in front of his own mirror, alone, working to imperfection the bad Ed Sullivan impression he will never share.

Resting, Pimletz loses himself in the rhythms of the newsroom. He takes it all in, but not to where it actually might register. There is a dull hum, not emerging from any one place or any group of places, but rather from the coalescing of activity around the large room. For Pimletz, there is no single, identifiable noise, just an insistent purr, like an engine. It is the noise of friction, activity, consequence. He likes to think he contributes in some important way to the general newsroom purring, but, as he checks himself, he realizes he is not making any noise at all. Even if his thinking made noise, he'd be quiet. He's done for the day, and what he's done has hardly mattered. He shuffles some papers in a show of consequence and logs on the in-house Lotus Notes bulletin board to see if there are any messages for him. It is late morning—Jesus, he only killed a couple hours with this Fleishmann obit!—maybe someone's wondering if he's free for lunch. Scrolling, he thinks, look busy, look busy, look busy.

Bill, in Classifieds, is selling his x-country ski machine. Cheap.

There's an office pool seeking wagers on whether Hillary Clinton will wind up in Westchester or Manhattan. (It looks like Long Island is pretty much out of the running.)

And here's one lingering from a few years back: the sports department peddling "Free Jack Clark!" bumper stickers—three bucks each, two for five—looking to raise funds for its annual bender on the back of the financially and otherwise troubled former Red Sox slugger who squandered both his personal fortune and his ability to hit a baseball in the same season. No one thinks to delete the posting, just as no one would think to display the bumper sticker anymore.

Pimletz scans the mess of unsigned drivel and mock headlines—HONK IF YOU LIKE SEXUAL HARASSMENT, BABE; NICE WEATHER WE'RE HAVING; THE CELTICS DRAFTED WHO?—until the screen finally flashes with a bulletin for him: "Hey, Axel. My dog died."

He gets this shit all the time. He looks up from his screen and sees Hamlin, next desk over, doubled up, laughing. Fucker doesn't even have a dog.

"He have any hobbies?" Pimletz hollers, playing along.

"What hobbies?" Hamlin shouts back.

"Like, you know, hobbies. What were his interests?"

Hamlin: "He liked to lick his own balls. That a hobby? That something you can use?"

=====

Here is Norman Wood, rail-thin, crew-cutted, twenty-three, smoking Camels, deconstructing *The Godfather*, lost in the swirl of making movies. Well, okay, he's not exactly lost and he's not exactly making any movies, but he is in the swirl. Here, in one of the screening rooms at New York University, he gets to sit in the dark with a dozen other pale and darkly dressed students and trade bombastic, overblown comments on what the people at NYU like to call the literature of the screen. He listens with a detached importance as the professor, a smallish man with smallish credits, offers his take on the American family, as seen through the eyes of Francis Ford Coppola.

The Godfather, to this smallish man, is all about the strength of family to withstand the disintegration of society. Anyway, that's what registers for Norman. He can't concentrate. He can't get past the way this guy stops and starts the picture to make his various points, the way he talks over the scenes to narrate what he thinks is really going on. This is where Francis does this, he tells, and here you can see Francis is trying to say that. He calls him Francis.

About the only things for Norman to get off on are that he is here at all—in film school, about to matter— and that they let him smoke. Everywhere else in Manhattan, you can't watch movies and smoke at the same time, at least not in a theater, but Norman lives to smoke in theaters, to look away from the screen at odd moments and catch the swirls of second-hand smoke as they pass through the light from the projector. He loves how, sometimes, an image from the film catches a cloud of smoke in such a way that he can actually see the light patterns filtered through the air above his head. It is, he thinks, an apparition of an apparition, the once-removal of an image that is already once-removed. It is the way movies were meant to be seen, the way he watched his father watch the rough cuts of his pictures back at the Woodman's house in the Hills.

The Godfather he can do without. It's not like it held any kind of defining screen moment for him, and he can do without the stopping and starting and dissecting the thing to its component parts. It's just a picture, and, anyway, he knows more about it than this smallish man. Probably, generally, he knows more about making pictures, about reaching into the heart of a purely American darkness and finding an essence of humanity and compassion and artifice and whatever the hell else it is a good movie can help you find. Absolutely, he knows movies. He's lived movies. Shit, he grew up in better screening rooms than this.

The smallish man interrupts the movie again, only this time to engage in whispered conversation with one of the department secretaries, who brings so much light into the room with her that the image on the screen is nearly washed out.

The professor looks up from his whispering and calls out to Norman. "Mr. Wood," he says. "It seems you have a phone call." He holds out a pink While You Were Out message slip.

"It's his agent," mocks Mona, an androgynous looking friend of Norman's, whose pictures are to the literature of the screen what Woody Allen is to estrogen. "He's got Warners on the line with a three-picture deal."

Everyone laughs but the smallish professor, who looks at his watch and makes notes on the legal pad resting on his angled podium. Norman collects his backpack and his smokes and his previously owned bomber jacket and walks to the front of the room to retrieve the message slip. Then he crosses to the bin by the door, where the professor has his students check their cell phones and pagers, switched off to avoid interruptions such as these. He grabs his phone from the loose pile and switches it back on, and, as he leaves the screening room and the picture starts back up, he can see the professor's shadow in the corner of the screen. He's gesturing toward James Caan's elbow, only his entire shadow is about the size of James Caan's elbow, and the effect reminds Norman of George C. Scott standing in front of that giant American flag in *Patton*. The man is dwarfed by the images on the screen, and Norman leaves the room thinking how cool it is to get a phone call in the middle of class, to give the appearance of some business cooking on the coast, to circumvent the professor's ridiculous cell phone check, to have a chance to put such a small man in an even smaller place.

====

News of Terence Wood's death stops the presses. Literally. Figuratively. And every which way, besides. Pimletz returns from his hard-boiled eggs and chocolate milk at the P&S Lunch and smells that something has happened. Place gets that way sometimes. A strange stillness develops underneath the purr of activity. He wills himself into it. It permeates the vast room, this strange stillness, and the people inside it, the way it did when Reagan was shot, when the stock market dropped five hundred points, when the shuttle exploded with that teacher on board. Not like when Pimletz wakes to a piece of news after the bulletin has a chance to establish itself. Those times, the story is already written, the drama complete. The weird hush comes in the space between tragedy and deadline. Someone, maybe Hamlin, told Pimletz that during the San Francisco earthquake, when the news hit, there was a pocket of about ten, fifteen minutes during which everyone sat frozen in front of CNN and ABC, waiting for pictures. It got to where you could walk into the newsroom from the outside, unconnected, and right away know something was going on. It was like a visceral thing. Pimletz was home, waiting on the World Series, but this was what he was told.

Today, back from his early lunch, Pimletz's nose for news tells him he is about to be floored. There, over by the assignment desk, six or seven reporters are huddled around a small television. Something's definitely going on. Most of the desks surrounding Pimletz's are empty, their monitors abandoned between thoughts, the dull green from the letters of their not-saved stories coating his corner of the newsroom with an uncertain light. He rests his still-warm Warburton's muffin—jumbo oat cranberry crunch— on his desk and inches toward the television huddle to see what the matter is.

"Got something for you," Volpe announces, approaching the same huddle.

Pimletz, startled, looks over his shoulder to see who's got what for whom. Nothing's ever for him.

"Axel," Volpe says.

"Me?"

"You."

Pimletz shrugs. "Okay, what? What's up?"

"Terence Wood."

"Terence Wood, the actor?"

"No, ass wipe. Terence Wood, the dry cleaner. We're holding the front page for Terence Wood, the fucking dry cleaner."

Pimletz wonders about the ass wipe. He wonders whether it's just newspaper talk, the kind he's been fielding for most of the last twenty years, or if maybe Hamlin has spread the word about his underpants. And why did he have to mention dry cleaner? Where did that come from? Volpe knows, Pimletz determines. He knows. Shit. Then he thinks, okay, wait, it's nothing, right? The ass wipe and dry cleaner business, it's just nothing. Just expressions. I'm being paranoid. You know, that's just the way Volpe talks. I've heard him talk that way. Probably he just thinks I'm an ass wipe. Good.

"Front page?" he finally says, up from wondering. "Jesus, what happened?"

"He's dead, that's what happened." Volpe fires a Marlboro Light, shakes the match onto the floor, in the direction of Sam Haskins, the health and science reporter who has been petitioning to declare the *Record-Transcript* newsroom a smoke-free environment. "Of course he's dead. Why the hell else you think I'm talking to you? Car spun out over some cliff in yesterday's storm."

"Here?" Pimletz can't think where Terence Wood might have found a cliff in downtown Boston. He hears it back and he thinks, okay, ass wipe, stupid question. Take it back, take it back.

Volpe: "Up in Maine. Acadia. National Park Police found his car this morning. What was left of it. Tide ran out along those rocks and cliffs and there it was. Still looking for the body."

A million thoughts queue for Pimletz's attention. Maine. Park police. What kind of car? What else did they find? How can they be sure he's dead without a body? Why Maine? Plus, what about that movie Terence Wood was supposed to be making? Scorcese, Tarantino, one of those guys. De Niro. Jessica Lange. He definitely remembers reading about this somewhere. "I can be up there this afternoon?" he says hopefully, asking, sort of, making room for what he has to do. "I've got a car I could use." He's thinking maybe they were shooting this Tarantino movie up in Maine, maybe he'll get to meet Jessica Lange out of the deal.

"What, up there?" Volpe says. "You're here. I want you here. I've got someone else on the story."

"Who?" Again, Pimletz thinks, take it back. Stupid question.

"Fuck do you care, who?" Volpe says, flat. "Someone else. Not you. You, you're on the straight obit."

"With no body?" Pimletz says, making sure. To the best of his knowledge, which hardly ranks up there with the best of anyone else's, the *Record-Transcript* has never run an obituary without a confirmed death. This has been discussed, from time to time. "It's an obituary you want, or something else?"

"Obit, tribute, fuck do I care what you call it?" Volpe barks. "Fifty inches. Life story. First break. Academy Awards. That *Playboy* interview he did, couple years back, made all the headlines. Talk to his wives, his kid, some Hollywood shits. The works." He snuffs his butt under his shoe and kicks the flattened filter toward Haskins. "And lots of local color. We're his hometown paper. Don't let those fuckers at the *Times* beat us on this one."

"He's from here?" Pimletz marvels. Everything is news to him.

"He's from here."

"No shit?"

"No shit."

"And Maine?" Pimletz tries. "Why Maine?"

"Fuck do I know?" Volpe snarls. "Maine."

"Oh," Pimletz says. "Good. Good to know." He nearly puts pencil to scalp with this mental note.

"Check the morgue," Volpe says, turning for his office. "Check the live file. We should have something."

With Volpe's leaving, Sam Haskins, a large man with delicate features, reaches into his center desk drawer and pulls out a plastic sandwich bag, zip-locked, from which he removes a small pair of tweezers. Then he stoops—a swooping kind of stoop, given his size and the statement he wishes to attach to the motion—pinches at Volpe's kicked butt with his tweezers, and walks the offending filter to the garbage can across the room. He does this with a dozen sets of eyes on him, unruffled. Then he returns the tweezers to the bag, the zip to the lock, and the bag to his center desk drawer. Then he makes for the Men's to wash up.

Pimletz looks on and doesn't get how there's a guy like that, just a couple desks over, and Hamlin still beats the shit out of him.

The newspaper's live file—banked obituaries of still-breathing heads of state, politicians, business leaders, aging movie stars, retired athletes, and anyone else rich or famous enough that their sudden but increasingly likely death might spark a scramble for biographical material—is stored in its computer system and retrieved by punching in the command "NOT YET," followed by the first three letters of the subject's last name. The drill, on slow days, is that Pimletz is supposed to fill at least some of his down time scanning magazine features, press kits, and unauthorized biographies for thumbnail life stories and anecdotal material, which he then plugs into working obituaries on notables of his choosing. Just yesterday, flipping through a back *Vanity Fair*, he noticed something interesting on Ross Perot and dropped it into the live file under "PER." Once, from scratch and from memory, he started a file on Fay Vincent after learning that the former commissioner of baseball was facing tricky back surgery and reconsidering the fact that the guy walked around with a cane. He even got one going on Macauley Culkin, the kid star from those first *Home Alone* movies, after catching an interview on *Good Morning America* or someplace, couple months back, and deciding the kid had an attitude.

NOT YET, but SOMEDAY. . . .

Always, compiling these epitaphs-in-progress, Pimletz is filled with a dizzying power. It is a kind of voodoo, he thinks, the way he writes off the rich and famous and still-breathing while his innocent subjects are left to meander through the balance of their lives unaware. He imagines what Barbara Walters would say if she knew her passing would invoke a graph in one of the Boston papers on her turn as a "Today Girl," dressed in a bunny suit for a Playboy feature, or if Boston Pops conductor John Williams had any idea his leave-taking would be accompanied by a sordid anecdote from the set of Steven Spielberg's forgotten opus, *1941*.

It is a special thrill for Pimletz, a wonder, knowing something so intimate about these beautiful people, something so benignly spectacular. Sometimes, it is all he can do to keep from calling Heather Locklear (or Larry Bird, or Boston University President John Silber) and letting loose the childish taunt, "I know something you don't know," sing-song, although it would also be more than he could do to get someone like Heather Locklear on the phone.

For the longest time, the running joke he played with himself was to change the lead on Rose Kennedy's file. The thing was mostly written when he signed on at the paper, but he kept topping it with one cause of death after another. Falling safe. Drive-by shooting. Scared to death by Dr. Kevorkian. It was, for a time, his daily amusement, and he wondered if there maybe wasn't a board game in here somewhere, on the dove-tailing theories that others might find some challenge in his callously trivial pursuit, and that he might as well make some money from it.

When Rose Kennedy finally expired in her sleep of natural causes, Pimletz couldn't bring himself to write the straight lead. Hamlin had to do it for him because, for Pimletz, the point wasn't at all how Rose Kennedy died, but that she finally did, and that he'd have to come up with some other way to pass the time.

He's back to the live file, looking to get himself going. Ah. There, right after Kerry Wood, the Chicago Cubs pitching phenom, he finds what he's looking for. Wood, Terence Upton (b. March 2, 1932; Boston,

Massachusetts)—American film actor. Then he scans from Wood on down to Mort Zuckerman to measure the file, study his output, kill time. Back to Wood. There're only about three screens of information on this guy, most of it pulled from a *People* cover timed to promote the actor's last relevant effort, but some of the entries show evidence of Pimletz's tired hand:

see *Tonight Show* appearance, 12/76, for comments on Vail run-in with Pres. Ford

note T.V. spots for some potato chip with Redskins running back John Riggins, early 1980s

panel participant, "Reinventing Hollywood: Will Big Budgets Kill American Cinema?" New York University Film School, spring, 1984, transcript available

Always, Pimletz's notes reflect a resigned shorthand, as if he were merely going through the motions of his job and never planning to linger at the obit desk long enough to have to work from his abbreviated entries. He does what he has to do, barely, but now that he is here, on deadline, he realizes it is not enough. This Wood file is a sorry example. There is reference to some recent out-of-town articles, including one on the dedication of a plaque outside the actor's boyhood home on Beacon Hill, and one profiling his first wife, Anita Tollander Wood Veerhoven, who apparently resettled in Nahant, where she opened a rug cleaning business with her second husband. But there are no corresponding dates or publications to help Pimletz now locate the real deal. There is also mention of an unauthorized biography by a British journalist, who claimed to hold evidence linking the actor to quashed bigamy charges in the state of New Hampshire, but there is no reference to the book's title, or author, or publisher.

Of course, he could look these things up like a real journalist, but he rides himself for letting what was once at hand slip so haphazardly away. The way Pimletz works, or chooses not to, this is hardly enough to go on.

=====

Petra Wood has got her phones rigged to sound an old-fashioned bell ring—two short bursts and a pause, two short bursts and a pause, just like in the old movies. The only problem with this ringing is the way the clang invades her sleep and jolts her awake. The peals are like fire drills to her at these times, but, for the rest of her day, she finds them calming and not nearly so intrusive. She even has the antiquated handset that looks like a dolled-up parenthesis to go along with the ring.

It is 10:30, California time, when the first two short rings jolt Petra Wood awake, and it takes her a moment to focus. By the time the second bursts clang through, she has noticed the clock; calculated there are still another two hours of sleep to be had before Wilton, her personal trainer, arrives for their early afternoon run; peered through her taupe mini-blinds to see what the day was doing; kicked the remote control from her quilted covers to the pickled wooden floor; and watched helplessly as the two triple-A batteries came loose and rolled to the air vent by her nightstand. She even found time in the pause between rings to worry how she might retrieve the batteries should they roll into the duct, if maybe she could just leave them there without a problem, or, relatedly, if perhaps the things were too thick to fit through the narrow openings. She abandoned these lines when one of the batteries stopped short and the other came to rest nearly perpendicular to the vent slats. All of this, along with another mess of thoughts having mostly to do with the way her mind races while the rest of her is too numb to move, and how later, when she's fully awake, her thinking will slow to its more accustomed pace, before the third set of rings. "What?" she says, picking up finally. "What?"

"I have news."

Her lawyer, she processes. In New York. With news. "Good or bad?" she says.

"Depends," says this guy, Andrew somebody, she can never remember his name. Smith. Zalaznik. Merlinson. Something. He's been handling her divorce for six months, just about, and she still can't get it straight. "Shall I spoon it out," this Andrew guy says, "or do you want it all at once?"

"That depends, too."

"It's Terence," the lawyer says. "I'm afraid he's had a terrible accident." He hates being the messenger on a call like this, wishes someone would come up with a way for him to deliver his news whole, all at once. Like a "send" button on a fax machine. *Here. Here is everything I know.*

"Terrible terrible?" she asks, anxious for the rest of it.

"Pretty terrible. There was a bad rain. Car apparently skidded off a cliff up by the house. They don't think he made it."

Petra Wood doesn't understand this Andrew guy's hand-holding, the effort he's making to ease her into what he has to say. "They don't think he made what?" she tries. Reservations? "What don't they think he made?"

"It," he repeats, presumably in clarification. And then, for emphasis, "It. You know, they don't think he made it. They haven't found his body, but they're pretty sure he couldn't survive such a crash."

There. The part about his body is Pet's first hard clue that something is wrong, that this call is anything more than another in a long series of updates on a hoped-for divorce settlement with her estranged husband. Now, with this body business, she's all over the place in her thoughts. First she's thinking, You know, okay, so Wood banged up the car a little bit. Not the first time. And then she's thinking about the cliffs up in Maine and it's still not registering. And then, inexorably, she knows. "When?" she says.

"Last night. Late, I think. Not really sure. Got the call just now."

"Shit." She falls back against her pillows, lets the phone drop to her chest. The truth of the moment nearly overwhelms her, but not to where she is lost in it. She is whelmed, just. A part of her is very definitely here, focused, thinking, you know, okay, this thing happened, it's a happened thing. She worries that, in her thinking, she has not made room to feel anything, that she has given these instants over to simply absorbing this new piece of information, that she is not letting it touch her in any substantive way. She is not transformed by the horrible news the way she thinks perhaps she should be. Then again, she catches, she must be feeling something because she is momentarily paralyzed, unable to move or think clearly. Wood, she thinks. Her Wood. She goes from hating him to wanting him back, desperately, in the time it takes for Andrew Somebody to deliver the news.

Petra Wood is swallowed up by her pillows and by the thought of her very nearly ex-husband tumbling on down to the stormy sea. She wonders, briefly, what it was like for him in those last moments—if he was conscious or afraid, if he called out to her or to someone else, if a lifetime of memories truly were unfurled before him or if his thoughts were blank, if he had the radio on, if he'd been drinking—and, in her wondering, she fixes on a vision of Mel Brooks in that Hitchcock spoof (*what the hell was that movie called?*). He's falling backward, spinning, flailing in a crazy, swirling vortex, screaming madly, almost comically, only in Petra's wild imaginings, Mel Brooks has become her Wood. The mad screams have exaggerated to where they are now joyous shouts of "geronimo!" and "look out below!" and there is no end to his falling.

Wood.

"Petra, I'm sorry," Andrew says, thinking that his client is still listening at the other end. "I know how upsetting this must be for you."

"*High Anxiety*," Petra says, remembering the movie, only the phone is by now buried beneath the linens and all her attorney can hear is the rustling of sheets as she rolls from her bed and thumps to the floor.

"Petra?" he says, "Pet?" but he gets back nothing.

Petra Wood, whelmed and cold and naked on the pickled wooden floor, crawls frantically to the air vent by her nightstand and fumbles for the batteries. It is an effort for her to pinch the things from their position against the metal duct, but she eventually manages. Then she looks under the bed, also frantically, for the kicked remote, and when she finds it, she struggles to fit the batteries into the trap and line them up against the vague markings etched into the black plastic, copper tops opposite. This, too, is an effort, and when she's satisfied with it, she spins on her seat and points the empowered remote to the television at the foot of her bed. She holds it out like a magic wand, a divining rod, only she can't get the thing to work. She presses every button. Then she spins the batteries in their trap and tries again. Then she holds the remote in her right hand and slaps it crisp against the palm of her left, over and over. Then she bangs it on the floor. Sometimes this helps.

In her deliberate frenzy, her thoughts arrive on the possibility that maybe this Andrew guy doesn't know what he's talking about, maybe he didn't even call, maybe she dreamed his call and she's only now waking from her nightmare. Maybe the ugliness over the divorce—and it has gotten pretty ugly—has left her feeling sentimental and willing to forgive the six or seven times she knows about Wood dipping his cock into any warm hole he could find. (And those are only the times she knows about!) Or, okay, he did call, the lawyer did call, there was very definitely a call, yes, but maybe it was just a wrong number, some other piece of bad news meant for someone else.

There, the television flashes on, and, for an instant, the screen confirms her frantic imaginings. She's landed on one of those mid-morning talk shows with bouncy supermarket music and an enthusiastic audience and a jump-suited blonde looking far too earnest for her day part. Today's topic quickly reveals itself: cosmetic mastectomies, something Petra Wood has never before encountered, and which strikes her, at this moment, as particularly repulsive. Still, she is momentarily drawn into the discussion—it's "a radical-feminist fashion statement," "a defiant, streamlined look"—and to the presumably tasteful before-and-after photos displayed on the screen, and then, underneath her watching, she remembers the phone call. It hits her all over again.

She switches channels. Surely, if something has happened to Terence Wood, the kind of larger-than-life Hollywood celebrity whose untimely death would almost certainly merit an interruption in regular programming, she will not have to flip too long to find out. And, indeed, she doesn't. CNN has got a tiny map of Maine inset over the blonde head of its anchorwoman, and right away, she knows. Again. It's like they've been waiting for Petra to tune in, only now that she has, she's not listening, she doesn't want to hear what this blonde head has to say. She's thinking of the last time she saw her Wood. She's trying to remember his last words to her, his smell, the way his balls would spin in their sack when she sucked him off, the sound of his voice, the rough of his beard sandpapered against her skin, that odd little whistle-puckering thing he used to do to clean his teeth after he'd eaten. She doesn't want to lose the slightest thing.

The map of Maine morphs into a headshot of Terence Wood as a young man, a still from *The Half Shell*, the movie that launched his career. He's smiling, his thick, dark hair breezed by a wind machine, and there is magic in his eyes. Petra wasn't even born at the time of that shoot, but his eyes seem to know her. She looks at the still and swears he can see her coming, and then her own eyes are drawn to the black border underneath the picture, with the still-open birth and death dates burned in (1932–), and she's thinking it is like a headstone, a video headstone, the way the television reports on the deaths of all these people. She's also thinking, well, okay, it's true, it must be true. They don't put up dates and black borders around pictures unless it's true.

The headshot fades and is replaced over the anchor-woman's other shoulder by one of Bill Clinton, which, in turn, is replaced by photo opportunity footage at some Rose Garden ceremony, and then a shot of Lloyd Bentsen on the floor of the New York Stock Exchange. As Petra Wood collects these various images, she wonders how it is that the stuff of her life has become also the stuff of everyone else's. She loses her Wood off a cliff in a storm, and here it is for the world to see, scripted and TelePrompted and sifted through the machinery of mass communications. Her kick in the stomach is news to CNN, and, after that, they're onto the next story.

She reaches for the phone to call Anita, wife number two, who's up in New Hampshire somewhere (she doesn't know the number, but it's on the speed dial). When she follows the cord and fishes the machine out from beneath the covers, she realizes she's left it off the hook. She clears the line, speed-dials, but the call does not go through. "Hello," she says, into the silence. "Hello?"

"Oh, good," she gets back. "Good, I was about to give up on you."

"Andrew?" Parker? Applegate? Wojiski? What is his last name?

"Yes," her lawyer says back. "Andrew. Me. Still me. Thought I'd lost you."

"You've been talking to me all this time?" She's confused a little, that this lawyer person has somehow remained on her telephone.

"Some, but then I heard the television. I stopped when I heard the television."

She considers this a moment, until it makes sense. "That it?" she says, when it does. "Anybody else die you need to tell me about?"

"No," Andrew says. "I just wanted to be sure you were okay."

"I'm okay."

"You're sure?"

"No, I'm not sure, but I'm okay. Really. We were split, right? That's why I hired you. I hired you because we were getting a divorce, right? We were about to kick his ass in court. It's not like we were together." She strings the words like a charm bracelet to make herself feel better. Underneath, she's thinking, This is how I feel, this should be how I feel. Then, suddenly: "Anybody else in the car with him?" She doesn't know where this comes from, but now that it's out she's burning to know.

"Like who?"

"Like anyone. I don't know. That sitcom actress he was banging."

"I don't think so," Andrew says. "I don't know."

"Which?"

"Which what?"

"Which?" Petra pushes. "You don't think so or you don't know? They're hardly the same thing."

"I don't know, then," Andrew says. "They didn't mention about anybody else. You'd think they'd say if there was somebody else."

"You'd think," Petra considers.

There's an overlong pause, during which neither of them has any idea what to say. Petra takes the time to think what she'll wear on the plane east.

Andrew, finally: "Okay?"

"Okay."

"Good. I'll call you later. That be alright, if I call you later?"

"Fine, call me later."

"Good. That's what I'll do. I'll call you later. Tonight. You gonna be okay?"

"Andrew," she says, exasperated.

"You got somebody out there to come sit with you, someone to call?"

"Andrew, I'm fine," she says, "just get off my fucking phone."

Petra dials again when he does. Answering machine. Anita can't come to the phone, but Petra's call is important to her. Really, really. Petra listens to the tape and wonders briefly what kind of message she should leave, if she should just spit it out and deposit it, or if perhaps the enormity of what she has to say is too great for the technology. She guesses Anita already knows, given the time difference. She's probably been up and about and caught it on the radio or somewhere. Step outside the house, turn on any appliance, and this is the kind of information that will find you before long. Plus, she's the mother of Wood's kid. (Oh, shit, *Norman*; she'd forgotten, for the moment, about Norman.) Surely someone's called. This is the kind of information probably flows pretty quickly to the mother of someone's kid.

"Hi," she finally says, caught short by the beep, "It's me, Pet. Our husband died. Call me."

==

Fifteen minutes to deadline, and Pimletz has got his fifty inches nearly filed. He's thinking this is probably the longest damn obit he's ever written, can't imagine any from his live file likely to surpass it. Ted Williams, maybe, but the way he's going he'll probably outlast Pimletz. He read somewhere that Ted Williams was admitted to some hospital somewhere, but that's one tough bastard, that Teddy Ballgame, and now that he reflects on it, there is no way Terence Wood is more deserving of space than Teddy Ballgame. Not in Boston. He'll be gone before long, and so will Red Auerbach, Kevin White, Betty Friedan, that channel five anchor lady, and any number of local heroes might beat out this Wood by a couple inches.

There are few surprises left in Pimletz's line of work, so he takes them where he can. With Rose Kennedy gone, about the only detail to keep things interesting is this right here, trying to figure how much space the Volpes will leave for each subject. That, the cause of death, and the order of assignments. He'll get to all of them, eventually. They'll all die of something, but who's next?

Right now, the day's only surprise for Pimletz will be his lead. He has no clue how to play it. Volpe's got someone else on the story, and Pimletz doesn't have it in him to check with the news desk to see how the paper is handling it. Far as Pimletz knows, Terence Wood's body has yet to turn up, the guy's been missing or presumed dead less than twenty-four hours, and the story can go any number of ways: tragic accident, crossed signals, foul play, mysterious disappearance, apparent suicide, colossal misunderstanding.

The way it goes will determine whether Pimletz plays his end as a straight obit, or a tribute, or something else. His lead, determined, will give the piece its tone and meaning. Whatever it is, he'll stitch it to the next graph so it all fits and flows.

Rest of it is all here: the infamous 1979 *Playboy* interview in which Wood challenged the Pope to a round of golf, incurring the ceaseless wrath of the religious right, left, and center; the actor's tongue-wagging protest of the Vietnam War during the Academy Awards, when he marched to the stage to accept his best actor Oscar, waited for the standing ovation to sit down, placed his statue firmly at the edge of the podium, and made to leave it there, offering one of the most stunning acceptance/rejection speeches in Academy history ("I'll come back for this when our boys are home"); his rumored romances with Twiggy, Cher, Madonna, and virtually every other one-named actress-model-whatever to have crossed the scene in the past thirty years; and his three dryings-out (a course record!) at Betty Ford—the last only a year ago.

Pimletz even wanders beyond the tabloid realm, with enough of Volpe's precious hometown color to fill a paint store. There are glimpses of Wood's growing up, the only child of immigrant parents, raised in a cold-water tenement in Boston's North End. There is Wood as a small boy, selling soda bottles to construction workers at the old Boston Garden site, chilling his inventory on blocks of ice stolen from the neighborhood ice man. There is Wood at twelve, sanding the raised letters on his father's tombstone; Wood on his high school debating team; Wood on the Philco Television Playhouse; Wood in Korea; Wood on Broadway; Wood roaming the Raider sidelines at the Super Bowl; Wood at the still-birth of his first son, a child he refused to name despite the pleadings of his wife, Elaine.

Not bad, Pimletz thinks, scrolling through what he's written, waiting for his lead to come to him. When it does, finally, there is Volpe attached to its other end. "Hey, Axel," he hollers across the newsroom, "you finished wiping your ass yet or what?" and, right away, Pimletz is back to yesterday. Jesus, he's thinking. He knows. Everybody knows. Then he's back to today, this. He's thinking, that's just the way he talks. Doesn't mean anything.

"Almost there," he says, as Volpe reaches his desk. "Just waiting on the lead."

"Fuck is that supposed to mean?" Volpe barks. "You're having it delivered? Domino's is writing your lead?"

About the only thing Pimletz can think to do in response is to stand and step from his desk, clearing the way for his boss. This is the routine when an editor comes to read over his shoulder. Volpe stares back at him contemptuously, sits, rolls the chair to the keyboard, pulls the obit up on Pimletz's screen, and starts writing:

A dramatic career came to an apparently dramatic end yesterday afternoon with the mysterious disappearance of internationally acclaimed actor Terence Wood, a Boston native whose life was the stuff of legend. . . .

Pimletz looks on and can't imagine how it is that someone can just sit down and write without thinking about it. Really, he has no idea. He can write, occasionally, and he can pretty much refrain from thinking, but it never occurs to him to try the two things at once.

"There," Volpe says, standing, "there's your fucking lead. Fresh from our keep-'em-hot vans." He holds out his hand, palm up. "I expect a tip."

"What about the rest of it?" Pimletz asks, overrunning the joke.

"Fuck the rest of it," Volpe says, pocketing his hand. "Deadline. No time for your dicking around. Just send it to Copy and let them deal with it." He backpedals as he says this, and, by the time he is through, he has placed six or seven desks between himself and the stormed Pimletz. At the third or fourth of these six or seven desks, Sam Haskins points a can of Lysol mountain scent air freshener at his boss's nicotine wake.

Pimletz sits back down, expecting to do as he's told, only he can't remember the commands for his computer.

He has to fumble through his manual to remind himself of the motions he goes through every day, but when he finds what he's looking for, he notices his screen has gone blank. Then it beeps, and there's a fake human voice through his speakers telling him he has mail:

Never mind, Axel. I'll do it myself.

Well, shit, Pimletz thinks, looking reflexively across the room to where he knows he'll find Volpe staring back at him with those menacing eyes of his. There. Over by the news desk. Only Volpe's not leaned over someone's terminal sending silent criticism the hundred feet or so to Pimletz the way he usually is. No, this time Volpe surprises Pimletz. Oh, he's staring, he's always staring, but this time Volpe has got a thumb plugged into each ear, he's waving both hands from the sides of his head, he's sticking out his tongue. It is like a cartoon tease—*nyah nyah, na nyah nyah*—and Pimletz has no idea what to make of it, except to think, well, okay, this is something.

=====

Petra Wood, middle-seated two rows deep into coach, is running on silent fumes. She does not understand why it is she is made to tolerate so many insipid little annoyances in the course of an already bad enough day. She just moves from one bother to the next, and each has got her so bent out of shape it's a wonder her leotarded Isaac Mizrahi pantsuit still fits the way it did when she first tried it on.

First, there was this protracted nonsense on the telephone with some guy from TWA reservations, who claimed the airline's discounted bereavement fares did not extend to first class tickets. Whoever heard of such a thing? What, people with presumed-dead husbands are not supposed to be comfortable on a five-hour flight? That it? Someone actually expected Petra Wood to sip from plastic? to pay for her drinks? at a time like this?

"Ma'am," this reservations guy wheedled into the phone, "I mean no disrespect, and all of us here extend our deepest sympathies, but I'm afraid there's nothing I can do."

Right, like all of them there had actually put their deepest sympathies to a vote. "Don't tell me there's nothing you can do," she insisted. "This is not some farmer's wife you're talking to. This is not some lemming. There are always things you can do."

"Not here," he said, trying to be pleasant. "I assure you."

"Well then, I'll just consider myself assured," she shot back, not trying at all.

"Look," he pressed, "ma'am, I'd like to get you on this plane so you can do what you have to do. I know you have to be somewhere. I can check if there's room in first, if that's your preference, but you'll have to pay full fare."

What's with this ma'am business, she wondered. She had dialed into some toll-free wasteland, with no way to tell whether she was talking to St. Louis, or Atlanta, or Dallas. Maybe if she knew she could place the ma'am: "Where am I calling?" she said.

"TWA."

Duh. "No, I mean, where are you right now, what part of the country?"

"We're not supposed to give out that information."

"What?" This she could not believe. "Why? What possible reason could there be for TWA to care if I know where I'm calling?"

"Policy, ma'am. Don't ask, don't tell." He said this in a Jack Webb staccato and waited for his laugh. "That's a joke," he said, when he got nothing. "Gays in the military. Don't ask, don't tell."

"That's a joke?" She really didn't see it.

"Well, it was," he said. "Guess it's not anymore."

"How 'bout you just tell me where you're from? Where you were born? You can tell me that, right?"

"Yes, ma'am, I s'pose I can."

"Well, then, do."

"New York," he declared. "Queens, actually. That's where I was born, although I wouldn't exactly say that's where I was from."

"Where, exactly, would you say that was?" Petra said, with a growing upset at having gotten tangled in such an unnecessary conversation.

"North Carolina, ma'am. The Piedmont. Folks moved there when I was in grade school."

That would explain the ma'am, she thought.

"Look," he said, finally warming to this strange, bereaved, and apparently pampered lady on the other end of his line, "I can always issue you the ticket and you can worry about the fare later."

"Meaning?"

"Meaning you still have to show up at one of our ticket counters with a death certificate and proof of immediate relations in order to qualify for the discount. Might be worth a shot to just go first class and play dumb."

"Like we never had this conversation?"

"Exactly, ma'am."

"Great," she said, "let's do that, then."

"What? Pretend we never had this conversation?" He waited again for a laugh, but Petra Wood was a tough room. "Ba-dump-bump?" he tried, to sell the joke.

"Another joke?" she asked.

"Guess not." Beat. "So, what'll it be?"

"Anything," she said, trying to move this too-polite reservations guy along with as much economy as possible.

"Anything, what?"

"In first. Is there anything in first?"

"Checking," he announced, adopting a chipper voice evidently meant to convey not only that he was, but also that he was about to place his entire being into some electronic investigatory mode. Again, from somewhere along the information highway, to fill the silence: "Checking."

Petra Wood, now fully impatient, suddenly decided she had spent enough time on this transaction. She should have been fretting over Anita, or poor Norman, or frantic to learn if there was any news from Maine, or setting up a meeting with her attorneys for when she got back to see about the estate, but there she was quibbling over a couple hundred bucks. What the hell had gotten into her, she wondered. "You know," she said, interrupting checking mode, "anything is fine."

"Good," the reservations guy said, "because anything is all we've got. Our last block of first just disappeared from my screen."

"What does that mean?" By "anything" she had meant aisle, window, or whatever. She hadn't meant to consider coach.

"It means first is full."

"Just like that?"

"Just like that. We went back and forth for so long someone else just snapped 'em up."

Great, she thought. Now it's either the huddled masses or another airline. She didn't have time to start all over again with another airline.

"Ma'am?" he said, waiting for instructions.

Oh, yes, him. "What do I want to do, right? You're wondering what it is I want to do?"

"Our next flight is two hours later, if you'd like to wait."

"Or?"

"Or, I could book you in coach and we could pretend we never had this conversation." He was running out of options. His tone was sunny, as if he didn't mind at all spending his days with a phone cradled to his neck, or maybe with one of those sleek headsets she'd noticed some of these telemarketing professionals had taken to wearing, as if helping to arrange the last-minute travel plans of distracted, discourteous persons like herself were a kind of calling.

"Coach, then," she said, "unless you'd just like to chat for a while, give all those empty seats a chance to fill up, too?" Her tone was dark, laced with a touch more sarcasm than she intended, and she regretted it right away, attempting to smooth her demeanor with a joke of her own. "Ba-dump-bump?" she said, thinking this would do.

Of course, it didn't, because by then the sunny bastard had consigned her to her middle seat, too close to the damn bulkhead to watch the movie and not far enough away from this unusually tall, elaborately bearded Middle Eastern fellow seated directly in front of her, wearing a turban and smelling like he'd been dipped in a vat of curry.

Okay, so that was the first thing. Or maybe the first and second things, if she counts her unfortunate seating as a separate nuisance. Next, there was some additional unpleasantness at check-in, when the agent attempted to check her carry-on bag, and some further words at the gate regarding the complimentary newspapers and coffee, and now that Pet has been settled uncomfortably in her seat, her nerves are in serious need of a good hem. Woman next to her, by the window, has commandeered what seems to Pet to be far more than her fair share of personal space. She's all spread out and organized and much too comfortable. Right at this moment, this woman is doing some annoyingly serious browsing in the Air Mall catalog from her seat-back pouch. She's making notes in the margins alongside some of the items, working a calculator to confirm her interest.

"This is something you can't do without?" Pet wonders, her voice still viscous with the sarcasm that put her here. She couldn't help but notice her neighbor's interest in a squirrel-proof bird feeder shaped to resemble Tanya Tucker.

"Oh, why yes!" the woman kindly drawls, happy for the chance to share her dueling enthusiasms for country music and bird-watching. "I've already got the

Judds side by side over the patio, and Dolly Parton is just a-smilin' away outside my kitchen window." The poor dear is tickled to have stumbled onto this common ground with this striking stranger. She just goes on and on: "Why, just the other afternoon, I was doin' the dishes when this little ruby-throated thing set hisself down right outside my window, and, wonder of wonders, I'll tell you, this little fella looked near set to go a-nursin' on poor Dolly." She laughs like this is one of the top ten funniest connections she has ever made regarding her country music bird feeders.

"Go on!" Pet exclaims, exaggerating her interest. "That must have been a picture!"

"Oh, darlin', it was somethin' to see," marvels this woman in the window seat.

"Me?" Pet starts in, affecting something like the same drawl as her neighbor, curling her every thought into a kind of question. "I called to order me a few a those Patsy Clines? And the fella, he says to me, you know, how would I like that delivered? And, I says to him, well, special delivery would be fine? And he reads off all the different special delivery options? You know, overnight express? two-day air? three-day ground?" Her accent is a caricature, she's swallowing her words to keep up with it. "Turns out, they can get these packages to you every which way? But I says back, no, no, no, that's not at all what I have in mind? And he wants to know what it was I did have in mind, and so I just said, suspended air freight? I don't know why I was funnin' with him so, or what put me in this kinda mind, but it just come to me. Suspended air freight, that's what I said, just like that. Naturally, this poor fella had never heard of suspended air freight, so I explained that I wanted my Patsy Clines flown to the Tennessee hills and then dropped from the plane and slapped against the side of one of those cliffs they've got there, until my desired items were reduced to recyclables? This is what I told him. Recyclables. They're plastic, right?" She laughs as if she might choke on her own good cheer, and embroiders this with a string of unnecessary breath-catching gestures. "Oh, my Lord!" she says, patting at her chest with an open palm, pretending to ease herself into a lower gear. "And then, oh, oh, oh"—she pats at the air in front of her unnerved neighbor, to make sure she still has what's left of her attention— "I'm leaving out the best part. I tell the guy, you know, if he could somehow fix it so that the pilot could be playing 'I Fall to Pieces' on the cassette when he dropped my package, I would consider that extra special delivery, and would be willin' to pay a few dollars more?" She builds to her best mock-cackle. "Extra special delivery?" she says, slapping at her own knee. She makes to catch her breath again. "Good lord!" she says, "that fella was off the phone quicker than if I were tryin' to sell somethin' to him!"

Petra Wood looks up from her performance and is nearly able to count the fillings in the mouth of the woman sitting next to her. This is what it means when they say someone's mouth is agape, she thinks. This is as agape as it gets. The woman, flabbergasted, manages to clutch her Air Mall catalog to her breast with one hand and reach for the orange "call" button at her armrest with the other, going to harumphing lengths to avoid eye contact with the devilish woman at her side, and when the stewardess arrives to see what the trouble is, the woman very demurely asks if there might be an empty seat toward the back. Something about the rumble of the engines makes it easier for her to fall off asleep, she says, although from the urgent, hushed tone of her voice she might be discussing matters of national security.

"That will be fine, ma'am," the stewardess says, and she helps the flustered lady collect her few things and inch her way past Petra Wood to safety.

There, Pet thinks, sliding over to the still-warm seat by the window, stretching out. Wasn't so hard.

═══

There is a coffee shop in downtown Bar Harbor, Maine, serves perhaps the greasiest mess of home fries ever to have fled a skillet. Place is landmarked for its home fries, which are larded and charred and coated with this heavythick glaze of some secret something that lets them slide past peristalsis for the nearest artery. They taste famously like burnt candied yams, and even the late-to-lunch locals can't inhale enough of them. Folks have been known to drive two hours out of their way for a plateful, and, in these parts, a two-hour side trip is pretty much a four-star review. This part of New England, everything is so spread out and remote that a one-hour trip is nothing, but two? Well, that's a high compliment.

The restaurant has got no name Terence Wood can easily determine, unless of course the Good Food and Coffee Shop signs out front are meant as more than exposition. Even the menus offer no clue: Menu.

About the best a first-timer like Wood can gather is a sanctioned nickname—Two Stools—which appears to have something to do with the overweight waitress working the room like a matron and with the limited seating at the lunch counter. The spinning seat discs are a memory on the half-dozen metal posts lining the counter's length, save for two at the end by the cash register, and Wood guesses there might be a story behind their absence. He won't have to wait long to find out.

Wood, dressed down in a straw fishing hat and plaid flannel shirt, has stumbled in to refuel and evacuate. He's got his long gray hair tied with a red rubber band he found lying on the street. He hasn't eaten since the sample pack of cheese-filled Combos he collected first thing this morning when he stopped by a roadside convenience store to see if his exit had made the early papers. Fuck did he know about newspapers and deadlines? Closest he ever came to the world of print journalism was a cut bit as a paper boy in *Citizen Kane*— his first Hollywood payday, a favor to his connected uncle. While this insignificant contribution to movie history may have been left to shrivel on strips of acetate in some forgotten vault, it also left Wood with the idea that if his car should somehow sail off a cliff during the night, there might be some mention of it on the front pages by morning. This was news. Surely there might be some paper boy, somewhere, urging early morning commuters to plunk down their coins for the latest on the sudden death of a Hollywood legend: *Read all about it! Terence Wood, dead at sixty-five! Entertainment world rocked by the news!*

But, alas, there was no mention of the actor's sudden presumed death. Wood idly thumbed the newspapers and magazines on display, strolled the few aisles with enough interest to forestall any suspicions of loitering, and, in this way, consumed some additional minutes on this first day of his new freedom. This last had quickly become one of his primary concerns. He hadn't figured on all the time he would now have to fill, hadn't decided yet if this was a good thing. Some other things he hadn't figured on were eating, shitting, showering, going through the rest of his life unnoticed, and now that these had taken turns occurring to him, he figured he'd deal with them on an as needed basis.

First, food. As he continued with his aisle strolling, he realized he was famished, and the brightly packaged snack foods leapt off the shelves to assault his hunger in a way he found strangely satisfying. Oh, he didn't do anything more than consider each package, maybe handle a few of them, hold one or two to his nose, but this was enough for Terence Wood. There is something filling, he considered, in staring down a box of Freihoffer's cookies, assorted, or a neatly stacked tower of Pringle's ranch-flavored potato chips, or individually wrapped Ring Dings, Ding Dongs, or Ho Hos, or the exalted fake-creaminess of a package of double-stuff Oreos, when your wallet is trapped in the glove box of your jettisoned four-by-four vehicle and you can't know how far the fifty-three dollars and change in your pants pocket will take you.

Wood was drawn to the Combos not for the promised bursts of zesty processed cheese or the ten-cent introductory price tag, but because he once had a thing going with a woman who sang back-up on the Combos jingle: "Combos really cheeses your hunger away." The line, between them, became a source of endless bedroom by-play. One of the singer's favorite gags was to grip Wood's cock like a microphone and croon to him like she was on Carson, like he was her first true break, and it was only underneath her sometime teasing that Wood could recognize the real omnipotence of his situation, that he felt he could actually stand before this girl and cheese away her hunger simply by being who he was, by letting her perform for him this unadorned act of raw tenderness, by accepting her supplication. He would fill her with the seeds of power and fame, he used to think, his celebrated greatness would become hers, and she would thank him for it, ask for more.

Cindy. Her name was Cindy, and this was how Wood remembered her. As he popped one of the Combos nuggets into his mouth this morning, he tasted again the stale sweetness of this singing Cindy. It came right back to him. The girl had kept what seemed like a lifetime supply of Combos in a corner of her studio apartment (one of the perks of her jingling), and in the few weeks they spent together, her lips could hardly brush up against Wood without leaving behind specks of pretzel and puttied cheese. Sometimes, Wood's tongue in her mouth would discover a coarse paste, and he would return to his own mouth and pretend not to mind. He recalled drinking a lot of water.

The Combos held him through mid-afternoon, when his stomach began to feel as if someone had inflated a balloon inside of it. Also, like he was about to give birth to an avocado pit. He had to shit, and he couldn't tell if the two developments were somehow related. Probably. Anyway, this Two Stools joint surfaced in time to cover both needs, and Wood slipped in and made for the back. Earlier in the day, he had found the apparently abandoned straw fishing hat on a park bench, and he pulled the brim down low, seeking obscurity. He caught a glimpse of himself in the plate glass window on the way in, and it didn't seem to him he looked like Terence Wood. He was dirty, and unkempt, and underdressed, and not at all himself. This was good. His plan was to slink to some back table, order the cheapest item on the menu, and nurse an accompanying cup of coffee until he could motivate his bowels. He asked the huge waitress for an egg sandwich, heavy pepper, and settled back to soak up what he could of the local color.

This is what he now makes out: Two Stools, the waitress, is the daughter of the restaurant's owner. It's his place, but she runs it. She's got two short-order cooks, each named Lenny, and herself, and that's it. Her father lives on a golf course in Florida. Eleventh hole. Dogleg left. She sends him a check every month. Summers, it's actually a good-size check. The deal with the stools at the counter is that, one by one, as the place fell into disrepair, they kind of spun loose from their mountings, the fitting grooves worn from more than fifty years of fidgety swiveling. This happened over a period of ten, twelve years, Wood surmises, and Two Stools was forever meaning to take care of the problem, fix the place back up, nice, but she never seemed to have the time or the money to make the repairs. 'Course, most of the folks seemed to prefer the mismatched tables and chairs she'd collected and loosely scattered about the restaurant, and it was a lot cheaper to scavenge some tables and chairs than it was to adequately replace a row of lunch counter stools. Before anybody knew it, they were down to just these last two stools. One of the regulars, guy named Joe Scapsi, finally looked up from his home fries one late afternoon and affectionately remarked on how fortunate the waitress was to have her chair still standing. "If there weren't two stools left together, honey, you'd have no place to sit down," he reportedly said, or words to this effect, and from that moment forward, the waitress and her father's restaurant went by their new name.

All of this comes to Wood in fifteen minutes, like a side dish to his small meal. Sure enough, this waitress is so big-butted he can't imagine she ever was able to balance herself on a single stool, even as a small child. Yet, when she sits every few minutes or so to tally up her checks or credit the tabs of her regulars, she manages to slither elegantly between the two remaining stools and hoist herself onto both seats. Really, she moves like a fat ballerina, but a ballerina just the same. Most of her excess fleshiness drops into the space between the two stools, which do an otherwise serviceable job of supporting her considerable weight.

Wood looks on and connects the woman to his old points of reference. She reminds him first of one of those dancing hippos from an old Disney cartoon and then of a story he read in *Variety*, couple days back, about a similarly overweight woman who had brought suit against her local multiplex for failing to provide what her lawyer called "wide-body seating." He wonders what it must be to go through life with such an added burden. Wondering, he upbraids himself for managing to translate even so innocuous a human condition as obesity into movie terms. Here he is, freshly disappeared into the middle of nowhere—or, more precisely, the edge of nowhere, this being a coastal town—and, first chance he gets, he comes right back to the trades, to the industry, to cartoons. This poor fat girl works two shifts to stay solvent, keep her father on the links and off welfare, sustain the out-of-work locals with her extremely reasonable prices, and shoulder the (mostly) good-natured taunts of her regulars, and she smiles underneath the indignity of having to use two counter stools to support her girth. It is all Wood can do to keep from optioning her life story.

"Refill?"

The voice startles Wood from his wonderings, principally because his mind was on something other than his coffee, but also because it sounds far too delicate to have come from such a big woman. Also, he is surprised that so large a woman could have sidled up alongside his table without warning. Here is her voice, again: "Most people, they order themselves a bottomless coffee, they drink maybe two, three cups." The waitress's tone is pleasant, playful. "They want their money's worth."

"Hit me," Wood says back, matching her tone, inching his cup forward, and as she pours for him, he fixes on the still-moving flesh of her arms, their doughy warmth, the way she seems to occupy this incredible space without encroaching on his own. "This place have a name?" he says, looking up from his filled cup, making conversation.

"Not really," she says, softly. "Folks know where to find us."

"How 'bout yourself?"

"Know where to find me, too." She laughs, knowing this is not quite what her new customer means to discern. "I'm always here."

"No, I mean a name," he clarifies. "What is your name?"

"Everyone calls me Two Stools," she says, with practiced pride. "You can do the same."

"I'd prefer to know your given name," Wood persists, "if you don't mind."

"Two Stools is fine," the waitress answers, stepping shyly away from the table in a way that perhaps suggests she does. "I don't mind it at all. Even my father calls me Two Stools."

"That's fine," Wood says, "but I'd prefer to know your real name."

"Grace," she announces, extending her hand. "Name's Grace. Pleased to meet you."

"Grace," he says back, in appraisal. "Grace. I believe it suits you." From any of Grace's regulars, this line would have sounded counterfeit, but Terence Wood has a way about him when it comes to women. All women. Fat. Skinny. Pound ugly. They are all made to feel beautiful around him. This is sometimes an effort, sometimes not, but here, now, it is no trouble at all. Up close, this Grace has an astonishingly pretty face, and she smells (wonderfully) like fresh bread. There is something about her Wood cannot yet identify, but, nevertheless, has got him bent to distraction.

He collects her hand and is startled by the meat of it. He's got big hands himself, but this woman can just about swallow him up with her paws. Her fingers are like sausages. Then, quickly, he's off her hand and back on to these pleasantries. Right. He needs a name. Hadn't thought of that. Okay, okay, think. Name. Something he can slip into, some new space he can occupy. A character, perhaps, from one of his pictures. Yes, that's it. Someone he's played before. Someone he knows. This way he gives himself not just a name, but a history, a personality. A plot.

His mind races over his credits, trying to place himself. There was that architect he played, lost his wife in an elevator accident, one of his own buildings. No, no, no. Too recent. And what would an architect be doing here, flannel-shirted, in a remote corner of Maine? What about that public defender, took up the rights of all those '60s radicals? Joe Justice? What the hell kind of name was Joe Justice? (Jesus, he's made a lot of shit pictures.) No, no, he needs something a little less assuming, something more generic. Whatwhatwhatwhat? Small-time circus owner. Neurosurgeon. Corrupt congressman. That gay guy he played, coming out to his family, his own kids. Nothing fits, until he hits on *Front to Back*, this all-but-forgotten draft-dodging picture he made opposite an undiscovered Goldie Hawn between campaign appearances for Humphrey. Played a guy, fled to Canada, built a new life for himself. Could work. Picture sank like a cinder block, but it wasn't half bad. The timing was just wrong, the director for shit, but this actually works okay for him now, this works it so that he can slip into this borrowed persona undetected. Far as he knows, the picture's never been released on video. He can't imagine anyone around here has seen it recently enough to remember it. Now he just needs to remember the fucking guy's name.

He considers all of this in a moment, the same moment this Grace has been using to make Wood's acquaintance. He's still got hold of her meaty sausages; it has not yet become an awkward exchange.

"Trask," he says, remembering the character's name. "Harlan Trask. Just passing through."

Alone

Pimletz shuffles into the *Record-Transcript* offices a half hour early and a couple hours shy of a night's rest. Sleep didn't come easy, and when it finally did, it didn't matter.

He's energized, still, by his swollen effort on the Wood obit, eager to soak up what there might be of collegial praise. He'll even take grudging acknowledgment. Anything. Been forever since someone's noticed something he's written. Last time he made the front page was during Reagan's first term—yes?—when the paper played the shooting death of a twelve-year-old Roxbury drug dealer way beyond deserving. Back then, the paper had a managing editor named Charlie ("King") Tuthill, and the man was legendarily hot for any story to accent the desperation of Boston's inner city youth. This was his thing. Janet Cooke's faux Pulitzer had come and not yet gone, and King Tut was on the prowl for anything that might put his own rag on the same map. Guy would rub two stones together and call it an avalanche. This Roxbury youth had been gunned down in an otherwise innocuous dispute over an ounce of pedestrian dope, and Pimletz was called in to dress up the kid's adolescent life and hard times with the kind of sorry prose for which he was not yet known.

This time, too, the front page was not awarded to Pimletz for anything he had written, but for what he was asked, by default, to write. It fell to him, is all. The significant play had nothing to do with Axel Pimletz and everything to do with Terence Wood. The front page was there to be filled.

Even so, Pimletz is plenty pleased with himself as he strolls to the paper's reception area to pinch a couple more copies of the four-star final. He wants a complete set, a front page from every edition (maybe he'll have them framed, side by side, for one of his bare walls), and he also wants some extras, just to have. You never know, he's thinking, as he lifts seven or eight copies from the stack by the main elevators. He hugs the papers close, partly to conceal his excessive filching, but also for the strange comfort and assurance they offer. They are like a blanket to him, these newspapers, a protective coating, and the heavythick smell of newsprint reaches him like he matters. Yes, he thinks to himself, inhaling deeply. Yesyesyes.

There is so much ink committed to the sixty-point front-page headline—WOOD'S EXIT?—that Pimletz's fingers and clothing are right away rubbed black with the residue. This kind of mess he doesn't notice, at first, and when he does, he doesn't mind. This kind of mess he can get all over his not-pressed white shirt and probably when he gets home, he'll just hang the thing in his closet and leave the stains where they are. This kind of mess is a validation.

In truth, Pimletz's obit/tribute/send-off is just a sidebar to the lead story, but he rubs up against the banner headline as if it were his own. He walks the stack of papers to his desk and brings his nose to the front page of the one on top, breathes it in like it could not have been the front page without him. Who knows, he considers, working at some perspective, while somehow managing to keep himself in the picture. The headline to his own piece is far smaller than the banner—TERENCE WOOD: A MAN OF PARTS, in twenty-four–point, uppercase—but he chooses to view it in context.

Inhaling, still, he reminds himself of the kids in his elementary school pressing the teachers' freshly mimeographed assignment sheets to their faces, breathing deeply at the hard scents of knowledge, importance, technology. The smells are nothing alike, but the essence is the same. It's been thirty-five years, and he's moved from there to here, just.

He follows his story to the jump at the back of the paper, to look again at the spread of accompanying photos. Often, in the writing, Pimletz tries to picture his fallen subjects in his mind, to bring them back to life, although it rarely occurs to him to seek out an actual photograph while it still might impact on his actual prose. With Terence Wood, it would have been nothing to stop at the photo desk or to pull some clips from the morgue to help with his half-hearted attempts at visualization. It would have been nothing and everything, both. Instead, now, taking in the dozen or so images chosen by the photo desk to illustrate the actor's noted accomplishments, Pimletz kicks himself for what he's missed. There's a lot. There's that famous windswept still from *The Half Shell*, which Pimletz has, by this time, seen all over the television news accounts, and with each sighting, moved further from fathoming how he had somehow neglected to discuss the guy's breakthrough movie. There was that fleeting relationship with one of the Nixon girls, captured here in an uncaptioned paparazzi shot from some years-ago charity function. The romance sputtered after only a few weeks, but, by the time it did, it had made enough noise along both coasts that there might have been some indication of it in Pimletz's piece. There were screen collaborations with more Hollywood luminaries than Pimletz now cares to count—and more, apparently, than he cared to mention. There is even a photo of a baby-faced Wood testifying before the House Un-American Activities Committee, but Pimletz seems not to have had the inclination to elaborate on the actor's role in these proceedings.

Oh, well. His glaring omissions are enough to counter his enthusiasm over the Wood story, but not enough to leave him despondent. Really, it hadn't gone that badly, considering. (In consideration of what, Pimletz is not quite sure, but it never hurts to qualify things.) He did get to do his job, on deadline, over fifty column inches. He did cover the basics, basically. He did get a quote from Scorcese—something about how Wood managed to occupy more space than he actually took up (a positive quality, Pimletz is assuming)—and he did find some compelling anecdotal material from Wood's early years. And the kicker is the front fucking page, deserving or no. There he is, for all of greater Boston to see, or dismiss, or gloss over. "By Axel Pimletz." That he's missed a few of the particulars does not dim the light he was able to shine on Terence Wood's life and presumed death. Hopefully. And anyway, who the hell will know the difference?

"You call this an obit?" Hamlin, two desks over, pulls Pimletz from his post-mortem like he's on a string. Either he's noticed the holes in Pimletz's effort, or he's jerking him around.

"You mean, apart from the fact that this guy may or may not be dead?" Pimletz says back. He means to hang tough, to keep Hamlin and anyone else with the same idea from spoiling his already uncertain sense of accomplishment. He's feeling good enough about himself, doesn't want to lose it.

"Apart from that."

"Apart from that, yeah, why not? It's all there."

Hamlin moves quickly for the kill: "Was it Julie he nailed, or Tricia?"

Jesus, Pimletz thinks, this guy doesn't miss a thing. He throws up his palms in easy surrender. "Fine," he says, not wanting to argue Hamlin on this one. "Fine. So I fucked up. Beat me, whip me, fuck me dead."

"Just making a point," Hamlin says, disingenuous, moving from the attack to the defensive.

"Point being?"

"Point being it wasn't just you who fucked up, it was the whole fucking process fell apart. It's this sorry ass rag we write for. One guy fucks up, it's not a problem, it happens, but there's no checks and balances. No system. That's the fucking problem. One hand's got no fucking clue what the other is doing."

Pimletz sees Hamlin is revving himself up, and when this guy gets going on what's wrong with the *Record-Transcript*, or newspapers in general, or the decline in the ability of the general population to distinguish between its ass and the couch it's sitting on, there's no derailing him. He's like a rollercoaster gone berserk. Here it comes: "This is just one thing, but it's everything. No one knows what anyone else is doing around here. Who's minding the fucking store? I mean, don't take this personal, Axel, but come on, if some goddamn hack is going to drop the ball on a story, then Volpe and whoever the hell he's got working the copy desk and running photos should know better than to call attention to it. 'Hey! Look! Our guy fucked up! Here's pictures to prove it!' What the fuck are these people thinking?" Hamlin's words generate their own momentum as he talks, he's picking up speed: "I'll tell you what the fuck they're thinking, they're not thinking anything, that's the fucking problem. Nobody's thinking. That's the crux right there. That's it. These assholes haven't had a thought in their heads since they thought to apply for their damn jobs, and who knows what they were thinking then?"

Hamlin runs his fingers through his not-baled hair, catches up with his breath. "Okay, fine, so you missed a couple points on this actor," he says. "Big fucking deal. But how in the fuck can they run those pictures without fixing the holes in your story? This is basic stuff. Either they shit-can the pictures or plug your story." Hamlin has whipped himself into such a complete frenzy it appears he might choke on the foam in his mouth. He slows, trying to determine if he's made his point. "Am I right or am I right?"

"This is a rhetorical question?" Pimletz wants to know.

"This is a rhetorical question."

"In that case, asked and answered."

"Fine," Hamlin concludes, and underneath his conclusion, he's wondering how it is he lets himself get all lathered around a guy like Pimletz. *Asked and answered*. What the hell kind of way to talk is that? It's like talking to a fucking sitcom lawyer, to a guy who's being paid by the ten-dollar word. Once, Pimletz made the mistake of confiding that he sometimes makes an effort to work new words and phrases into his conversation, and Hamlin has been able to spot his lame attempts at vocabulary-building ever since. Asked and answered. Jesus.

"Fine," Pimletz echoes.

"Civet," Hamlin says.

"Civet?"

"For your precious vocabulary. It's the fatty secretion of an animal. As in, the fucking cat got its civet all over the fucking place."

"Fuck you, Hamlin."

"Fuck me," Hamlin concurs. "Put me in my place." He's had about enough fun at poor Pimletz's expense. There's no sport in it. It's like the Red Sox playing those fuckers out at Harvard. Unchallenged, disinterested, he retreats to his desk and turns on his computer. By the time the prompts appear on his warmed screen, he has rolled his sleeves, sugared his coffee, sorted the mess of papers at his desk, and speed-dialed one of the mayor's top advisors for a comment on the just-proposed city budget.

Pimletz looks on and can't help but marvel at this guy. He gets going like that on what's wrong with the paper, on and on, and then he just lets it go, moves on to the next thing. Plus, he's got more next things than anyone. He's exceeded his quota of next things. His next things are corralled into one of those snake lines they've got at the bank, waiting for Hamlin's next available piece of attention. With Pimletz, it's the other way around. He's the one on line, endlessly waiting for some next thing to fill his day, to move him forward. He can look up *civet* in the dictionary, but that's about it.

"Hey, Axel," Hamlin hollers, when he's off the phone with city hall, waiting for his next call to go through. He's gotten a second wind with his razzing. His eyes are fixed on his terminal as he talks, he doesn't swivel to face his target. He doesn't need to look at Pimletz to know he has his ear. "This is what I'm thinking," he says, typing, leaning over to lap at his coffee. "I'm thinking either it's Ash Wednesday, or whatever it is you people celebrate, or you've been moonlighting as a fucking chimney sweep." He keeps typing as he talks, working his budget story.

"Say again?" Pimletz tries. He's got no idea where his heckling friend is going with this one. Somewhere. Usually he can tell.

"The newsprint, Axel. What's with the newsprint?"

"Oh," Pimletz says, "that." He holds out his hands to check the damage. "Hands could use a wash."

"Fuck the hands," Hamlin says. "Look at the rest of you. Look at your face. You look like you been working in a fucking mine."

Pimletz has no idea what Hamlin is talking about, can't tell from his reflection in his dull terminal screen, but then he flashes back to a picture of himself putting his nose to the front page, and he thinks, Jesus, what a stupid fucking thing to do! Things are difficult enough around here, and he has to go compound his problems by getting caught smelling the goddamn newspaper.

Hamlin, swallowed once more by his next things, is deep into his story, back on the phone, so Pimletz slinks a couple desks over to Sam Haskins's station and cracks the box of Baby Fresh baby wipes his fastidious colleague keeps by his terminal. Haskins isn't in yet, most people aren't in yet, and Pimletz pulls one of the aloe-scented, hypoallergenic sheets and rubs at his hands. The wipe is wetter than it needs to be. It's supposed to be alcohol free, according to the label on its box, but it smells faintly medicinal as Pimletz reaches it to his face. He keeps one eye on Hamlin as he wipes himself. He's satisfied he's not being watched, but he lets his other eye take in the Baby Fresh packaging. He is satisfied to learn that he is not only cleaning the newsprint from his face and hands, but he is also moisturizing his skin with benzoic acid and grapefruit seed extract—a good side benefit. When he finishes, he tosses the spent wipe into Haskins's lined waste bin, dries his hands against his pants, and returns to his own desk, largely unnoticed and somewhat refreshed.

"Fresh as a baby's bottom?" Hamlin chides, his back still to Pimletz.

"You working or keeping tabs?" Pimletz says. Fucker is all over him, riding him, all the time, and this is the best he can manage. Once, just once, Pimletz would love to come up with something that might put this guy in his place.

"Both," Hamlin snaps back, punching out a new number, from memory, on the telephone. "I'm also chewing gum and cleaning my oven." He swivels around to face Pimletz and reclines his chair. "See," he says, chewing loudly. He rubs at his stomach and pats his head. "I can also do this," he continues. Then he switches to patting his stomach and rubbing his head. "And this."

"The Amazing Hamlin!" Pimletz teases back. "Miracle reporter!" He's not sure whether to play along or to lean into the guy for his baiting.

Hamlin swivels back to his work, leaving Pimletz to figure if what has just passed between them has really just passed between them, if it was simply some stressful, one-sided interoffice rough-housing, or something else. He can never be certain with Hamlin, and just as his figuring has got him leaned to where he can imagine some affection underneath his colleague's steady ribbing, Hamlin delivers a final blow to tilt his figuring the other way. "Maybe your friend Sam would be kind enough to leave a box of his moist towelettes in the Men's," Pimletz hears from the back of Hamlin's head. "Never know when you might need to freshen up."

Great, Pimletz thinks. Just fucking great.

═══

One thing about Anita Tollander Wood Veerhoven: she is famous for the way she can't make coffee, even instant. She never remembers if she should round off her spoons, or level them, or what. This was one of Terence Wood's running complaints during their years together, one that ran with him to his next marriage, to Pet. His replacement, Nils Veerhoven, a Norwegian rug cleaner with unnecessarily curly hair and a smear of moustache, doesn't seem to mind. Nils's drink is cocoa, and he makes it himself.

"Just some bottled water," Petra Wood says, when Anita asks her to join her in a second cup only five minutes after pouring her first. "If you have."

"Tap," Anita replies. "This is New Hampshire."

"Tap, then." Beat. "It's okay to drink?"

"Yes, it's okay to drink. You're drinking it now. That's what's in the coffee."

"Maybe that should tell me something," Petra says, laughing gently at her friend's expense. (Back home, she makes her coffee with Evian.)

It is late morning, but early for Pet, forget the time difference. Plane arrived at Logan about ten last night, and by the time she pulled into her friend's drive, after some trouble with her bags, it was past Letterman. Nahant is, like, nowhere, she was thinking, driving, following the directions in the beam of map light supplied by her rented Sunbird. Make a wrong turn up here and you're gone.

Anita laughs back, happy to have so much shared history suddenly perched across her kitchen table. She needs this. With Nils, there's been a surface comfort—*Oh, Nita, how awful it must be for you! Tell me what you need*—but there's no connection, now, about what's happened to Wood. How could she expect a connection? He tries, Nils, he wants to be there for her, but his there is not the same place as hers. She's in a completely different zip code. It's been more than twenty-four hours since she first heard, and she's walking around like someone's cut her arms off, that's how helpless and desperate the accident has made her feel. Alone. She's been left lost, crazy, unfocused, and she's hoping maybe Pet can pull her back in time for Norman.

God, Norman. Don't even get her started about Norman. He left New York early this morning, borrowed his roommate's car, said to look for him around lunch. At least she didn't have to tell him. Some jerk wire service reporter took care of that, and as enraged as she was to learn of the way her son absorbed word of his father's probable death—in the hall, outside some screening room, delivered cellularly by some interloping journalist who thought it appropriate to pull Norman from class for a comment—she was also grateful. What would she have said? *Oh, Norman, by the way. . . .* There're no words to tell something like this. There's no way to hear it. This way, at least, he knows.

Pet's mind isn't focused yet on these unfamiliar surroundings or on the unsettling tragedy that seems to be happening, still, to some other set of people. It's happening, sort of, but it's not happening to her. It's like she's not paying good attention, like she's watching a documentary that can't quite hold her interest. (Plus, she's in New Hampshire.) She thinks this is something she can undo, reinvent, that the facts of her estranged husband's apparent demise can be rewritten as easily as one of his lousy scripts. She thinks this must be what people mean when they say something is surreal.

Also, she's not fully awake, and she has yet to move after the endless drive of the night before, or the long flight that preceded it. "Live free or die," she says, in mid-distraction. "What the hell is that?" This has been troubling her.

Anita's thinking, we should be doing something here, must be someone we can call: police, lawyers, private investigators, someone. There's this psychic down in Jersey, some sweet old lady, she's been on all the talk shows with her knack for discovering dead bodies and missing persons, maybe she has some ideas. Then she's thinking, no, we should leave the line clear, case someone is trying to reach us, that's what we should be doing. She's thinking she should have had that call waiting put in by the phone company back when it was being offered, free installation, even if she can't stand it. Times like this are when you need a feature like call waiting. Maybe Norman's having car trouble, maybe he's trying to call. Maybe Terence has turned up on a piece of Pathfinder or driftwood a couple miles down the coast. Maybe he's delirious or comatose. Maybe he's lost his short-term memory. Maybe he's asking for her. There are, like, a couple dozen things to consider, viable things, and she is startled when Pet introduces yet another. "What the hell is what?" she manages.

"On the license plates," Pet explains, as if it were plain. "Live free or die. I'm driving here, middle of the night, I pull over for gas, and every car at the pump has to tell me this. Live free or die. Live free or die. Like I need all these cars to be telling me this."

"It's the state motto."

"Figures," Pet says, realizing. "But what does it mean? Think about it. Live free or die. What the hell is that doing on everyone's car?"

"You know, I don't really know," Anita allows. She's never considered the question before, and this surprises her, now that she's been asked. She's lived in New Hampshire a half-dozen years, and it's never come up. "Probably just a patriot thing," she guesses.

"Patriots, the football team?"

"No, patriots the patriots," Anita says. "American Revolution. Paul Revere. Taxation without representation. That whole deal."

"Oh," Pet says, realizing again. "Right." For a moment, she'd forgotten where she was. She downs her tap water in one long pull, presses the cool of the empty glass against her forehead, rolls it around up there like she saw someone do in a movie. Faye Dunaway, maybe. She's trying to startle herself awake, into focus. Pay attention, she summons herself. Pay attention. "What's to eat?" she wonders, thinking food might help.

Anita stands, peeks into the fridge. "Eggs," she announces. "I could make omelettes."

"Omelettes sounds good."

"Better yet," Anita continues, now by the pantry closet, "there should be a box of matzos in here, still good." She's rummaging among her shelves, back to where the hardly used containers of honey and syrup have left their gooey imprints on her flowery shelving paper. There's rice back here from the day she moved in; she's afraid to open the package to see what's inside.

Pet sees where her friend is going with this and smiles, remembering. Wife number one, Elaine (or, "the Jewess," as she is alternately known to wives two and three), used to cook up this breakfast thing called matzo bry, which was basically just scrambled eggs and crackers. Wood went crazy for the stuff, and he was always asking Anita and, later, Pet to whip him up some. He was no more Jewish than Billy Graham, but this was his idea of a treat, and he had Anita collect the recipe from Elaine, and Pet from Anita, like it was some goddamn heirloom. And it's not like it was any big deal of a recipe, just eggs and matzo, hard to screw up eggs and matzo, but he liked it prepared with Tabasco sauce and dill leaves and whatever else Elaine used to throw into the mix. (Also ketchup, in the pan, if she's remembering it right.) Tell the truth, Pet developed a taste for the stuff herself, although not to where she would ever fix a plate without Wood. "You keep matzo?" she asks her friend. "What's that all about? Nils is Jewish? Veerhoven is a Jewish name?"

Anita, from inside the pantry: "About as Jewish as Mamie Eisenhower." She doesn't know where she gets this, but the connection makes her laugh.

Pet, too, and, for a moment, the two wives are lost in a wave of shared silliness. "So?" she presses, out from under her laughing.

"I cook with it," Anita says, emerging from the pantry to explain her matzo stash. "Puddings, soup stock, things like that. Not much lately, but I keep some around." She places the box down on the counter and begins breaking sheets of matzo into bite-size pieces.

Pet steps from the table to help with the eggs. She cracks them awkwardly with two hands, as if she hasn't spent much time in a kitchen. She has her thumbs do most of the work. "One or two?" she asks, holding up an egg. "Eggs."

"Whatever," Anita says. "Might as well do them all. Maybe Nils will want."

Cracking, Pet tells how once she left the matzo to soak in the egg-beat for something like four or five minutes, and how when she cooked it all up, she was left with a plate of what basically amounted to eggs and wet soup crackers. "Wood didn't say anything, though," she says, "just cleaned his plate without a word."

"He'd eat anything."

"Telling me."

"Him and his Oreos," Anita recalls. "Remember?"

How could Pet forget? She still has a shelf full of them in her own cupboard back home. She's been doling them out to herself, one a day, since Wood moved out. She tells this to her friend.

"You're holding on to him," Anita interprets. "When you eat the last cookie, that's when you can let him go. I'm surprised you don't see it."

"You think?"

"Yes, I think. I don't see what else it could be. You don't eat Oreos. Why else would you be eating Oreos all of a sudden?"

Pet shrugs. "It's just one a day."

"This is why," Anita concludes. "My God, this is exactly what you're doing. Exactly. You're usually so on about these things."

"But we were getting a divorce," Pet says, trying to understand herself. "This is stupid. We were divorcing."

"But there's a piece of you thinks maybe you would have worked it out, am I right?"

"What, worked it out? There were teams of lawyers on this thing. It was ugly. It wasn't a work-it-out kind of thing."

"What about maybe underneath the ugliness, maybe there was some secret hope, something, that things could get back to how they were?"

Pet looks at Anita blankly.

"Don't tell me you never thought of it," Anita says.

"Okay."

"Okay, what?"

"I won't tell you I never thought of it."

"Seriously, Pet."

"I am being serious. What we had was gone. Just like what you had was gone. That's Wood."

"But privately, in your most secret, secret places, tell me you're not still in love with him." Beat. "Forget me. Tell yourself."

She's fishing here, Anita, but she fishes with such conviction that Pet begins to recognize herself. She wants to accept what Anita is saying. Of course, she lets herself think. She's too close to have seen it, but suddenly it's clear. It's so obvious. Of course she still loves him. This is just her way of keeping him near. Oreos. One each day. Now and forever. And now especially. She can't let go. It doesn't occur to Pet that Wood is dead or even that he might be dead. She's forgotten, for a moment, the dreadful news that brought her here.

She's thinking in terms of the day before yesterday, of calling off her attorneys, of going back home to her husband. She's thinking everything is as it was, and maybe she'll just go back into therapy to figure this further. Maybe she'll find some way to control herself and bring her emotions into better check, or maybe, when she gets home, she'll simply take all those unopened bags of Oreos over to the food drop by her dry cleaners. But, as she's thinking these things, her friend is busy reeling in an even better explanation for her behavior.

"Of course," Anita continues, this time with not nearly so much conviction, "there's always the possibility that maybe you just like Oreos. Maybe after all these years he just wore you down." She laughs as she says this, mostly because it strikes her as funny, but also because she wants Pet to know she's just fooling around.

Petra Wood ponders this and feels taken, duped. First Anita gets her going on what might have been a momentous personal revelation, and then she makes like she's just kidding. *Boom. Never mind. Ha ha.* "Fuck you," Pet says. She's pissed, but she's trying to return Anita's playfulness. "Fuck you very much." She grabs the empty egg carton and tosses it at her friend. It lands at her feet.

"My pleasure," Anita says, stepping over the carton to the stove. She flicks some of her own saliva into the saucepan to see if it sizzles.

"Gross," Pet says, noticing.

"Oh, come on. Like you've never done it."

"Not when I'm cooking for someone else," Pet insists. "And not when someone else could see me, no."

"Well, we'll just pretend you didn't see, okay?"

"Easy for you to say," Pet says, and then lets it drop. Her mind is someplace else.

"Dry or runny?" Anita asks, spilling the egg-beat into the pan.

Pet comes back from wherever she was and thinks they're still talking about the spittle, but then she gets that it's about the eggs. "In between," she says.

Nils's pickup rumbles unmuffled into the carport. He was out on an early flood job this morning before the rest of the house was awake, and he's not sure what he'll find back inside. This has troubled him all morning.

Pet hasn't seen him yet—he couldn't wait up last night with Anita—and she goes to intercept him and make trouble. "Nilsy!" she cries, throwing open her arms. She's wearing one of Anita's robes, no sash, and when she spreads her arms, the robe opens with them. Underneath, she's got on an *Everything's Archie* T-shirt from Wood's last movie, nonmerchandized panties, and that's it. She knows poor Nils will blush from the exposure. "How's my Swedish meatball?" she says, collecting him for a hug and adding all kinds of color to his face. She doesn't care that he's from Norway. Norway, Sweden, it's all the same to her. Denmark, even.

Petra Wood is everywhere on Nils, all at once. She kisses him on the lips, cups his ass, runs her fingers through his thick curls.

"Pet," he says, untangling himself from her groping. "Good that you're here." He's flustered, his cheeks the color of cartoon embarrassment. "You might want to do something about that robe."

"Oh, don't be such a prude," Pet chides, and then she snaps the robe open and shut, and open and shut, like a flasher. "Wake up, Nahant!" she screams across the street. "It's showtime!" Then to Anita, who has joined them on the front walk, she says, "He's mine, you know. I'm next in line." To Nils: "I get all her leftovers."

"I'm not through with him yet," Anita says, moving to rescue her proper husband from Pet's teasing. She wraps his arm around her shoulders like a stole.

"Yeah, well, when you're done," Pet says, taking Nils's other arm. To Nils, in a hot whisper: "We share everything, you know."

Nils laughs uncertainly and walks the two women to his kitchen door. This is not a comfortable thing for him. This is not the way he is with people, not what he expected to find here this morning, but he can't think how to move the situation to where he can relax around it. There is no gentlemanly way for him to squirm free of Petra without also losing hold of Anita, so he leaves his arms where they are. And there is no way for him to silence his wife's friend or voice his disapproval without setting an unpleasant tone for the rest of the morning. All he can do is wait for it to pass. This is not the way he expected his day to go. He spent the morning pumping three inches of water from a flooded basement, hauling the wet vac down and up the stairs, and when he stopped to think about Nita and Pet back here waiting on breakfast, he imagined they'd be all over themselves with tears and grief and worry. Last thing he expected was to find them whooping it up, laughing, like their ex-husband hadn't just driven off a cliff, like there was nothing going on.

"I'll just wash up," he says, when they finally reach the door. He steps clear of Pet and makes for the stairs, thinking, okay, I'll go change my clothes and catch my breath and by the time I come down she'll have tired of this game. By the time I come down she'll be back in the kitchen, brooding over her precious Terence, weaving her worst-case scenarios together with Anita's to where there will no longer be room for such flirtation.

"Not so fast," Pet says, grabbing for his shirt. She's not finished with Nils just yet, and he can't think quickly enough to stop her. She untucks the back of his shirt and pulls herself up the stairs toward him by its tail. He doesn't want to appear rude or unfriendly, so he doesn't shake her off the way he might. She throws off her robe and turns to Anita on the landing below. "Me and Nilsy," she says, mock-sweet, "we got time for a tumble before breakfast?"

=====

Wood needs cash and coffee. He's down to about thirty dollars, with no place to stay and no prospects. Last night was dry and reasonably warm, and he didn't do too badly on a bench in an unlit corner of a municipal parking lot, but he feels like shit this morning. Looks like shit, too, he imagines, although perhaps this last is not quite so unfortunate. He thinks maybe it'll be easier to blend in if he's not himself, if his two days growth of beard and dead skin cells leave him looking, smelling a shade more like the day laborers crowding into Two Stools's coffee shop for their morning caffeine, and a little less like the hulking, tortured presence of an untethered movie star he had only recently been. Like shit is a good thing, probably.

"Harlan," Two Stools greets, as Wood sits himself at one of her loose tables. Her tone is agreeable, but she's got her head down. She's wiping at the table with a once-wet rag from her apron belt and righting the ash tray, sugar tower, and salt and pepper shakers into a kind of arrangement at the center. Her entire upper body sways with the choreographed effort, even after she is through. She goes through these motions a hundred times each day; she's all business, and yet Wood can find no dullness to her routine.

"Grace," he says back.

She smiles shyly, recalling her first encounter with this unusual man. "Coffee?" she says, stepping away from the table after she's set it right.

"Decaf?"

"No," she says. "Coffee. My people drink it straight."

"Coffee, then." Actually, he can always use the caffeine, now especially.

"Black?"

Wood nods and watches as she retreats, reaches behind the counter for the coffee pot, a cup and saucer, and returns with these to his table. She carries the cup and saucer individually, each pressed flat between the flesh of one forearm and breast and not fitted together collectively the way Wood is accustomed to seeing. He notices this, thinks it strange, but it doesn't do any more than occur to him.

"What kind of name is Harlan?" Two Stools asks, setting down the saucer and cup.

"Gaelic," Wood guesses.

"Gaelic?"

"Maybe. I don't really know. I used to know when I was a kid."

"Gaelic, like Celtic? Up here, we know about the Celtics."

He's about to be tripped up and quickly shifts to safer ground: "I've always thought it's not where a name comes from that's important, but where you take it, what you do to make it your own." Drivel. This is what these people are good at. This is what he'll have to learn.

Two Stools weighs Wood's nonsense, but it proves too much for her. "I've never known a Harlan before," she manages.

"Well," Wood says, "here I am." He twirls his right hand against the air with a flourish, as if he might take a bow the way Carson used to do in his Carnac bit.

"Only other Harlan I even heard of was Colonel Sanders," Two Stools offers. "You know the Colonel Sanders I mean?"

This Grace, Wood's thinking. She moves from one thing to the next and expects the world to follow. That he has strikes him as remarkable. "Colonel Sanders, the chicken guy?" he says.

"That's the one. Colonel Harlan Sanders's Famous Recipe Chicken."

"He's a Harlan?" Wood asks. This might be a good thing to know.

"Was," Two Stools reports. "Dead now, pretty sure."

Wood files this away, wonders how it is that the kind of woman who would retain a piece of information like this hasn't yet shown herself to be the kind of woman who would also recognize his hulking, tortured self. Probably, she picked up this morsel on the Kentucky Fried Chicken guy from *People* or *Entertainment Tonight*—where else would she learn something like that?—and it follows that a frequent consumer of such infotainments might have come upon an item regarding Terence Wood, with accompanying photo, at one time or another. Surely, if this Grace can identify the Kentucky Fried Chicken guy by his given name, then it's only a matter of time before she identifies the internationally famous Terence Wood. Maybe she already has. Maybe she's seen the papers and heard the news on the radio and put it together and figured it wasn't a big enough deal to say anything about it. Maybe she's showing great restraint in not revealing Wood to her other customers, keeping him for herself. Maybe she's picking her spots, working some unforseen angle. Maybe she's some backwater Kathy Bates, stalking him, planning to inflict unspeakable miseries on his presumed dead body, deep fry his body parts and serve him up in a red and white bucket.

She disappears for a bit and returns with what appears to Wood to be a plate of corned beef hash. Where it comes from, he's got no idea. Doesn't seem to Wood she had time to slip back into the kitchen to pick up an order, but here it is, and it looks to be heading his way. This must be considered. Last time Wood ate hash was from a vacuum-packed tin on maneuvers, and the idea of interacting with Two Stools's version is perhaps more than his uneasy stomach can manage. Still, he does not want to appear rude or suspect, so he prepares himself for a couple polite mouthfuls. Better to accept her good will, he overthinks, than to send it back untouched.

"Look here, sailor," Grace announces, laying the plate before Wood with importance. "Jimmy over there said he wasn't much for hash this morning." She flits her eyes across the room to indicate an oily little man with someone else's name stitched over the pocket of his mechanic's overalls. "Said he'd rather just have a bowl of oatmeal. H'only took but a few bites. Shame to waste it."

Wood doesn't catch Two Stools's meaning straight off, and when he does, he is thrown: she means for him to finish this oily man's breakfast. This is what he looks like to her, a man who might welcome a hardly touched plate of used hash. This is what he has become overnight, and the realization leaves him pleased, uncertain, disoriented. He gets a thick noseful of the gestured food and it mixes with the idea of where it's been to leave Wood feeling queasy—happy at the ease of his transformation and yet unsure of his ability to walk about in his new role.

"Coffee's about all I can manage," he says kindly, inching the plate from his range of smell.

"Suit yourself," Grace sings back, and she collects the hash and reconnoiters with it to an already-started plate of same, two tables over, apparently occupied by a diner with less discriminating tastes. She slops the hash from one plate to the next without a word. She doesn't even step back to notice her breakfasting customer—a large, also-oily, also-overalled man, who receives the extra helping as if he has it coming, as if everyone around here eats from the same pot like it's nothing at all.

This, Wood thinks, might take some getting used to.

＝

Here's Norman: half-orphaned, half-paying attention, halfway home to deal with his mother, this guy she married, Pet, every damn thing. Woodman. This right here's the hard part.

It's like it's not real. Half real. Half assed and half real. The way Norman heard, what he heard, what he knows, it's all like something out of one of Woodman's movies. It's happened, it's scripted, but it's not yet finished. He's been redirected, his whole life set off course, but then there's this gaping loophole, another way around. His father's dead, but maybe not. He smirks at his own melodrama, but he is held by it, taken. Poor Norman's been ripped apart and left hanging, half orphaned, but maybe not. Better: quarter-orphaned. Still, he's more orphan than not. He considers the phrase. Movie title, he thinks. *More Orphan Than Not.* Something he can use.

The loaner he's driving lost its radio to an unfortunate piece of parking a couple weekends ago on Riverside Drive, so Norman's got the headphones on full tilt: "It's a Sunshine Day" retooled by some industrial band. His roommate's tape. He remembers the song from a *Brady Bunch* episode and wonders what it's doing now in his ears. *Everybody's laughing. Sunshine day-ay-ay. Everybody's smiling. Sunshine day-ay-ay.*

Maybe in 1973, he thinks. Now's another story.

Norman ramps onto the Massachusetts Turnpike underneath a helmet of grunge-kitsch. He's got the windows down, the sunroof cracked, but the traffic sounds don't reach through the headphones. He's cocooned himself from whatever else is going on, denied to the rest of the world, like he's driving in one of those boothed arcade games: Killer Grand Prix. If he drifts from his lane, he'll never hear the bleat of horn to scare him back in line.

He's in his own head, a straight shot into Boston. Nothing to distract him, but, at the same time, there's nothing to keep him focused, rooted. His thoughts bounce from school to home, friends to family, from the picture he was deconstructing before he heard to this right here, right now. There's *The Godfather* and the destruction of the American family, and there's the Woodman and the destruction of his. There's nothing to hold him to the moment, but this doesn't register as a concern, at least not on any conscious level, and certainly not at first. Anyway, it's not like the road twists and turns all that much. What the hell is there to pay attention to anyway? He can watch *The Godfather* and still drive this road. There's a slight curl off the Pike onto Interstate 93, north to New Hampshire, but that's it. If he keeps his eyes between the lines, dead ahead, he should do just fine.

To Norman—unfocused, driving—the Mass Pike has got to be one of the most boring stretches of asphalt ever committed to high-speed, intrastate travel. Absolutely. In truth, there are sparkling lakes, lush valleys, and here and there, pockets of great natural beauty, but to

Norman the road just unravels and keeps going and going. The only dots on the landscape are the rest stops and food courts that reappear before it even occurs to him to eat, or piss, or stretch his legs. It's like his needs have been programmed into the road. Also, it's like one long strip mall with no good stores. It's like a lot of things, he thinks, and, at the same time, like nothing at all. Even the songs blasting through his head are no distraction. What the hell kind of songs are these, he wonders. Who programmed this fucker? He's way up on the volume, but he's not truly listening. He keeps flashing back on images of his father: speedboating in Cannes, high-rolling in Vegas, limelighting in Hollywood, uncoiling in one of his ridiculous fucking cabins. . . . Stills from a long life lived someplace else.

They are everywhere for Norman, these images. Everywhere and in no one place. Here's one: long time ago, on vacation in Sun Valley, Idaho, his father ditched a perfectly good snowmobile into a perfectly passable gully. He wanted to see how long it would take rescuers to track down his missing self and wanted to impart to Norman his strange values of patience and place and purpose. For several hours, father and son sat huddled against the cold in a crude snow bank, awaiting salvation, weighing the mysteries of the peculiar lives they shared. The picture reforms in Norman's racing head as if it never left. He was only ten or twelve, too young to be placed into such danger or introspection, but it's all here for him still: the fleeting closeness with his father, the taste of the old man's breath bouncing off the packed snow, the strangely adolescent notion that through Terence Wood's eyes the world must seem a sorry fucking place.

He does not remember being afraid.

"Bad for business, them to let us freeze to death," Woodman told his only child, presumably in reassurance. The words reached Norman's nose before they found his ears. "You'll see."

And he did. The sun didn't set on the valley before the father proved his labored point to his young son, the boy he saddled with the eery-queery name of Anthony Perkins's *Psycho* character years after it mattered that Wood had lost the part. When mountain patrol workers arrived breathlessly on the scene, the actor was appropriately stoic. It never occurred to Norman to reveal the purposefulness of the incident to rescuers, to his mother (God, she would have just shit!), to any of the dozen reporters who had gathered at the Idaho hospital where father and son were choppered and treated for frostbite, and it was never again discussed. There were the requisite mentions on *Entertainment Tonight*, CNN, and a two-page spread (with "exclusive photos") in *People*, but the incident was pushed from public attention by a staged reconciliation between Dean Martin and Jerry Lewis and a flare-up at a gala Holmby Hills picnic for the preservation of the rainforests, during which the actress Blythe Danner would not accept that the organizer's choice blend of Brazilian coffee was being served and warmed in nonrecyclable styrofoam cups. There followed, respectively, a flap and a scene, and after such as these, the news of a celebrity snowmobiling mishap seemed a trifle, even if it seemed to Norman Wood the largest, most defining fucking moment of his young life. In the movie he keeps in his head, this was a key scene.

Still, it happened and it was over. To talk about it would have been to put his father on the defensive, to question the precepts he had put on display. It occurs to him now, naturally, because of the similarity to yesterday's accident. He imagines the headline: GAS-POWERED VEHICLE DROPS FROM THE FACE OF THE EARTH, but also because of the manner in which it reveals his father: impetuous, impervious, self-important.

Now that Norman Wood's put his unfocused head to it, virtually every memory of his father reveals similar aspects of character. There was that time, this is going back now, when the Woodman went on the Carson show to endorse independent presidential candidate John Anderson and wound up referring to Ronald Reagan and Jimmy Carter as "a couple dumb fucks." (Norman's seen the tape, with Carson's classic doubletake, the censor's transparent bleep; it made the anniversary show, couple years running.) Or, just this past summer, when he called a press conference to announce his application for the post of Commissioner of Major League Baseball. (Come to think of it, what the hell was that all about?) Or, when the maitre'd at Lutece wouldn't seat him without a reservation, no matter who he was, and the old man simply walked to an empty, not-bussed table and sat himself down, without reservation, at a table next to Liz Smith, who made dutiful note of the incident in her next column.

And even this. This business with the car over the cliff, the body missing, the terror of not knowing what happened, the raging doubt surrounding his father's last moments, if they were indeed his last moments . . . it all seems to Norman like a part of the same package. It is all just the Woodman, as ever, on his own kick, manipulating his world to his own rhythms, having his way.

Tollbooth guy, just off Route 128 outside Boston: "No pennies."

Norman, who had counted out the toll with what change he had: "Why not?"

"Read the sign."

Norman reads the sign: No Pennies. Okay, he thinks, so now we can all read. "Okay," he tries, lifting the headphones from their perch and sliding them down around his neck like a collar, "but why not? Maybe they screw up the machines or something, but this is the full-service lane, right?"

"Sign's not there for my health."

To Norman, this seems an arbitrary nuisance. He holds out his coins, palm up, sixty-five cents. Exact change. "Either you want my money, or you don't," he says.

Tollbooth guy looks back at Norman from inside his own bad day. Norman sees that he's got his tiny workstation decorated with pictures of Selena and Jesus, the slain Latin singer and the crucified son of God. Funny how Norman'd never heard of Selena while she was alive. And funnier how he'd been raised to think he, Norman, was the son of God, crucified by his very birth and the burdens that came with it. Lately, before he heard, he tried not to think about his father, to place himself in some unvarnished context, but these last couple hours, he can't lose the old man. A part of Norman believes his father is in the car with him, spiriting him through these next paces, telling him what to do.

A fruity-smelling stick of incense, not unpleasant, burns alongside the cash register inside the tollbooth. Gloria Estefan is scratching her way from a Tandy transistor radio hanging from a hook on the far wall. "Turn the Beat Around." Tollbooth guy's got a sterling silver cross dangling from his left ear, a jail-green tattooed serpent slithering from his right shirt-sleeve. He flashes a gold-toothed, fume-sucking smile that tells Norman he's up for the hassle. "I could write you up for the headphones alone," he says, reaching toward the incense for an official-looking pad. "Take down your plates, send you out a nice fucking summons."

"You want my money or not?" Norman says back, palm still open.

"I'm tellin' you, kid. Bust my hump and I'll bust yours."

At this, Norman turns his open palm over and lets the coins drop to the pavement. Some of the coins are stuck to his sweaty skin, and these he scratches off with the fingers of his other hand. "Don't bother counting it," he says in his best Woodman impression. "It's all there." Then he stomps on his roommate's gas pedal and speeds from the toll plaza, itching for a chase. The car doesn't respond the way he'd like it to—it goes zero to sixty in a time no one would advertise—but it does the job, and, as he pulls away, Norman thinks he doesn't have to put up with this shit. Nobody should have to put up with this shit. Not someone who is more like his father than he knows.

======

Phone.

It takes Pimletz a half-dozen rings before he realizes it's his own line and not Hamlin's. It's not like anyone ever calls, not unless he's left a message and is waiting to hear back. On his voice mail, he tells people he's either away from his desk or on another call, but he's never had to use the damn thing. He's hardly away from his desk, and he's rarely on another call. If he leaves a message for a coroner or a funeral home director or a grieving family member, he waits around until he hears back. It's been two years since the paper spruced up its phone system, and he's never even bothered to consult the memo the office services people sent around telling how to use it. It's not that he doesn't trust the technology; he doesn't trust people to make themselves available to him a second time.

"Pimletz," he barks into the handset, the way he's heard Hamlin bark his own name forty-three times already today. And it's not even lunch.

"Axel Pimletz?" he hears back. "Obit desk?"

No, he wants to say. Axel Pimletz, tax attorney. Synchronized swimmer. Horticulturist. Systems operator. Instead, he says, "This is he." What the hell kind of way is that to talk? He scolds himself, soon as he's said it. *This is he.*

Guy on the other end introduces himself as Warren Stemble, senior editor at Asterisk Books in Manhattan. "You may have heard of us," he says to

Pimletz, coaxing at recognition. "We've had quite a lot of ink these past months."

"I know the name," Pimletz concedes. He's thinking, I thought Asterisk was a magazine. He's thinking, books and magazines, they're becoming the same thing.

"Good. That makes what I have to say that much easier. I find it awkward having to introduce myself. I never know where to start. Don't you find that, Mr. Pimletz?"

For a guy so concerned about making what he has to say that much easier, this Warren Stemble doesn't seem to Pimletz to be in any great hurry to reach his point. "No," Pimletz says, "not really." He's got his own introduction down to where it doesn't mean a thing.

"Fine," Stemble follows. "Good. Well, then, here it is. I have a proposition for you."

"I'm listening."

"As you may know, my company owns world rights to Terence Wood's life story. He was at work on the manuscript at the time of his accident. We've seen only a few pages, but what we've seen is brilliant. Just brilliant. But that's Terence Wood for you, right?" He gets back nothing, continues. "I understand there are notes to be found among his papers and hours of unedited interviews on tape. Hopefully, somewhere, there's another few hundred pages of manuscript, possibly an outline of some sort. It had been our plan to publish Mr. Wood's autobiography late next year, but, in consideration of yesterday's tragedy, we would like to come out with it sooner."

"And?" Pimletz wouldn't recognize a proposition if it breathed hotly in his ear.

"And, naturally, we need a writer, someone to pull all the loose ends together. It must seem ghoulish, I know, for me to be on the phone to you the very next day, but you understand that time is of the essence."

Pimletz's first thought, also naturally, is that this polished, big time book editor, with his polished, big time moniker, is merely seeking a recommendation, a couple names from the *Record-Transcript* rank and file to start him on his search, maybe a confirming vote of approval. But then it hits him. It's not the rank and file this guy wants, just the rank.

"Me?" he checks. "Why me?"

"Don't be modest, Mr. Pimletz," Stemble pushes. "We saw the obituary in this morning's paper. Your paper. Front page, no less. Guy who writes like that should be writing for us."

Pimletz does not wish to argue the point, but he can't help himself. "Yes, but, still. . . . " He lets his mini-protestation hang, hoping Warren Stemble will be kind enough to upend his thought, or to keep him from having to finish it himself, but when there is no help forthcoming, he attempts a kind of follow-through: "There are, like, what, a million writers in New York? Another million out in L.A.?"

"Give or take," Warren Stemble agrees, "but how many up in Boston?" He doesn't wait for an answer. "You're New England. Terence Wood is New England. Christ, you live in his hometown."

I do, Pimletz wants to say. Then he's thinking, okay, I'm in the right place, but I'm also cheap. And available. He's thinking, it's not yet noon, but probably these Asterisk assholes have called every other hack who knows how to type and come up with shit. Probably, I'm a last resort dressed up to look like first choice. "What you read was a clip job," Pimletz says, damning his chances.

"And a fine clip job it was, Mr. Pimletz."

Jesus, this guy won't go away.

"Look, Axel," Warren Stemble says, "if I may call you Axel. I know how newspapers work. I know what you do. I did it myself for a time. I know that if you're like most writers, if you're like me, you have time on your hands. I know you can do this shit sleeping, and that you'd probably not like to be doing it for the rest of your life." Beat. "You'll let me know if I'm getting warm?"

"Go on."

"I also know that you're probably making, say, fifty-five thousand a year? Sixty, tops?"

"Warm."

"There's money to be made here, Axel," Warren Stemble says. "Good money. For all of us. For Wood's family, too, if that's a concern."

"How much?" Pimletz asks. "What are we talking about?" This he has to know.

═══

There's a town square, just outside Bar Harbor, actually looks more like a town parallelogram. What it is, basically, is a small, unevenly shaped patch of grass dropped into the middle of one of the busier intersections, making itself a much-angled rotary and the center of attention. On it, there's a bench and a plaque and a flagpole and two dormant flowerbeds.

He crosses onto the green without thinking about it, although perhaps he should. The center of attention is the last place a guy like Wood ought to be right now, and yet here he is, sunning his famous face on the most prominent bench in town, awash in the harsh glint of midday sun. He's got the place pretty much to himself, save for a couple terns. Or maybe seagulls. He's never been any good with birds. One thing he knows is they're not pigeons. Pigeons, he knows. Egrets, he thinks. They could be egrets.

He's got a Free! Take One! local newspaper tucked under his arm—*Acadia Week*—but he hasn't cracked it yet. He's figuring how to access his trapped, once-considerable funds, without giving himself away. This is both a nagging concern and a daunting puzzle. He might have thought of this beforehand, would have made things a whole lot easier, but his instincts did not anticipate any great need for financial planning. All he wanted was out, and there's no way back in without money.

Until yesterday, money was always one of the last things on his mind. There was someone to pay to think about his money for him. Now, he thinks of little else but what's left in his pockets, and from there it's a short trip to what he might find in the *Acadia Week* classifieds. In his head, he runs through the kinds of jobs he can handle, if it comes to that: he can paint houses, inside and out, if someone shows him how; he can lift things, heavy things, long as he doesn't have to navigate any stairs; he can trap lobsters, cut grass, clean toilets, read the news on the radio; hell, he can middle-manage, if he can find a local businessman fool enough to give him a shot.

Ah. He can also steal. Yes. This he's already done, at least in theory, for a time in rehearsal. Yes, this he can do, and here's why: early '70s, he was signed for the lead in a picture called *Harry in Your Pocket*, one of those benign caper comedies that were, for some reason, popular at the time. In the interest of verisimilitude (which was also, for some reason, popular at the time), he studied for weeks with a master pickpocket named Snake, a crappy little accountant from Nutley, New Jersey. Snake happened to discover his particular gift of dexterity when he abandoned his sleeping first wife on an Amtrak train headed for Virginia Beach. Snake, then known as Bernie, hopped off in Philadelphia after pinching two thousand dollars in travelers' checks and a complete set of credit cards from the inside zippered pocket of a baby blue rain slicker, which his sleeping first wife happened to have bunched up and put to use as a pillow to cushion her head against the hard window. Not bad, Bernie the Snake thought at the time, and for some years after. Guy landed in Vegas and made a quick name for himself. Regrettably, Wood was such a dedicated pupil and committed actor that he started to put his new pickpocketing skills to full use. After all, he justified, where was the challenge in lifting a wallet from a hanging suit of clothes when there was the real deal to consider? He wound up making his own name for himself, caught red-fingered on a casino video monitor, working his craft on an old man in a fishing hat who appeared to be from somewhere in Missouri. It made all the papers, and, in the fallout, Wood lost the part to James Coburn, a tough sonofabitch whose fingers were nowhere near as light, but who came without the excess baggage of a Nevada police record and a fucking file cabinet, legal, full of bad publicity.

So, anyway, he can steal. Definitely. Or, at least, borrow. Shouldn't be too hard to get the touch back in his fingers. Then, he'll set himself up, find a way to get the pinched wallet back to the duped tourist, make good on the monies, eventually. He doesn't have the head for outright thievery. There's a way to live with what he has to do, he thinks, if this is what he has to do. Can't go pinching from one of the locals, that would be like shitting on his new front lawn, but there're enough out-of-towners to get him going: just line the suckers up and pluck 'em off, one by one. No big thing.

Wood's got his scheming head tilted so far toward the other side of the law that he doesn't notice the short-legged, short-tempered police officer step onto his patch of grass and make a not-so-tentative approach. The cop kicks at Wood's bench with a scuffed black shoe, the heel of which has worn thin in such a way as to suggest a pronation problem. "All right," the police officer says, in a tiny bark, "move it along."

Wood, with guilty conscience, worries that the police officer has somehow read his mind, wants to pick him up on premeditation charges. He can't think of a thing to say in his own defense.

"Don't want no trouble here," the officer keeps at him. "Move it along." He waves his billy club at Wood like a paintbrush, back and forth to where he just might black out the whole scene.

Reflexively, Wood lifts himself from the bench, but then he sets himself back down, reconsidering. This, too, is reflexive, but it takes a while for it to kick in. He's not breaking any laws here, Wood quickly realizes. It's not a crime merely to ponder an illegal act. Hey! Far as the law knows, Wood's just a guy killing time on a public bench, minding his own. Who is this squat little man with bad shoes and a possible pronation problem to try to move me along? Where does he get off? Cop doesn't know who he's dealing with, Wood thinks. I'll move myself along when I damn fucking feel like it. A part of him wants to bark back at the officer in the same brusque tone, but he is checked by common sense. He crosses his legs, clasps his hands behind his head, leans back and says, "Friend, I'm in no particular hurry."

This, he believes, is an appropriate response.

The badly shoed police officer, believing otherwise, slaps the billy club in the pit of his own left arm and reaches for his holster with his freed right hand. He wants to be ready. Last time he met up with some belligerent psycho, the fucker nearly tore his head off. This guy looks big enough to give him trouble. He wonders what the lunar cycle is looking like these days. Usually, he doesn't pay attention, but he read somewhere that these assholes get going all kinds of weird when there's a full moon. He's careful to tread lightly here, doesn't want to set this guy off, not without back-up.

Wood sees he's got the cop all bent with worry, and he plays to it. "Friend," he says, "I'm thinking Boggs gets into the Hall on the first ballot."

=====

Norman pulls his borrowed wheels into the parking lot of a package store just outside Nahant. It's not a grand plan, but the idea and the store present themselves at roughly the same time and seem to get along. No way he can face what's going on in his mother's house without a splash of something, he is made to realize. Vodka, probably, this close to home, this early in the day. Anything else will leave him smelling tanked, when all he wants is to top himself off, dull his senses a bit before dealing with whatever the hell it is he's going to have to deal. He certainly doesn't want to throw any pain-in-the-ass questions or recriminating stares into the mix.

There's a poster out in front of the package store advertising a new line of flavored vodkas—citrus, currant, pepper—and Norman is drawn by the bright colors and the promise of refreshing sweetness, escape, a life without worry. (Good things, all.) Inside, there's a display of, like, a dozen flavors, all spread out as if in a spice rack, and it strikes Norman that even this last, urgent need has been thought out for him, programmed into the road home. He lifts a few of the flat, four-ounce flasks and, for some reason, brings them to his nose one by one, thinking this will help him decide. The smells of glass and label and plastic seal are interchangeable, but he is pushed to choose a citrus for now and a cherry for later.

Good, he's thinking, walking his bottles to the counter. This will be good. He grabs a couple swizzle-stick straws from a plastic container and fits them in his pocket with the change. Something to chew on.

Back in the car, he twists the seal from the citrus-flavored bottle, brings it to his lips, and right away realizes that the notion of flavored vodkas is probably something better left to brightly colored posters than to his own circumstance. What stands out is more of an aftertaste, really. Nothing too terrible, but nothing too terrific. And nothing that's exactly alive with flavor, either. A couple sips later, and he starts to think maybe it's his situation that leaves the vodka tasting flat. Surely, this is not the way flavored vodkas are meant to be consumed: alone, in the middle of the day, in a borrowed car idling outside a state-owned package store. Surely, he fits into some demographic the marketing people hadn't anticipated.

Norman, anxious to turn his situation around, fishes in his pockets for one of his tiny straws, thinking maybe the citrus flavoring will have a better chance of locating his buds through a small sip than through a full-throated gulp, only the straw is too short to stand in the flask and too narrow for any significant sipping. Still, he's determined to complete his experiment, and he pinches at the straw with the fingers of his right hand while tipping the flask gently with his left so that it might find vodka. This proves more trouble than it's worth, so Norman places the wet straw on the dash and downs the rest of his four ounces in a single swig.

Gulped, the vodka tastes faintly antiseptic, almost like cleaning fluid, like what he imagines Lemon Fresh Mr. Clean must taste, and the alcohol buzzes through Norman's head like it belongs to someone else. (The head, he means, and not necessarily the vodka.) Also, it's like the static on a still-warm television screen. These are the connections he makes. It's there, this buzz, but not so anyone would notice, except maybe to the touch, timed right. It's there and it's like cleaning fluid, a little.

He tries to shake the buzz from his head, almost in a shiver, returns the headphones to his ears, and pulls from the parking lot like Starsky and Hutch. This connection, too, just comes to him, peeling from the lot, and now that it has, he's all over it. Starsky and Hutch. Damn. He's got their lunchbox, still, in one of Woodman's houses somewhere, unless maybe his mother or the fucking Swede threw it out. Only now that he's onto it, he realizes that even if he's still got the lunchbox, that whole Starsky and Hutch deal's been wrecked by what's happened to that guy's family. Starsky, or Hutch, he never could tell them apart. One of them. Guy's wife got AIDS in a blood transfusion and passed it to her kids, and pretty soon he's the only one left. That's the story as it registered for Norman, and now that he's landed on it the sadness of what's happened to Starsky and Hutch overcomes him and becomes greater than his own. Strange how the tragedies of other people seem larger to Norman than those in his own life. After all, he's also the only one left. His father's gone and driven himself off some cliff, his mother's gone and married the Swede. There's just him, alone, headed north in a borrowed car to a house that is so unfamiliar he must consult directions.

He starts to cry, only in his head the tears are for Starsky and Hutch. And it's more than just tears. Stuff comes out his nose, bubbles form at his mouth when his lips part, his face is suddenly slick with sadness. It passes over him in a moment, this cry, but even in the calm, he is left whimpering. Wet and whimpering. He pulls over to the side of the road and dabs at his face with his sleeve, rubs at his eyes with the butts of his palms, checks himself in the rearview mirror, wishes for tissues.

He reaches over to roll down the passenger window, and then back to roll down his own. He wants to get a breeze going, figures maybe somewhere in the whoosh of speeding, mid-afternoon air he'll find a way to blow-dry the tears and slobber from his face, the red from around his eyes, the ambiguous ache from his heart. He figures on these things—counts on them, really—only, when he gets going again, he finds the manufactured breeze too much of a distraction. Out of nowhere, it's like a twister inside the car. Toll receipts are lifted from the dash by the cross currents; the pages of this morning's *Daily News* are rifled in the back. For a moment, he imagines his father in the back seat, flipping through the newspaper to measure the coverage, searching so frantically for his obituary that it might be another bad review of another bad picture.

In the whoosh, Norman remembers a car his father used to drive, some kind of convertible, cherry red. He remembers the way the Woodman would pull up at Anita's with the top down, whatever the temperature. He'd tool around L.A. on his occasional weekends with Norman with the heater on full. "Don't want to hear your crap, son," the old man dismissed, whenever Norman complained about the cold. "In this town, you put up with a lot. This is nothing."

Soon, Norman is off I-93 and scrambling for directions. He wrote them down on the back of a Tower Records receipt, only the tiny square seems to have been blown from the shelf beneath the handbrake. He can't recall whether to turn east or west at the stop sign, but decides to go from memory. It'd be no big deal to pull over and fish around for the receipt, but this seems easier to Norman, more practical. It's not like he's never driven here or anything.

And so he follows the scent home, ticking off the familiar landmarks as they pass: Dairy Queen, Stop 'n' Shop, BayBank, the pond where he would've learned to play ice hockey had he grown up here and shared the local passion for the sport. As it is, he can't even skate. As it is, he's only spent a half-dozen nights on his mother's couch.

There, just around the bend, across from the school, he can see Nils's pickup in the carport, a rental job out front. Must be Pet's. Must be everyone is inside, finishing lunch, waiting on word. Waiting on him.

Waiting.

He pulls up along the curb in front of the house, a couple car lengths back from where he would park if he felt like he belonged. He checks himself in the rearview, runs his fingers through his hair, makes himself presentable.

They're out to meet him before Norman's exited the car: his mother, Pet, even Nils. A regular fucking welcome wagon. All he needs.

"Oh, baby," his mother says, reaching him first, collecting Norman, tight, in her long arms. She grabs onto him like there's nothing else left.

Nils pats Norman tentatively on the back, not sure he belongs inside the hug with the boy, but wanting to make some physical connection.

Pet steps back from the car and onto the sidewalk, choosing to leave the moment alone before inserting herself into it. A part of her wants to turn away from it. Poor Norman looks so much like those old publicity shots of her Wood that it hurts to see him. Kills. There's this thing they each do with their face, a kind of flared-nostril, curled-lip snarl Pet had mostly seen on Wood during orgasm, which now appears on Norman. She never noticed the similarity before. She likes to think it is every emotion, all at once, bursting from wherever it can find expression, and she takes it in wondering what Norman is trying to keep inside.

Norman loses himself in his mother's fierce hug. He gives himself completely to it. He doesn't mean to, at first, but he can't help himself. Soon, he's not even thinking about it. In the folds of her robe and the smell of her same perfume, he is a small child again. His knees buckle. He seems suddenly unable to support his own weight. He starts to weep uncontrollably, and it is only through the sounds of his own sobbing that he becomes self-conscious again, aware of his letting go. "Daddy," he cries out, trying to fight back the hard flow of tears.

"It's all right, baby," Anita says, stroking her son's hair, working to keep him from collapsing right there on the street. Holding him—indeed, lifting him, almost—she starts to think of Ray Bolger. She's inside the moment, but also on its edges, thinking of Ray Bolger. Yes, Norman's gone all limp like a scarecrow, and, for a moment, she fights the impulse to look around the yard for extra stuffing. That's the way things are these days with Anita. Even now. She's either not all here, or too much here, or someplace else. But then she's back to it, instinctively, finding the right way to hold her grown son, and soon she's rocking gently with him, almost in a dance, back and forth on the curb in front of her house. She hums a tune neither one of them recognizes and no one else can hear.

"It's gonna be all right, baby," she whispers sweetly into his ear. "Everything's gonna be all right."

Pet steps to Nils and wraps a robed arm around his skinny shoulders. She's not flirting, or goofing, or anything at all. She just wants something to hold onto, and Nils is in easy reach. He'll do, she thinks, and then she wonders if maybe her knees might buckle and her friend's husband will have to struggle to support her weight.

Nils wonders the same, realizes this reaching out of Pet's is not the same as her earlier playfulness. This reaching out is real, but it makes him uncomfortable. He wills himself tall against it. He does it for Anita, and for the boy.

This, all of this . . . this is not what any of them were expecting.

Not Thinking

Hamlin, back from a late lunch, lands himself at his desk like he's got a job to do. His own ancient oak swivel chair receives him without wheeze, or wobble, or whatnot. Pimletz, waiting for someone to talk to, figures his efficient colleague must oil the springs himself, tighten his own screws, maybe even cart the contraption out for repairs. There's no explaining the noiselessness of the thing. Jesus, Hamlin certainly keeps that chair purring. On it and swiveling, the man goes about his business like it should be set to string music: he logs back on to his terminal, speed dials an aide to the police commissioner, triages his message slips, milks and sugars his half cup of coffee, kicks off his shoes. He does these things in a strange, seamless choreography, rolling here and there and back, here and there and back, riding the grooves he's made in the floor with the years.

"You about done?" Pimletz says, one desk away.

"No," Hamlin replies, head down, his mind every place but the interruption. "You're about done. You. Me, I'm just getting started."

Great, Pimletz thinks. Guy probably slams me in his sleep. It's like a reflex with him, but he goes at Hamlin again, and, like a fool, he goes at him from inside the conversation he's been having with himself since he got off the phone with New York. "So what do you think?"

This gets Hamlin's attention, this starting in at mid-stream. He steps down his stockinged feet (gold-toed!) to stop his chair from rolling and swivels to face Pimletz. The chair responds like a show dog. "A lot of things, actually," he says, gearing for another slam. "I think it's strange that nobody makes tomato pie. Why is that, you think? I think Ted Kennedy is looking more and more like a float in Macy's Thanksgiving Day Parade. I think national health care reform is a fucking pipe dream. I think, for Halloween, I'll be going as George Pataki." Volley, volley, volley. . . . He pauses, runs a spot check on his sarcasm levels, absorbs the blank look on Pimletz's face, continues. "And I think the day Drew Barrymore is worth twelve million dollars a picture is the day the women's crew team over at Harvard starts jumping rope with my dick. These the kind of thoughts you're looking for?"

To the rest of the world, Pimletz may appear thick, but there aren't so many layers to him he can't see the point. He rips into himself for being so stupid, starts back in at the top. "Okay," he announces. "Wood. You saw the obit in this morning's paper. We talked about it, remember?"

Hamlin nods. "So it was both Nixon girls? Julie and Tricia? The Doublemint twins." Beat. "Talk about your whitebread sandwiches. This is what you're telling me?

"No," Pimletz tries. "Hear me out." You sonofabitch.

This is tough for Hamlin, to sit on his chances, but he rolls back his chair a few feet, indicating to Pimletz that the floor is his.

Pimletz: "So I get this call, hour ago, maybe two. Guy from New York. Senior editor at Asterisk Books."

Hamlin, bounding from his chances and onto Pimletz's floor: "Wanted to talk to you about the Wood book."

Fuck, this guy knows everything. "You know about the Wood book?"

"Come on, Axel!" Hamlin shoots back. "Pay attention. It was in your goddamn obit."

"Oh," Pimletz says, and guesses it was. Right.

By the time poor Pimletz gets his story out in a form poor Hamlin can comprehend, poor Wood surely has begun to decompose. Pimletz tells what he knows about the shape of the manuscript, the outline, Wood's notes, the situation with his wives and entourage, tells how what the editor is looking for is someone to capture the New England aspects of Wood's character. He tries to cover everything. "Warren Stemble," Pimletz says, as if the name might mean something.

"Never heard of him."

"No, but he checks out." (As if Pimletz did any actual checking.) "Wants me to come talk to him. Tonight. Maybe catch a late dinner."

"And?"

"And what?"

"And you're telling me this because?" Always, Hamlin is leaving room for Pimletz to work for his point.

"I'm telling you this because I want to see what it looks like to you. I'm telling you this because who the hell else am I gonna tell? I'm just telling you." An uncomfortable note hangs between them, and Pimletz moves to play over it: "I mean, you're always saying it pays to have the conversation, right? It pays to go to New York, hear what this guy has to say?"

Hamlin stands, re-shoes his feet, fills the few paces between himself and Pimletz, pats his associate on the head like a small child. "Ooooh, Axel," he mocks. He pinches his cheeks. "Look at you. Such a big boy. Jetting down to New York to take a meeting."

These had been Pimletz's thoughts, although not exactly. In his own head, he does without the condescension, but he can't shake the abrupt turns his life might be taking. He can still count the number of times he's been on a plane (fourteen, not including his annual puddle-jumps to the Vineyard to stay with cousins, off-season), so it's not even close to an everyday thing for him. Think of it: down and back to New York just for dinner. He's never been the kind of guy to go down and back to New York for any reason at all. Even the idea of it is intimidating, and now, through Hamlin's taunts, it also seems ridiculous.

"What?" he says, suddenly unsure of his plans. "Tell me. This is something we should do over the phone? Me and Stemble? You think this is something we can talk about over the phone?"

"What the fuck difference does it make, you meet with this guy in New York or on the phone? Go. Have dinner. Move and shake."

"So it could be something?"

"Shit, yeah, it could be something."

"Like?"

"Dinner, for one thing."

"No, I mean, there could be something here?"

"Listen to me, Axel," Hamlin says, underneath a long sigh. "Best I can tell, you've got no shot here. At the paper. Be honest with yourself and you'll say the same. You've been doing this for like a hundred years. With a rotary phone, you were doing this. With carbon paper and copy boys, you were doing this. Great, so you've got it down, but it's also got you, and if you've got a chance to break out of this grind, well, then, you've got to take it. How can you not take it?" He takes in a long breath, lets his words find their mark. "Man," he finally says, "anything's better than cranking obits. It's a long time, Axel. You want to be a writer, be a writer. Doesn't matter what you write, long as you write something else." He means to be constructive, but he can't help himself. "If I were you, a fucking grocery list would start looking good to me."

"I'm not a hack," Pimletz asks, tentative, "if I take a job like this?"

"Yes, you're a hack," Hamlin rides, "but you're a hack now. Been a hack long as I've known you. Fuck do you care if ghosting some dead guy's memoirs isn't the most prestigious gig in the world?"

Pimletz weighs the truths in what Hamlin's saying against the perception he has Velcroed to his self-esteem all these years. Yes, he defines himself as a writer, but he is no writer. Yes, he toils, ostensibly, at journalism, but he is no journalist; he has a profession, but he is no professional. He works for a newspaper is about the best he can say for himself, and this may be his one shot ever to say anything more. Or different. Hamlin's right, he can't do this shit forever, even though he probably will. He considers these things—everything, all at once—but his face is blank, without aspect.

Hamlin watches for Pimletz's reaction, but he picks up nothing. Jerk-off never shows his hand, probably doesn't even know what he's holding. For all Hamlin can tell, Pimletz is thinking about Olestra, the environment, the federal trade deficit, what the short trip to New York might cost in terms of what he'll miss on television. "So you're going?" Hamlin finally prods, not wanting to leave things loose.

"I'm going," Pimletz says, playing at determined, but beneath his surface resolve is another layer. Fuckin'-A, he's going. That, or he's gone.

===

Place has emptied, pretty much, save for this interesting Harlan person, just passing through. Gets dark early these days, and most of the Two Stools regulars are quick to get back out on the water, see about their traps, set 'em down again before nightfall. Nothing like the long, shiftless stretch of summer, when a cup of coffee after lunch can reach to just this side of the six o'clock whistle.

This new fellow, though, this Harlan . . . well, he seems content to fritter away his entire afternoon. Isn't that something? Grace, she keeps to herself, but she's got an eye on this one. Oh, she relishes this time of day, this time of year, knows it better than anybody, but even the tiniest shift in routine can set her to wondering: this stranger, in back, nursing his coffee until it heals. Doesn't take more than that.

She tries to put her mind on something else, but it won't move. She sits uncomfortably on the two stools by the cash register, half working her receipts. She wills herself inside the stillness, the contrast from the rest of her day. She wants everything else to melt away. She wants the feeling of being in the eye of a storm.

Jerry Springer's on, although just barely, coming as he is through the portable black-and-white, rabbit ears pointed south and west for the signal. There's not much to look at through the fuzzed reception, but the audio's coming in clear enough. Today's panel: unattractive women (some with teeth missing!) who've cheated with their husbands' best friends. From the tone of his voice, Jerry's never heard of such a thing, but Grace doesn't get the fuss. In a small town, everybody knows everybody. Who else is there? Why, she can think of a half dozen of her customers, right off the top of her head, who have driven their marriages (or someone else's) to the same place.

She's half-listening, half-working, half-lost in thought. Three halves in all. Grace laughs at the way things just never add up. Like with her receipts, she's always coming up short, even when her regulars are paid up in full, even when there's nothing to figure.

There's a cup of lemoned hot water on the counter in front of her, cornered by the elbow of Grace's massive left arm. It's like she's guarding it. And here's a funny thing: she brings her face to the cup when she's got the taste for a sip, rather than the other way around. Been drinking her tea and coffee and hot lemoned water like this since forever, never thought it strange until a girlfriend pointed it out, couple years back, in her kitchen, and, even now that she's been made aware of it, she can't quit the habit.

Wood's never seen anyone go about their sipping in quite this way. He considers himself a student of human behavior, an estimation he developed after a brief stint at the Actors Studio, under Kazan. An actor observes, Wood was taught, and so he observes. Always. Observing, more times than not, he can find something off in behavior others regard as not worth noting. He's spent some time on this. Life is all about nuance, he believes, and best lived in the details. Most folks bring the cup to their lips, maybe meet it halfway, but this Grace leans herself full onto the counter and laps at the cup like a cat at a saucer. She doesn't touch the cup with her hands at all, except (eventually) to tilt it slightly, to help the liquid to her lips. This is her essence, what he finds in her details.

There's a lot about this woman that strikes Wood now as extraordinary. He watches from a makeshift table at the back of the restaurant between more customary sips of his own. Her movements are not without effort, he notices, but she manages them with a kind of artfulness—he's back on those dancing hippos from *Fantasia*—a grace that belies her size and yet justifies her name. Where she gets it, he can only imagine. And what it's doing to him? Well, he can only imagine that too. It's been just a couple hours, but already this Gracie Two Stools is all he can think about: the way her fleshy arms wipe down the tables between customers, the trace of perspiration at her upper lip, the give and take with her crew, the whole damn package. It surprises him, this rash attraction, especially with the way he'd been thinking he'd run out of drive, but it isn't in him to question something so basic. It's almost primal. She's pretty enough, and sure enough of herself, and she smells altogether wonderful.

Ah, yes, this last gets him going most of all—or, at least, most recently. Someone should bottle the way this woman smells. When she passes with a fresh hit of coffee, she leaves behind the not-incompatible scents of just-baked bread, and bacon, and fabric softener, and (for some reason) lilacs, which mix with the coffee and her own sweetness to leave Wood solidly distracted. He's all coiled up with what's going on in his head. He's thinking, maybe if I just sidle up from behind while she's distracted by her paperwork, press myself against her, spin her around to where she's facing me. Then he's thinking, well, no, he can't quite spin her around, not with Grace camped like she is on two stools at the same time, not without spilling her to the floor, but he still likes the idea of sneaking up on her. There's no one else around, the short-order Lennys are off for the few hours until dinner, everyone else is out doing what they can to make a buck. He's got the place and its owner to himself.

From the television: "You, the man with the tie? You're not bad looking, you got a good job, you could do better."

"Her, on the left, she nothin' but trash!"

"Wouldn't talk if I was you."

"Let's keep it civil, folks."

"Don't be runnin' your mouth 'bout what you don't know."

"Tell it, girl."

Applause.

He slinks up from behind, presses against the fat of Grace's ass, reaches for her hair. He moves in a kind of zone without thinking. She doesn't notice the pressing—not at first, there's just too much of her—but she's distracted by the hair. Startled. Let her tell you, she loves it when they touch her hair. Oh. My, oh my. She rests the pencil she's been using to scratch out her figures on the counter in front of her, closes her eyes. She doesn't want to think about what might happen next.

"Well?" Wood says softly, a beat before the exchange can turn clumsy. His not thinking has turned to where he is now keenly aware of how exposed he's left himself, how close to being found out. No way he should be connecting with another human being—not now, not like this. Disappear, he cautions himself. Disappear.

"Well, what?" she answers, her eyes still closed. She's lost in some serious not thinking of her own, and in the gentle tug and pull of her hair, and in what should be her response to this most recent development.

Wood steps around the stool, wedges himself alongside, reaches for Grace's chin, coaxes her to face him. If he can't spin the whole of her, he'll settle for the highlights. She turns, and he catches, for the first time, the soft peach fuzz of her cheeks, the light of her smile, the taste of her breath: lemon, heat, grease from the deep-fry, overworked Trident (spearmint). "Well, hello."

Grace, flustered, considers how to play the moment. Okay. He's an interesting man, this Harlan Trask. Interesting, she guesses that's the right word. Unusual. Something about him. Different than the guys she sees up here, that's for sure. The way he plays at her hair is like nothing she would have imagined, although the simple fact of his playing with her hair is also like nothing she would have imagined. This never happens. Guys up here just don't see her like this, so it follows that she never sees herself in this kind of situation. Only now that she has, and is, she doesn't want it to play out on its own. She wants to contribute something, to be herself, to give over fully to this moment, and yet she doesn't want to think things through to where she loses the spontaneity. "So," she says, also softly, "you're short on cash? You lookin' to work off your tab?"

Good, she thinks, having offered her contribution. Exactly right.

He smiles, keeps at her hair. "Lunch," he says. "Need to work off what I ate."

She laughs, then teases. "What ate? You've been mostly coffee all day long."

"Just an expression."

"A girl could lose her shirt offering a bottomless cup to someone like you." Also, good.

Wood thinks so too. He could get used to this one. "Kinda what I had in mind," he says. He reaches for the top button of her once-white blouse, and when she doesn't move to stop him, he unfastens it and slides down to the second. By the third, he catches the precipitous drop made by the space between her enormous breasts and the rest of her shirt, still unbuttoned. Could hide a textbook in there, he thinks. An encyclopedia.

Grace, not without interest: "You goin' somewhere with this?"

"Hope to," Wood replies. "Before long."

"I see."

"Bet you do." Wood has no idea what he means by this, what she means, if together they mean anything at all. Just words. For his part, he means to keep her talking. That's basically it. Talking and interested. There's nothing but silliness between them—a Paul McCartney song without the melody—but as long as he keeps up his end, he'll find his opening. This he knows.

Grace knows it too, only she finds one first. She hoists herself down from her stools and saunters to the front door, as ladylike as she can manage. She can feel Harlan Trask's eyes all over her, but she moves as if she's not being watched. Tries to, anyway. She reaches to a shelf above the doorjamb and pulls down a frayed rectangle of cardboard with the message, ERRANDS, BACK IN TEN, block-lettered on one side. The sign is fixed to a triangled string tacked to a shelf above the door, and she leaves it to hang against the glass, at eye level, facing the street. She drops the blinds behind the door and twirls them shut, then does the same at the half-dozen picture windows at the front of the restaurant. She moves self-consciously back to the counter.

"Quittin' time?" Wood says, reaching for the tucked parts of her blouse.

"More like a break." She slides confidently up against him, presses her dry lips against the scratch of his beard, and when he opens his mouth to receive her she's overwhelmed by the taste of coffee. Figures. And she doesn't mind!—the scratchiness or the coffee—which figures also.

He kisses back, struck by her cool-warm wetness. And the gum.

"Upstairs," she says, gently pushing him away. She indicates the swinging doors to the kitchen and beyond. "There's a back way. No place for us to get comfortable down here."

"You live up there?" Wood says, grabbing Grace's meaty hand, letting her lead.

"Just a small apartment," she says, climbing the stairs. "One room and a bath. No need for a kitchen."

"Not a bad commute."

He likes to talk, this one. Grace supposes he's the kind of man who's terrified of the normal silences that form between normal people, the kind of man for whom small talk runs big. *Sally Jesse* did a whole show on this just the other day. "Jesus, you," she says, opening the door to her place, closing it behind them. She leans into him again, wanting to take charge the way the *Sally Jesse* expert recommended. "Shut up and fuck me."

Wood, happy to comply, maneuvers his prize to the unmade bed, and by the time he climbs aboard—it and its owner—he realizes he's in for a bouncy ride. In truth, he had no idea what to expect. This Grace appeared big enough when she was wrapped in unnatural fibers and questionable blends, but there are whole sections to her he's never encountered on a woman. Never even considered. Naked, she looks like a giant genie let loose from a bottle, and he contemplates the crumpled-up clothes at the foot of the bed and wonders how she ever fit inside. (He thinks, also, of the blue-cartooned genie from *Aladdin*, and the voice-over gig for which he reduced himself to audition.)

For a moment, initially, his mind is everywhere but on this sweet, gentle giantess waiting to receive him, although he is soon enough absorbed—by the possibilities, yes, but mostly by the woman herself. He's never seen such fleshiness! Such abundance! He allows himself to be swallowed up by her folds and crannies. He buries his face in her chest and worries jokingly for his own safety, first to himself, and then out loud. "If I'm not back in twenty minutes," he says, pretending to come up for air, "call in the National Guard." He hopes she takes this the right way.

She nearly does. She also takes it as a cue for some playful teasing of her own. "You call this a cock?" she says, reaching for him.

He's embarrassed, a little, but he joins in when he sees the turnabout in her heckling. And the truth. Next to her, his very nearly erect penis looks very nearly like nothing at all. "Just look at me!" he cries out, truly amazed. "I'm a fucking toothpick!"

She flips him over on his back, works her way smoothly down his torso, and collects him, full, in her mouth. She moves, Wood has room to think, like a woman her size should not be able to move: like a dancer, a cat, a snake. A dancing hippo. His thoughts shift to what he's doing—here, now, like this—then on to where he's going, where he's been, what he'll do next. He'd forgotten about his circumstance, his supposed death, but now he's back on it. It just comes to him, comes and goes, been that way all day. It's not yet a part of him, and yet here, in this moment, on the unmade bed of this too-large woman, it finally takes hold. He is here and gone and back. He is reborn, reclaimed, and absolutely untethered. At fucking last.

Nothing can touch him, he thinks. No one.

"Gracious," he says, playing with the name of this moment's lover and again with her hair. "Goodness, Gracious."

===

There's been this thing between Pet and Norman going back to, like, day one, since about the time the boy first jizzed his shorts. Not a big thing, not anything at all really, but a thing just the same. Lately, this thing has been with them whenever they're in the same room. They each recognize it, Pet feels certain, but neither one has chanced to give it voice or action.

Anyway, this is how she sees it, and when Norman, dressed in a towel, steps innocently from the guest bathroom to the living room couch on which he'd left his overnight duffel, it's all she can do to stay focused. Used to be she could slap herself back to reality, but now, with Wood gone, it's more than she can take. She's sitting there, thumbing the pages of a perfumed fashion magazine, trying not to think, when she gets this eyeful. Lord. In the middle of everything else, she has to confront this and the dreadful weirdness that comes with it. Like this is what she needs right now.

It's not like it's her fault or anything, not like she can help it if the kid looks just like his father. Look! It doesn't make her a bad person—does it?—if the sight of him, wet still from the shower, gets her going the way only Wood could get her going. There's nothing morally wrong with a runaway thought. She didn't ask for any of this. And besides, she never knew Wood as a young man; it's only natural she would wonder what he was like, right? Come on, he was fiftysomething when they met, old enough to be his own fucking grandfather. There was this image of him, the one she had throughout her growing up, and then, finally, there was him. She'd seen Wood's early movies over and over, and once she met him, she longed for what she'd missed, and wetsweetnaked Norman is simply a manifestation of her longing. That's all. Nothing wrong with that.

"Hey," Norman says, reaching for his bag, catching Pet's stare.

"Hey." Hey. That's all. *Hey, get the fuck out of here and give me a minute to save me from myself. Hey, take me with you to how it might have been with your father.* Norman grabs his bag and retreats to the back room with the pull-out sofa to get dressed. Pet watches him leave and tries to harness her thoughts. Come on, she tells herself. Come on, come on, come on. This is nothing. This is everything. Her head runs to where she sees this non-thing with Norman as not unlike the real thing she reads about in the tabloids. That's it, it's like Woody Allen and that thing he had with Mia Farrow's kid, what the hell is her name? This is how it is with Pet, over such as this; she tends to filter the stuff of her own life against the sensational headlines of a lifetime (or a week ago), and here is where she lands with this one.

Okay, right, fine, so she's Woody Allen, lusting after her lover's kid. At least now she's got a frame of reference. Pet and Norman. Woody and Mia's kid. It's the same thing, complicated by biology, and by the fact that Norman's mother happens also to be Pet's closest friend, and by the fact that Wood is gone, and by the fact that Woody Allen probably has a bit more going on upstairs than she does. Okay, so it's not the same thing at all.

"Jesus, Pet, you look like you've seen a ghost." Anita, back from the kitchen, from cleaning up after lunch. Leave it to Anita to find cliché in high drama. You look like you've seen a ghost.

Yes, Pet wants to say. Yes, I have. Our ghost. Our Wood. Right here in this room. Yes. She wants to tell her friend everything, but she catches herself. Now is not the time, she's caught enough to realize. Never is the time. Shit, Anita is Norman's mother, no way Pet can tell her where she is with this. "Just sitting," she says instead. "Trying, you know, to get my mind off things."

"I know," Anita says. "I just cleaned out my spice cabinet. I'm actually thinking of running down to the store for shelving paper. Can you believe it?"

Pet can't recall ever thinking of running down to the store for shelving paper. What kind of store even carries shelving paper? Hardware? Grocery? Office supply? "Want company?" she says.

"I've lost the impulse. Think maybe I'll just stay here by the phone."

"Good. I had no intention of actually going with you."

"Nils was saying maybe we should drive up to Maine to where the accident was, maybe see about the cabin, if there's anything we can do."

"You think?" It had never occurred to Pet to do anything but sit right there flipping through perfumed magazines for the rest of her life.

"I don't know. Maybe."

Pet doesn't respond, leaves it to Anita to figure their next move—truly, she doesn't have a decision left in her—but after a few beats, feels compelled to move things along. Any direction will do. "What kind of shampoo do you use?"

"What?"

"Shampoo." She rustles her hair to illustrate, like she's signing to Marlee Matlin, whom she met once at a square dance for the homeless. "Left mine at home." Somewhere between Norman's exit and Anita's entrance, it occurred to her that a shower might be a good thing, a way not to think about Norman, or Wood, or what's happened. She doesn't recall processing the idea, but here it is. Again, without sign language: "I've got a hotel bottle of something in my bag, but that stuff dries me out."

"I keep a whole assortment. In this weather, I've been using some natural crap from this place in Cambridge. Supposedly milk and honey in it."

Pet imagines some foul-smelling curdled ooze. "Gross," she says.

"It's actually not bad," Anita offers, patting her hair like a model in a commercial, pretending at perky. "Leaves me sure and shiny." She crosses the room to Pet, head down, like a battering ram: "Smell."

Pet smells. "Actually, not bad."

"There's like a vat on the shower floor, upstairs."

"Yeah?"

"Help yourself."

Pet leaves the room committed to the notion that a shower and shampoo will carry her past the day's uncertainties, only by the time she reaches the staircase Norman has reemerged from the back of the house, looking for his mother. Pet, redirected, lingers at the foot of the stairs, choosing to overdose on pure family dynamic, from the source, instead of bottled milk and honey.

"What's this about Maine?" the kid says to his mother. "We going?"

"I don't know," Anita says. "What do you think? Nils is thinking maybe we should."

"Screw Nils," Norman says, with a shade more disdain than the moment requires. "You think it's a good idea, then we should go. Pet thinks it's a good idea, then we should go. But don't tell me about Nils."

"Norman," Anita admonishes. "This is his house, remember?" She had thought her son might have gotten past his little differences with Nils by now.

"Of course it's his house. How can I not know this is his house? There are like a million pairs of clogs in my room. All these carpet remnants." Norman lifts the square of industrial weave at his feet—brown, with rainbow flecks—to illustrate his point.

Anita's smile is like a patronizing pat on her son's head. "They're not clog clogs," she tells. "You can't wear them or anything. They're just decorative. He collects them. They're handmade."

"Great. That explains it." Silly him.

Pet listens in and thrills at the tension. It's a regular soap opera, what goes on in this house, with her in the other room. Also, she thrills at the way Norman validates her being here by including her in his argument. She gets a vote. She matters. She sees the way he treats Nils. It'd kill her to be cast in the same role.

Anita: "So?"

"So, I guess. Yeah. I mean, if that's what everyone wants."

"I didn't say it's what everyone wants, just it was something Nils suggested. I'm just putting it on the table."

Norman hates it when his mother puts things on the table, which usually means she wants to gather support for whatever it is she already has determined. With his mother, you either put things on the table or in your computer or on top of the "in" box. "Let Pet decide, then," he says. "I'm not exactly up for any big decisions."

"Oh, and like I am?" Pet, from behind the living room wall, on the staircase landing.

"Pet, you're a child," Anita reprimands. "Eavesdropping. Nice."

She gets back a laugh. "I'm not eavesdropping," Pet insists, not quite sincere, still in hiding behind the wall. She puts on a wee voice. "It's a small house. I couldn't help overhear."

Norman pokes his head around to where Pet is crouched on the bottom step. "Pet's in trouble," he sing-songs. "Pet's in trouble."

"Oh, Norman, shut up," Anita says, following her son to the stairs. She's about run out of good cheer.

"Norman's in trouble," Pet taunts back. "Norman's in trouble." She stands, makes to climb the stairs, turns and shakes a finger at Norman: "You wait till your father gets home, young man!"

She's a sitcom mom, lampooned, only as soon as she says it, she wants to change her lines, replay the scene. *Wait till your father gets home.* What's that? She struggles for a way to un-say the words, but Anita's not waiting for any explanation. She flashes her friend a look that could chill soup. She's not like this, Anita, not usually, but this is not usually. She surprises herself with her reaction. The line strikes her first as no big deal, just a slip of the tongue, but then she hears it from Norman's perspective and she gets all twisted up inside. She goes a little crazy on his behalf. She bounds up the first few steps to where Pet is now standing and leans into her at the waist.

It's a good, clean hit, and Pet is abruptly rag-dolled over Anita's shoulder with the force of it. Then she straightens and slumps to her seat, where she tries to reclaim her wind and her bearings. "Jesus, Nita," she says.

"Don't 'Jesus Nita' me."

"Mom," Norman intercedes, pinning his mother's arms to her sides in a tight hug. "It's cool. Be cool. Everything's cool." He can feel his heart, up against his mother's collarbone, racing, like, a million beats a minute. Anita can feel it too, and she wishes her own beat in synch with her son's. That would be nice, she thinks, to feel what he's feeling, to be in synch.

But it's too much for Anita. All of it—too much, too soon, too everything. Instead of racing, her heartbeat goes flat, near as she can tell. She feels suddenly faint, overcome. She doesn't black out, but she's close enough to know how it might feel. *Oh, yes, this.* . . . She goes with the feeling and lets herself fall against Norman, limp. He tries to lower his mother gently to the steps alongside the slumped Pet, only when the dead weight of her is more than he can handle, he is pulled down as well, so that eventually all three of them are slumped and draped across the middle steps like the victims of a shooting spree.

They lie in this haphazard way for what feels to Norman like a long time, underneath the sounds of their breathing and the unfocused thoughts of what just happened. What an odd picture they must make. They are puzzled together in roughly the same formation Norman remembers from the adolescent game of Ha!— a human circle linked head to stomach, head to stomach, all the way around, allowing laughter (or tears, or whatever) to pass from one body to the next like a contagion. Ha! Used to play it with his friends in the atrium at the mall on rainy weekend afternoons when he was about thirteen, when the thought of lying his head on a girl's stomach was the biggest thing in the world. Now it's just his mother and Pet, but he gives it a try. "Ha," he says, without much conviction.

His mother and Pet, lost in their own reflections, do not respond. Anita's got her strength back, but she's not up for doing anything with it.

"Ha!"

Nothing still.

"Ha!" This time Norman's canned laughter turns somehow genuine, and he is collected by it—hahahaha-ha—and transported to another frame. Really, he can't help himself. His laughing gets bigger and bigger to where he is doubled up in such uncontrollable fits that it begins to hurt. There's no explaining it, but there's also no stopping it, and soon Pet and Anita can't help but join in. (It never worked like this when he was a kid!) They've got no idea what they're doing, or why, but they are taken in. It's like a wave, a shared release: the three of them, laughing, wiping away tears, desperate to ease the same pain.

Nils, in from the carport, where he'd been sorting his screws, happens onto this scene like an immigrant to some strange shore. Norman's right, they do make an odd picture, and Nils struggles to filter what he sees against what he knows: his wife, her son, her best friend, splayed across the steps, giggling helplessly like children, waiting for the other shoe to drop on Wood. They all know what's coming; what they don't know is when or how. It's like they refuse to acknowledge the poor man's fate. Listen to Nils. In death, a bastard like Terence Wood is elevated to pity. He works to understand it, Nils, the way these people are coping. He's missing something: how they've contorted into such an unlikely position, how things like appearance and propriety don't seem to matter, how they can laugh at a time like this. It makes no sense. A death in the family is a solemn thing. A tragedy like this, time should just stand still.

"Nilsy!" Pet cries, when she notices him at the foot of the stairs.

The others turn to look, and their doubled-up laughing swells by the powers of three and four. The sight of poor, staid Nils strikes them all as about the funniest thing they've ever seen.

"Nilsy!" Norman shouts.

Anita tries to stifle her laughing, but even she can't control herself. She doesn't want her husband to think they're making fun of him—it's not like that—but even if she could find the words, there'd be no place to put them. She tries to calm herself, to slow her thoughts, but, for some reason, she starts gesticulating madly, patting the air in front of her like a spastic traffic cop. When she realizes what she's doing, she makes to halt Nils and his passing judgment, but in that same realization is the knowledge that she is having the opposite effect.

"Anita," Nils says, making his disappointment known. He doesn't know what to make of her mad gesturing except to think it strange.

"Anita," Pet mimics. "Get a fucking grip!" She notices, for the first time, Norman's head on her stomach, and, in this instant, her laughter subsides. She wants to run her fingers through the boy's hair, touch them to his lips. She can't remember a time he's been in her lap like this, wonders if he even notices, if this whole set-up means anything to him. She leans close, wanting to smell his hair, the back of his neck.

"Oh, Nils," Anita says, finally composed, hands still at her sides. She's nearly out of breath. "I'm so sorry. It's not what you're thinking."

What could he possibly be thinking?

=

Pimletz, shuttling to New York to take a meeting. Last time he took the shuttle, it was run by Eastern, but the wings of man have long since been clipped. Now it's

Delta, or USAir, one of those. He has to consult his ticket to make sure. On his own dime, he'd have taken the train, maybe even the bus, but this Stemble guy said he'd reimburse him for the fare, and time was tight, and no way he'd have gotten there and back the same night on the ground. Anyway, there's a kind of heightened sense of importance, flying. No reason Pimletz need deny himself a taste of the high life—especially if someone else is paying for it. Especially if he wants to matter.

It's been a while. Last time Pimletz took the shuttle, Ed Koch was still mayor. He remembers because Koch was on the same plane, couple rows back, a good head taller than anyone else on board. Kissinger, too, on the same flight, other side of the aisle, average height. The former secretary of state was giving a talk at the Kennedy Center, at Harvard, there was an item in that day's *Record-Transcript*. Nothing in the paper about what Koch was doing, and Pimletz had to fight back the impulse to ask.

Still, Koch and Kissinger on the same plane, what were the odds on that?

No one worth noting on today's flight, not that Pimletz can tell. He's wondering if anyone's looking at him, thinking if maybe he's someone important, the way he's been studying everyone else. He longs to tell someone his business, to justify his being here, to leave the guy next to him with a story to tell. *Yeah, interesting fellow, that Axel Pimletz. Writes for the* Record-Transcript. *Surely you've seen his name. That's right. He's Terence Wood's biographer. Going down to meet his publisher, have some dinner, maybe a couple drinks.*

Guy next to him appears to be no one special, no one better. Pimletz thinks maybe he should engage him in conversation—interact!—but he's never been any good at that sort of thing. He worries that his breath, up close, is not what it should be, that he hasn't done such a good job on his ears, past couple days, that he'll run out of small talk before anyone recognizes it for what it is. You know, what does he have to say to these people? He grabs the in-flight magazine from the seat back in front of him and turns away with it toward the aisle to avoid the possibility of confrontation.

"Sir," he hears, from an officious voice, "we'll need to pass."

It does not occur to Pimletz that he might be the designated "sir." Why should it? People are always addressing each other respectfully, in ways that have nothing to do with him. With Pimletz, it's always more like, "Hey, you!"

"Sir," he hears again.

This time he looks up from his not reading and sees a beat-up drink cart at his shoulder being slowly wheeled and badly steered by a beat-up flight attendant who looks way too old for the job. She must be fifty, easy, and pushing not only the drink cart, but the FAA limits on makeup and hairspray, as well. One look at her and everything about this airplane seems suddenly too old for the job. Even his armrest, Pimletz now notices, has logged a few too many miles. The worn plastic cushion is duct-taped to the rest at his elbow; the hole where the recline button used to be stares back at him like an empty eye socket; there's muted, tinny sound spilling from twin headphone jacks. He takes in all of these things, wondering at entropy, at how circumstances evolve, in the same moment he works the exchange with the too-traveled flight attendant. He straightens, pulls his legs in from the aisle, leans away. "Don't mind me," he says, good-naturedly.

She doesn't, apparently. She's in too much of a hurry to wait for Pimletz to finish rearranging himself in his seat, rolls the cart directly over his left foot, and scrapes the sharp metal corner against his pant leg, tearing the fabric and leaving a good-size abrasion on his calf.

"Sonofabitch!" Pimletz whisperhollers, reaching for his wound, thinking what it'll look like tomorrow. It doesn't really hurt, not in a releasing adrenalin kind of way, but he is surprised. And indignant. Just the idea of it gets him. What kind of flight attendant rolls her drink cart into customers? This doesn't happen to other people. This doesn't happen to Ed Koch or Henry Kissinger. She's already a couple rows up, hasn't even turned to see if he's okay. It can't be she didn't notice. How can she not have noticed? Pimletz doesn't know what to do about it, if he should do anything, maybe contact this woman's supervisor, keep the skies safe from runaway drink carts and beat-up airline employees.

Indignant, Pimletz does nothing but sit and stew. What is it with these people? What is it with him? He wonders if maybe there isn't something in his demeanor lets people roll all over him, literally and otherwise, if maybe he sends out some kind of signal, some show of weakness, some veiled Kick Me! sign he can't quite make out. He thinks about this, rubbing at his calf, seeing if the tear in his pants is something Warren Stemble might notice, trying not to call any more attention to himself. Rubbing, he thinks that perhaps his musings on how the world has tilted since his last shuttle flight have more to do with him than with any dramatic shifts in air travel, that what really matters is how time has marched on without him.

As the world turns, Pimletz holds fast. This is mostly true, even though he has changed in his own way. He has to remind himself. Absolutely, he's changed. He just hasn't kept pace.

Last time he took the shuttle, Pimletz had a reason to get up each morning. He was not yet mired in complacency and routine. There was a God, and there was Eastern, and there was hope. Now everything's all turned around. Yes, perhaps there still is a God, but Pimletz can strike the other two. Yes, he's in the same job, and in the same apartment, and yes, he somehow manages to get up each morning, but it's not the same. Last time he took the shuttle, he had something to look forward to.

Pimletz doesn't know when he became the kind of man with more life behind him than in front, when it started to matter, why it matters now. He doesn't know what he did with all those years. Well, he does know, now that he's dwelling on it: nothing, jack-shit, bupkus. It's just that he doesn't know how he got away with it for so long.

===

Pet—milk-and-honeyed, fine-and-not-fine—steps from the shower and into a thirsty red towel, then onto a mocha and mauve shag remnant her friend seems to want her to use as a bathmat.

Okay, so this is a given around here. For all of her finer qualities, Anita doesn't keep much of a house, that's for sure. Pet doesn't want to say anything, but she can certainly make an observation. Like with this bath-mat. It's not just an isolated thing, she'll have you know. Anita's got this odd collection of carpet remnants strewn all over the place, in every fucking room, in colors and styles that have nothing to do with the rest of her decorating, and whenever Pet steps her naked feet to the synthetic fabrics, she wonders at Anita's thinking. Also, she wonders at these used carpets, at their histories. Mocha and mauve! Who the fuck picked this one out in the first place? And, believe Pet, this one's not the worst of them. The fact of them, now that she thinks of it, that's the worst part. That they're here at all. Nils salvages these scraps from his cleaning jobs, and Anita sprinkles them about like crumbs. Pet doesn't get it, decides maybe it's a New Hampshire thing, a thrift. And it's a thrift gone to extremes. There're more remnants than Anita knows what to do with. Nils keeps a pile of them out in the garage, squared and stacked, and somewhere in his head he's got a story to go with each one. Don't get him started. Either you're stepping on a section of Mrs. Needle's paisley weave, the victim of a frozen hot water pipe in the blizzard of 1993, or you're on a piece of primary-colored, broad-loomed hopscotch board left over from an overly thorough delousing at Nahant's cooperative nursery school. That's how it is in this house. It's just been a day, but Pet already has passed more than a few idle moments mapping her escape from each room. She's got it figured so she can hopscotch over every square foot, like a child traipsing across stepping stones, without dipping her toes on any primary flooring, and when she tires of this she might also navigate her way in the negative, leaving the remnants untouched.

Truly, Pet's not much of a thinker—she'll be the first to tell you—and here she is with too much time to think. This right here is the problem, but she can't see what to make of it. There's not much else to do but sit and think and wait, which is why she's all for Nils's idea of heading up to Maine. Why not? It'd be something to do, right? Some way to distract herself from the emptiness and uncertainty, get her mind off Norman and back on Wood, where it should be. God knows this shower didn't help.

She looks into the mirror and considers the lines on her face, the red in her eyes. She hasn't been crying much, but she's all bloodshot and flat. Her eyes don't give her away, the way she's been told they often do. Right now, they don't reveal a thing; even she's got no idea what's behind them. And the lines! Jesus, she's like one of those Hirschfeld caricatures, those drawings in the Sunday *Times*. She can count the fucking NINAs on her face. When did this happen? Where was she?

She cracks the mirrored doors of Anita's medicine cabinet and searches the shelves for facial cream. All she finds are some old jars of CVS house brand—another thrift!—so she leaves them untouched. Better to let grief and nature run their course than to risk what's left of her skin to generic lotion.

The medicine cabinet doors are accordioned in such a way that Pet picks up her reflection exponentially, and in the fractured images she grows confused, frightened. There's more of her than she wishes to consider. She steps back from the mirror and lets the red towel drop to the ground. She examines her many breasts, refracted, not all that closely at first, but enough to catch the effect. She's onto the idea of them, as much as she is the specifics. She wonders how many breasts she might find in the too many folds of mirror. She starts to count, but leaves off at twenty-seven, twenty-eight. She's disoriented, can't remember if she's doubling back, if she's covered this set already. She ends up with an odd number.

It is a weird thing to see yourself like this, naked, over and over, into infinity. Pet has to blink her eyes to refocus, to step back farther, and finally to reach up and push the mirrored door closed before she bangs her head against the glass in frustration. There is just too much of her, too many. She shudders her head clear. Think, she coaches herself. Think.

Thinking a little, she finds the switch to the make-up lights rimming the mirror, leans in close. She's got the mirrored cabinet pressed flat; there's only the one image now, but she wants to take it all in. The light is good. She needs to see what's going on here, to really see. My God, these lines on her face are pretty much stenciled in, she notices up close. She's way past the point where even the most expensive creams will do any good. And these tits! Christ, they look like they've been put through a fucking car wash and wrung dry. They're the tits of one of her mother's friends from down at the beach club from when Pet was a girl: Aunt Wynnie—not her real aunt, just someone who was always around. She's gone all sorry-looking, Pet, all of a sudden, all over, but here is where it gets her. She can even spot hairs growing from the aureole of her left breast. Hairs! Five or six of them, not clumped together, but black as night and wiry as the frayed edges of a Brillo pad.

Jesus.

She cups herself with both hands, pushes up to where she's her own personal WonderBra. She lets her imagination go. She casts herself as one of those *Dangerous Liaisons* actresses—Glenn Close (yes? Michelle Pfeiffer would be pushing it), only a bit younger, all busting out and ready for anything. She pouts her lips, like from the other era. Then she lets herself drop and her entire body seems to sag with the lack of support, the lips included. Her posture's for shit when she's deflated like this. She straightens willfully, rolls back her shoulders, juts out her jaw. People are always telling her she should have modeled, but here, at least, she adopts a model's pose. There, she's thinking. There. Okay.

Actually not bad.

Pet looks deep into the mirror and what she gets back is a face heavy with living, a body worn by time. It's someone else, someone older, someone whose husband just drove off a cliff. She thinks back on the vibrant young woman she has always defined herself as and marvels at the transformation. She doesn't remember looking like this yesterday. She doesn't remember growing Aunt Wynnie's tits. She didn't sleep much last night, but it's more than that. She wonders if it's all Wood, the way she looks now, if the thought of him gone has sapped the glow from her appearance. Lately, she's done a lot of reading on mood and body image and positive emotional health, and she's thinking maybe this is the way she processes her grief. Maybe that's all it is. She's not weeping or wailing or anything, but the way she feels has manifested itself in the way she looks. This is how it happens with some people.

Then it hits her: she doesn't have to look like this. Wood, here or gone, wouldn't stand for it. Pet doesn't have to have lines on her face or hairs growing from her tits. She doesn't have to drag her ass around looking like shit. It's not the feeling like shit part that's a problem, it's how she looks.

She comes up with a loose plan. She reopens the folding doors of Anita's medicine cabinet. She's looking for tweezers. She means to pull the wiry hairs from her tits, but she's distracted by a disposable razor—black, it must be Nils's—and an ancient-looking dispenser of Edge shaving gel, the rim at the top gone to rust. She moves to Loose Plan B. Where it comes from, she's got no idea; where she's going with it, only some. She reaches for the Edge, shakes the can, listens for the rattle, squirts some of the stuff into her left palm. Still works, comes out green and runny. She checks for a date on the can; she's thinking maybe the congealing properties have somehow expired, but after it sits in her hand for a bit, the gel appears to harden. She works it until it turns white and creamy.

Then she goes to it. She steps to the sink, close enough so her mound of pubic hair is pressed flat against the cold counter tile, and runs a slow stream of water into her cupped right hand, dabbing at herself, again and again, until she is wet enough to take the cream. She rubs the Edge into her hairs until she is well lathered, working slowly, careful not to make a mess of Anita's bathroom. She needs another few dollops to complete the job, and when she is through, she steps back to admire her neat preparation in the glass.

Well. Pet's never seen herself like this down there: a near-perfect *V*, filled in. The German lady who waxes her works with a sheet and no mirrors, so this is a first. This is a one and only. Talk about weird. One minute she's her mother's friend from the beach club, and the next she's one of her own friends at ten or eleven in the bath playing with Crazy Foam, waiting for puberty.

She rinses Nils's razor under the faucet until the water starts to steam. She leaves the water to run, hot. Then, almost without thinking and yet somehow with great care, she slides the blade in a straight line through the cream, then again. She worries if she should shave in a down-and-away motion or up and back, figures it probably doesn't matter. Either way, it'll do the job, long as she doesn't cut herself. Actually, it's her lips she's worried about, the soft folds, so she's careful to leave off just under the pubic bone. South of that, she'll leave to a professional. Or just leave.

She shaves until there is nothing left but a racing stripe down her middle, a Brillo-y line about one inch wide and running straight to her core. That's how it strikes her at a glance, like she's reaching down to find herself, to discover something. She rubs away what's left of the cream, fluffs out her hair, steps back once more to examine herself in the folds of glass. Her next thought is she looks ridiculous, but she tries to come at it from another way. She looks at her stripe as a

Mohawk, a genuine Down There Mohawk. In her head, she makes herself a fierce warrior, a savage. For the moment, to Pet, this radical pubic hairstyle is not just a fashion statement, but also a statement of purpose, a reflection of how she feels. How she wants to feel is empowered, ennobled, resolved, but she's back to feeling ridiculous. Also conflicted, disbelieving, supernatural. She's all over the fucking place, and, when she realizes her new 'do has done nothing to root her in one reality or another, she reaches again for Nils's razor to finish the job.

She reclaims a smear of already-gelled Edge and reapplies the cream to what's left of her pubic hair. The used cream is runny, but she's hoping it'll do the job. This time she makes one last swipe toward the bottom of her long road—enough, say, to remove the 'stache from a Hitler or Chaplin—leaving off just where her mound of hair returns to full flower. She makes it like a firebreak cut into a hill: there's this stripe of hair, then a bare inch or so, then the full-flower patch surrounding her pussy.

Done.

Now when she steps back the effect is startling. Now it's something. She does a lousy model's twirl, indicates her new bush like one of the *Price Is Right* girls displaying a wall of EZ-Brick, a Brand New Car! She steps one foot ever so slightly forward in a tentative pose. With the cream rubbed away and her hairs refluffed, it looks to Pet like she's wearing a furry exclamation point. She smiles, finally. These things just happen to her. A goddamn exclamation point. How about that? Wood would basically shit. And that Hirschfeld character from the *Times*, he'd go just about blind, trying to hide his NINAs now.

She's pulled from her musings by a knock on the door.

"Pet, honey, it's me," Anita calls, from the other side. "I need to grab a couple things. Looks like we're mobilizing." She flings open the door.

"Hey," Pet says, moving quickly to cover herself. "Some people knock, you know."

"Knock, knock," Anita suggests, reminded of the endless childhood riddle.

Pet plays along. "Who's there?"

"Anita."

"Anita who?"

"Anita grab a couple things. Looks like we're mobilizing." She takes a moment to turn sardonic. "Stop me if I'm repeating myself."

"Real fucking funny," Pet begrudges. "Like that's the first time you ever used that one."

Anita turns serious and pissed. "You been in here for like a month." Seriously pissed.

"What, you want me to reimburse you for the hot water? Nils is outside reading the meter?"

"No," Anita says, turning to concern. "It's just, you know, a long time. I was starting to worry." Serious concern. She looks around. "What the hell you doin' anyway, all this time?"

Pet drops the towel in answer, and Anita turns in the direction of the heavywet thwomp! on the floor and sees her friend's strange handiwork. Pet does another pose, this time for an audience, only this time her hand gestures are closer to Vanna White than to the *Price Is Right* girls. This time, in her head, she's a star.

Anita struggles to understand everything that's going on: her best friend naked, their husband dead, her family downstairs, all of them wondering how to move forward, when the rest of their life will kick in. There's all this shit, all this not moving, and now, on top of it, there's this unusually shaved pussy commanding her full attention. It stares back at her like a cheap toy.

"Why an arrow?" she wants to know. She can't think of anything else to say. She's thinking maybe there's some psychology to what Pet's doing, maybe the arrow pointing down has to do with her spirits being down, maybe she's laid out a map to reclaim her soul. Something.

"What arrow?" Pet asks. "It's an exclamation point!" She says this with the same emphasis she hoped to convey with her haircut.

"Meaning?"

"Meaning, you know, ta-da! Exclamation point! Yes!" Another model's pose, like at a car show.

"So, this is a good thing?" Anita asks, making sure. "What you're doing, this is a positive thing? You're not going slowly crazy on me?"

"Absolutely, it's a positive thing. It's my own little exclamation point. Since when is an exclamation point not a positive thing?"

Anita steps closer to inspect the design. "You sure it's not an arrow?" she says. "To me, it's an arrow. That's what I'm seeing." In the brief moment she had to consider it, she felt sure this was the design Pet was after. Look, the way the hair returns to its natural mini-V, right there, where it matters. Definitely an arrow.

"I should know if it's an arrow or an exclamation point," Pet insists. "Right? If anyone should know, it'd be me."

Anita steps closer still, touches her friend gingerly where her skin has been rubbed raw, where her hair used to be. "Jesus, Pet, you could have cut yourself," she says. She notices her husband's disposable Bic on the sink. "Could've at least found yourself a decent razor. Nils uses these things into the ground."

"It's just irritated," Pet dismisses. "I'll be fine. Maybe some cream."

"Look how red you are."

"It's fine."

Anita still can't believe what she sees. "My God, Pet, what were you thinking?" she says. She rubs herself, in sympathetic pain. "Next you'll go off and have your clit pierced."

Well, I wasn't thinking, Pet wants to say. Not at all, and that's probably the point. I'm just moving, acting, doing. There's no other way to be, now. All we can do is get sucked along, just be. Do. That's all that's left. Who the hell has time to think anymore?

"Come on, Nita," she says instead, just being, reaching again for the Edge. "I'll do you. Take your mind off things." She shakes the can until the rattle fills the small room like silly thunder.

Great, Anita thinks, this is just what Nils needs to see later. This is just what we need to be doing—dulling his already-dull blade with our pubes, giving ourselves a kinky makeover. Then she thinks, you know, what's the big deal? It's just hair. She's up for being sucked along, like her friend. Do. It's as good an idea as any.

Of course, an exclamation point wouldn't suit her mood. She's never been an exclamation point kind of person. A question mark, that'd be Anita's call. If that doesn't just fit: a giant WHAT? to let the world know she's got no fucking clue.

═══

He's not quite himself, Wood.

Hell, he's not quite anyone. In less than forty-eight hours, his life has been recast and undone. True, it's been Wood's own recasting, his own undoing, but everything seems to be running away from him just the same. It's like he's got no say anymore, like he doesn't matter. He guesses that was the idea, but his life has taken a life of its own, and he's not even left playing the same role. He is here, in the upstairs apartment of an overweight waitress, momentarily alone in her bedroom area, listening to a heavysteady stream of what sounds like horse piss coming from the pocket door to the bathroom at the foot of her bed.

True as well, this last is not an unpleasant realization to the overindulged (as ever) Wood. Recast, undone . . . it doesn't matter. The essentials are the same. Absolutely, the thought of his enormous new friend squatting mightily over her dwarfed toilet has an undeniable appeal. It runs alongside competing thoughts of his son Norman, his wrecked car, his first wife Elaine, the turmoil he imagines in the preproduction offices of his next picture, the calm he feels at being left alone, at last. Also, Anita and Pet—as much a part of him as they are now of each other.

Probably the biggest thought is for the general uncertainty he has unleashed around him, all of which looms as this wild cacophony, while Wood—somewhere in silence, somewhere in the middle—struggles to understand the foofaraw. He listens to Grace, pissing, and, in the sound of her water meeting the town's, he finds genuine release. There's a peace and quiet inside the moment that he hasn't known for way too long. Just last month, he paid $139.95, plus postage and handling, for a white noisemaker—the deluxe model Heart and Sound Machine from the new Sharper Image catalog—with settings to simulate the soothing sounds of rain on the roof, waves on the shore, critters in the night forest, to which he might lose himself and the world around him enough to facilitate sleep. Yet, there was no setting to match the sound of Grace pissing. Too bad. To listen to her now is to lose the wild cacophony, to drift off into the rhythms of silence, into nothing. If she can keep it up (and for a while it seems she can), he might just sleep for the next hundred years. As it is, he lightly nods off, flitting at the edges of a sound sleep for just a few beats, but long enough to become disoriented until Grace finally runs out of need. In the cruel sound of her flushing, Wood is returned to his shifting reality.

He wills himself alert, reclaims his bearings: ah, yes, here. This is where I am. This is what's happened. This is me now. He looks about, takes it all in, plans to think ahead. The one-room apartment is decorated with framed posters advertising out-of-town art shows and a lobby poster for Scorcese's *Alice Doesn't Live Here*

Anymore, which Wood figures must be the *Easy Rider* of waitress movies. There's not much in the way of furnishings: tattered loveseat, a single straight-backed chair, full-size bed (a mattress, box spring, and frame, just), Formica coffee table, two mismatched floor lamps, the windows dressed only in shades. There's a counter and two stools pulled close enough they might be kissing; the counter tops are showroom clean, save for some loose packets of Equal sugar substitute, the new issue of *Entertainment Weekly*, an open box of Kellogg's Corn Pops, some personal mail. The room is dominated by Grace's one apparent extravagance: a kick-ass Mitsubishi entertainment system, complete with wide-screen television, side-by-side four-headed VCRs (for dubbing), high-definition DVD player, and fully integrated stereo.

The tiny apartment is in only slight disarray, most of which seems Wood's doing: kicked pillows, rumpled linens, a happy forest of pink stuffed animals floored by an errant elbow from a shelf alongside the bed. His clothes are bunched in a ball in the far corner of the room, and, in their bunched position, they appear somewhat ratty, uninspired, out of fashion. Now that he's noticed them, he can't find any accompanying plans to put them back on. Oh, he'll be out of the apartment soon enough, and back about his strange new business, but he is in no hurry. He stays under Grace's sheets, waiting for her to return from her ablutions, trying to keep warm (it's like the whole town's in need of insulation), angling for a way to parlay his good fortune at being here into a shower, possibly a change of clothes. He's worrying what kinds of stories he'll need to pin on Harlan Trask in order to win Grace's accommodation.

Grace, meanwhile, loiters at the other side of her pocket door, wanting to allow this Harlan person time to get dressed—maybe even to leave, if that's what he wants. No reason to expect anything more. She's seen enough *Sally Jesses* to know this is the way things usually go. It's the way of the world, and she should just get used to it. Besides, it wasn't like it was even his idea or anything, this getting together in the middle of the afternoon. Well, it was, but it was also hers. It was a mutual thing, a consenting adults thing. Matter of fact, if she wants to get particular, it was mostly Grace's doing. She's a big girl, she's got her own impulses, and if she's big enough to act on them she'll have to find room for the notion that there's someplace else the guy needs to be. There's actually someplace else she needs to be, too: downstairs, fixing for the dinner crowd, touching back down on the rest of her life.

"You're still here," she announces, sliding open the pocket door, noticing Wood between her sheets. She is pretending at surprise and truly surprised, both.

"Something I need to ask you," he says, patting the bed at his side, smoothing a place for Grace to sit. He wants to get through this.

"Something big?" Grace wants to know, not moving from the doorway.

Wood hedges. "To me, you know, I guess it's pretty big, huge, but that's me. That's where I'm coming from. You, I don't know. You, I'm hoping maybe you'll see it like a little thing."

Grace is interested as hell, but determined to play it cool. She read a book once, *Interacting to Advantage*, in which the author told how she should present herself without giving anything away. Her mood, her emotions, anything. Doesn't matter that she's shared an intimacy with this man, that they've exchanged bucketfuls of bodily fluids. It should, but she won't let it. Sport fucking, her regulars call it, no more meaningful than bumping carts with your neighbor at the Stop 'n' Shop: *oh, excuse me, nice to see you, yes, love that little thing you're able to do with your hips, let's get together again soon.* She wants to come across as guarded, indifferent, like it tells in the book. She knows enough to know that you never know—right?—and that this is the only way she's got to keep from being too exposed. "Now?" she says, trying on indifference. "You need to tell me this right now?"

"Or later, doesn't matter." Wood allows himself an actor's pause (if anyone's entitled, it should be him) before lapsing into melodrama: "But soon, though."

She buys into it, full price. "What?" she says softly. "What is it?" She has to know.

"Basically a favor. That's all. Don't mean to make it sound like such a big thing, but I'm at a place in my life where I could really use a good turn." Of course, he does mean to make it sound like such a big thing. That's his plan exactly. He bites back his lip as if to hold off tears, congratulates himself for the "place in my life" phrasing. The way she watches *Jerry Springer* and all, this Grace is probably a sucker for pop psychobabble. He's thinking maybe he can muster some crying if he sees that it's needed. Matter of fact, he gets close to it here: "I've forgotten what it feels like to lean on some-one else."

Grace, suckered, reaches for his hands, sandwiches them between her own, waits for the rest.

Here it comes, closer still: "Grace, it's like this. I need a place to crash for a while. Crash, settle down, whatever. I need to get back on my feet." He dabs at his eyes with the top sheet.

"What can I do?" She knows, but she wants to hear.

"I'm wondering if I can't maybe stay here a while, get myself a job. Like I said, get back on my feet." He doesn't wait for a response, figures it's best to keep talk-ing. "I'm not looking for a hand-out or anything, just a place to stay, maybe a couple weeks, until I can put together some money, get a place of my own. I'll pay my own way, soon as I get some money coming in, it's just that all the rooms to let in town, they want the money up front. Like a week's worth. You know these people." She nods to confirm that she does, but he keeps talking. "They need to make their nut for the winter, I can see that, but that kind of money I don't have. Not anymore." He touches her hair. She seemed to like that. He's to where he'll try anything. "I know you don't know me or anything. I mean, who the hell am I, right? But I think you can sense I'm a good per-son. Two people don't share what we just shared with-out trusting each other, at least a little. All I'm asking is that you keep trusting me, maybe trust me a little bit more. I just need a shot."

She has questions. She doesn't want to scare him off, but there are things she's dying to know. Like, why here, in Maine? Why her? To look at him, you'd never guess he had no place to go, no money in his pockets. He's well-groomed, articulate. Clothes could use a wash, now that she thinks of it, but they were nice looking once. And recently. Him, too. Still, the package doesn't fit with her idea of desperation. Something must have happened. Something worth knowing. "You want to tell me about it?" she says, softly still.

"Long story short?"

"For now."

He comes up with something. He works from the script, sticks to Harlan Trask's story, but there are whole chunks missing from memory. Anyway, what Wood does recall doesn't entirely fit. In the picture *Front to Back*, Trask uproots his young bride to Canada to avoid Vietnam, leaving his conservative father with an office products business he can no longer manage and the indignity of having a draft-dodger for a son and partner. Wood no longer remembers where in Middle America the story was set— Idaho, Iowa, one of those—except that it was the sort of place where youngsters did what they were told, where patriotism was absolute. Here, for Grace, he's got to embroider things to get what he wants. He borrows the backstory, but that's about it. He throws in a bit about losing his wife to cancer, no children, and, from there, it's just a short leap to the White House pardon, to a less forgiving reception back home, to vagabonding the country, running from what happened, looking to put down some new roots. It's not hard to see how just a few wrong turns might have led to this sorry place.

"Harlan," she says, pulling close. "I had no idea." She's thinking, if this is what he wants to tell me, then this is fine.

"I'm okay," he says. "I'm really fine. I just need a break, is all. A change of clothes."

"A fresh start. Like you said, someone to believe in you. Everything'll just fall from there. You'll see."

"You think?" He starts to dab at his eyes with the sheets again, maybe ask for tissues, but he catches himself. Doesn't pay to overdo it.

"Yes, I think." Grace has all the answers. She tells him what. She'll get dressed, get the dinner menu started, leave him alone up here just to relax. There's meat loaf tonight on special, and that's always a job and a half. Harlan can just use the time to rest and think. Lord knows he must be tired. Just look at him. Probably a shower'd do a world of good. She's got some sweats in her closet, he can help himself, they should fit. He needs to get past the color, is all. They're lilac purple, she's sorry to say. Not exactly gender neutral, but who's gonna know? She'll send one of the Lennys up later with a plate of food. Something hearty, she promises, with built-in seconds. She'd come up herself, but she hates to leave the place during the rush. She's not exactly the poster girl for delegating responsibility, she hopes he understands. Anyway, she should be done around ten, maybe eleven, it's not a late crowd around here, and after she closes up they can talk things through some more, see how tomorrow's gonna look, and the day after that. "One day at a time, Harlan," she says. "Remember that show?"

He does, but only because Papa John's kid played one of the leads back when they used to run together. The man was always meaning to drag his friends down to one of the tapings in a charade of pride and doting, but it never happened, leaving Wood with no knowledge of the show other than the casting. Nobody watched television, then, at least nobody in the business, but they all read the trades, and news of Papa John's kid landing a CBS sitcom spread like a bad chain letter.

"That it, then?" Grace says, sensing he doesn't want to talk television. "Anything else you might need?"

Wood stands, pulls close. "No," he says. "I'm good." And he is. He lets the sheet drop to the floor, leans into Grace and places gentle butterfly kisses on her brow, her nose, her lips, the fleshy gobble of her chins. He means to overcome her with these tiny, soft kisses, with his famous naked self, but to Grace he's merely naked. To her, this is more than enough, but Wood was hoping for more of an impact. Either he's losing his touch, or she's had enough, or he's had whatever effect on her he's going to have. Maybe there's some place else she needs to be. Probably she's thinking about dinner, opening up downstairs.

"Car," she suddenly announces. "What you need is a car. Get out. See the sunset. Take in the town."

A car? He hadn't even thought to ask. "You think?" he says.

"I definitely think," she insists. "It'll be the best thing. You won't feel so trapped up here waiting for me to close up downstairs." She grabs a set of keys from a hook by the front door and hands them to Wood. "It's the Brat out back," she says.

"What color?"

She has to think about this. "You know, I'm not sure," she allows. "That's so weird. Gray, basically, I'm pretty sure. Maybe blue-gray. It's always dark when I drive. That tells you how often I get out of the restaurant, right? Anyway, it's the only one in town. You won't miss it."

"A Brat?" He likes that she calls her place a restaurant.

"A Brat. You know, like a pickup. It's got those two seats in the bed, facing back. Totally useless. Very big in the seventies."

Wood nods. So was he. Big in the seventies. True, there's not much he remembers from that time other than his bigness, but there's not much he remembers from the night before last. He couldn't even swear to the color of his ditched Pathfinder.

"Still runs great," she continues.

He puts the keys on the counter and pulls Grace back to where she was. "Not going anywhere just yet," he says, a famous catch-phrase from *The Half Shell*, delivered with trademarked inflection. Right away, he wants to draw it back. What's he thinking, mimicking his own material now? The line was the closest he ever came to a classic here's-looking-at-you-kid moment on the big screen. For a while, there were T-shirts and bumper stickers all over the place echoing the sentiment—and here he is, falling back on it like he was at some party. Go ahead, make his day. Jesus. He covers his blunder with another round of gentlesweetallover kisses, hoping she won't notice.

She doesn't, but the kisses are at last getting to her. It astounds her, all this kissing. "There's not like a quota?" she says, gentlysweetly pushing him away.

Wood is still worried about the catch-phrase, doesn't get what she means.

"Kisses," she says. "You're not gonna run out or anything?" She grabs at his balls and kisses back, hard, wet, over and over. She works her hands around to his ass cheeks and presses herself against him; when she feels his excitement, she steps back. She hadn't meant to get him going again; she's really got to get back down-stairs to see to her regulars. "Here," she says, reaching for his hand, guiding it to his cock. "Hold that thought."

She spins to leave, this Grace, and Wood's thinking, okay, so this is what I'm into here. This is what I've got to work with.

All this, and a car.

═══

"Tell me about yourself, Axel."

Pimletz doesn't know where to begin. It's just been fifteen minutes, but already Warren Stemble has gotten two drinks into him. Vodka martinis. This is what pub-lishers drink, apparently, and how quickly they drink it. Fifteen minutes, two drinks, and a load of shit. This must be the formula, and Pimletz fumbles through the mix. He's not used to all this drinking and talking. Either one on its own would be a challenge.

"Nothing to tell, really," he manages, "more'n you seem to already know."

"I don't know shit," Stemble dismisses. "Just enough to get you down here."

Oh. He knows he's being foolish, but Pimletz had been hoping that for some reason this guy had been following his career. (Yeah, right. The only thing following his career is his retirement, and even that's in doubt.) "Well, Mr. Stemble," he says, "I don't know shit myself." He's drunk, a little. He's trying to gather his thoughts in a neat little line so that he might retrieve them as needed.

"Warren."

"Warren," Pimletz laughs. "Still don't know shit, but I can certainly call you Warren." He laughs again, louder than he needs to. It's not even funny.

The silence that surfaces between the two men would be awkward, were it not for the two martinis. As it is, it is simply there.

"What are you reading?" Stemble asks, making to fill it.

Pimletz hadn't realized that he was. "What?" he says. This is hard for him. Reading? He figures these publishing guys are pretty proprietary about the printed word, but there's no reading matter in Pimletz's view other than a tented cardboard advertisement for blendered tropical drinks, which he now holds out for his host's inspection. He attempts a joke: "Don't spoil the ending."

Stemble doesn't get it. Or he does and it's not worth having. "On your night stand," he clarifies, "on the plane down, on the crapper. Everyone's got a book going. Me, I've got three or four. I can't keep track."

Oh, what am I reading? They expect me to read and write, these people, to have a book going. Hamlin would say that costs extra. Pimletz does a quick review of his recent readings and figures the newspaper doesn't cut it. "The new Grisham," he finally manages, hoping this might cover him. All he knows of the new Grisham is that it probably resembles the old Grishams, which he also hasn't read. He hasn't even seen the movies, but he gets the idea.

"We published his first book," Stemble offers, "before anyone knew who he was."

Pimletz gets that this is a good thing, although he's not certain why. "I'm a bandwagon kind of guy," he says, permitting the drinks and the lie to reveal more about him than he would bare on his own. "Ten million people can't be wrong."

"Does that include foreign?"

"What?"

"The ten million readers. Is that just domestic?"

Pimletz has no answer. It was just an expression, and now he can't decide whether to play it out or come clean. What does he know from sales figures? "We should have such worries with Terence Wood," he instead suggests, boldly inserting himself into the deal before it is formally offered, while, at the same time, neatly side-stepping the manner of his embellishment. Neither response is particularly like him, and yet to accomplish both—on the same pass, and under the influence of two vodka martinis—is a kind of triumph. He allows himself a slight smile and a tinge of confidence, but he's not enough used to either to pull them off.

"Indeed," Stemble says, raising his glass in toast, and showing himself to be the kind of person for whom the word "indeed" indeed has a place.

"Indeed," Pimletz tries, toasting back, the word rising from the desperate atmosphere of the bar to where it just might pass for hope and possibility.

Indeed.

—

They decide on Pet's rental—a two-door Omni coupe, cherry red. Anita's car is in the shop, Norman's roommate's car is way too small, and Nils's truck is so totally not what Pet has in mind.

Nils, driving: "You're sure you listed me as one of the drivers?"

"They give me a form, there's a space for additional drivers, I put down you and Nita," Pet assures. "Doesn't cost me anything. Who else am I gonna put?" She gives Norman a look across the back seat that says, yeah, right. She'll tell poor Nils anything.

"Good," Nils says. "That's good. I don't want trouble with the insurance."

"Nils is very particular about insurance," Anita translates from the front passenger seat. "It's one of his things."

"Which is why I made sure to put him down on the form," Pet pours it on. "Do I know my Nilsy or what?" She reaches forward to tousle her Nilsy's hair, and he flinches from her touch.

They are lost, most of them, in the mundane logistical matters of the moment: directions, insurance, what to listen to on the radio, dinner. And yet, from within these mundane matters, from time to time, they are each hit by what has happened, where they are going, what they expect to find there. It comes and goes, and, when it comes, they move so uncomfortably against it that it gets pushed aside. The weight of Terence Wood's death is too much for them, to where it can only be processed in little bits, by not thinking about it. It will come to them, in time, when it needs to; until then, it is left to fill the interior of Pet's rented car in such a way that it only occasionally sets down in their heads. It's there, and then it's not. It's a part of them, and then it's gone.

Nils, driving, is the closest to acceptance. He is a practical man, removed enough from Wood to acknowledge what has happened, but even he has his moments. He allows himself to worry about the insurance because it is easier than worrying about Anita, what she must be feeling. He allows himself to forget because he doesn't like what the remembering has to tell him, the way it makes him look to his lovely wife, the way he looks to himself in the reflection. If Terence Wood can be said to have been larger than life, then surely Nils Veerhoven must be smaller, and surely Anita will now recognize the correlation. It was tough enough competing with the bastard when he was around, and now there's the way he will be exaggerated in memory.

For Pet and Nita, there is a pocket of comfort in these momentary denials or, at least, a hold on how things were. If they choose not to believe it, then perhaps it hasn't happened. If they focus on something else, the rest will go away. This is not a conscious thing, this inability to accept Wood's death, this not thinking, but they are both taken by it. And linked. For a while, last night, they were able to talk about what they were feeling, to reach deep for what it means and where it leaves them, but they have since turned away from it and from each other. From Wood, even. They will talk about everything but their shared loss, even though there is no one else for whom the loss could possibly mean the same. There's Elaine, but she's so far removed from Wood's recent life and times that she's hardly a thought.

There is also Norman. Anita can't fathom the way this must be registering for him. She hates that they hadn't been close, Wood and Norman, the way fathers and sons are meant to be close, but then there's always been something between them beyond her understanding. They have this strange shorthand, the two of them, a telepathy. All right, so maybe they are close, but their closeness, if that is what it is, has nothing to do with proximity. They don't spend time together, not really, but they have come to define each other. Anita sometimes thinks Norman can actually feel his father's legacy, that the weight of who he is and where he comes from has some kind of structural impact on her son's existence. It's why he's in film school. It's who he is. Certainly, they look alike, the two of them, but she sees it also in the way her Norman carries himself when his father is around, or even when he isn't. He's a skinny kid, and tall, but he takes on a hulking demeanor that is more than he was meant to carry, and he looks the part for the moment. It's a striking transmutation and exactly right. He's thin, and shy, and unassuming, but when he's with his father, or in his orbit, or even just at one of his pictures, he takes on new dimensions. He goes from decorous to devilish in, like, nothing flat. She wonders what will happen to all of that now. She wonders if anyone else sees what she sees.

For Norman, the wondering is all about these other people here in the car with him. He doesn't get why it is he has to deal with Nils. What's that all about? Pet he doesn't mind, actually likes it when she's around, but Nils is like a tourist. The guy's got no fucking clue and no claim. Back at the house, Nils called him over and whispered something about wanting to be there for his mother, and Norman was like, yeah, well, where the hell else you gonna be? Why are we even talking about this? Norman's in and out of acceptance just like everyone else, but when it hits him, it hits him hard. Like now. He gets a picture in his head of what has happened, and he works it against the noise about the insurance and Nils's generally annoying presence, and what he's left with is a giant frustration. It's pretty fucking huge, like nothing he's ever known. He doesn't know what to do with it, but he has an idea. Just like this, it comes to him. He pulls his knees to his chest and then he kicks, hard, against the back of the driver's seat, whiplashing Nils to where his chin is knocked against the steering wheel and his glasses thrown to the dash.

"Pull over!" Norman screams, slipping into one of his father's famous tantrums.

"Norman!" his mother shoots back, without much conviction. She spots the devil in her son for what it is.

Nils rubs at the sharp pain in his chin and pulls to the side of the road—not because the boy told him to, and not because of Anita's apparent upset, but because, at the moment, he is too stunned to do anything else. Forget driving. He wonders if the thing to do is comfort his wife or lean into Norman for his outburst. Another option: get out of the car and walk, leave these people to themselves.

"Finally," Pet says, "some fireworks." She smiles at the excitement.

Norman throws open his door, steps from the car before Nils brings it to a full stop, and with the momentum, storms to the front of the car and glares at his mother's new husband through the tinted windshield. His mother and Pet are frozen by his fit. Nils is just waiting for the rest of it. So is Norman. This is his father's doing. Norman moves without thinking. He kicks suddenly at the front headlight with his sneakered feet, and, when the glass does not shatter, he goes at it again. And again.

"Insurance," he rambles, scanning the shoulder of the road for an object that might do the job for him. "Insurance. I'll give you insurance." There. A rock. Boulder, almost. He lifts it with two hands and walks it to the driver-side headlight. He goes so slowly about his business that someone might make it theirs to stop him, but no one is moving. He presses the rock to the light, hard, as in a pounding motion, but it won't give. Then he steps back and shot-puts his find at his target, which finally shatters, and, from the sound of the shattering, seems to have been made from heavy-duty plastic. No wonder. Anyway, Norman's just about made his point. He picks the rock back up and lofts it onto the hood of the car, where it leaves a good-size dent and a good-size thud and a couple good-size scratches. That should do it.

"See if that's covered," he says, loud enough for them to hear inside the car. Then he cleans his hands against his pants, slinks calmly back into his seat, and wills himself whole.

Pet bursts into applause and laughter, and Anita reaches over from the front seat to slap her into silence, biting back her own smile.

They sit there, the four of them, for so long Nils can't think of a thing to say or do except to ease the car back onto the road.

Anita, who has been looking back at her son, wondering how it is he's become so much like his father and when, turns ahead with the car's movement. She grabs Nils's right arm, to get his attention. "Rock," she says, pointing out the window to Norman's boulder, still on the hood. "Honey."

"Fuck the rock," Nils says, pulling onto the highway, picking up speed. He turns sunburn red with his exclamation. He doesn't usually talk like this. Once more, softer, as in an apology: "Just fuck the rock, okay? Excuse me, but that's all I have to say."

"Nilsy," taunts Pet, unfrozen and back at it. "Such language."

=====

As advertised, Grace's Brat has two black plastic seats, all-weather, facing back, right there in the truck bed— probably the most useless things Wood's ever seen. Who the hell came up with these?

Still, he climbs in, sets himself down along the curves of the seat backed against the driver's, and tries to understand how he'd missed such a significant moment in the history of automotive design. Seat's working overtime to hold him (it's not exactly built for hulking presences, still tortured or no), but Wood's not so uncomfortable he can't adjust. *There. Better.*

He pulls the top on a can of Coors Light pinched from Grace's fridge upstairs, sucks the foam from the arrowed opening, considers his new circumstance. He's got all night and a lot to consider. He still can't get his hands around what he's set in motion. All he knows is he's got no place to be, nothing to do, and in this he finds contentment. Fuck, he's not jumping for joy or anything, he's not spinning cartwheels, but there's a mighty weight gone, the kind of weight he never fully measured until it was lifted. He feels twenty years younger, twenty pounds lighter, twenty times richer. He doesn't dwell on what the rest of the world has made of his apparent death, only on what he has managed, and what he has managed is something. What he has managed is to get through the better parts of a day without thinking about his asshole agent, his next project, his back taxes, his divorce lawyers, his too-high profile, his goddamn cellular phone, his hangers-on.

Well, okay, so this is not entirely true. He's thought of these things, all of them, and a whole lot more besides (he's even thought about calling his machine at home to check for messages), but what he hasn't done is think about them too seriously or for too long. Before his disappearing act, when something or someone commanded Terence Wood's attention, he neglected it at great risk to his karma and equilibrium and general good feeling. Now, he simply puts his mind on idle, like it was an appliance setting, and, when he happens on an unpleasant thought, he quickly jumps to something else. There's nothing to hold him down.

He needs to act it out to understand it. He stands in the cab, rubberstretches his arms at his sides, goes all floppy, like a dropped marionette. Then he slinks back into the uncomfortable seat. He's got no strings to hold him down. This is his idea of improvisation. He takes a long draw from the Coors Light. This is what untethered looks like. This'll show that fuck from Chicago with his thumb up his ass. This is me, hopelessly lost, without tether.

Only thing Wood can't get past is Norman. He hadn't figured on this, although if he'd thought about it at all he'd have come to it eventually. Everything else he can do without, but he can't face losing the connection with his kid. That, and he's got poor Norman thinking his old man has met a ghastly end off the side of a cliff. How could he do this to his own child? To strip him of his father just because his father wanted to shake things up? He can't forgive himself, or justify his grand act, or even understand it, but he wonders if he might make repairs. Yes, he's got to find a way to get to Norman, he suddenly thinks, to make him get what's happened in a way that doesn't leave him hating him for the rest of his life or running to tell his mother. He can't decide which would be worse. He's got to bring the boy back into his life, into his secret, before the thought of his dying takes hold. He can't do that to his own son. Okay, so he already has, but he can't let it stand, not for too much longer. If he does, and he's found out, he'll be left doing Rogers and Hammerstein in dinner theater, which he guesses is a kind of hell. Plus, he can't sing for shit.

He resolves to make things right with Norman and soon, although, for the moment, he's got no idea how to accomplish this. With his resolve comes an impulse to move, and so he downs the last of his last beer, hops down from the bed and into the cab, and fires up Grace's truck like it has some place to go. It does, for a time, until Wood, not thinking, veers wildly from the side of the road into one of these little protected marsh areas he'd seen along the coast, here and there, during the day. They've got these too-tall egret nests every couple hundred yards along this stretch of town, built and lovingly maintained by the local wildlife weirdos. There's not much in the way of street lighting, but he can make out the resulting skyline in the night air. In his headlights, at varying high speeds, the towered nests look like telephone poles against a stark Texas landscape. Of course, there are signs and shit to help tell the difference, but these don't register in the darkness. About the only thing that does, and this Wood remembers from his wanderings on foot this morning, is that there are way more nests than egrets, and yet he manages to run Grace's Brat head-on into one of each.

Wood, hitting and running, continues on his nocturnal chase, not sure where he's headed, not thinking anything of the strange *ka-thunk*! beneath his tires, the snapped base of the nest stand as it rips from the ground and flips over the length of the speeding pickup.

Winter

"There is a time for laughing, and a time for not laughing, and this is not one of them."

--Inspector Clouseau

Up-Gathered Now Like Sleeping Flowers

Norman, dead drunk but not really, turns to his dead-but-not-really father and frames a question. It doesn't matter what he asks, only that he does. The trick, he's learned, is to get this ghost of Woodman started. When he appears like this—late at night, as in a vodka-soaked hologram—it doesn't take much to get him talking, and in the run-on, Norman can sometimes discover the truths of his growing up. He hears what he wants to hear.

"You bought Microsoft at what?"

This is what Norman comes up with because this is what's on top. He's sorry about this, but lately, with all the estate nonsense, and the back and forth with the lawyers, and the persistant hounding from certain elements of the media, and the not-quite-Sotheby's auction the widow Pet is considering to consolidate all the unagreed-upon stuff (custom shoe horns!), Norman has been fairly preoccupied with the financial aspects of his father's life. Stocks. Trusts. Safe deposit boxes.

Limited partnerships. Art. Insurance policies. It's all that's left. That and his pictures, but Norman can't watch a Woodman picture without thinking also of what's to come. Or, what has passed. Even the early ones—*The Half Shell* and *Straight On till Morning* and (especially) *Sixes and Sevens*, where his father actually buys it in the end in a badly orchestrated bar fight over a badly dressed woman—they're all tied up in the same thing.

Norman looks at these old movies, piped in on Ted Turner's cable empire or pulled from the worn DVD and video sleeves in his haphazard collection, and in his father's eyes he sees the future about to happen and slip away. It's like he knew. All along. Like he was just waiting.

And so he's left with the mundane, the temporal fuel that fed his father's private life. Elaine. Pet. His mother. Money. Houses. Some cars. Microsoft. Woodman was in at the beginning. The story Norman heard was he'd met Bill Gates at some party, although he could never imagine Terence Wood and Bill Gates at the same party. The young Gates made an impression on Woodman, although Norman could never imagine his father leaving an inverse imprint other than by reputation. However it happened, the stock split itself a dozen ways like a fucking Breck commercial, and, in the end, Wood was holding approximately three hundred thousand shares.

Norman chokes on the math.

"Sid put me into it," the actor says to his not-really-dead-drunk son—or, at least, this is what his not-really-dead-drunk son wants to hear. It is a voice from another dimension and a reference to one in a long line of money managers who, with this great exception, succeeded mostly in mismanaging Terence Wood's funds. What Norman guesses he is after with this line of communication is a fix on how it was that his father ended his life with the taint of money troubles when he owned approximately thirty million dollars in Microsoft stock.

"It was pure profit," Wood spirits back to his son. "I couldn't touch it without giving it all back in taxes. You know that."

Yes, of course, he does. It is an argument Norman had heard a dozen times before his father's death and another dozen since. (He's counted and rounded off.) "But you didn't have to go making those piece of shit pictures!" he rails. "You could have borrowed against it on margin. Something. You didn't have to go taking your teeth out on screen!"

"No, but—"

"Like a fucking character actor!"

"What can I tell you, son?"

A lot, Norman wants to say. Everything. Like, for starters, what the hell is he supposed to do about Pet? Tell him that. He likes her and all, Norman does, they're connected, always have been, but she's been all weird around him since Woodman died, a little too . . . what? Here: she's been a little too wetly affectionate. He can't think how else to put it, but that about cuts it, and anyway, there, it's out, they can finally talk about it. She's always eyeing him, rubbing up against him, finding reasons to be left alone with him in otherwise empty houses. She calls late at night—like really late at night, like three or four, too late, even, for the coast—

and then has nothing to say. Poor Norman's got no idea how to be around her, what's expected, what's going on. Once, back in L.A.—this was pretty extreme, even for Pet—she walked naked into the media room, where Norman was just in from some club and winding down in front of Conan O'Brien, and she sat next to him like nothing at all and said, "You think he's funny? I'm not so sure I think he's funny." Like sitting around naked was the most natural thing in the world. She sat and watched David Cassidy do a number from *Shenandoah*, which he'd just mounted in some dinner theater somewhere, and then suffer the predictable late night taunts on his fallen teen idolhood.

"I used to love him," Pet said. "God, look what happened to him. That hair!" Then she leaned back against the cushions, set her legs Indian-style like Sharon Stone auditioning for Disney's live-action remake of *Pocahontas*, dipped into the potato chip canister she found at her hip, and, for a while, said nothing. When she tired of this and the nonresponsiveness of her stepson at the other end of the couch, she quietly stood and left the room—carrying, the nonresponsive Norman couldn't help noticing, a couple Pringle crumbs with her on her pubes.

Okay, Woodman, what's the deal with that? And with the way people have been looking at him since Maine? Like he's contagious. Like he, all of a sudden, has this ominous background music announcing his coming and going, as if his life had been scored recently by that drummer from the Police, alerting perfect strangers to his now-troubled presence. If music isn't the tell, it must be something else, because he can't go anywhere these days without someone picking up on something. Before, he lived in the once-removed glow of his father's fame. He didn't advertise it, but it tailed him like one of those fucking bowls of oatmeal from those old commercials. (Maypo, he thinks.) People knew. And now they know. This. It's all around him, what's happened. It's a part of him. It's in the air, and on his shoes, and no one wants to get too close for fear it'll rub off.

And the giant question: how the hell is he, Norman, supposed to make a place for himself in his father's wake? This is one for a team of psychologists—assisted, perhaps, by a bunch of brown-nosing graduate students—but, as long as he's on it, he might as well throw it out there. It's like when he was a kid, staying with Woodman, and, in the morning, he'd bounceflounce into that great big bed with him. In the grand landscape of sleeped-in sheets and too many pillows, he'd start to feel misplaced and alone and incapable of filling the spaces his father left behind. On the man's chest alone there were, like, a couple acres of uncharted territory. He was like a climbing apparatus. There was just too much of him and not nearly enough of Norman, who'd eventually roughhouse the covers to the floor, where he could make his own room.

"I thought you were just goofing around," Norman hears. "Horseplay."

"No," Norman says. "I was hiding."

"From what?"

Norman shrugs. He thinks about this. "I don't know. You, maybe?" He's guessing, fishing. They never talked when his father was alive. Not like this. Like this is a revelation. Like this is the way a father is meant to talk to his son, right? Like this is how they do it in the rest of the world. (On television!) When they had it to do for real, it was long distance, through the gossip columns, passed along comments from hangers-on. There were some shared photo opportunities—at charity events, in airports, courtside at the Lakers—but there was nothing ever natural about their time together, not that Norman can now recall. For a stretch, late 1980s, maybe early 1990s, Wood communicated with his son only in one-word postcards: "Persevere." "Agitate." "Listen." During another stretch, between Anita and Pet, there were, like, a dozen girlfriends, each introduced to Norman through the pages of some tabloid or other. (One of them, a redhead named Katrinka, was sent to the airport to meet Norman for a weekend visit with an introductory note from Woodman to prove she was legit.) Always, it was what was not said that mattered most. Or, what was said to someone else.

In film school, Norman is making a movie about a father and son, only the father's dead and the son has a little trouble dealing. The bone of the piece is the way the two of them still have this relationship going through these same kinds of late-night visits. Well, they're not exactly the same, but sort of. There's another movie he wants to do, not totally unrelated, about a father and son who fly all over the world to these different Planet Hollywood openings, but Norman doesn't have the budget to pull it off. What he's got is, like, no budget at all, and so he's going with the smaller, more intimate story. In the script, which Norman's calling

Special Effects, he's written it so the dead man's ghost actually inhabits his scenes—he can move objects, occupy real space, you can see his reflection in the mirror—partly because it's easier to tell it without any convoluted narrative tricks and to film it without any special effects (that's where he gets the title), but mostly because that's how it always seems to Norman.

Here, now, late at night in his shitty little apartment, it is as if his father has pierced some fourth wall of his near-dreams to invade his senses of time and space and order. He's drunk, a little, but that's not it. This registers for Norman as a sobering thing. He's got this image of his father, this fading memory, and it's lit up on some big internal screen. Then the image steps from the screen and into the room like Woody Allen had it set up in *The Purple Rose of Cairo*. When it happens, it is as if the Woodman, Norman's Woodman, is truly here. When he leaves, if he's been drinking, he leaves behind the glass; if he's been sitting, the sofa cushions hold his shape.

"Don't tell me you've got one of your freak film school friends lined up to play me," Norman hears.

"Actually, I was thinking of Brian Dennehy."

"Brian Dennehy?" The voice is insulted, incredulous. Norman does not respond.

Again: "Brian Dennehy?"

"I've got a way to get it to him," Norman justifies. "He's a friend of one of the professors here. He likes to help out on these student projects. He's good at what he does."

"This is what you think of me? Brian Dennehy?"

"Lighten up, Woodman. It's just a movie. Like you used to say."

Daniel Paisner   201

"Yeah, but Brian Dennehy?" The ghost of Terence Wood is seething. "He makes television movies! He couldn't carry a cartoon!"

Norman lets this hang in the still air of his shitty apartment alongside his father's visage. What he wants to say is, yeah, well, at least he didn't think to try, Weatherbee. At least he hasn't sunk that far. Instead, what he says is, "What makes you think it's about you?"

"Yeah, like it's about some other father and son. It's about Kirk Douglas and one of his boys. It's the *Martin Sheen Family Christmas.*" You could cut a wheel of hard cheese with his sarcasm.

"No, I mean, it's not like anything we ever had. Where the fuck were you all those years?"

"Where the fuck am I now?"

"My point exactly. It's a fantasy. It's not based on you and me. It's not anything we ever shared."

"Fantasy is you thinking you can make a movie. Fantasy is you thinking that candy-ass school can teach you how to make pictures." This stings, but Norman waits for the rest of it: "It looks easy to you, what I do."

"Did, Woodman. What you did. You don't make movies anymore, not since long before you drove off that cliff, and even when you did you were just reading someone else's lines." He pauses to consider his point. "Making pictures. That's such shit. Doesn't take much to read someone else's lines."

"Ouch," the voice pretends at hurt. Then, almost in admiration: "Jesus, where'd you get that nasty streak? And to your old man."

"From you, you sonofabitch." Norman takes a final swig from the flavored vodka bottle (peach) on the Pioneer speaker at his side.

"Damn right, from me. Don't go saying I never gave you anything."

Norman makes a note of this, thinks it's something he might be able to use.

====

The cabin where Pimletz has been holed up since forever has got this massive stone fireplace at its center, which seems, to Pimletz, bigger than his entire apartment. In the hearth alone, there'd be room for his dresser, his straight-backed chairs, and the crate he uses for a kitchen table. Here, for some reason, he's set up his writing desk, run an extension cord for his laptop, piled his sorted and foldered notes, and put the remote phone to rest on its base. There's a picture window with a great view of the woods and a sky-lit loft over the living room. There's even a little breakfast nook back in the kitchen, which would have made a nice place to work, but here he is in the dank, cool grit of fitted stone, working at what it is he has to do. He doesn't know why he hasn't put the fireplace to its intended use, which would have been a good thing, considering the bite of New England winter. He figures his decision to use it instead as an office must have to do with wanting to get a little heat going in his writing, to light a fire under this project.

He sees things a little too literally sometimes, Pimletz does, and he's tucked himself into Terence Wood's stone hearth expecting sparks. What he gets, instead, is an inventory of false starts and misguided notions, including the giant fucking one that put him here in the first place. *Yeah, right, Axel. You can write a book. On some other plane, you can write a book. In your dreams. . . .*

Predictably, this is not turning out to be the book of his dreams, but Pimletz isn't sure it ever was. It's an assignment, he keeps telling himself. A good gig. The deal is, for twenty-five thousand dollars up front, he gets to slog thigh-deep in the life and times of Terence Wood, the blustering movie actor whose mysterious death a couple months back vaulted him from a waning celebrity to just about legendary status. He gets to live in the great man's cabin, thumb through the great man's papers, consume the nonperishables in the great man's pantry, wipe his ass with the great man's Charmin, and call down to Boston on the great man's nationwide calling plan. All of it's with the sanction of the great man's estate and all in the ostensible name of research and atmosphere-soaking. And, here's the kicker: if Pimletz does all of these things to the estate's satisfaction and, in the process, produces a posthumous autobiographical manuscript written, natch, under the great man's name that, in turn, meets with the satisfaction of the publisher, then Pimletz will receive another twenty-five thousand, a vaguely delineated piece of the back end, and the thin chance at lending new shape to his career.

In the meantime, he deludes himself into thinking he is in control, at least in editorial control, at least until he relinquishes the first draft of the book to Wood's various people. Right now, tucked cozily into the opening of Terence Wood's stone fireplace and slipped easily into the great man's open-toed sheepskin slippers, Pimletz is not about to give up control.

It is not for reasons of artistic integrity that Pimletz expects to remain in charge, but rather for reasons of sloth. From his perspective, on page thirty-seven, Pimletz is not expecting to finish a first draft any time soon. He's made about full use of the scant notes and log entries Wood left behind at the time of his death, and he's come up dry in his efforts to pull salient note and comment from the great man's wives, his kid, his famous friends. Past week or so, he's busied himself screening old Terence Wood movies on the great man's big-screen television to see if they might suggest some way to fill a few paragraphs. And he's thumbed through a coffee-table reference book, *The Films of Terence Wood*, to where the pages are fairly stained with margin notes and Cheese Doodle residue and turned-over pages. The book includes production notes—dates, credits, and locations—for every movie Terence Wood ever made (and a few he merely thought of making, but never quite managed), beginning with a small part in the 1953 thriller *Magnificent*, in which, the coffee-table author is quick to note, Terence Wood wasn't.

Hamlin, at the front end of this misguided notion, suggested to Pimletz he keep a list of Wood's dead co-stars so that he might let his imagination run. Trouble is, Pimletz's imagination runs like a drugged tortoise, so he hasn't gotten much past the list itself: Rita Hayworth, Marilyn Monroe, Natalie Wood, Lucille Ball, Barbara Stanwyck, Lee Remick, Ginger Rogers, Ingrid Bergman. . . .

"Now what?" he said to Hamlin one afternoon, back in Boston for a change of clothes and scenery. He actually brought the list with him for Hamlin's approval.

"Now what?" Hamlin echoed, mocking, working the lead on a piece of his own, not paying full attention. "I'll tell you now what." He rolled his chair back from his desk, turned to face Pimletz to focus on this particular piece of show-and-tell, flipped through the oranged pages of Pimletz's reference book, and landed on an idea: "*Trouble No More*," he read, without looking up. "This is fucking paydirt. United Artists. 1969. Durango, Colorado. Richard Widmark, Lee Remick, John Wayne in a cameo. Janis Joplin, even, in her first screen role. First and only."

"I can read, asshole," Pimletz interrupted, not sure he wanted to hear how what keeps him up nights is no trouble at all for the next guy.

"It's not the reading I'm worried about, my overwhelmed friend," Hamlin taunted, swatting Pimletz playfully (and a little too hard) on the head with the book. "It's the comprehension."

"Fine," Pimletz said, rubbing his head, "I get it. I com-pre-hend." He drew out the word. "So now what?"

"Now is where you sit down and write that the filming of *Trouble No More*, down there in sleepy Durango—population, what, like, twelve, couple dozen more in summer maybe—calls to mind a memorable moment. Now you write that Wood and Lee Remick and Janis Joplin were tripping one night on some mushrooms or some shit, this was the sixties, right? This was what people did. It's not that much of a stretch.

"They were sitting uncomfortably in one of those phony mining cars they had strewn about the set because, you know, Durango is one of those old mining towns. There was that scene in the movie where Wood's character was trapped in the mine, and Janis Joplin, who played his daughter, had to go running through the town one afternoon to find her mother, Lee Remick's character, to tell her the trouble with Pa down in the mine. Then there was that great moment where John Wayne swept in to lead the rescue attempt, and the whole fucking town had gathered outside the mine to see what the matter was. He took one of those beat-up cars from outside the shaft and hurled it right at the opening, in one giant frustration. Only, you know, the Duke was getting on in years, so the car he picked up was pretty flimsy, like it was just painted plastic, or balsa wood, or whatever they use in those Hollywood prop departments. But there were also a couple real cars strewn around, for authenticity, and it doesn't seem possible that even the Duke in his prime could have hurled one of the real deals, least not all that far.

"But anyway, now is when you establish about those mining cars and tell about what a dead-end town Durango was—throw in some local color. Then you get back to how Wood was just tripping his brains out and running around bare-ass naked with his wife and daughter—his screen wife and daughter—and how they somehow managed to squeeze, all three of them, butt-naked, into one of those little cars, one of the real ones because, you know, what the hell else is there to do in Durango, right? I mean, this is fucking Durango,

Colorado. The Toenail of the West. Fuck it, the In-Grown Toenail of the West.

"And then you write how Wood doesn't remember Janis Joplin being all that good-looking, but she was limber as hell, and she tasted, sweetly, of lilacs. That's the way you write it, just like that, 'she tasted, sweetly, of lilacs.' And you write how Lee Remick was just one of the great beauties of her time, a real presence, how she was into some real wild shit, how, after a while, the three of them talked themselves into this car just for laughs, you know, just because it was there, because it was Durango. But then one of them looked up, probably it was Lee Remick, yeah, definitely Lee Remick, and realized they'd fitted themselves in too tightly. It was all just a little too cozy, and they couldn't pull themselves out, not without help or external lubrication, certainly not without a clear head.

"It slowly occured to them there was nothing to do but start screaming until help arrived, only the problem with this was that it was, like, two o'clock in the morning, and there was no one around. They ended up spending the night in this way, amazingly, or at least a couple hours, long hours, and the screaming was kind of half-hearted, but still.

"Along the way, Wood remembers having to take a leak. Jesus it was bad. He even remembers mentioning this to Lee Remick, who was awake most of the night and who thought it was one of the funniest fucking things she'd ever heard. Joplin was out cold by this time, but Remick was up—fuckin'-A she was up—and she kept telling Wood to just let it go, let it go, he was among friends. Soon she started saying she had to go too—she's got a pee coming on is how she put it—and after a while, with the way she was just laughing and laughing, hard, she started to stream against the cold metal of the car. Even then, Wood couldn't bring himself to go. He just couldn't. The thought of sitting in a puddle of his own piss with a sleeping Janis Joplin and a stoned-out-of-her-mind Lee Remick was an execration to the great Terence Wood, even as the noise of Lee Remick's pissing put him in pretty much the same position, biologically, psychologically. Practically.

"Anyway, pissed, they sat awake a couple hours. They'd run out of screaming and laughing and fondling. They didn't have it in them to try to squiggle free. It was warm enough with all that flesh pressed tightly together, and all that was left was to sit and wait for the early crew to start its shift and get things ready for the day's shooting. Finally, one of the technicians came by and noticed the trouble these three stars had gotten into, this laughable trouble, and he set about finding someone to help him hoist them out of the car and back into their clothes.

"Then you write that, before it was over, Richard Widmark came by to take pictures. Richard Widmark, this is the kicker to the whole deal. Someone woke Richard Widmark up at the hotel in town, and he came down to take pictures. For the rest of his life, Wood was after him to make copies; it was like a running thing between them, but he'd never seen copies. Then you write that he knows that somewhere out there, somewhere there are copies of Widmark's photographs of the three of them, Wood and Lee Remick and Janis Joplin, all fried and naked and tripping and stuffed uncomfortably into a mining car on the set of this otherwise forgettable picture. You write that his secret hope, Wood's abiding hope, is that they turn up, these Richard Widmark shots, not in the *Enquirer* or the *Star* or on one of those ridiculous tabloid television shows, but out there on the Web for the whole world to see on someone's homepage, where they can be downloaded and hard copied into every fucking home on the planet because this, to Wood, is what celebrity is all about. This is the point of the whole fucking anecdote. Hell, it might as well be the theme of your whole fucking book, if you ever manage to write it. To be photographed by Richard Widmark, naked and stoned and tired and sitting in a puddle of Lee Remick's piss, with Janis Joplin along for the ride and unable to keep up, this is the essence of what it means to move about in the strange light of Hollywood, to be above the laws of human nature and polite society. This is what it means to be Terence Wood. This is what you write about. This is your now what."

Pimletz can't get over it. He doesn't know whether to ask Hamlin to start in again, slowly this time, so he can get it all down, or to stand up and applaud. He doesn't know whether Hamlin was yanking him or taking him to someplace he might need to find again. "Just like that?" he asks.

"Just like that."

"But it never happened!"

"Everyone's dead," Hamlin says, turning back to his own work. "Who cares it never happened? Write it and it might as well have."

Pimletz thinks about this for longer than he needs to. "You can do this? It's ethical?"

"Fuck ethical. It's celebrity pap. It's ghostwritten celebrity pap. Legal is all you need to worry about."

"Okay, so what about legal?" Pimletz wants to know. "Can't the estate be sued?"

"What estate, doughboy? You. Read your contract. No one's suing the estate of Terence Wood without dragging your ass into it."

Damn. "But there's insurance. Someone said something about author's insurance."

Hamlin usually relished in confusing his usually confused friend, but he was on deadline and didn't have the time. "Yes, there's insurance," he finally said, typing underneath his dismissal. "Probably there's insurance, but who's gonna sue? Everyone's dead, asshole. You can't libel the dead. Journalism 101."

Pimletz all but groans in relief. He hadn't yet committed anything to paper—Jesus, he hadn't even committed it to memory—but he was relieved just the same. This meant it was a whole new enterprise, a whole new book deal. Trouble no more. Anything was possible. "So, like, I can use that?" he asked, begging permission, wanting, at least, a place to start. "There's no problem with me using that?" It sounded good, this naked assessment of the convoluted values of Terence Wood's world; it sounded like something the great man would write, like it would kill a few pages, maybe lead to a few more. Plus, in an unbelievable way, it struck Pimletz as moderately believable. Shit, he bought it, and he's not as naïve as Hamlin would have him think.

"What?" Hamlin sends back, no longer paying attention.

"You know, Lee Remick? Durango, Colorado."

"Fuck do I care? Go. Use it. Have a party." He was three paragraphs into his lead on his own piece, had the rest of it pretty much written in his head. Today's business: a mini-scandal surrounding a State House official caught high-ending it at the Super Bowl on the taxpayers' dime. If it weren't for Pimletz, he'd be on to the next thing.

"Great," Pimletz says, trying to remember Hamlin's exaggeration. "Good. Thanks." Janis Joplin, he prompted himself. Don't forget the part about Janis Joplin. That's key. And the piss. And the Richard Widmark thing with the photos, with what it all means. He looked on at his typing friend and marveled once again at Hamlin's ability to fill an empty page, to think on the fly. To do, write, be. Pimletz wished he could be so effortless, so completely without fear or hesitation. He wished he could open those same valves and have the work flow out of him and have it not be shit.

His admiration might have been transparent if Hamlin had cared to look.

"Tell me, Hamlin," Pimletz said, tentatively, not wanting his esteem to show any more than it has, "how do you do it?"

"What?" Already, Hamlin's piece was about to be zapped to the copy desk.

"You know, think. Come up with that shit. Have it pour out of you on deadline."

Fucker makes it sound like diarrhea, Hamlin thought. He tapped out a final, flashy keystroke for significance, sent his copy on down the line, and, done, swiveled back to Pimletz to rub his nose in it. "Axel," he said, shaking his head, "you can't imagine."

No, he can't. Or at least he hasn't been able to. Yet. But he means to get there. And soon.

He sits at his makeshift desk in Terence Wood's hearth and tallies his next moves. There's the cut-and-paste job to be done on the stack of cheapie star bios piled on the bottom steps of the spiral staircase leading up to the loft, anecdotes to be culled from the *Record-Transcript* clip file and from an Internet search, but these are only filler. The real work will come in fabricating for Wood the kind of storiedfrenziedtortured existence that readers have come to expect from their celebrated auto-biographers. They don't want the raw honesty; they just want the raw, and it is up to Pimletz to give it to them.

Happily, for Pimletz, his dilemma has become a showcase for the turbo-imaginings of his friend Hamlin. Better, a parlor game. In the months since Hamlin's effortless recounting of the Durango myth, Pimletz has reached out for more of the same, and Hamlin has obliged: a three-way with Lucy and Desi, an aborted child with Natalie Wood, a quashed breaking-and-entering charge with RFK. Lately, Hamlin has become so amused by the possibilities that he sends them, unsolicited, by fax or e-mail. Pimletz never knows what he might find. Just today, he booted up the laptop and was greeted with an elaborate compound regarding Howard Hughes and a former child actress from the old *Our Gang* series.

Hamlin's stories remind Pimletz of the game he used to make of his father's leaving back when he was a kid—the at-home version of the game he used to spin at work writing off Rose Kennedy. His father, though, that was a whole other muddle. The asshole was gone pretty much at conception, far as Pimletz could ever determine. His mother used to say he was killed in a car accident, but, to Pimletz, he always was kidnapped by aliens, drawn and quartered by horse thieves, thrown from a speeding train by Russian spies. Even after he learned the truth, that his old man was just a shit, Pimletz couldn't keep from imagining a different twist: food-poisoned at his own sister's wedding, felled by a Sears air conditioner, struck dead by a Frank Malzone liner to the owner's box at Fenway.

It's the same thing with Hamlin. Pimletz doesn't know what to do with the windfall of stories, but he is determined to make them all fit. They are instantly a part of the Terence Wood legacy, as told to Axel Pimletz. They belong as surely as if they had actually happened. Anyway, he's got nothing else to go on, and a bunch of pages to fill, and a deadline to meet, so he's hit on the not-too-original literary device of mixing them together in a loose, internal monologue, the whole business linked with self-aggrandizing and grade school punctuation. Probably, there are more ellipses in Pimletz's thirty-seven pages than there on the New Releases: Nonfiction table at Barnes and Noble—and, thanks to Hamlin, more irrefutable bullshit.

The bleep of Wood's remote phone echoes up the stone flue like a high-tech fart. There's even an echo as the ring runs up the chimney so that it comes back again and again, sounding like the fart-around-the-campfire scene in *Blazing Saddles*, acted by droids. This is how it strikes the unimaginative Pimletz, and, for some reason, perhaps because he hasn't been out of the cabin much, past couple weeks, perhaps because, developmentally, he's moored back in junior high school, the connection strikes him funny. He covers his nose to amuse himself further.

"Yeah," he says, the phone to his ear, his hands now away from his nose. "Pimletz." He answers like he's still in the newsroom, like that's where he belongs.

"Axel," he hears. "Good. I'm glad I got you."

Pimletz is glad to be got.

=====

Okay, so maybe Terence Wood wasn't built to paint houses or fish commercially or work construction. He was built, that's for fucking sure, but not for much. Hard labor and him, they don't get along; hard living is about where it ends for him. And heavy lifting he can just forget about. For a while, just after his not entirely thought-out exit, his Polar heart rate monitor cast off into the sea with the rest of his Pathfindered belongings, he not-entirely thought through the idea of starting his own moving company, leasing a couple trucks, and hiring local college kids to do the jobs, but Grace talked him out of it. There's not much in the way of coming and going up here in Maine, she convinced him, and, anyway, the folks who do move tend to move themselves.

About the only job left to him, at least the only one that didn't have him exerting himself too terribly much or asking customers if they wanted fries with that, was this right here (and an acting job, to boot!): inhabiting the character costumes at Maritime Merrytime, the theme park by the sea. The people who run the place actually have gone and trademarked the tag line, "the theme park by the sea." There's a little TM trademark thingy on all the T-shirts and tote bags and signage, and it always strikes Wood as ludicrous every time he sees it. He gets this picture in his head of a team of Down East lawyers dressed in unnatural fibers discussing over some lunch counter how people would be climbing all over themselves to use a tag line like this one, how it would be smart to tie it up while they could. *The theme park by the sea"; that'll be in play before you know it.*

Funny, how things work out. This is what he did, and now this is what he does, and here he is, acting, ludicrous or no, dressed as Larry Lobster, posing for pictures with the thinned winter crowd of Merrytime visitors, trying to sign autographs with the foam rubber claws they've given him for hands. When he started out as Crabapple Jack, the cantankerous old fisherman with the corncob pipe, he didn't have this trouble with the autographs; his hands were his own, but he worried people would recognize him underneath his flap-eared yellow rain cap. In the beginning, he worried constantly that he would be found out, but here especially. Everywhere else, he could fuse into the background, but at Maritime Merrytime, as Crabapple Jack, he was calling a little too much attention to himself. True, no one would have believed that an Academy Award–winning actor would willingly dress up in flea-infested costumes and greet tourists for six dollars an hour—forget a dead Academy Award–winning actor—but Wood couldn't be too sure. Plus, he didn't like the way the little kids always ran from him in terror, the way the bigger ones kicked him in the shins or asked him when it was he last had a bath, the way the parents pretty much ignored him. He wasn't used to playing secondary characters, and he wasn't about to start. Fuck, it just about killed him when he was asked to do it for real, in pictures.

He's since put on about twenty pounds and nurtured a full growth of beard, which has come in a lot grayer than he hoped, almost white. There's no way anyone would spot him for who he was, but he's more comfortable draped in red polyster. He's come to cherish the anonymity of the lobster suit. And it's not just the anonymity that's got him. Larry's the character he was born to play. He's the Mickey Mouse of shell fish, the star of the whole show, and Wood sometimes thinks his Larry Lobster is the best acting of his career. He believes this wholeheartedly, actually puts what he's doing in context, compares it to the work he did under Kazan and Peckinpah, sees the connection he makes with the runny-nosed kids as a pure and wonderful and immediate thing, unlike any connection he'd ever made with any other audience, anywhere. It's all so . . . *right here*. And now.

He wonders what that fucker Strasberg would have made of a gig like this. What freedom! What drama! Every day, it's a full-bodied, fully realized performance, one that permeates his entire being when he's out there. Inside that lobster suit, he is Larry. It's not so much acting as reacting, he presumes, better, interacting. He's constantly evolving, expressing emotions he never knew were available to him through nothing more than cloaked hand gestures and body language; he becomes a part of his environment and lets the environment claim a piece of him in return, and he does all of this without speaking a word.

It didn't start out this way. For a while, after Crabapple Jack, they had Wood working the Libby Lobster suit (Larry's girlfriend), and then he subbed a couple times for the guy who wears Crusty Crustacean. Once they even let him try out his own character, Scrod, the nebulous sea creature of uncertain form, although, it turned out, the Merrytime children preferred their villains to be somewhat more discernible. Scrod never made it past the few complaints it generated down at Guest Relations.

But Larry suits him. He's on all the T-shirts and shorts and the pennants, and there are Larry Lobster hats with wiry tentacles and shit. There's even an interactive CD-ROM piece of crap, and Wood looks on at all the preexisting merchandise and sees himself. He is at the core of this particular universe, precisely where he belongs.

Maritime Merrytime is not much in the way of a winter attraction. On a scale of county fair to Disneyland, it barely registers, but it's all they've got up here, and Wood can't blame the owners for trying. They've got a pretty spot, hard by the national park and right on the water. The real estate must've cost them, and they've put some money into it. They've got a world-class rollercoaster, the Typhoon. They've got a local cable show, live action, featuring Larry and his pals, and they're working on a syndication deal, but what they haven't got is the weather. There's not much of a pull during winter. Place is only open weekends from Labor Day to Memorial Day, and, if it's particularly cold or if they're expecting snow, they don't open at all. It's not worth it. Most of the outdoor rides—the Typhoon, Twister, the Wave, the Water Snake—are shut down for the season. All that's left are the indoor arcade and the carousel and the live shows, the chance for kids to greet their favorite Merrytime characters without the hassle of the summer crowds. The real attractions for parents are the Lobster Pounds sprinkled throughout the park, serving enormous lobster rolls and lobster salad platters and lobster claws at enormously reasonable prices.

And, as ever, there is the Catch of the Day, also trademarked, the Merrytime ritual wherein one unsuspecting young guest is scooped up in a big fishing net and placed in a giant lobster trap by the Dancing Waters fountain at the main entrance to the park. The idea is that the sea-dwelling characters are turning the tables on their land-dwelling friends. Get it? (It took Wood a while.) If people can go fishing, there's no reason Larry and his pals can't go "peopling." There's even a song to signal the charade: "We're a-goin' peopling, a-peopling, a-peopling. We're a-goin' peopling, a-peopling today."

The owners defend the practice by suggesting that it gets children to think responsibly about the sea and by reminding customers that if they don't want to participate, they can avoid the performance. Besides, they insist, it's all in good fun. Everything about Maritime Merrytime is all in good fun, even the miscalculations. The lobster trap is friendly enough looking, done up in bright colors (anything but the beaten-down hues of the briny deep!), and filled with pillows and Merrytime comic books and good things to eat. At the end of the day, the caught kid and his family are treated to a free dinner and T-shirts and set loose in the park for an hour after it closes, but there is no changing what it is.

It falls to Larry and a half-dozen Helper Crabs to do the trapping. Wood can usually tell, when the Catch of the Day song starts to play on the loudspeakers and he begins to circle the park with his giant net, which kids would make good candidates for Merrytime's all-in-good-fun brand of cruel and unusual punishment. The chickenshits usually run for the safety of their parents' legs or hide behind the trashcans, while the ones who are into it tend to chase after Larry with their hands in the air, yelling, "Pick me! Catch me, Larry! I want to be caught!"

If he can, Wood looks for a kid somewhere in-between, someone too cool to hide, but nicely terrified of the prospect. Today, though, as on most winter days, he must catch what he can. He sifts through the slim pickings and lands on a six- or eight- or ten-year-old kid (he can never tell) with a Marcus Camby/UMass jersey worn proudly over the outside of his down jacket. The jersey reaches to the kid's knees like a skirt, and it gets in the way of his fleeing at the site of Larry Lobster and the Helper Crabs. The kid's clearly not game for this particular game, but he runs awkwardly in his heavy winter coat and the stretched-over and loose-hanging jersey. Wood doesn't move that easily in his costume either (the suit weighs another twenty pounds on top of the additional twenty he's been carrying), but he doesn't have it in him to redirect himself. It's his job to catch this kid, but it is also his nature.

A-peopling, he wonders if he ever chased after Norman in something like this way, if he ever mistook his laughter for fear, if he was more inclined to respond to his own kid's signals than he is to these kids' in the park. He works to remember what it was like to be a father to a small boy, to matter—hell, not just to matter, but to matter like nothing else in the world has ever mattered, to have whatever it is the kid is going through to matter right back. He connects with these kids, but he can't connect with his own, can't for the new life of him reach back across the great divide he's dynamited into their worlds and set right the pendulum.

For a moment, Wood loses himself in thinking how he might make repairs with Norman, to reconnect without doing any further damage—Jesus, it's been three months, and he still hasn't told him!—but he's gone for that one moment, just. Introspection and him, they also don't get along. Besides, he's got a show to do.

The Helper Crabs lift the poor Marcus Camby fan carefully into the net, which Larry Lobster and his crustacean pals have balanced on their shoulders like pallbearers, impervious to the near screams and mild flailings of today's Catch. Kid's parents are no help, either. Dad's got the video camera out and Mom's pushing two kid siblings into the frame, and everyone else is milling uncomfortably around the fountain, waiting for what will happen next to just come on and happen so they can get back to their own dysfunctions.

The little boy is resisting, big time, but Wood and the crabs struggle to get him into the trap. Kid's not screaming or fighting back, but he dead weights himself to where anyone paying attention can see he's being moved against his will. The boy's mother, who apparently is, crosses the square to her netted son. When Wood catches sight of her, late, his first thought is she's going to make this even more difficult. This happens, sometimes. Once, in late fall, some burly looking goon in an "I'm with Dickhead" T-shirt with an arrow pointing to his crotch, stepped purposefully to Wood and kicked him in the groin—or, at least, in the place where he thought he might find groin on a lobster. The only things that saved Wood were the goon's evident misunderstanding of marine biology and the costume designer's evident inattention to detail. Also, Wood's relative lack of peripheral vision inside the Larry suit likely prevented him from retreating in fear in the moment before the attack and likely saved him from a more-than-necessary embarrassment.

"Just don't give him any ice cream," the woman whispers into what may or may not be Larry's ear, as if this had been Wood's secret plan.

Wood holds up his claws so that they frame his costumed face in sharp parentheses: a lobster's shrug.

"He's lactose intolerant," the woman explains.

Wood nods, as if to give his word that he will do no such thing, and turns back to the boy. As Larry Lobster, he is unable to speak—it's one of the basic rules of employment, that the actors inhabiting the Merrytime characters not make a sound—and so the only assurances he can offer his unwilling participant must be delivered through foam-rubbered gesticulation. He pats at the air with his claws to suggest to the boy that he calm down; he holds a pincer to his lobster lips, to suggest quiet; he rubs the boy gently on the back to make nice; he borrows the camcorder from the neck of the boy's father and motions the Dad into a shot with his son. He *acts* like he has never acted before, and the rare and wonderful thing about it, for Terence Wood, is that the boy plays off of him as if it all were real, as if Larry Lobster and the Helper Crabs were truly holding him against his will.

When the kid is finally trapped and hushed, and his family no longer fascinated by the photo opportunities, and the few other tourists diverted by the few other attractions, and Wood is momentarily full of himself and his ability to improvise with a crowd of oblivious tourists, it occurs to the great actor to break for lunch. His twenty new pounds have come mostly from the all-he-can-eat lobster rolls, and he's learned to get them while he can. He retreats to the employee entrance at the main Lobster Pound by the Dancing Waters fountain, where he is handed a brown paper bag with Larry's face on it, which he, in turn, carries awkwardly between the pressed-together heels of his claws to the fenced-in employee picnic area out back. Another basic rule is never to be seen eating or drinking or ducking into the bathroom or engaging in otherwise human behavior. The ducking into the bathroom part is never a problem for Wood because it's such a bitch to get in and out of the lobster costume that it's not worth his trouble. He goes without fluids so that he might go without peeing, although he wonders what it will be like inside the Larry suit in the heat of summer. The thing about his wondering is that he lets himself go out that far. Here it is, late January, and he's already out to June in his head. Last time he was this settled was basically never.

Grace, from outside his limited vision: "That you in there?" She taps at his lobster head.

"Grace of my heart!" he says, surprised to see her. They are the first words he's spoken all morning, and his voice comes out scratched, as if from sleep. He sounds far away underneath his thick Larry head.

"Thought I'd bring you something to eat," she announces, fumbling under his lobster chin for the tucked-away buttons and zipper so that she might unfasten his lobster head and tilt it back like a hood. It is not a chore Wood can perform for himself, not without undoing the intricate lacing on the costume gloves (although this last is not something he can do for himself, either), and Grace doesn't like the thought of someone else performing such an intimacy on her Harlan. She takes the bag from his claws and sets it aside. "They put so much mayo in that stuff I'm surprised you can taste the lobster," she says. "I'm surprised your cholesterol isn't off the chart."

"What's instead?"

"Instead is tuna, like you like it."

Like she thinks he likes it is with Miracle Whip, which Grace insists is better for his cholesterol than mayonnaise, and chopped-up celery on whole wheat. The chopped-up celery pieces are like hidden enemies when he finds them in his mouth, and, with his claws, he won't be able to pick at the gristle they leave behind in his teeth. But this is the way they do tuna down at Two Stools, and he doesn't have it in him to carp. "You spoil me," he says, not insincerely, getting his voice back, wiping at his brow with the synthetic fur of his costumed sleeve. "You're not careful, I'll never leave."

"Then I won't be too careful." She takes over on the brow-wiping with one of the coarse napkin squares from the dispensers down at the coffee shop, but it feels to Wood like she's leaving behind scratch marks. Then she licks her thumb and slicks down his graying eyebrows, which she's told him tend to go all wild and absent-minded professorish when he's been inside the suit a couple hours. "You want your hands?" she says, taking his lobster mitts in her own meaty paws.

"No," he says, "don't have time. They want me back there to check on that kid."

"I can feed you," Grace offers, "if you want."

"I want," he says. "I want, I want, I want." He opens his mouth like a small child.

Grace pinches bites of the tuna with celery on whole wheat and places them tenderly in Wood's mouth. They make an uncertain picture, the two of them. To a Merrytime colleague looking on in the employee picnic area, with the way Wood's fake Larry head is tilted back and his real Wood head angled also to receive the tiny sandwich bites, he must appear helpless, attached, and Grace like a mother bird returned to her nest to feed her babies. To Grace, she is simply caring for the man she loves in the only way she knows; it doesn't occur to her how it looks. To Wood, eating, how it looks is everything, and how it looks to him is like that scene in Kubrick's *A Clockwork Orange*, the one where a recalcitrant Malcolm McDowell opens wide to collect the succor that is his due. He doesn't like this picture, but he can't shake it, and every time he swallows a bite of tuna sandwich, he opens his mouth and waits for the next one, like he has it coming, like Malcolm McDowell; he can't help himself.

Grace doesn't have it in her to notice. All she knows is she at last has a reason to duck out during the lunch rush at the coffee shop; that her two Lennys have the place basically under control; that this giant of a man in the red lobster suit has somehow found enough to like about her to stay put, even if he hasn't come entirely clean; that without her here to feed him her Harlan would just melt away inside that suit; that he waits without asking for her to open the can of Arizona Iced Tea she's brought with her from the coffe shop, diet peach, and twirl the angled straw to his lips.

=====

"You sure you don't mind?" Pet asks for the third or fourth time, taking off her coat and absurd winter hat, shaking out her hair to set it right. "I'm not interrupting?" She moves as if it doesn't matter whether or not she is.

"No," Pimletz says, his own mess of hair quickly fingered through to where it doesn't look too bad. "I could use the distraction."

"Yeah, like there's not enough for you to do without me dropping by."

"Technically, you called first," Pimletz corrects, trying to put this stunning Petra Wood person at ease. He's even taken by the absurd hat, figures it's something the beautiful people are wearing these days. He gives her the benefit of every doubt, and a few more he hasn't even considered. Petra Wood is, after all, a kind of client; he serves at her pleasure, hers and Anita Tollander Wood Veerhoven's, on behalf of Wood's kid. If they don't like what he writes, he'll never see that second twenty-five thousand. "That shouldn't count as just dropping by," he sucks up. "That should be for something, that calling."

"From the car phone," Pet insists. "I called from the car phone. In the drive. Right outside. Any decade but this, that's just dropping by."

Pimletz gets that it's important to her that she just dropped by, and he lets it alone. The woman did live here, once. Probably, after the estate is all figured and he finishes the book and clears out, she'll live here again. Her stuff is all around. She shouldn't have to call first.

Pet, after a beat, not about to miss another: "So, like, what page are you on?"

"Thirty-seven."

Pet laughs like he's kidding. "Fine," she says. "Don't tell me. Keep me in the fucking dark. It's not like I'm the wife or anything." She moves about the place as if she's reorienting.

"Coffee?" Pimletz offers, not knowing how to act around this woman in her own home. "There's instant."

"Fuck coffee," Pet says. "There's wine somewhere, if you haven't polished it." She leads Pimletz into the kitchen. "There," she says, pointing. "Top of the fridge. Can you reach?"

Pimletz reaches.

"Great," she says, taking the bottle, dusting it off. "Friend of his had a vineyard up in Napa somewhere.

Gentleman farmer type deal. Guy was an asshole, and his wine was shit, but Wood was always begging for cases. They did a Riesling one year, wasn't too bad." She rubs her hands together in a gesture of warming. "Jesus, it's cold in here," she says, even though it's not. She switches subjects like channels, Pimletz is getting. Like Hamlin. "This is how you keep it?" She doesn't wait for an answer, presses her hands to her face. "They're, like, ice cold," she announces. "Feel."

She touches the backs of her hands, both, to the sides of Pimletz's cheeks, also both, and he pulls back, thinking, this is not what's supposed to happen. Terence Wood's wife is not supposed to be touching me on the cheek, in a cabin, in the woods, no one around for miles. Her hands are cold, but they're cold from outside, from the car, and against her cold, heavily ringed fingers, his face feels like the kind of brown paper towel that gets dispensed in public rest rooms.

He needs to switch his own channels, move this encounter back to a show he's seen before. Wine. He can't find a corkscrew, makes an elaborate show of his looking. "Any ideas?" he finally says. "Swiss army knife?"

"Here." Pet reclaims her hands, sniffles as if she must, grabs the leather duffel she's slung over the knobbed back of one of the kitchen chairs, and pulls from it a worn pocketknife with a dull corkscrew folded to its side. "Try this." She hands the knife and the bottle to Pimletz, and, in the exchange, the cold of her hands shoots through his fingers and once again sets him to distraction.

Focus, he tells himself. "That's it?" he asks, meaning (he thinks) the pocketknife. *Focus.*

"That's it."

"Nothing more, you know, dedicated? That thing they bring to your table at the restaurants? What the hell do they call that?" He's fishing here, Pimletz is, trying to seem on top of things.

"This is it," Pet sings. "We're roughing it, we're making do." She does a twirl about the place, like a trade show model for a kitchen convention. "Place's not exactly outfitted," she says, meaning the kitchen. "Might have to drink it straight from the bottle." She crosses to a stool by a kitchen counter, brings her fit legs with her to the small oval seat, hugs them to her chest, keeps talking: "Me and my dead husband's ghostwriter, swapping spit, talking 'bout how it was." She seems to Pimletz entirely too cheerful for an encounter such as this, although, in truth, he's got no idea what the appropriate levels of cheer might be. He's got no idea about the appropriate levels of anything.

He sinks the rusted corkscrew into the cork and does what he can, but the bottle had been on its end and the cork gone dry and the stopper goes all crumbly when he tries to pull it out. There are tiny pieces of cork all over the up-high countertop in front of him—a whole litter!—and he considers these as his head fills with bad ideas on how to salvage the situation. "Cork's gone bad," he says, stalling, hoping his virtually unannounced guest will find some reason to reach for the bottle and brush her hands up against his, just one more time, pleasepleaseplease.

"I'm guessing you were never a waiter," Pet says, taking the bottle back from Pimletz (and grabbing only glass!) and pushing the cork down past the neck with a still fused-together pair of take-out chopsticks. She finds these in a drawer by the sink, where Pimletz has let them accumulate.

"What about the cork?" Pimletz wants to know.

"It's just cork," she says, working the last of the stopper down the bottleneck. "Not like it'll choke you or anything." She brings the bottle to her mouth and takes a long pull, and the wet, left-behind glisten on her lips is enough to make Pimletz forget about her hands. He wonders if her lips are cold. Then she sets the bottle down on the counter, brings her hand to her mouth, and spits cork into her cupped fingers. She does this with a kind of artful poise that belies the act itself. "Pretend it's pulp," she says. "Okay? It's just pulp. It's fresh-squeezed orange juice and there's just some pits and some pulp. That's all. Strainer didn't do a very good job." She pushes the bottle across the counter to Pimletz. "Join me?" she says.

=

He wasn't expecting his mother.

Last he spoke to her, she was running on about how busy they were at work, she and Nils, about how things were really taking off, and wouldn't it be great if Norman could just scoot on up there for the weekend (just scoot on up there, that's just how she said it), maybe help out a bit, go out on a couple calls. She talked about everything but what she meant to talk about. It'd be a good chance to get together, she said, get things back to normal. Norman was thinking, Yeah, like, this is pretty much the first thing on my list to do, to scoot on up to New Hampshire, to suck the dust and muck and apple pie from the rugs of Mr. and Mrs. Smalltown U.S.A. Yeah. If this is normal, he'll be someplace else.

Still, he's glad to see her—here, now—landed in the not-quite vestibule area of his shitty little apartment late in the day, with an oversized package wrapped in plain brown paper and criss-crossed packing string, like on a cake box, under her arm. The thing is too big for her to carry comfortably, and so she's got a couple fingers curled under the taut packing string, which serves as a kind of handle, except that it cuts off her circulation at the knuckles and tears at her skin. It's not the best arrangement, but it's how she managed up the few flights of stairs.

"What's that?" Norman says, noticing.

"No hug? No how are you, dear mother? What the hell kind of sewer were you brought up in?"

"Nice, Mom," he says, collecting her for a hug, helping her to set down her package. "This is the way you talk around your Nilsy?"

Anita smiles at him like they've both been caught smoking. This is her new thing. The tension between Nils and Norman has troubled her since the beginning, and it's worse since Wood's gone. Lately, she's chosen to play it from both sides. She doesn't want to get into it, and so she dances around it on the theory that if it isn't there, it isn't there. When she's with Norman, she adopts a kind of conspiratorial tone, as if she would like to acknowledge that her new husband is about an inch short of ridiculous, but would prefer it if she and Norman could just keep this fact to themselves. When she's with Nils, she's a little too quick to join him in his subtle castigations. They are hard on Norman together; they worry what to do about him. "He's got this thing about casual profanity," she says, back in us-against-him mode. "Nils. You know that."

"Too well, mother dear," Norman says, hugging still. "Too fucking well."

"Norman!" She slaps him on the butt, playfully, the way a mother would her teasing child.

"Enough of this shit-chat," he says, emphasis front, pointing once again to the oversized package. "What's in the bag?"

"What's in the bag is just a little something," Anita announces. "Plus, it's not a bag. It's a package. You're just like your father. It wouldn't kill you to be a little more precise."

No, Norman thinks, but maybe it's what killed him. He doesn't know what this means, except that it is something to think. Certainly, the Woodman was never known for his precision. There was nothing exact about his father that Norman can call to mind.

Anita leans the bagged package against the wall. "Been lying around the house," she explains. "Thought you might like to have it."

Norman slips the taut string over a corner of package and struggleslides the loop down its length. Then he tears at the brown paper wrapping, and from underneath the tear—from, like, before he's even got the paper all the way ripped off and bunched to the ground—he catches his father's eyes staring back at him, and the immediate effect is that he's being watched, as ever. It hits him like one of those forgettable Vincent Price horror movies, the ones with the long-forgotten family portraits hanging over dusty mantels, the eyes moving predictably about the room, catching everything.

He is momentarily alarmed.

"Here," his mother says, reaching for the package to open it the rest of the way. "Let me."

Norman has to step back a couple paces to take it all in. There, behind the promise of Panavision, is the Woodman himself, as advertised, in a lobby poster for *These Things Happen*, a fairly unnoticed Paramount effort with Sebastian Cabot and a young Ann-Margret. Norman tries to figure the date from the fine print, but it's laid out in Roman numerals, and he can't get much past the MCM. They didn't teach Roman numerals in his fancy-ass school. Something something something. Early 1970s, he thinks. Whenever.

In the picture, Wood played an Indy race car driver, Trim Tompkins, whose broken-down car couldn't quite handle the drill, and the drive of the movie was the way Trim kept patching his vehicle with spit and hope and plugging on. *The Little Engine That Could* with fast cars and too-tight jeans and early-1970s sex. Ann-Margret played the love interest, the daughter of some motor oil executive whose company was sponsoring Trim's car, and Sebastian Cabot the pit boss. What stayed with Norman, other than the incongruity of seeing his beloved Mr. French in garage overalls, was the way this Trim Tompkins refused to be beaten down. It was so unlike his father, a man who would have kicked and screamed and somehow managed to trade his broken-down race car for a new set of wheels just before the starting gun. He was never the type to shoulder his rough circumstances and hope for the best. He was the loud asshole at the front of the line getting what he wanted, never the shrinking sap at the back willing to acquiesce.

In the poster, there's Wood underneath a store-bought frame in racing gear, working his pretty boy smile, a helmet crooked under his arm. He was never much of a matinee idol, Terence Wood, but, for a while in there, also early 1970s, the studios were on him to make like Paul Newman and Ryan O'Neil, only he never could manage it without seeming like he was on the knowing side of an inside joke. They kept handing him these shit pictures, and he kept looking like he could just choke on the charm, like he knew something the rest of the planet couldn't possibly imagine. It wasn't him, but no one seemed to notice, or care, or think it was up to them to say anything about it. This poster, this Trim Tompkins, this isn't him, but Norman takes it in as if it might have been. He loses himself in his father's put-on smile and wonders what his life might have been like if the Woodman had been more conventionally Hollywood, on screen and off, more conventionally glamorous, but then he remembers what happened to Ryan O'Neil's kid and thinks maybe he didn't have it so bad. Least he's never been in rehab. He wonders what his father was thinking when they took the shot, if he was thinking what it would be like to do good work again, what it would be like to have a kid, to matter.

"I thought, you know, the title," Anita says, tentatively, trying to pull her son back into the moment. "These things happen." She pauses to get Norman to consider the deep meaning of the phrase. "That's one way to look at it."

"Oh, Mom, please," Norman says.

She throws up her arms as if she doesn't know what else to do. (She doesn't.) "Excuse me for trying to make this make sense," she says.

"It doesn't make sense. That's the whole point."

"No, Norman. It has to. It has to mean something, his not being here."

"Dying, Mom. The word is dying."

"Fine, dying. It has to mean something."

"Okay, then," he challenges. "What does it mean? Go ahead. Enlighten me."

Anita hadn't thought things through to this point. She came to New York knowing only that they should talk about Wood's death, but not knowing what to say. With Nils, at home, she gets to play it at the surface, but she wants to reach down deep when she's with Norman. She's talked about this with Pet. She wants to let Norman know the ache she feels for him, for what he's lost. Hell, for what she's lost, too, but a lot of that is tied up with what Norman's going through. She wants to put it in a place where it will touch her without leaving her spent, hopeless, obscured. Still, she can't think what to say. "Why does everything have to be so confrontational with you?" she finally manages.

Now it's Norman's turn to have nothing to say. He crosses the not-quite vestibule to his mother and collects her once again in a hug. He's never liked to see her upset, now especially. Hugged, he helps her out of her coat and then he folds it, inside out, and rests it on the floor. (He's got no closets.) Then he takes the framed poster in one hand and his mother in the other and leads her to the not-quite living room, where he searches his cluttered walls for a spot to hang the poster. He wonders if his mother sees any irony in gifting to her only child a poster of his dead father dressed in racing gear, about to don a helmet and step into a defective car and drive off at great speed to an uncertain fate. He wonders if she makes the connection, if it's even worth mentioning.

====

Harlan Trask, sleeping, takes up more room on Grace's bed than there actually is. Or maybe it just seems that way. Or maybe it's just how when he's bushed, he drops onto the mattress at whatever angle he can most easily manage. However Grace looks at it, the man takes more than his share, and she sits at what's left of the foot of the bed cataloging new ways to accommodate him. Don't get her wrong, she's not complaining or anything, but when she's working late at the coffee shop, closing up, and he knocks off early after his shift at the park, she comes upstairs and there's, like, no room.

It's just a full, Grace's bed, and even when it was just her, it sometimes felt a little too confining, so she's willing to take that into account, but now that she's got company long-term, it's a serious crapshoot, getting comfortable. It's out of hand. When they go to bed at the same time, if they've both been reading or messing around a bit or something, then it's easy to drop off together before either one stakes out too much territory. Then it's no problem because then she doesn't have to worry about Harlan's crazy angles, and anyway there's always spooning, like normal people, even though they're each about one hundred pounds north of normal people and their spooning is more like ladling.

She's watched that show *Roseanne* for years, and now that it's in reruns she's watching it all over again. She's never once noticed how Roseanne and Dan sleep in a full-size bed. Until lately. What's that all about? They're six hundred pounds between them, easy, and the producers have got them squeezed onto this tiny mattress, only Grace never paid good enough attention until she got this thing going with Harlan. Now she watches those bedroom scenes with Roseanne and Dan and fills with sympathy. They're always in there talking about their kids or whatever problems they're having; it's, like, one of their regular sets, and now that she's noticed, she can't get past it. How can people not notice something like that?

Maybe they think it's a blue-collar thing, the producers, this sleeping on a full-size mattress, or maybe it's a queen, hard to tell on the television, but the way Grace sees it, it's a logistical thing. It's making the effort to make the change, it's moving away from something old into something new. No way it's a money thing, she's thinking. The difference between full and king is probably no more than, like, fifty, sixty bucks.

They did a *Sally Jesse* on this, once. They had on this one big-sized couple, and they were saying how there wasn't enough floor space in their bedroom for a bigger bed. And how, anyway, they were trying to hold back on any major expenses because they were trying to get enough of a stake together for a down payment on a house, and how it was just something they'd gotten used to. But she couldn't see it. She couldn't see how people would choose to sleep this way. Once in a while, you know, okay. She can even deal with it for a short period of time, but she's pretty much to the point where a new bed is a mandatory thing, only to bring it up, to bring herself to make a change, would be to bring up all kinds of other stuff. Getting a new bed now would tie in to whatever's going on between them.

But maybe they do need to take a look at this thing long-term. It's, like, way past indefinitely already. She loves her Harlan, but she needs her sleep. And so does he. That's the thing. She can't deny him that. She steps from the foot of the bed and lifts his feet by the ankles, lovingly, but also purposefully, and walks with them so that his whole body pivots to a right angle with the headboard. There, she thinks. That's a little more workable. Then she slips his feet from the red furry pant legs the poor baby didn't bother to take off after work. She moves like a mother doting on her child.

Then she pulls an afghan from the chair by the bed and covers him with it. She's tried, on other nights, to slip the tucked-in sheets and quilt down from under his butt and then draw them back up and tuck them in again around him, but she doesn't have the effort in her tonight. Plus, you know, it's pretty nice out, not too cold, she's got the windows cracked and everything. He'll be fine with just the afghan.

Then she slips out of her own clothes, drops them in the pile on the floor of her closet, pulls from the pile the extra large Maritime Merrytime night shirt she's worn now for a couple nights running, and slides away the hangered clothes to get to the videos she keeps stacked on a shelf in the back. Something she hasn't seen in a while, she's thinking, something to take her back. She thumbs through her library of mostly store-bought titles, although, for a while, she was pretty good about keeping blank tapes in the apartment, studying the *TV Guide,* and dubbing some of those hard-to-find old movies straight from the cable. She bought the tapes six to a box, sometimes ten, whatever was on special down at Blockbuster. Turned out to be a real money-saver. She pulls out a few of the store-bought tapes to read the thumbnailed storyline and reviewers' comments on the back, but settles finally on one of her homemade dubs that definitely could stand another viewing. It's been a while. Then she slides back the clothes, closes the closet door, crosses to the big-screen television, and presses the videotape into the VCR.

Usually, she likes to keep a couple months cushion between her repeat viewings. Any longer and she loses the familiarity she cherishes; any shorter and it's like a broken record. There's a fine balance. She wants to feel connected to the movie, like the characters know her, but not to where her knowing them gets in the way. She likes to space it out so that she doesn't remember the dialogue, or the subtle plot twists, or who might turn up in a supporting role, or whatever. She knows what happens, but she doesn't want to know what happens. She likes to be surprised in her own small way, and, tonight, in her own small way, she surprises herself.

She's been too long away from this one, and she wonders why. Actually, she knows why; she just wonders. She listens to the lone violin at the start of *The Half Shell.* The simple melody has rarely left her head since the first time she saw it back at the Tivoli, back when there were lightbulbs on the marquee, back when you couldn't hear the loud action from the movie playing in the theater next door because there was no such thing as the theater next door, and on through the years, when the only way to see it was at the revival house in Bangor, or on late-night television, cut up by Ginsu knives and time constraints. When the rest of the orchestra comes in behind the solo, and the theme song swells, and the opening credits roll, she looks over toward her too-small bed and her sleeping hulk of Harlan Trask and wonders when he'll get around to telling her.

What It's Like

Pimletz can't get over it. Really, stuff like this never happens to him, and it's been so long in not happening, he's begun to think it never really happens to anyone else, either.

What it is, though, he isn't sure. How it started is about the best he can do. How it started was one afternoon, day after she arrived, this Petra Wood person began inching a little too close for polite conversation. Closer and closer, to where Pimletz could almost taste her breath against his lips. She was all amazing looking and good smelling, and it's possible he was reading more into her behavior than she was putting out, but he didn't think so. It was a little obvious, even to Pimletz, a man to whom a double-talking politician might seem a surprise. That she was like something out of one of those lingerie catalogs he keeps around his apartment didn't help, but even if she'd been plain, his imagination still would have managed to get ahead of him. At his depth, he can't rule anyone out.

It started right away. Subtly, but right away. Or maybe not so subtly, but still. First it was just Petra Wood touching her hands to Pimletz's face to show how cold it was. But then it was leaving the bathroom door ajar while she was toweling off after a shower, leaning over Pimletz while he was at his desk, not writing, in such a way that her breasts were made to brush suggestively against his head. It was Petra telling him her heart was beating super fast after lifting a wicker trunk filled with old magazines and pulling his open hand to her chest so that he might feel for himself, sharing unsolicited intimacies regarding Terence Wood's sexual prowess and her appetite for same. ("You need to know this," she kept saying, "don't you, Axel? I mean, for the book?") It was Petra asking if he kept any C batteries in the cabin because she'd brought with her a small bedroom appliance, she claimed to be embarrassed to admit—her little joystick, she called it; said she never travels without it—which seemed to be running out of gas. "Even us grieving widows need a poke every once in a while," she said, playing at sheepish, holding out her rebatteried dildo like it was medicine.

She decided she'd stay a couple days, long as she'd made the trip, long as there was nothing else doing, and there was plenty of room. Pimletz assured her she wouldn't be in the way, but, in truth, he wasn't sure he could get past the distraction. Jesusmotherfuckingchristalmighty, it's not like you have to beat him over the head with what's going on. He jerked off twice, maybe three times, the morning after the business with the cold fingers against his face and kept up the routine as Petra Wood kept up her temptations. He was determined to drain himself, to guard against the likely possibility of shooting his wad the moment she finally reached for him—a defensive maneuver he'd had to employ his entire pubic life, to be ready by not being ready.

For Pimletz, age and an extremely limited experience have done nothing to diminish the response time between sexual thought and dick-preparedness, and since there's never any time between sexual thoughts, he is constantly prepared. He's always reading these letters in the advice column in *Playboy* from these guys who can't get it up, or hearing some talk radio caller with the same problem, or catching some episode of *Montel* about related dysfunctions, but, with him, it's the other way; he can't keep it down. He's hard all the time, for the slightest reason, for no reason at all. He gets hard watching those Nice 'n Easy, Tender Loving Care shampoo commercials, or Tipper Gore giving a speech, or Dominique Moceanu straddling the balance beam at the Olympics. He gets hard watching Jessica Rabbit—a fucking cartoon! And it's not just a naked-woman-in-the-shower type thing, or the *Sports Illustrated* swimsuit issue, or a finely drawn piece of animated ass; it's the idea of any physical contact that gets him going. Apparently, it doesn't even have to be human.

He's got no control of himself in this area, to where even a trip to the doctor's office for his annual physical leaves him wondering if his dick will turn him in. He jerks off before the appointment (by his calculation, it should be within an hour or so), so that when the guy examines him for testicular cancer or whatever the hell it is he examines him for, he doesn't show any interest. That would just be too weird. That would just be the bottom of the bottom. He's thought about switching to a female doctor, but then he thinks that would just be a too-weirdness of a different kind. What if she's old, like sixty or something, and she goes to examine him, and he just loses it, right there?

It's the same when he goes to buy pants and has to be measured for alterations, except with the tailor he doesn't have to piss himself clean to wash away any of the residual semen to make sure he's presentable down there. Jesus, he would just shit if the doctor spied any caked-over come at the tip of his cock (and, with a lady doctor, he'd shit and die!), but, with the tailor, it's just about avoiding any telling bulges, any movement.

He's thought this problem through to the floor-boards, Pimletz has, although it never helps when the real deal presents itself. When the real deal comes, he's a force of nature. Here he is, thinking he's walking around the cabin with nothing left, but Petra Wood at last presses herself against him from behind and starts to nibblesuck at his ear, and he's variously thinking how stuff like this never happens to him, and how he hopes the ear cheese that has surely formed on the ridge between ear and skull since his last shower is not too terribly noticeable, and how during that last shower, just this morning, he should probably have jerked off one last time, just to be sure, because already the skin of his cock is stretched so taut he's thinking it might crack.

"How about a little break, Axel Pimletz?" Petra Wood says, his ear still in her mouth, her voice reaching him as if through an imbalanced Walkman. "All work and no play, Axie," she says. She lets go the ear and walks a tight half-circle to face Pimletz from the front. She keeps a hand to his clothes as she walks around like he's a fucking maypole, which, in a way, he might be.

"Remember that line?" she continues, "From *The Shining?* From the way Nicholson just kept writing it and writing it, over and over? Page after page, it was just the same thing. 'All work and no play makes Jack a dull boy. All work and no play makes Jack a dull boy. All work and no play makes Jack a dull boy.'" She makes her voice smaller with each repetition, appending ellipsis to her performance. He gets the idea, but she keeps going. "'All work and no play. . . . '"

She starts in playing with his hair, removes his glasses, moves on to the next thing: "I'll tell you something. What he saw in that Shelley Duvall, I'll never know. We met her once at some charity function, and her mouth was, like, way too big for her face. You think? In person, it's like way too big for her face."

Pimletz doesn't think, or at least he's never thought about it, and now that he's been made to, he's not much interested beyond supposing it is so. For a beat, he's thinking the obvious Jack Nicholson impression is a back-handed hint that he get moving on this Wood manuscript, implying as it does that even a deranged Jack Nicholson was able to compile hundreds of pages of the same fucking sentence, while Pimletz has only managed a repetitive thirty-seven, but mostly what he's thinking, now, is that his ear's a little too wet for him not to dab at it, maybe with his sleeve or with a casual brush back of his hair, but he doesn't want to get caught at it and leave this woman thinking he's dabbing at his too wet ear. She might get insulted, and he's also thinking, Axie? No one's ever called him Axie, and it never occurred to him anyone might. Mostly, though, he's thinking he needs to reach into his jeans to adjust himself. He's angled in the wrong way, pointing down, so that when Petra Wood entered the room and got him going, his straightaway swelling cock pressed up against his boxers and jeans like it was trying to lift weights.

He allows himself a small joke by association—just a punchline to start, something about the "clean and jerk," a simple weightlifting maneuver, but then he marries it to the soaped tug and pull of his morning showers—before returning to his dilemma.

"You'll have to excuse me," he's got no choice but to say, standing, turning his back to Pet and reaching into his jeans to right himself.

Pet, noticing, fills the few paces between them. "Here," she says. "Let me." She turns Pimletz to face her and reaches for his belt, only when she unloops the front end and drags the hasp back through its hole, she sees that maybe she's too late. Or, too soon.

(Better, too much.)

"Jesus," Pimletz says, coming, crazy at the thought of this exotic Pet reaching for his pants as much as at any actual friction occasioned by her reaching. He can't help himself. "Jesus," he says again.

Pet rubs at him through his jeans—she doesn't want *not* to participate, after all—and purrs wetly in his ear and keeps rubbing until he's well past through. "It's okay, baby," she purrs. "It's okay."

"Fuck!" Pimletz cries out, done, pissed at himself for not keeping control. He slams his hand into the cabin wall in an embroidered show of frustration. He hurts his hand doing this, his friction hand, but he wants to sell the point that this isn't how things usually are with him, that he's as surprised as she is. What the hell is this all about? he means to suggest. Hey! When the hell was the last time a couple layers of denim and cotton-polyester weren't enough to keep a grown man from spilling himself at the near touch of an amazing-looking woman? Tell him that.

"It's okay," Pet says again. She strokes at his hair with one hand, finishes with his belt with the other. She's up so close against him he can smell the fabric of her clothes, the kind of shampoo she uses, and Pimletz is so caught up in her smells and his disappointment he doesn't notice what she's doing, not at first. She unbuttons his jeans, slips her hand under his shorts and around to his ass, slides his pants down over his hips. He doesn't know how to tell her to stop.

"You must be a mess," Pet says sweetly, somehow producing a moist (and somehow hot) towel and working it tenderly around his dick and balls, like a waitress in a deservedly popular Japanese restaurant. The towel reaches his spent cock like a redemption, a forgiveness.

Jesus, this woman comes prepared, Pimletz thinks. Not him. He just comes.

"I was in a band once," she says, out of nowhere, working her towel, "back in school, we called ourselves Nocturnal Emission, we did a song about this. 'Emission Control.' Get it? It's like a play on words. Nocturnal Emission? Emission Control?" She looks to see if he does. "It was like our theme song. That, and 'Emission Impossible,' which was like the flip side to the whole deal."

She looks up at Pimletz, gets back nothing, continues. "Oh, don't mind me. It's just, you know, you reminded me." She seems to drift off, onto another line of thinking, but then she's back: "God, I haven't thought about that in years. I was on drums, can you believe it? A girl drummer, back then." She bunches the towel and tosses it aside, then drops to her knees and takes him in her mouth and works him like a mother cat. She licks at the messed hair around his balls like he's a kitten in for his bath, like it's her privilege. Her tongue is warm against his wet skin, the inside of her mouth like the mattress side of his pillow.

"Nice," Pimletz says, thinking he needs to keep up his end.

Pet isn't listening. She's back in school, banging the skins, rocking the house. She starts to sing: "If you can't come when you're invited, what's the point of coming at all?" It's the chorus, apparently, so she sings it again and again. It's one of those songs that just drifts away, so this time her ellipsis is a fade. She looks up, sung, to see how Pimletz is doing. "Maybe you saw us?" she wonders. "We were up at Smith, but we played Boston all the time. The Rat. The Paradise. Some place in Cambridge, I can't remember. Late seventies, around in there. Girl groups were pretty happening. The Pretenders. Blondie. All those strung-out chicks." She laughs. "Hey, the Strung-Out Chicks. That's what we should've called ourselves."

Pimletz can't think what to say. He looks down at this amazing-looking woman with his dick near her mouth and thinks if he had a million bucks for every time he found himself in this pose with a woman in that one he'd still be scrambling to make his rent.

"It's okay, Axel," she says, standing to face him. She's back in the moment now, back to her soothing. "It's no biggie." She laughs, not meaning to. "Sorry."

"Thanks," he says, smiling, as if he can laugh it off as well. "Thanks a whole fucking lot."

"Sorry."

Me too, Pimletz wants to say. Jesusfuckingchrist, him too.

Pet retreats to the back bedroom for her little joystick. It'll just take a sec, she tells Pimletz. They can finish her off, you know, if he doesn't need to get back to work. Pimletz stands there, momentarily alone, his pants bunched around his ankles. He's replaying what just happened, fast-forwarding to the next scene with the dildo and the finishing her off, and he's hard in his head, but nowhere else.

===

Norman can't write the truth without understanding the scene. It's easier for him to visualize the piece if he sees himself in the role, if he sees the set, the props, the particulars. It's a layering kind of process. Right now, it's just Norman Wood in his shitty little apartment, but the effect is the same. The juice of the story is Norman and Woodman, but it's also about Norman and Brian Dennehy, or, as it turns out, maybe Charles Durning, or whoever he gets to play his father. It's about what's missing, now, in their relationship, what will be forever lost to Norman with his father's passing. But it's also about how much easier it will be to film the relevant scenes if he confines his search for these missing and lost aspects inside his apartment, just, if there's no reason to take the story anywhere else. He reaches for the truth of his own story, but he's careful not to let his reach exceed his budget.

This is how he works. This is how everyone works around here. It's this, or get nailed. The deal is, he's supposed to produce a shooting script by the end of next week—forty pages, tops, it's just a short—and yet he's managed only a couple sketchy scenes. He knows what he wants to say, what's universal in his relationship with the Woodman, but he doesn't know how to narrow the focus. They've taught him this, in theory, but he doesn't get it. (Not just in theory, but in Theory, an actual class.) He wants to tell the whole story, all at once, fully-realized, but he's stuck having to pick and choose from among his experiences. He gets these flashes in his head, these different scenes, and they have nothing to do with each other or with the piece as a whole, and what bogs him down is that the distance from where he is to where he wants to be is, like, way fucking long. He doesn't see a solution.

Stuck, he flips on the television. Maybe a half-hour or so of tube will spark something for him, or at least leave his head sufficiently numbed that he might better recognize a new idea. Plus, he's up for anything might keep him from writing. Always. Even *Three's Company*. This is where he lands, so he gives it a try. This is Norman for you. He'll grace even the most dubious entertainments with the benefit of his doubt. Maybe it's because he grew up on the industry's fringes, but he feels an obligation to watch what passes in his view. He knows the work that goes into it. He knows the people involved, or people who know the people involved. He owes it to them to watch.

He never noticed *Three's Company* much as a kid. Its first run was a little ahead of his time, but the premise is somehow a part of him: this guy Jack pretends to be gay in order to fool his stuck-up landlords and live platonically with his two attractive female friends in a great apartment. Norman wonders how he knows this, but, more than that, how it passed the dozens of rewrites and story conferences and network suits to emerge as a viable concept for a situation comedy.

Here, now, Jack is dressed as a woman trying to pass herself off as a man, so he's kind of back where he started with just this extra complication thrown in. It is not immediately clear to Norman how this complication came about or how it fits with this episode's story, but he is mildly distracted by the effort. It all seems to matter to these earnest people on screen. There's some shtick with Jack's fishnet stockings underneath his suit trousers, with the way they show when he crosses his legs at a job interview. Then the camera cuts to show a dangling hoop earring left behind on his ear, and the laugh track lets on that this is funny. Norman is stuck marveling at the effortless physicality of the guy who plays Jack and at the difficulty he's having with his own material. This, what he's watching, seems written without a thought; this other thing, what he's working on, has been thought through to the ground without his having written a word.

A commercial break lets him change channels without hurting anyone's feelings, and he bounces remotely along the dial in search of diversion: infomercials, soaps, talk shows, old movies. Ah, here we go. On TNT, they're showing *True Grit*. It looks from these first couple scenes like he hasn't missed much. He sparks to the connection. Usually, with these old movies—late 1960s through, about, early 1980s—there's a connection. With Wood gone, Norman can't look through the cable listings without drawing a line from whatever's showing to some aspect of his father's career. It's like that Six Degrees of Kevin Bacon game, the one that holds that everyone in Hollywood is linked to Kevin Bacon by a flow chart of no more than six pictures. (His roommate is friendly with one of the guys who thought it up.) He maps his own path from Wood to Kevin Bacon: *Sixes and Sevens*, with Yul Brynner, who also appeared in *The Magnificent Seven*, with Steve McQueen, who also appeared in *Papillon*, with Dustin Hoffman, who also appeared in *Kramer vs. Kramer*, with Meryl Streep, who also appeared in *The River Wild*, with Kevin Bacon. There are shorter paths, but it's more of a challenge by way of *Papillon*.

Norman and his film school buds have made the same game out of Woodman's career. (They can get to Darth Vader and back in just four pictures!) He worked with everyone, by the time it was over, rubbed, in some way, against virtually every studio production. The *True Grit* connection is hardly once removed. Wood originally was signed to play the Glen Campbell part, actually showed up for the first day of shooting. But the story he told was that he got into this right-out-of-the-gate pissing contest with John Wayne, and when it became clear to Wood that the Duke was producing a mightier stream at that time in his career, there was nothing to do but kick up some dust and walk. Hal Wallis, the producer, had been an old friend until

Wood's walking caused this great falling out; as far as Norman knew, they never spoke again.

The more likely version was that Wood arrived on the set to find that *True Grit* was clearly John Wayne's picture, and also that he wasn't inclined to help him carry it. No way was he working in support of a bigger legend. Plus, it turned out to be a nothing role. For Glen Campbell, maybe it was a big deal, but for Wood it was insignificant. He might have known, but in the script he'd read, and in the novel on which it was based, there'd been a little more balance to the story. Wood seized on this as the basis for his dissatisfaction. Norman, when he was old enough to get what was going on, never understood his father's surprise. Come on, he always thought, this was John Wayne. John Fucking Wayne, a goddamn legend. What the hell did the Woodman expect? What, he wanted the Duke to dilute the role of a lifetime to leave room in the picture for an upstart pain-in-the-ass like Terence Wood? Yeah, right.

The truth, Norman later found out, was that Wood had a hard-on for the Rooster Cogburn role and couldn't stand that he wasn't long enough in the tooth to battle it out for the lead. (The Duke had about twenty-five years on him!) No way he was gonna sit back and watch John Wayne act the shit out of a part that, in another lifetime, might have been his. Which was why Wood, unnominated, passed the Academy Awards ceremony in Squaw Valley that year, watching from a slopeside condominium with his first wife, Elaine, and the reaction shot to John Wayne's best actor Oscar was the Woodman running outside to take a shit in the resort's heated pool. He had to pay to have the pool drained, cleaned, and even regrouted, but he made all the papers, borrowed some of the wind at the Duke's back, and made himself feel a little better at what he'd missed. It was never his to miss, but Wood didn't see it that way.

Norman, watching, not thinking of his script, tries to imagine his father in the Glen Campbell part. There's no easy fit, but he works at it. There's no edge to Glen Campbell, no danger, and Wood was always a little wanting in the sweetness and hope departments. It would've been, like, a completely different picture, like *It's a Wonderful Life* with Edgar G. Robinson as George Bailey. Toward the back of the movie, there's this scene with Glen Campbell's dead body being dragged along the plains by his horse, and right away Norman flashes to an image of his father, body-bagged, being dragged down Sunset Boulevard by his beloved Pathfinder. It's the weirdest thing, this leap from Glen Campbell to Woodman, from the horse to the sport utility vehicle, but Norman worries it won't leave him. It's with him, still, when the closing credits roll, when he goes to shut off the television manually and press his hand against the static of the screen. It's with him as he crosses to his desk, to return to his script. It's with him when he looks for something to eat in the refrigerator. It's with him when he leaves the apartment for a slice of Ray's down the street, or maybe a two-frank special at Papaya King up the block in the other direction. It's with him, he's guessing, for the next while.

===

Don't talk to Grace about patience. Don't get her going. She's about had it with the wholesaler she's been dealing with, the guy who delivers her milk and cheeses and ketchup and other foodstuffs. Some guy named Howie, tall drink of water, too big for his hats, calls from his cell phone to tell Grace he's just around the corner, the kind of guy who actually refers to himself as a tall drink of water, who seems to be having entirely too much fun at a job that's got no right being any fun at all.

She buys in bulk, naturally. There's a standing order for three times each week—she doesn't have the refrigerator space to go longer between deliveries—and on each pass this Howie's supposed to leave two five-pound bricks of processed American cheese, presliced, one hundred sixty slices. Only, the last couple times, the cheese was all crusty at the edges and moldy in the middle and she could only salvage like fifty or sixty slices from the whole damn order, and even those she wasn't so sure about. No one complained or anything, but for, like, a day or two in there, she was expecting a pissed-off call, or a summons. For, like, a week now, she's had to send one of the Lennys to the Stop 'n' Shop out by the highway for the individually wrapped Kraft slices, which run like a thousand dollars a pound, just so she can offer cheeseburgers, cheese omelets, and grilled cheese sandwiches to her good customers. Everyone else can just wait for this wholesaler to get his deliveries together, thank you very much.

The fisherman crowd, they're a couple decades behind the rest of the world. They hear old Two Stools's not serving cheeseburgers, and, right away, they're into this old John Belushi routine from *Saturday Night Live*. It's like a time warp. They're clapping each other on the back, bellowing "Cheeseburgah, cheeseburgah, cheese-burgah," doubled-up like they've never heard it before. Maybe they haven't. Maybe the routine's just come to them on its own. Maybe the joke's been so long in the atmosphere, from all those reruns and retellings, that all the air's been taken out of it, and it just touches down in their fishermen heads. "Cheeseburgah, cheese-burgah, cheeseburgah."

Bar Harbor's always been safely removed from the cutting edge—the kids up here are just now starting to wear Airwalks and flannels—but it's like these fisher-men haven't been near a television set in decades. Ask any one of them—Mike, Lem, Chester—and he'll tell you the only reason he hasn't seen Carson on the *Tonight Show* past couple years is because he and the wife haven't been staying up.

There's a piece in the *New Yorker*—Grace's sub-scription just started—about the geography of cool, about how, in matters of fashion and trends and music, New York and Los Angeles are generally a month or two ahead of Chicago and Boston and San Francisco, while cities like Dallas and Orlando and Indianapolis drag by another few months. She started reading the article, and she was thinking, you know, what with tel-evision and the Internet and movies and everything, the whole country should be wired pretty much the same, but it turns out it has to do with the way different types of people from different parts of the country respond to that wiring. It's all tied up in how these different prod-ucts are distributed, how they connect in each commu-nity. The article tells how it's actually someone's job (a marketing job, Grace guesses) to track how long it takes the huddled masses in each of our major metropolitan areas to catch on to the next big thing. There's a whole formula for it, and Grace figures, if this is the case, then her particular corner of Maine must be about ready for disco and leisure suits. Even the phrase, the geography of cool, would be meaningless to her fishermen. They'd think she was talking about Canada.

Like with sneakers, okay, you've got your Nikes and your Reeboks and whatever else it is you see on those basketball player commercials, but, up here, everyone just wears what fits from the sale bin at Cuthbert's Drug Store and Emporium. There's the New Balance factory, but everyone knows at least one person who works there to poach on their employee discount, and, besides, they sell all the slightly damaged seconds down at the outlet store. There's this one guy in town, one of her regulars, still wears the canvas P. F. Flyers he had back in high school. Salamander, they call him. Real name is Salmon, Jimmy Salmon, but he goes by Salamander, and his sneakers are shot through with holes, but they're still on his feet. The point is, the day these good people have one hundred thirty-nine dollars to spend on a pair of sneakers is the day Grace wears a thong.

"Chester," she says, leaning over the fishermen to bus their table, refill their coffee mugs, see about pie. She wants to get a conversation going. "You know the Bushes? George and Barbara? You've met them? Took them out on that boat of yours, I recall?"

Lem laughs. "Chet thought he was in the charter business," he says. "Had half the Secret Service thinking that boat would be their death." He laughs again. "They were going down with their president."

"It's a fine boat," Chester counters.

"It floats," Mike offers.

"For the time being," Lem roars. "It floats for the time being." He slaps his palm against the table, hard, as he says this.

"But you met the president?" Grace continues. "And the first lady?"

"That there's no lady," Lem contributes. "That's Babs." He's slapping, still.

"But you met them, right? You know the kind of people they are?"

"I s'pose," Chester says. "I mean, they're not having me down to Houston or anything."

"Fine. So here's my question. What kind of president d'you think his son would make?" She's got their three plates stacked on the muscle of her left arm; she's working the table with a no-longer-wet rag pulled from her apron belt; she's not cleaning so much as she is moving stuff around. "Junior. Primaries just around the corner. What kind of job you think he's done down there in Texas?" She's thinking, okay, this is a good line to pursue, this is something they can get their hands around: local kid, sort of, making good on the national stage. Next-door neighbors in New Hampshire about to cast the first nods in his direction that count for anything more than publicity. She replaces the rag, picks up the coffee pot, and goes to rest the dirty dishes on the counter. Coffee shop's not so big she can't have a conversation from the other side of it. "I'd really like to hear your thoughts on this." She really would, that's how hungry she is for an exchange of ideas.

"I thought it was Florida," Mike interjects.

Lem: "No, that's the other one."

"The one owns the baseball team."

Chester, trying to think this through: "He's got, what, two kids, then?"

"More like a million," Mike figures. "Remember all those White House Christmas cards? Them all dressed up? Greta Cuthbert'd set 'em out behind her cash register every year like they was close personal friends?"

"Six. Pretty sure." This is Peter, some guy who paints houses. He's sitting over by the window. It's his slow season, it being winter and all. Grace can't say what accounts for the slowness of her fishermen.

"There was that Vietnamese kid," Lem contributes. "They adopted this Vietnamese kid, I'm remembering. Didn't look nothing like 'em."

"Not like Jack Kennedy," Chester says, with the reverence New Englanders reserve for their own. "With Jack Kennedy, you knew it was Caroline and John-John and that's it. They didn't have to go adopting."

"Hop Sing Bush."

Apparently, Kennebunkport or no, the Bushes don't cut it as New Englanders.

"Dog looked nothing like 'em, either."

Acky, used to own the hardware store at the corner of Brown and Bartlett, reaches his coffee mug into the air and waves it about. "Coffee," he says.

"What Vietnamese kid?" Mike wonders. "Since when was there a Vietnamese kid?"

"Millie. A collie, I think."

"Since she was in all those Christmas cards."

"She or he?"

"There you go, Ack," Grace says, pouring. She holds the coffee pot out for her other customers to see. "Don't make me make a special trip," she warns with what's left of her good nature. "Ask me now." Peter the painter holds out his cup, and she moves to fill it.

"No," Chester corrects. "It was a grandkid. Wadn't his kid, and it wadn't no Vietnamese kid, either. Korean, I think. Something like that."

"Sh'wrote a book. The dog. Remember?"

"There was those miscarriages Jackie had. They had a devil of a time with those miscarriages. 'f'was up to them it wouldn'a been just Caroline and John-John."

"A spaniel. Some kind of spaniel."

"What miscarriages?"

"Read a book, why don'tch'ya?"

"No," Lem insists. "It was Vietnamese. I'm telling you."

"What the hell is a spaniel, anyway?"

"If a dog can write a book, then I don't see as I have to go and read it."

"Since when can you adopt grandchildren?" Mike wants to know. "You can do that?"

Grace, back now to the other side of the coffee shop, has reduced her listening to just one ear, her hoped-for exchange of ideas reduced to the standard foolishness. She's brought the dishes to the sink and cleaned the rest of the tables and set herself down on her remaining stools and started figuring her lunch checks. One ear of this is about all she can take. She meant to get a conversation going, but it's like she started a brush fire.

"Hey, Two Stools!" she hears. "Mike here thinks you can adopt grandchildren!"

"Well, then, it must be so," she sends back. There is no arrogance in her voice, but there's no effort, either, and there's no trace of the good nature that had been running thin. "If Mike thinks it, it must be so." She doesn't turn around when she says this, keeps figuring her checks. This time of year, she's got to reach to make ends meet. If the building wasn't paid up in full, she once told her father, she'd be out on her substantial ass.

"Mexican, maybe," Mike tries. "For some reason I'm thinking the kid was Mexican."

Into this foolishness walks Grace's Harlan—bearded, pale, and looking like he could sell pipe tobacco, or cough drops, maybe even flowers. All he needs is a sweater. (Grace makes a note of this for when he tells his birthday.) He's caught the gist of the conversation, past few minutes, from the doorjamb to the back stairs. He's down for a bite to eat and gets this earful from Grace's chowderheads. "How 'bout she's American?" he says, when he's heard enough. "How 'bout her father was the president of these fucking United States, and we'll just leave it at that."

The others hadn't heard Wood come in, and they turn to face him. "Hey, lookie here," Chester says. "It's Larry Lobster."

"Time for his bottom-feeding," Mike announces.

Grace chuckles at this. It's a good one, especially for Mike, especially with the way Harlan has to come downstairs to eat. She wonders if Mike put this much thought into it, if he thought of it just now.

"Trask," Lem says, kicking out a chair. "Just in time for pie."

They're glad to see him. They've known each other their entire lives, these fishermen, and yet in just a few months they've allowed this stranger into their midst to where he's nearly one of them. He doesn't fish, but he gets the idea. He gets the rest of it too.

"If Harlan eats, the pie's for free," Chester calls over to Two Stools.

"Like hell," she says, her good nature restored now that Harlan's around. She likes the sweet mood he brings with him, wants to hold on to it for later, but she hates the idea of free pie. It's one of her biggest profit margins. That, and coffee. "'He's not careful, I'll charge him too."

"Oh, I pay, Gracie dear," Wood says, sidling up to the counter, pressing himself against Grace from behind. "I pay dearly." He kisses the back of her head, sweetly, then he plays absentmindedly with her hair, then he crosses to the other side of the counter and helps himself to what's left of pie. Blueberry. She's sold about six pieces, but she cuts them so thin there's more than half still in the tin. He grabs some forks and walks his bounty back to the table to join his friends.

"What kind?" Lem wants to know.

"Blueberry."

"Stains my teeth," Chester says.

"Who's having?"

"They're not even yours," Mike says. "Just take 'em out and soak 'em."

"Ammonia," Lem declares. "Someone told me ammonia does a good job."

"On denture stains?"

"Absolutely, on denture stains. This is what we're talking about. Denture stains."

"They're not dentures," Chester insists. "Mike knows shit. They're capped, is all. They're still mine. And it's just these front four, top and bottom." He opens wide, in a cheesy smile, to illustrate.

"And who's paying for all this?" Grace wants to know, meaning the pie party. She's back at the table. She's brought plates. She doesn't want to hear about Chester's teeth.

"It's on the house," Mike says, indicating Wood.

"Since when is Harlan the house?"

"He lives here, don't he?"

He's got her there. "So what if he does? Still don't make him the house."

Wood puts a five-dollar bill on the table. "Here," he says. "This makes me the house."

Grace pushes the money back across the table to Harlan with the tip of her pie knife. "I don't want your money, Harlan," she says, and then she waves the knife at the fishermen. "I want theirs."

Lem laughs at his own joke before he can give it voice, and when he does, it doesn't come out funny. "Trask can work it off in trade," he says, hopeful.

"Got any apple?" Chester says, when Grace slides a thin piece of pie in front of him. "This blueberry really does stain."

"It's just blueberry today, Chet," she says. "Sorry." She really is. They were on sale, the blueberries, flash-frozen, from Oklahoma. She didn't even know they grew blueberries in Oklahoma, thought it was just wheat fields and maybe corn, but Howie, the whole-saler, swears to it. Says it's peak growing season down there. "There's ice cream," she says, "if you prefer." She's off to the painter's table to see if he wants. Acky never takes pie. Says it clots the arteries. She's never heard this except from him.

"What kind?"

"Chocolate." Also on sale: two-for-one.

"Well, that stains too, chocolate." Chester pouts as he says this. These caps of his have become a big both-er, especially around dessert.

"Aw, Chester, quit whining," Lem says. "Just take your fucking teeth out and put 'em in your pocket."

"He'll have the pie à la mode," Wood says, and the fishermen howl—Chester, too.

"I suppose you're payin' for the mode," Grace says to Wood, returning to their table. She's asking and telling, both.

Mike doesn't know why he's laughing. "What's mode?" he wonders, catching his breath. "Ain't never seen that on the menu."

This is true, Grace thinks. He ain't never. She gets her boys served and recaffeinated and returns to her stools to total their bills. They've got tabs going, but she's let them run up pretty high. Money's tight for everyone this time of year. Harlan, too. She can't imag-ine he'd have enough with just his winter paycheck from down at the park if it weren't for her room and board. He's got, like, no expenses. She doesn't have it in her to be on him about work, but she's thinking a man like that should be working more than just week-ends. He should be doing more than just managing.

He's strong and healthy. There must be something. She's also thinking, you know, he must have some real money somewhere. There must be some resources he can call on, if it gets to that. He's not the type to go hungry. Just look at him. The man's put on about thirty pounds since he drifted into town, and most all of it has come from her refrigerator. She doesn't mind, but it's something to think about.

"Vanilla's really a better match for pie," Lem says. He's put some thought into this. "Goes with everything."

"Mmmm," Mike says, presumably in agreement.

Chester (stained): "Vanilla."

"D'you hear that, Gracie?" Wood thunders across the restaurant. "The chowderheads seem to think the chocolate dominates the blueberry."

"That so?" Grace shoots back. She and her one ear are only half-listening. She's still on her bills, and the mess-ups with her wholesaler, and the way it takes forever for the latest trends to find her, and how Harlan has fitted himself into her world. It's like there was a place for him, waiting. She's back and forth and all over. She's thinking how tomorrow's *Oprah* is one of those book club shows (she saw it in the listings), and how she hasn't read the book, and how she's got nothing to show for her forty-three years but a small coffee shop with mismatched tables and chairs and more money going out than coming in, how in winter she should probably cut back on one of her Lennys, but then she's back on Harlan, on what to do with a sixty-six-year-old man who isn't sure who he wants to be, or where, if he wants to be there with her. She looks over at him, laughing with his new friends, contented, and wonders at her feelings for him.

She feels alone, and yet she's not alone; she's somewhere in between. She wonders if what she feels is love, or if it's just that she loves the attention, the rough of his beard, the salt of his kiss, the way he likes to fall asleep against her breast, watching Nick at Nite. Maybe she just loves the idea of him. It's not like they're banging down her bedroom door, the men up here, so maybe she's confusing Harlan's banging with something deeper. Maybe it's just banging. Maybe she's just a place to park, something to do while he figures what he really wants, and she's fooling herself into thinking it's anything more. She's relaxed around him, herself, but his own uncertainty is beginning to tear at her. And this place—Maine, the coffee shop, the mold on the cheese, the being overweight and alone and forty-three—is beginning to tear at her too. She doesn't want to grow old, like this, here. She wants a better spot in the geography of cool, to be somewhere, to matter. She doesn't want to spend the rest of her days perched on her two stools talking blueberry stains and George Bush's adopted Vietnamese grandchildren with her regulars. She doesn't want to keep reaching. Or, if she has to keep reaching, she wants whatever it is she's reaching for to stay wherever the hell it is and give her a chance to catch up. She wants Harlan Trask to rise from his chair and cross to the counter and take her in his arms and carry her upstairs and come clean. She wants it to be like that scene in *An Officer and a Gentleman*, the one where Richard Gere comes into the factory and collects Debra Winger into his arms and fireman-carries her to a happy ending, and everyone in the coffee shop will just stand and applaud and surge with good feelings. She wants to look like Debra Winger. From the back. From the front, she wants to look like that actress from *The English Patient*, the one who has sex in the bathtub with Ralph Fiennes and then dies in the cave. Sometimes she thinks she'd even take dying in a cave if it came with having sex in the bathtub with Ralph Fiennes. It seems to Grace as good a way to go as any.

===

"Here," Pet says, emerging from the front hall closet, handing Pimletz a pair of Wood's sheepskin mittens and his flap-eared woolen hat. "It's cold."

"I'm okay," he says, pulling on his own parka. "Shouldn't be too bad." He doesn't like the idea of wearing other people's hats. He especially doesn't like the idea of wearing dead people's hats. Slippers, he doesn't mind; he could even see his way into a coat; but there's something about a dead guy's hat leaves him queasy. He opens the door and steps one foot across the threshold. "See," he says. "A regular day at the beach."

In truth, it is cold—about six degrees when they got up this morning—and there's a dusting of snow to cover the few fresh inches they had the day before yesterday, and neither one of them is dressed for it. Pimletz is determined to make like it doesn't matter, and what does Pet know about winter? She's a California girl. She looked outside and announced that a walk would be a good idea. Through the frosted panes of the kitchen window, the woods seemed like something out of a storybook, and she thought she could use a good story. She ached to be out in the swallowed-up silence of the fresh snow. Anyway, it's been a while since anyone picked up the mail in the box at the end of the road, and she thought they could maybe make a special trip out of it.

"Cold enough for you?" Pimletz says. It's a stupid thing to say, but he's got nothing else.

"Maybe just a short walk," Pet suggests, stepping all the way out the door. "To the mailbox and back." Right away, her ache shifts to wanting to be back inside. This looked good, all this softsilent snow, but the coldness cuts through her. All she's got on, really, is a T-shirt and a sweater and a fleece pullover. She could use a couple more layers, a pair of proper boots, maybe some thermals. The knit hat and scarf she pulled from the top shelf in the closet seem mostly for show; she wonders if maybe they're Anita's or one of their weekend guests'. Pet certainly doesn't remember buying them; there are enough holes in the pattern to test the theories of insulation through negative space; she wraps the scarf around her neck three or four times, like she's winding a yo-yo, and she leaves enough play in the wrap to slip it up around her mouth and nose and cheeks, and then she tucks what's left of the scarf's loose end under its middle. Her ears she can just forget about. No way is this hat keeping her warm.

"Least there's no wind," Pimletz says. Again, it's all he's got.

"Like at this temperature, it really fucking matters."

"Move around," he suggests, hopping up and down as they start to walk so that he gives the appearance of being in a sack race. "Get the circulation going. Warm you up in no time." His breath, when it leaves, turns to ice against his upper lip.

Pet is not about to hop up and down the length of the drive, a half-mile or so, to the mailbox and back. She'd rather get frostbite, or hypothermia, or whatever people get when they're too long in the too cold. She doesn't want to look ridiculous, even though she realizes her wrapped-around scarf is no help in this regard; the hopping business would just increase her ridiculousness exponentially. She'd rather lose a toe and look ridiculous in the privacy of her own home. "Let's just get this over with," she says.

"You make it sound like it was my idea."

"Sorry," she says, "but this wasn't what I had in mind."

"I can run up ahead? Save you the round trip?"

She's too cold to answer.

"You can start back without me." He doesn't wait for a response. He darts ahead, slipsliding over the mostly packed snow. Last night's dusting has barely covered the packed, iced-over driveway leading out to the road. It looks good on the trees, but it doesn't offer any traction, and with his seventh or eighth step, he is on his back, his legs tripped out from underneath like a drunk on a log. The snow collects him with a resolute crunch. "Shit," he says, fallen, but he scrambles to his feet and shakes off the loose snow and continues to the road. He doesn't look back to see if Pet noticed his falling, but, when he's down in the snow and scrambling, it occurs to him that the thing to do is pretend nothing happened. The thing to do is press on.

He wills himself to not look back. It reminds him of a game he used to play on himself, as a kid, when he left the apartment for school each day. They lived in a Storrow Drive high-rise, same place his mother lives now, and she would walk with him through the meandering streets of Beacon Hill on down to the Common, after which it was just a straight shot across the park to his school. He always tried just to leave his mother there without looking back or waving or checking to see if she was still watching, but he could never make it all the way without turning over his shoulder. She was always still there, matching his gaze, waiting for him to disappear inside the safety of the school. He used to hate that he had to look, but he couldn't help himself. If he'd been thinking of something else, he would have been fine, but he laid out this test like it was important. Or maybe it was a test for his mother, to see if she loved him enough to keep her watch, or maybe to pinpoint the day when she stopped loving him enough to keep her watch. He tries now to remember the day he made it across for the first time without looking back, because eventually, of course, he started walking to school on his own, except now he figures he must've gotten to that point by degrees because he can't recall that first day. He wonders if there was triumph in it, for him, or if mostly it was tinged with sadness, or if maybe he didn't notice it at all. Maybe it was just a day, like the one before.

Today, though, he makes it. It bugs the shit out of him, not to look back to see if Pet is watching, but he makes it, and he wonders if this signals a kind of growth or just that he's finally learned a measure of control.

There is no triumph in his reaching the mailbox without turning around. There's no sadness. It just is.

Terence Wood's mail is bundled and waiting. Up here, rural route deliveries are only twice a week, and the mail comes bundled in thick rubber bands. (If the locals need their mail on a daily basis, they can pick it up at the post office.) Pimletz collects the half-dozen bundles, and he can see without sorting that it's mostly circulars, some bills, magazines. In the whole pile, there are only a few pieces of real correspondence. He doesn't see the point in collecting a dead man's mail, especially when the temperatures are in the single digits and the mail is mostly circulars, but this is what Pet wanted. He wonders what she'll do with it.

He turns back with the few bundles cradled in his arms, and he notices Pet halfway down the drive, about where he left her, only she seems to be doing more than just standing still, or less. She seems to be not moving at all, frozen, and as he quickens his pace he notices she's stuck with one arm up in the air and the other at her hip. This strikes him as the kind of strange he might need to do something about. "Pet," he calls out, racing back. "Pet."

She makes a noise, but Pimletz can't make it out.

"Pet," he says again.

She makes the same noise, and Pimletz strains to hear it. He's just a few yards away, and then he's on her, and then she says it again. Her lips, far as he can tell, are not moving behind the wrapped-around scarf. What he can't tell is she's smiling.

"Oil can," she squeaks, in her impression of a tinny voice. She's gone from being too cold to breathe, to just being cold, to thinking it's really not that bad out, once you get used to it. She's out here, she's cold, she might as well have some fun. She holds her pose like a statue. "Oil can." It comes out sounding like oyolkin, oyolkin.

"What?" Pimletz says. He's not catching on.

"Oil can," she squeaks again. Then, in a stage whisper: "You're supposed to get me an oil can and lube up my joints and get me moving again. Tell me you've never seen *The Wizard of Oz*."

Pimletz, wanting to please, pantomimes the getting of an oil can and the lubing up of joints, which allows Pet to pantomime the gift of movement after a rust or a thaw. "Better?" he says, playing along.

"Better." Pet goes into some elaborate stretching, and then she laughs, and then she pushes Pimletz playfully in the chest with both hands—a you-don't-say! gesture that catches him off guard and knocks him back down to the snow. He clutches the bundles of mail as he falls, doesn't think to break his own. "You just can't seem to keep your feet," she says. "You're like the scarecrow." She laughs again, and races in a zig-zag toward the cabin.

Pimletz scrambles back up and goes to catch her. He has to think about it, though. He has to think if this is what he's supposed to do. He's not used to such playfulness. He's not used to getting other people's jokes— not on just the first or second pass, anyway. He's thinking, at last, a Hollywood reference he can understand. *The Wizard of Oz* he knows. He's also thinking he's got no playfulness of his own to contribute to the occasion.

Petra Wood is not thinking at all. She's no longer cold. She's beyond cold. She's to where the temperature is accepted. There are other things. She's lost in what she's doing and in what she's lost. She did this, once, romped in the snow with Wood. It was warmer, but they were out here on these same grounds, making snow angels, laughing, ducking behind trees, throwing snowballs, running around like they were the only two people on the planet. She wants to reclaim that moment, to taste it again and measure how it is now against how she remembers it. She wants to put her life on rewind and see how it looks on second viewing.

====

"Norman," Terence Wood writes into the ether. "There are some things I need to tell you."

He is hunched, uncomfortably, over one of the user terminals in the electronic room of the Bar Harbor Public Library, just a few beats after having gotten over the fact that there even is such a place. The library he knew about, but the electronic room is a revelation. He wandered in, thinking he might thumb through some magazines, maybe read the flap copy on some of the new celebrity autobiographies, check out the indexes, see if he's mentioned, and he stumbled on all these Packard Bells. Without even thinking about it, he logged on to one and started writing. It was something to do, a place to put some of the things he's been thinking, and it was almost as if it happened without him. Once he got going, he couldn't stop; it was like he was being pulled under by the riptide of what's happened. He didn't think it through to where it was about saving what he writes, or printing it out, or sending it out to be read. He didn't think it through to where it was about thinking it through. All he wanted was to not be swallowed up by it. All he wanted is for what he had to say to find its way out of his head and down through his fingers and out into the world. He continues:

There's no easy place to begin, except to say I'm here. Still. Yup. How the fuck about that? Okay, so that's a start, right? I'm still here. Boom. Big opening scene. Roll opening credits, right?

But really, Norman, it just kicks the shit out of me I haven't been able to reach out to you until now to tell you, you know, what I've been doing, what's behind what I've been doing. I'm not even sure I know myself, except to say it might surprise you. Surprised the shit out of me, that's for fucking sure. Still does. Every day. Surprises the shit right out one end and back in the other. Surprise, surprise.

It just hit me, is all, how it started. That night, in the rain, on that road. Boom. Exit, stage left. Remember that cartoon we used to sometimes watch when you were a kid? The one with the tiger? One of those Hanna-Barbera pieces of shit. I think it was a tiger. Maybe a lion. Some big cat. "Exit, stage left." What the hell was that tiger's name? Some great character actor did the voice. Guy I worked with once. Why am I not thinking of this asshole's name?

Bah. Here's a better question. Who cares? Better to talk about my presumed death, right? About what the hell was going on with me. Is. About what the hell IS going on with me. This is why we're here. Okay, so what can I tell you? It just seemed the thing to do, to check out like that, because Jesus, things were just shit. I mean, you know. You know the kind of shit I was in, the kinds of pictures I was doing, the people I had around me. There was all that shit going on with Pet. And there was your mother, and that asshole Swede, and that whole thing.

I was miserable. I thought I'd never be happy again, and I probably wouldn't have been, that's the truth. I probably would have developed some expensive drug habit, or started drinking again, or found some new way back to one of those fucking clinics, but not before I made such a public ass of myself that I became a running joke on Letterman, or woke up in a pile of my own piss or vomit, or was arrested at some airport for carrying a gun through the security gate, or something pathetically ridiculous. Me and Robert Downey Jr., right? Me and my cry for help. And then, when Betty Ford or whoever the fuck it'd be decided I was okay to check out, I'd have been on the cover of People or the National Enquirer, one of those magazines, telling how it was just a miracle that I made it through, thanks to all these good people at the clinic, and to my fans, and to the love of my family, or some fucking shit like that. I'd have to hire a publicist to smooth out my image. Or maybe I would have found religion. Now that's a sorry fucking thought: me and organized religion getting along. But that's what I would've become, the poster boy for hopeless des-peration, that's where I was headed. I was so out of the fucking loop, my agent would have killed for me to be a running joke on Letterman.

Pathetic, right? Let me tell you, I was for shit. When was the last time we spoke before that night? I can't even remember. I was just plugged out. You were off at school. We left messages for each other, but we hardly spoke. I was hooked up with some piece from one of those reality shows on MTV. She was closer to your age than mine. (Shit, she was probably younger than you, now that I think of it!) So there was all that, and Pet was out of her fucking head about the divorce. She hired these fuckwad lawyers who barricaded me from the house. Did I ever tell you that? I don't think so, but they actually had her change the locks, can you believe it? They had her freaked. It was over, but it wasn't over, and it was still a let's-leave-the-door-open kind of thing, but there were all these suits around telling her to grab what she could before I pissed it all away. There was no prenup, I didn't have the balls to ask for a prenup, and they had her thinking she should clean me out. On her own, she was thinking, you know, maybe we could work things out, get back together, find a way to patch. I don't think she knew about the MTV thing, I hoped not, but they're on the phone filling her head with how she needs to make a complete financial disconnect, how I'm no longer a bankable property. These are actually quotes. A complete financial disconnect. No longer a bankable property. I mean, shit. And I look at the way she's carrying on now, I've seen the interviews she's given in some of the papers, the way she's playing at the grieving widow thing. She was on Good

Morning, America, couple weeks after that night talking about how she wanted people to remember me. Did you see that? Jesus.

So it wasn't the money. You can understand that, right? I've got no fucking idea myself, what it was truly about, but I don't want you thinking this was about the money. (I certainly don't want Pet thinking this was about money; I don't want her thinking anything; far as she should be thinking, I'm just gone.) So, no, it wasn't money. I've had no money before. I've got no money now. You'd shit to see the way I'm living since that night. So it wasn't that.

Maybe it was the principle. Maybe I was just tired and needed a long fucking rest. Maybe it was that she let these assholes in to submarine whatever we had left, that she didn't trust it enough to find out, that she didn't trust me to take care of her if it didn't. Maybe it was that even these fuckwad Hollywood lawyers thought my career was for shit. Forty years, I'd been making pictures, and I was no longer a bankable property. They weren't even born when I started making pictures. Pet wasn't even born. What the fuck did they know? They had her poisoned against me, that's for fucking sure.

Then there was this other picture I was signed to do next, this futuristic piece of crap down in New Zealand. We were supposed to begin production in a couple weeks, that was a whole other thing I had weighing down on me. They had me fitted for a codpiece, can you believe it? Me in a codpiece? And there was that book I was supposed to be writing. Did that ever make it back to you? That I was writing a book? Jesus. I mean, I didn't even read the shit my partners had me optioning, back when I had my production company, remember? S.O.S. Shit on a stick. People were always asking if it stood for anything, our production company, or if it was just another actor's inflated ego cry to be taken seriously. S.O.S. That was before you, by a little bit. We didn't produce a fucking thing. I just read the coverage. Once or twice a week, I'd go in and see what everyone was reading on my behalf. Like I said, I didn't read. My reviews, maybe, sometimes, and scripts when they were a done deal, but that's it.

And here comes one of my asshole agents, talking me into writing a book. Said it wasn't for the few million the publisher was willing to pay, but for what the book would do for me when it came out. Said it was just like picking out exactly the right tie to complement a great new suit. This was the analogy he used, and I was in such a fucked-up zone, I bought into it. Plus, I needed the money. Man, I always needed the money back then. The idea was the book would get people thinking about the old Terence Wood again, people in the business, but the truth was, people in the business were still thinking about Terence Wood, it's just that they weren't thinking much. Hah! What a fucking joke . . .

Wood runs out of time before he runs out of things to write. One of the librarians comes by and tells him they're closing up, he should think about finishing. He doesn't know what's happened to the time. It was light outside, still, when he came in; now it must be like nine or ten; probably the library closes at like nine or ten; probably he should do something with what he's written. He's not thinking clearly, but he's moving quickly, and he's taking what he can manage of his thoughts with him. To lose it all now would invalidate the effort he put into it. It would be as if he hadn't even bothered, as if whatever discoveries he's made in the writing would once again be unclaimed.

But what can he do with it? He can't print it out—there're pages and pages of rambling stuff. There's no time. Plus, he's not even sure there's a printer. There's no way to save what he's written on a public terminal, and he doesn't have a disc or any other place to store it. So, in confusion, he decides to send it to himself. To who he used to be. It's something, at least. Some place. He can't just zap all this effort and have it disappear; he's been conditioned to keep what he writes in case he ever needs it, since boarding school, and already he's begun to look on these few pages as a kind of lifeline to what he's left behind. It doesn't occur to him he could just write them again. Shouldn't be too hard to call these same thoughts to mind, especially now that he's had them. They're his, after all. But he goes the other way and, on an impulse, directs the computer to send it to his old e-mail address. He sees this little mailbox icon in the corner of his screen, is where he gets the impulse, figures there must be some way to send this shit back out there. Someplace else. Why the fuck not, he's thinking. At least it's a productive, forward-looking decision. If he ever needs it, there it will be, accessible, assuming his account is still valid. He let it lapse once before for a stretch of about a year, and the Prodigy people didn't shut him off.

He's thinking, they're so desperate for customers they'll even count a dead guy among their ranks, and, anyway, it just gets billed direct to his credit card. If Wood knows Pet and her fuckwad lawyers, those accounts are still open. And if they're not? Well, at least he tried. At least he didn't submit to the electronic equivalent of balling up a stack of typewritten pages and tossing them in the trash. At least he meant to do something with it.

He decides on this course, but then he can't remember his code. It's been so long, his e-mail address has gone the way of old PIN codes and passwords. It all strikes him like some ancient cryptography. He never had any trouble with safe deposit keys back when he was still around, back when that was all he needed to keep track of, but these fucking passwords were always a bitch. Now that he's been so long away from his own computer, from his long distance carrier, from his automated teller machine, the codes have faded from memory. Something to do with the movie he was making, maybe, back when he first signed on. He runs through his few parts, last four or five years, but nothing strikes him. Then he runs through his important dates—birthdays, anniversaries—but still comes up blank. Then he thinks maybe he just used his name, maybe the fact that he was using a stagnant provider like Prodigy would be protection enough from the nuts and fruitcakes out trolling the Internet. Nobody would find him there. Nobody uses Prodigy anymore.

But it wasn't just "Wood," straight out. It wasn't "Terence" or "Terry" or any predictable rendering of same. No, he realizes now, it was Norman's own corrosive nickname—"Woodman"—hinting, as it did, at the suspect superpowers that attach to celebrity, and confirming, as it now does, those suspicions.

Yes. Woodman@prodigy.com. He sends what he's written and he's gone. And back. In no time.

=====

This afternoon at the Stop 'n' Shop, Anita bought Oreos on sale, three-for-one. She bought them for the bargain, but also for the way they got her thinking about Wood. It doesn't take much these days to get her thinking about Wood, and today it was just cookies.

There she was, wheeling up and down the super-wide aisles with the super-wide carts, when the display grabbed her attention and took her back to the life she used to have. And here she is, now, at her own kitchen table, dead solid center in the life that has claimed her; she's tidying up after dinner, emptying the contents of one bag into one of the large canning jars she and Nils use for keeping cookies, brushing the left-behind crumbs from the table into a saucer of milk she's poured for dunking.

Nils didn't understand. Of course, he wouldn't. He joined her in the kitchen to unpack the groceries and remarked at the Oreos. "Tell me, they were giving these away?" he asked, in that way of his. He also enjoys a creme-centered sandwich cookie, but he enjoys them generically and only from time to time. Three bags at once of the name brand needed some explaining, but Anita couldn't find the words to tell how her ex-husband used to stack his Oreos into a tiny tower and flick them, from the top, into a saucer of milk on the table below. The grand finale to Wood's routine was when he reached the Oreo at the bottom of the tower and allowed himself the small cheat of putting the saucer on a chair tucked part-way beneath the table and shot the cookie across the messed table top like a hockey puck. Altogether, it was the target practice of a small child, and it never lost its appeal. The milk would splatter all over the place—on his shirt, on the floor, on the chair legs. Sometimes, Anita would wake up the next morning, and there'd be little speckles of cookied milk in corners of the kitchen unlikely enough to suggest that perhaps her husband wasn't a very good shot. But for some reason, Anita never minded cleaning up after one of Wood's midnight snacks. There was a maid (a tiny girl named Resa, from Ecuador), but Anita couldn't leave this chore for her. Always, on those mornings, crawling on the kitchen floor with a wet rag, looking for the previous night's splatter, she got to thinking how her husband wasn't like other husbands, how she relished his differences. She couldn't think how to tell Nils, her new husband, who doesn't own any differences except, of course, in comparison to her ex-husband, how she still misses the man to whom she was once married, the man with whom she produced her only child. They'd been divorced going on ten years, she and Wood, he's been gone another few months, and yet she can't walk past a display of on-sale Oreos at the Stop 'n' Shop without getting all wistful.

She builds her own Oreo tower, then picks them off one at a time and dunks each cookie between the pinched fingers of a more refined adulthood. The Oreos never leave her hand, so that when each cookie is nearly soaked through, there's still a small section of solid crust between her wet fingers. She swallows them whole and marvels at the contrast between hard and soft, then and now.

Nils is just in the next room watching a tape of today's *Jeopardy!*, which goes on too early for him to catch at its original time. Anita Tollander Wood Veerhoven, for some reason, can't bear the thought of flicking the stacked Oreos across the table to a waiting saucer of milk and making such an elaborate mess and having to explain to her new husband what she's doing. Actually, the thought alone has a nostalgic appeal; what she can't bear is the thought of being found out after acting on it.

Anyway, she convinces herself, like this is better. Like this is basically the same thing, she thinks, dunking, listening to her new husband bark out his *Jeopardy!* answers from the next room. Like this makes more sense.

===

It's late for Pimletz to be working. Usually, he puts in his couple hours of not writing around the middle of the day. That's the routine. Sleep late, read the paper, flip around some of the morning talk shows, sit down at the computer, maybe take a walk, run into town to do his shopping, maybe pick up a video to watch that evening, turn in after the local news. Early mornings, late afternoons, evenings, he doesn't even bother trying to work, only now that Pet's on the scene, his habits are up for grabs. She's got him romping around in the snow, or trying on Wood's old clothes, or taking wine and cheese in front of a fire she's had him build and jump-start with a Duraflame brick. (The fires, not incidentally, have forced him to move his writing station from Wood's great stone hearth to the breakfast nook.)

His days have gone from a string of empty rituals to one of those phony montage sequences in bad television movies. He still accomplishes little, in terms of Wood's book, but he's frayed by the changes to his schedule. Pet just keeps him going and going, and she mixes in a generous helping of spontaneous fondling and grinding. Well, for Pimletz it's spontaneous; it just touches down around him, from nowhere; to Pet, it must be calculated and precisely what she has in mind, but, to Pimletz, it's a gift. She's way into grinding, this Pet, says it gets her off bigger and quicker than the real deal. He's never heard this, Pimletz, but she likes it when he goes at her through his jeans, hard, says the feel of denim against her trimmed pussy sends her completely overfuckingboard. That's her word for it. It's wetifying; that's another one. She's got all these different words for the things they do to each other, for how they make her feel. When she cleans him off after he comes, it's a spitshine. When she pulls him and his jeans down atop her soft naked body, it's another bushwacking.

What the fuck does he care? It's actually easier on him, not to have to worry about staying hard after his inevitably premature ejaculation or spilling himself all over the damn place. Friction is friction, he thinks, grinding, and besides, this Pet's wired in such a way that he can pump at her pubic bone with a thimble and get her off. So it works out. Let her call it what she wants.

She's just thrown him off his schedule, is all. That, and chased him from his cozy fireplace. This last sets him back. He liked the way he had things all set up in there, the way the occasional tap of his fingers against the keyboard bounced off the cold, clammy stone walls like a caved echo. It's not like he got any work done before Pet arrived, but at least he worked at his not working. Now he has to work at his not working when she's asleep, and he has to do it in the kitchen. He shuffles in his Wood-stockinged feet to the breakfast nook and switches on Wood's computer. He's got his own laptop with him, but the great man left behind this monster flat screen with killer resolution; usually what happens is Pimletz just winds up online anyway, before too long. Wood's attorney left behind his client's old Prodigy password, allowing Pimletz to roam cyberspace on the estate's dime. He does this usually on the fooling-himself premise that he needs to look something up on one of the filmography pages he's found, or to check the bios on some of Wood's dead costars, or to make sure he's got his chronology straight.

Once he's online, he's all over the place—not writing, but making a show of it. He's got his nook lit by a lone floor lamp, the rest of the cabin is dark, and as he taps at his keys the color of the light changes with what he's doing. The nook is tinted by reds and greens and yellows, depending. There, on the Prodigy menu, the place goes all rainbow-y on him. Then he looks down and sees his fingernails are blue, the white of his T-shirt lit up like a black-light poster. He doesn't notice the effect during the day with the abundant sunlight, but here at night, with only a sixty-watt bulb, the effect is enormous.

The colors on some of these screens leave the small nook area looking like it's across the street from an all-night diner with a flashing neon sign. But then he thinks it's more subtle than that. It's more like watching the people across the courtyard in his mother's apartment complex, watching them watch television. This is what he used to do as a kid; he used to try to figure out what channel the people across the courtyard were watching from the way the light patterns changed in their otherwise dark apartment. They were always watching something, every night, and always with the lights off. He'd look through his binoculars and guess what was on from the tinted glow on their faces. Then he'd lower the binoculars and cross to the set in his living room and try to find the same channel; the idea was to get the light changes in time with theirs. This was back before cable and all those damn channels that came with it, so it never took Pimletz very long to achieve synchronicity, but he wonders how long he'd have to work through today's one hundred twelve–channel capability to reach the same end. Plus, you know, what if they had a dish? Then he'd be at it all night.

He switches off the floor lamp to heighten the effect, and what he gets back is still more of the same. It's more intense, but essentially the same. There are a dozen sites he can check out before having to start making excuses to himself for not returning to his manuscript, and he means to hit every one of them. There's a celebrity chat room thing going on with that actress from the *X-Files*, that alien detective show on Fox, and it's set for ten o'clock. Pimletz doesn't watch the show, but the actress is pretty hot, and he's thinking he might check it out. Soon he's on to the ESPN sports ticker service to catch the box score to this afternoon's Celtic game. They're in Vancouver, of all places, and he's thinking, Vancouver? It's the Bruins should be in Vancouver, not the Celtics. Next, he bounces on to a gardening site because he's been thinking of getting a garden going out back, long as he's here. He's checking out the projected temperatures for early spring to see about setting up an appropriate planting rotation, when he starts to hear some strange chime noises coming from the speakers bracketing the screen. He's never heard these noises before, but he gets that they're coming together in a kind of tune. It's a tune he recognizes, but can't place. Some sixties shit. Hendrix, maybe. The computer chime reduces the song to a kind of muzak, but it's clear: "Purple Haze."

Pimletz's first thought is maybe the music has something to do with the *X-Files* promotion, maybe it's a way to get people to visit the site, but then he's thinking this doesn't make sense. He doesn't know much about computers or Internet technology, but he knows the song's got nothing to do with *X-Files*. Must be it's a signal for him, an e-mail alert, but he's never gotten an e-mail on this machine before. Usually, he gets his e-mail back in the newsroom; he's got to link up to the *Record-Transcript* on the laptop he brought up with him, and, in those cases, he is interrupted by what was once a human voice telling him, "You've got mail." He's never heard these musical chimes, and yet it makes sense to him that they're a kind of mail call. He's seen that at other people's desks, but then, in coming to this realization, he only gets more confused. He can't think who has his address. He doesn't know it himself. The lawyer, maybe. Must be he's got it written down somewhere, or maybe it's Anita, the second Mrs. Wood, trying to reach out to the third. Could be anyone. Probably it's just a solicitation from the Prodigy people, trying to sell the user on some new service or pricing scheme. Nevertheless, he wonders at the etiquette on intercepting e-mail, figures it's not the same as opening a misdirected bank statement. Anyway, it's not like he's trespassing or anything, or poaching on someone else's equipment; he's here on full authority. He'll just say he had no idea.

And so, clueless, Pimletz closes the gardening page window, and the ESPN sports ticker window, and the celebrity chat window, and retraces his steps to the Prodigy menu. He clicks on the tiny mailbox picture that presumably houses his unsolicited message. Ah. There. Yes, indeed, he's got mail, and, in the beat it takes for it to appear on his screen, he rubs at his legs in excitement.

It takes him ten minutes to read the document. He's scrolling down the screen as fast as the Page Down arrow can take him, and when he reaches bottom, he shoots right back to the top to read it again. It's more than anything he could have imagined. He reads it a third time just to make sure he's got all of it, and then he presses the commands to print it out, and to save it, and generally just to keep it at hand.

Next, he walks to the phone on the kitchen wall and dials Hamlin's number at home. He's dialed it only once before (they don't exactly have the kind of friendship that transcends the workplace), but Pimletz has got the same prefix and the rest of it is the kind of number even he can easily remember: 1717.

Hamlin's out pursuing truth, justice, and the American way, his answering machine tells, but Pimletz is welcome to wait for the beep and leave a message of any length, after which Hamlin may or may not get back to him, depending on whether or not he gives a shit.

"Hey, asshole," Pimletz says at the beep. "It's me. Axel. You've outdone yourself."

Spring

"Pay no attention to that man behind the curtain."

--The Wizard of Oz

Antennae

This Pimletz knows: he knows Warren Stemble of Asterisk Books has been on him for the manuscript, for some pages, something to show his salespeople and counter his concerns over what was to have been the lead title for his fall list; he knows Hamlin's dispatches have about dried up, leaving Pimletz to fill in the blanks of Terence Wood's life or just to leave them blank; he knows Pet has cooled somewhat in her all-over affections, realizing (it had to happen!) that Pimletz might be living in Terence Wood's house, and wearing his clothes, and sleeping with his wife, and opening his canned goods, and writing his autobiography, but that he is not, in fact, Terence Wood; and he knows that Volpe has been trolling for some kid out of Boston University's journalism school to take over Pimletz's job on the obit desk at half the salary and one-third the aggravation and probably twice the result.

This last is only momentarily unsettling to the stalled Pimletz, after which it blossoms into a full-blown anguish. Yes, there are a couple weeks to go on his leave, and, yes, he's got a contract and the Newspaper Guild behind him, but Pimletz does not want to fall any lower on the *Record-Transcript* depth-chart than he already has. He wonders how deep a fathom is, or a league, or whatever measure people use to calculate an abyss. Whatever it is, he can't see covering high school sports or taking personals over the phone.

It's late, late enough for Pimletz to be thinking of things other than the chances of completing his unlikely book project or jump-starting the business he had going with Petra Wood or reclaiming his place of indistinction at the paper. He goes from thinking nothing at all to everything all at once in the time it takes to scratch his head. Lately, when his mind wanders, it takes Pimletz to considering viable, four-headed groupings for the late-night talk show *Politically Incorrect* and wondering if there is any way to make money from this preoccupation. Alistair Cooke, Alannis Morrisette, Macauley Culkin, Madeline Albright. Iman, Pele, Madonna, Fabio. He tunes in, with nothing else to do, and watches with passing interest. The celebrity clusters keep coming to him, uninvited, just as they must keep coming to the show's producers. Surely, it must be somebody's job to put together these panels every night. Mike Nichols, Pat Sajak, Margaret Trudeau, Malcolm-Jamal Warner doesn't happen by accident. He's thinking, if things don't work out with the book or at the paper, maybe he can give Bill Maher a call. He can do this shit, no problem. Warren Buffet, Jimmy Buffet, Buffy St. Marie, Sarah Michelle Gellar. Brad Pitt, Eartha Kitt, Katarina Witt, Slim Whitman. He trips up on the fourth. That's where it gets hard. Three is a walk, but that fourth can be a killer. Robert Bork, Peter Tork, Michael York, Sarah Ferguson? Damn.

He's also thinking, you know, maybe he should try Hamlin, see what's happened to his e-mailings. Been four or five weeks since the last diatribe, a couple dozen pages on the vagaries of Hollywood and the inconsistencies of fate. It was crap, but crap Pimletz could not recognize and certainly crap he could use. At this point, he'll string random words together and see where they take him. Any thoughts but his own, that's what he's looking for.

He picks up the phone. Hamlin keeps all kinds of hours. (Not Pimletz; he keeps only one or two.) Up here, after *Politically Incorrect*, the ABC affiliate has reached the end of its broadcast day and switched to paid programming, but, down in Boston, who knows what the fuck Hamlin is up to? Could be out on a story, even. Or a date.

Hamlin answers on the first ring. "What?"

"What happened to hello?"

"What happened to not calling people after one in the morning?"

"It's me, Pimletz."

"I know who it is, diphthong."

Pimletz has to think about this one. Diphthong. Also, he has to think about directing this call back to where he wants it. If Hamlin gets going on him, Pimletz is done. Focus, he tells himself. Get in, get out. Don't be a diphthong. "What happened with you and Terence Wood?" he tries. "You guys have a falling out?"

"The fuck you talking about?" Hamlin says.

"Wood. Your little e-mailings. Faxes. All that shit you used to cook up and send along."

Hamlin beams. "Oh. Those." Beat. He's remembering an early embellishment regarding Margeaux Hemingway and a large-mouthed bass. "You need another one? You called for another fabrication?" Hamlin makes his voice like a dealer's. "You want another taste?" Then he goes exotic: "My American friend, he is desperate for another taste?"

"The letters to his son, Norman," Pimletz says, wanting to be sure he's understood. "Those weren't just stories. You know, the words. They cut right through me. The parts about how connected they were, even when they were disconnected. You know."

"What letters?" Hamlin says. "What cut right through you?"

"You know."

"This a scalpel we're talking about, or something that has jackshit to do with me?"

Pimletz refuses to let Hamlin beat him back on this one, or push him from the point. "Come on, man," he says. "Don't make me beg for it. Those letters were my book. Wood to Norman. Wood to the world. They were fucking brilliant. They were, like, you know, half of what I had to work with."

"Brilliant?" Hamlin bounces back. He's never heard the word used to describe something he may or may not have written, and he is charmed by it, although he's not sure it means all that much in Pimletz's estimation.

"What?" Pimletz says, sensing he's crossed some kind of line. His antennae are pitched to where he picks up a transgression. "It's too strong? Brilliant is too strong? I mean, if it's all that brilliant, I should be paying you for it, right? You want to be cut in on the book deal, is this what you're saying?"

"I'm not saying anything," Hamlin corrects. "This is all you." What he means to tell Pimletz is the day he wants in on his book deal is the day he shits quarters through his ears, but he's too tired to rip into the bastard with his usual enthusiasm. "You're the one doing all the talking," he says instead. "Do you hear me talking?"

"You mean, other than now?"

Hamlin doesn't respond, and Pimletz gets his point soon enough. "Okay, so it's not brilliant," Pimletz allows. "Strong, though. It's definitely strong."

"I don't care what it is," Hamlin says, "and I'm no closer to giving a shit."

It begins to register to Pimletz that his hard-to-figure friend does not, indeed, have any notion what he's talking about, that these most recent electronic mailings from Terence Wood to Norman Wood have been originating someplace else. But where? And, if Hamlin didn't write them, who did? Pimletz doesn't have any idea or the first idea where to begin looking for one. No one else comes immediately to mind. Shit! he thinks. Shitshitshitshit. Then he thinks the letters could be something Wood maybe wrote and left behind for his kid, maybe formulated his server to send them out on a kind of time-release program. Pimletz doesn't know enough about high technology to know if such a thing is possible. Maybe what he's tapped into is a genuine record of communication from father to son, from grave back to cradle, a reaching out of book-length proportions, the real deal. (The fatherlode?)

The missing piece to the confounding puzzle of Terence Wood's compressed life and times. Or maybe it's just some stream of Internet consciousness, cooked up by some unknown hands, out there, in the ether.

"You're shittin' me, right?" Pimletz tries one more time. "This is one of your yanks?" He gets back nothing. "Hamlin?" he says. "You still there?"

"Still here."

"And this isn't you, these letters?"

"Like I said."

"Jesus," Pimletz says, his voice trailing his thoughts.

"Probably not Him either." Hamlin permits himself a creased smile beneath his aggravation, but then he goes soft. He doesn't see the point in smiling if Pimletz can't see it. This surprises him, this turn. There was a time—just the other day!—when Hamlin could have laughed his ass off at something Pimletz had done (or, more likely, hadn't done) and not given a plain shit if the guy understood his humiliation. And, suddenly, this. Hamlin doesn't know how it happened or why, but, where there was once joy in his Pimletz-busting, there is now shame. Well, okay, it's not quite shame, but he does feel a little shitty about all his jerking around. Dirty. Maybe it's the late hour, or the utter hopelessness of Pimletz's situation, or the leverage he always feels in relation to his mediocre friend, but something gets to him, finally, leaves him thinking he'll ease up, just this once.

"You can source them, you know," Hamlin says, meaning to help, meaning to tell Pimletz there's a way to figure where his phantom messages are coming from. "Like tracing a call."

This is news to Pimletz. Everything is news to Pimletz, but this comes with a banner headline. "No shit?" he says, incredulous. One of the nice things about the computer, he'd always thought, was that you could hide behind it; to go online was to go underground in anonymous search of useless information and idle chatter. He could be a fourteen-year-old cheerleader from Topeka, Kansas, a technodrone from MIT, a Hollywood producer, and nobody could smoke him out. He was like an ostrich in these ridiculous chat rooms; he couldn't see anyone else, so no one could see him. "Who else knows about this?"

"Who doesn't know?" Hamlin says. "Come on, Axel, get with the technology." He refers him to a registration service known as InterNIC, and an internal search program called WHOIS, and he walks him through the commands he'll need to access each. He talks slowly so Pimletz can write it all down. Then he walks him through a second time, and his patience thins to where it's nearly transparent, to where he's about ready to resume his yanking.

"You're sure about this?" Pimletz says.

"I'm not sure about anything," Hamlin says. "I'm not sure why I even bother."

"But this works?"

"Most of the time, this works. Institutional systems, banks, libraries, schools, government offices, you can pretty much trace everything back unless they put a block on it, but most places don't think to block it out."

"And regular people?" Pimletz asks. "Some asshole in a cabin like me?"

"Some asshole in a cabin like you?" Hamlin considers. "Well, then you're fucked. If that's what you're dealing with, you're fucked."

—————

This kind of feeling doesn't usually find Grace, and, when it does, she usually knows to chase it back to the place in her head where other people's wonders don't register as her own. There's just no room for this way of thinking, and, where there might be room, there is no precedent. Her father used to tell her she was built to work, whatever that meant. "Girl as big and strong as you, won't be breakin' too many hearts," was how he indelicately put it once, and the truth of what he had to say became a part of her. She was built to work, to take care of her father, to feed his steady stream of hungry fishermen even after he had given up on them. Lord knows, she wasn't built for happiness.

Always, she sees herself through the eyes of her father and her regulars, Lem and Chester and those others. What she sees is a good-natured, big-hearted, essentially middle-aged woman with too many mouths to feed, too many extra pounds to carry, and too many years in the rearview mirror to be taken seriously in the broken-hearts department. Too this. Too that. Too too too. That's been the way of it, and the way it still is. Yes, still. Harlan Trask can't change it. Terence Wood. Whatever he wants to call himself, he can't just breeze into town and lift her from her life and drop her back down onto some other way of being. That's not how it goes. How it goes is he touches down, and she is momentarily transported to where she starts to think how her life might have been, but it can never be more than a supposition. She has so fundamentally worn through her routine it can no longer absorb change. She reflects it, really. That is about the best she can manage. It bounces off of her, change, and transforms the people around her. Like with Harlan. He comes into her coffee shop and collects her in his reinvention, but the way she thinks of it is she was sent to him, to help loose the cobwebs of the way his life was going, to see him to the other side of what he's looking for.

She wonders at how the same thing can look two different ways to two different people. Forget the way it looks—it can *be* two different things. It comes down to perspective. She could be watching a movie of her life and thinking, you know, this is fairy tale princess time, this is the happyhappy ending, with the way she wins the heart of the big old movie star who wanders into town unannounced, unattached. But from where she sits—at her lunch counter, on her two stools, working her receipts, and recovering from the breakfast rush—it's not that way at all. She's won the heart of the big old movie star, apparently, but he won't cop to who he is. More than that, he won't lift her from the way she is or the way she sees herself. He won't, or he can't, or she won't let him. And besides, the apparently gets her. In the movies, it's never unclear, the way the characters fall for each other; in the movies, there is no apparently, but she can't keep from qualifying Harlan's feelings. He's only apparently fallen for her, and, if he truly has, then there must be some explanation.

Oprah's on. They run it twice, the station up here, only the morning show is a repeat of the afternoon before. The idea, she guesses, is you catch people on different schedules, but they've got it so the times fit right into the two quiet pockets of Grace's day, so she is made to watch it twice, once for real and once on the rebound. It's not so bad. She's got all this other stuff going on, and sometimes she's only half listening, so it works out. You take the half listening from the afternoon and the half listening from the rerun the next morning, and it adds up.

Just this morning, not incidentally, she read in the paper how Oprah's considering ending her long run in the talk show business and moving on to other things, and this moves Grace to think how she relies on her little routines. She can't imagine a time without *Oprah*, and yet she knows from the article *Oprah*'s only been on the air for fourteen, fifteen years. Something like that. First she wasn't there, then she's always been there, and soon she'll be gone. Grace imagines she'll look up one day from these same doings and wonder what ever happened to her old friend Oprah, to her routine.

Things change, Grace realizes, but she doesn't catch them changing. Flowers bloom. Hair grows. Governments topple. Even the planets realign without her knowing. This is a new one on her. She grew up thinking Pluto was the furthest planet from the sun; it was drilled into her. There was even a little poem thing she committed to memory to help her remember the order: My (Mercury) very (Venus) energetic (Earth) mother (Mars) jumped (Jupiter) sideways (Saturn) under (Uranus) nine (Neptune) planets (Pluto). And now she's got kids coming in to the coffee shop after school and they've got textbooks saying it's Neptune that's furthest from the sun. Out of nowhere, without any kind of warning, it's Neptune. That's a major deal, she thinks, for the planets to switch places without her knowing, but it happens. The butt-end planets realign, you'd think there'd be a story on it, somewhere. They've interrupted her favorite shows for far less. The stock market drops one hundred points, there's a bulletin on *Geraldo Rivera*. (She used to watch him too.) But there's nothing on the planets realigning. Then she read in one of the textbooks how they're supposed to flip-flop back to how they were after about twenty years, Pluto and Neptune, only in her case she'll probably miss out on the switch a second time. She'll probably just be getting used to Neptune being furthest from the sun, she'll have learned a new little poem thing to keep things straight, and then it'll be Pluto's turn again, and she won't know until way later. The flip-flop won't make the news either.

So, yeah, things change. Very definitely. But it has to do with degrees. Perception and degrees. Pluto and Neptune don't switch places overnight, and *Oprah* doesn't disappear from the airwaves, and cities don't get new area codes, and Grace herself doesn't connect with this mysterious stranger in such a manner that it reconstitutes her entire way of looking at the world or her place within it. Maybe someday, you know, she'll think in terms of being happy, of allowing herself to grab at something she has not yet known, but she has to get there by degrees so that she doesn't notice. Or maybe she's already there and just doesn't realize. Maybe she needs to look at it differently. Maybe if she looks back at how she was, and holds it up to how she is, she can see the contrast. Maybe this is what happy looks like on her.

On *Oprah*, they've got these three women from somewhere in Indiana, these three neighbors. They started up an investing club and turned a few thousand dollars of pinched pennies and cookie-jar money into a six-figure portfolio. Grace listens to this one woman with big, hooped earrings go on about her investment strategy and wonders if she'll ever get to the place where what she owns could be looked at all at once and considered a portfolio. She's got some money put away in CDs, and—oh, yeah!—she's got those zero coupon bonds Walt Jamesly sold her back when he took that brokerage-type job down in Bangor. She's got her interest in the coffee shop and her little Subaru Brat pickup truck, which she owns outright, but she wouldn't exactly call these things a portfolio. Her furniture. Her big screen television and home entertainment center. These are just things she has.

She doesn't hear the truck pull up outside. She's lost in what she has, and she's not paying good attention to any one thing. Underneath the dissonant noises of the television, and the two Lennys in the back, and the few customers left lingering over coffee, and the general traffic sounds from the street, she manages to miss the pulling up of a big white truck with the initials ATQ stenciled on the door panels and a New York City phone number. She doesn't notice her Harlan pull up behind the truck in her Brat and step out of the pickup and around to the truck bed and start helping the overalled truck driver with his heavy lifting. She doesn't turn her head until the overalls lift the truck bed door and slam it shut, and then she turns to the direction of the noise and sees her Harlan straddling a huge, rectangular cardboard box resting on its edge on the sidewalk out front.

She assembles the picture in her head and tries to understand it. Harlan's got his feet pressed tight against the edge-up box as if he doesn't want it to wobble and fall over on its side, which, in fact, he does not. The driver is back in the lock box on the truck bed, fumbling with tools. There's a ladder in the bed too, and soon he goes about sliding it to the street as well.

Grace is pulled toward the window with the commotion, and then out the door.

"Aw, shit," her Harlan says, when he sees Grace emerge from the door to the street.

"Aw, shit, to you too," Grace says back.

"What I mean," he tries, "is 'aw, shit,' as in, I thought you'd be out at the bank. Or shopping. Usually you're out at the bank this time of day."

No, she wants to say. Usually I'm right here watching *Oprah*, doing the receipts. This is usually how it goes. Thank you for noticing. "What's in the box?" she says.

"Present."

She figured. "For me?"

"For you. For the restaurant, but mainly for you."

"Something I need?"

"Something you deserve."

Good answer, she wants to shout back, the way Richard Dawson used to shout on *Family Feud*. She finds room in her confusion to remember that show, which she used to watch in the mornings before *Oprah*.

Good answer. Something she deserves. "And where'd you get money for a present?" she says instead. "My deadbeat boyfriend."

He smiles. "Been saving," he says, motioning for her to cross the sidewalk to him. He'd go to her, but he doesn't want to leave the box standing on its edge in such a precarious way. While the New York City truck driver sets up his ladder and tools and a drop-cloth, Harlan's job, it seems, is to keep whatever it is in the box from falling flat. When Grace reaches him, he positions her so that she's also straddling the long box, facing him, and then he pulls her close enough Grace can nearly taste the left-behind mayonnaise on his breath from a late morning lobster roll. "Those kids we catch," he says, directly into Grace's mouth, "for Catch of the Day? We hold 'em upside down and sometimes change drops from their pockets and then we clean up."

He's kidding, Grace thinks. He wouldn't do that. Anyway, he couldn't, not her Harlan. "With those claws?" she says. "Those Larry Lobster claws? You can pick up change?"

"One of the helper crabs, Gary, he's working with me on it. Split everything down the middle."

"Really?"

"Really," he mock insists. "There's not much opportunity for those bottom-feeders."

She smiles. They turn their up-close talking into a kiss, and Grace pulls away from it licking her lips and making like she's just kissed a bad lemon. "How many of those suckers you had already today, Harlan?" she asks.

"What?"

"Lobster roll. How many?"

"Just the one," he lies.

"It's ten in the morning."

He wants to tell her they're free, and he doesn't always eat the bread, and they don't stuff 'em as full as they do for the paying customers, so it's probably not as bad as she thinks, but he realizes these are only small points. Anyway, she's not through: "Who the hell eats lobster roll at ten in the morning? Who the hell is s'posed to be watching his cholesterol and eats lobster roll at ten in the morning? Tell me, Harlan."

He won't.

"They're even open at ten?"

"Well, no," he at last allows. "The stands, at ten, they're still selling muffins and danish. Those shrink-wrapped danish from the factory?"

Grace nods to say she knows the ones he means. "But that still doesn't explain the lobster roll, how it wound up in your mouth."

"The lobster roll I get from the kitchen. They're back there at sunrise, spreading that stuff into those frankfurter rolls. Two or three guys, friends of mine, you've probably seen 'em, they're around, they run the whole operation, probably sell a couple thousand a day, easy, but not until eleven or so. They don't wheel 'em out to the stands until later, but I get it fresh."

Grace smacks her lips and wipes them against the back of her palm. "Yeah, well, from the way you taste," she says, "you should probably check the date on their mayonnaise jar." She kisses him again to shut him up a little bit, and also for the hell of it. It's not as if she's spent so much of her lifetime kissing that she can't put up with a trace of turned mayonnaise. This time, when

she comes up, she kicks gently at the standing-up cardboard at her feet. "What's in the box?" she says.

"Ah," he says, a little too theatrically. "The box."

"Ah," she mimics. "The box."

He ignores her teasing and asks, "How lame would
it be if I asked you to guess?"

"Lame."

"One guess."

"Still lame."

"Humor me," he says, defeated.

Grace shrugs, defeated too. "Okay," she says. "One
guess." She looks at the box, and then up at Harlan, and
then back at the box. Then she rests her head on her
right fist and her right index finger on her cheek to indicate deep thought. Then she smiles. "Record album,"
she says, not really playing. It's a joke to her, this guessing. "*Fiddler on the Roof.* Original cast recording."

"Grace," he insists.

"Bundt cake."

"You're not playing?"

"I'm not playing."

"Trask!" the overalls interrupt. "All set. Let's get it
up and get me out of here." He throws his hands up in
the air in a show of exasperation.

"Get what up?" Grace asks, working on some exasperation of her own.

"He's got a long drive back to New York," her
Harlan explains feebly, not wanting to upset his hired
hand. "How 'bout you step inside for a bit, and I'll call
you out when we're through?"

"Through with what?" She looks down at the
long box and up to the door of the coffee shop and

figures out a piece of it. "You're putting this up outside my restaurant? Whatever this is, you're putting it on my restaurant?"

"It was supposed to be a surprise."

"Yeah, well, surprise, surprise." She stoops and starts to pull at the heavy-duty staples holding the cardboard together, and then the overalls step over and hand her a beaten-up X-Acto knife—warm, still, from its pocket—to help with the opening.

"Just cut it," the overalls say.

"Fuck that," Grace's Harlan says, reaching for the knife. "It's supposed to be a surprise." He slides the blade back in its holder and slips it in his back pocket.

She has an idea. "Some kind of antennae?" she tries, unfolding to her full height. She can't think what else would need to go on the top of her restaurant. "Box is the about the right size. Something for the reception?"

He shakes his head no.

"Satellite dish, then?" She thinks she's onto something, won't let it go. "DirecTV?"

"How 'bout it has nothing to do with your television?" he says. "How 'bout we move on to some other line of thinking?" He pulls her to him, but she pushes him away. "This from a girl who already gets every television station on the fucking planet."

"Listen to me, Harlan," she says. She means to be firm, but not ungrateful. No one's ever gone to such elaborate lengths for her before, but no one is refacing her restaurant without her approval. "I can't let you put something up on the storefront without my knowing what it is. On the roof, over the door, wherever. Right? I mean, there's codes, there's the local business district codes. If I'm not in compliance, I get hit with a fine. They could shut me down."

"No one's shutting you down," he counters, quite reasonably. "They all eat here. All those business district assholes, where they gonna eat if they shut you down?"

She smiles, becomes somewhat less firm, tries another approach. "Well, what if it's ugly? What if, whatever you're putting up there on my restaurant, what if it's so ugly it scares people away?"

"Place is pretty scary looking as it is, Gracie dear. People still come. There's no place else."

She's thinking, as endorsements go, this one's up there. Eat here. There's no place else.

"Hey," the guy in the overalls shouts. He points at his wristwatch, throws his arms up in the air. He's big into hand gestures, this one.

"He's a little anxious, your friend," Grace says.

"Trust me," her Harlan says back.

"That a question or a command?"

"Pick one," he says, "but you can let me do something nice for you, once in a while."

"I can?" she says.

"You can."

Beat. She shakes her head. "Apparently I can't."

"Fuck apparently," he says gently. He turns her around as he says this and points her toward the coffee shop. "Just get your substantial ass back in there and start making these people some lunch."

She notices, for the first time, that a crowd has gathered to see what the matter is. It's not every day a truck from New York pulls into town and unloads a huge rectangular box into the middle of the street.

When you add two overweight people kissing and groping and bumping uglies and talking heatedly astride the box it's a rubbernecker's picnic. "It's not hideous?" she asks, meaning what's in the box. "Whatever it is, it's not too hideous?"

"You can always take it down, Gracious. You don't like it, you can take it down."

Oh. Right. She hadn't thought of that.

====

The thing with Norman—on a drunk, or underway—is the zone. He can't think how to explain it, what to call it even. A zone is about the best he can manage, a fold in his universe, a place in his thinking. A fractured pocket of weirdness transporting him to some other plane. How it finds him, he's never sure, but, when he's in it, he knows. When he's in it, in a blinding instant, the whole world washes over him, lifts him in the tide. Transported, he considers himself in his apartment, in his building, in his neighborhood, in his citycountrycontinentplanetgalaxy. . . . Or maybe it's like this: he's on a rolling camera cart careening away out into space, looking back at himself in a rapid-fire unfolding of images to where he is reduced, exponentially, by his own circumstance. You are here! No, wait, you are here! No, here. Here. Hereherehere. Backbackbackback.

Whatever it is, it happens in the time it takes to occur to him and before he can stop to think about it. When his perspective is pulled all the way back, it locks on Norman Wood as an infinitesimal speck on the universal landscape. He's Vincent Price in that great last scene from *The Fly*, only more so. And yet, he's not so small he can't still see himself. He can't even strain to hear himself, calling meekly for help. He's there, a world away, so small he might as well be meaningless, and then he locks on to this one final picture until it falls to static and fades away.

There're sound effects, too: a giant *whoooooooooo-ooooosh*, a sucking sound he guesses is meant to draw him more dramatically into the fold, and then a staccato machine gun trilling, a *chukka-chukka-chuk-ka-chukka-chukka-chukka* over and over until it becomes one sound, one long line of noise pulling him with it, inside it, all around. *Whooooooooooooooo-ooooosh! Chukka-chukka-chukka-chukka-chukka-chukka. . . .*

He can go weeks, months, without locking onto this way of seeing himself, without hearing all this noise, and he can will himself into these folds without success. He's got no control. It just grabs him, unprepared, and takes him with it, and rattles him with its staccato sounds and images and drops him back to where he was, shaking his head. Sometimes, at the other end of it, he has to cover his face with his hands and hold still, he's so dizzy from the ride.

And it's not just when he drinks, his getting this way. Norman remembers these sensations, or versions of these sensations, from when he was a kid, from before he ever climbed on his father's lap to the great, good cheer of Wood's famous friends, to sip from the Woodman's vodka, rocks, no fruit. Out of nowhere, it would find him, and take him, and drop him back down, shaking his head, wondering what it meant.

Whoooooooooooooooosh! Boom! Here we go! Again! Lately, though, it finds him more frequently, this zone, and alongside of this Norman finds himself drinking more frequently, so he wonders if maybe they aren't connected. It happens more often, he's drinking more often, so maybe it's just a boozy distillation of how he sees himself, and the world around him. Or maybe there's no correlation. Maybe it's just something that happens, some cosmic thing he can't know about, some force outside himself.

Who the fuck knows? All he really knows, Norman, is that when he is picked up and pulled back and made to consider things in just this way, he is left in a deep despair, a fold of emptiness so overwhelming he is swallowed up by it, lost. He can't see himself. He can't know. He gets the same feeling—in a sustained way, an intellectual way—when he looks at those pictures from the Hubble Space Telescope, the blue-white spirals of the Antennae galaxies colliding, and, underneath the bursting, he imagines the planet Earth in its own display, five billion years from now, the houses he grew up in all lit up in brilliant colors. He does more than imagine; he actually sees. The *New York Times* finally prints color pictures, and they get these fuzzy splashes of color from galaxies colliding, light years away, and the images alone aren't much more spectacular than the spin-art pictures Norman used to make at Disneyland at those fundraising photo opportunities he used to have to go to with his father, but it's what the pictures *represent* that gets to him. It's what they have to tell him about what will happen next.

He goes out five billion years and connects these pictures to how he is now, not really drunk, not really thinking. The pictures just take him there on their own. There can be a picture in the same newspaper, next column over, of a six-day-old baby abandoned on a Pittsburgh street corner by its twelve-year-old mother, or a story of some psycho charged with hacking up a busload of senior citizens, and this Hubble crap will be what gets him, this notion that someday, billions of years from now, our world will collide with some other and leave everything in a giant fireball. It's more than he can grab onto. It gets him wondering about the point of his being here, the efficacy. He looks forward to the troubles he will undoubtedly face, the movies he will make, the children he might have someday, and they disappear. They fade from view before they even exist, and Norman is left thinking how small he must appear, how redundant. He gets to where he's making a little progress in this area, to feeling like he matters, like he's part of some giant plan, and then he locks into one of his zones and is left shaking his head and covering his face with his hands and not knowing a single fucking thing.

Roaming Charges

Wood has got his sign bolted to the brick facing outside Grace's restaurant. All that's left is for Jim, the maintenance guy from Maritime Merrytime, to run a line from the electric box and generator down in the basement, in exchange for which Wood has promised to make an appearance in his lobster costume at the birthday party of one of Jim's kids.

The sign itself is draped in sheets and bungee cords—Wood's version of "under wraps"—but there's no longer any mistaking it for something else. It's mounted/bracketed into the brick at precisely the spot for a significant sign, occupying precisely the area a restaurant sign is meant to occupy. It's the right shape. It is, very clearly, what it is, and there's no fooling Grace at this point. She's stepped out of the restaurant every couple hours, at first under some pretense or other, but by now she's got it figured. "Not a record album?" she asked, last time out.

Wood nodded. "Not a record album."

"Good, then," she said, turning back for the door. "Good we cleared that up."

He wanted her to ask what it said, the sign, but he didn't want to tell her. He liked what was left of surprising her. He liked that she knew, but that she didn't push it on him, her knowing.

Gracie's regulars haven't been showing the same consideration, but Wood guesses he doesn't really mind. As the work drags, their constant steppings-out to imagine the sign's message are a tonic, a distraction. Plus, he likes the attention, that this is a big deal, that something he's doing is once again something to talk about. Been a while. He hadn't realized, fully, how strongly his being at the center of things had informed his perspective. He teeters atop his ladder getting the wires ready for Jim, wondering what's keeping him, collecting the speculation of Grace's chowderheads, and relishing in the small thought that what he's doing seems to matter to all these people, that the stuff of their days seems at last to hinge on the stuff of his.

"Over ninety-nine served," Chester jokes, hollering up to Wood. "Get it? Like the McDonald's sign?"

Wood gets it.

"You know, like, business is good, but it's not all that good."

He still gets it.

The rest of them have their own ideas.

Lem: "Free winter tune-ups."

Acky: "Fine antiques."

The guy who fixes the snowblowers and leafblowers down at Best Hardware (Wood can never remember his name): "Griswold's Emporium and Shake Shack." Smitty. Smith. Smithy. Something generic.

Joe Scapsi, who claims credit for the place's sanctioned nickname: "I should get a royalty, you put Two Stools up there. Free coffee. Something."

"Tourists go home!" suggests Jimmy Salamander, behind a giant laugh.

"Yeah, but not before you give us all your money!" offers Lem, back outside for another look-see, with a giant laugh of his own.

"Fuckin' tourists," Salamander says.

This is turning out to be great sport to Grace's regulars, this guessing at the sign, and with each entry Wood is reminded of the forces that had driven him from his past life into this one right here. These new friends of his are something, he thinks. That he even has friends to consider is something. His entire fucking life is something—brand new!—but he's never had friends like these. He's never known people who can find something to get excited about in a storefront sign; people who measure themselves by what they've built, or hauled, or caught, or sold; people who keep to yellowing the presentimented Hallmark cards they hand out to each other on birthdays and holidays. He still thinks he can get used to these people. Hopefully. He can get to appreciating people who don't wake up early Monday mornings to consider the weekend box office or think any less of him because he dresses in a synthetic lobster costume to earn his meager living.

Yes, these are his people, he convinces himself, now, definitely, and he's nearly right in the middle of being the same way. In convincing himself of this, it occurs to him he's put about as much of the continental United States between himself and the life he used to live as geographically possible. He hardly recognizes the man he was, the people he once knew, the choices he made. Out there, in L.A., it was like he was being pulled along by a giant momentum, and there was never any thought to where he was going or where he might have to go next or what the fuck he was doing when he got there. He was just pulled along, and kept moving, and pulled along, and just like everyone else and everything had to be up and up and up and bigger and bigger and bigger. He was either up or out, and the people around him were either up or out, and everyone was too busy grabbing at the same prize to even think what they'd become. Here, though, in Maine, he's filled with thoughts of what will happen next, where his decisions will take him. Here, there's no such thing as momentum. There's nothing but time: to think, to argue a small point, to act on a crazy whim like putting up a new sign outside Grace's restaurant. To take up with someone like Grace in the first place.

But then it turns on him, his thinking, and not because his thinking of Grace gets him started on what he's missing, but because after Grace, he runs out of argument. He's still with the here and there, still with the weighing of Maine against L.A., but now the scales tip the other way. Here, he starts to think, the only prize is making the rent, making it through the long, cold winter. Here, he's had about all he can take on the weather; on the merits, in deep winter, of dry heat versus moist; on this new kind of outboard motor meant to start sure and steady—first time, every time, or your money back.

Shit.

"What'ya waitin' on, Harlan?" It's Mike, another one of Grace's chowderheads, on his way in. He hasn't quite got the situation figured. "She finally gettin' 'round to tarrin' that roof?"

"Just a sign," Wood shouts down. "Go on inside. Gracie'll fill you in."

Mike steps to the door and then pulls back. He looks up at his friend Trask. "I'm pretty handy with the tools," he says.

Wood waves him off. "I'm good, Mikey-boy," he says. And he is. Good and charged and almost like new. He's also about as far removed from any kind of life anyone would even recognize.

=

It's not like Norman to be caught dead driving a Buick, but it's not like he has any choice. Guy at the rental counter, a buzz-cutted pain in his ass with a septum retainer showing through his too-large nostrils, said it was a Buick or dick, and Norman wondered whatever happened to trying harder. Then he wondered if he was even at the trying-harder counter, and just who the trying-harder people were, anymore, and if they were even still in business. Then he wondered how it was they were still making these cars—LeSabres, Park Avenues—without his fully realizing it, which went to show him the Buick people didn't exactly have him in their sights, demographically speaking. You know, if they wanted a fuckwad film student to really rather have a Buick, they'd find a way to get him the message. They'd buy a page in *Details*, sponsor a film festival, something.

Car's got like two miles on it, smells like a showroom, and it drives, he's come to realize, like it's out at sea. Like a fucking cabin cruiser! A sloop! He wonders if they even call them sloops anymore. (What the fuck's a sloop, anyway?) He pulls out in this boat of a car and takes the small hills in the now-winding road like swells in the open sea, and this is what he has time to think. The only reason he even knows the word "sloop" is from some fucking Beach Boys song. *I wanna go home.* He grows up on the ocean, pretty much, and the Beach Boys are the extent of his sea-faring knowledge. *This is the worst trip I've ever been on.* Repeat and fade.

Wheretogo? Wheretogo? Wheretogo? Where the fuck to go? Somewhere, is all. Anywhere. Just go. Move. Do. Be. Do-Bee. The fucking *Romper Room* Do-Bee. Christ, when was the last time he thought of that? When was the last time he thought of any of this shit?

Norman's mind, racing, reaches back over every emotion he ever had, every impulse, every thought, the whole of his experience, all at once, and he pulls with it a joke from his growing up, an inside joke he was too fucking plugged in to not get, even back in Kindergarten:

What did Sinatra sing on *Romper Room*?

Do-be-do-be-do.

Kid who told it to him lived in a house once owned (or maybe rented, but at least lived in) by Dean Martin's kid, Dino, so it came with its own Rat Pack lineage. It wasn't just a joke, it was an inside joke, and young Norman knew to laugh at the connection as much as the punchline. That's how it was, how he grew up—on the inside, looking out. His father knew the people who did the voices on his favorite cartoons. Adam West, in a bad career patch, showed at one of Norman's birthday parties and let his friends try on his cowl. The Starland Vocal Band (shit, remember the Starland Vocal Band!) came to his friend Bradley's bar mitzvah and played a memorably painful version of "Sunrise, Sunset." (People still talk about it.) It left him thinking the whole world was crammed into the same front row.

North, he decides. He'll head north, maybe unspool for a couple days in New Hampshire. Pet keeps saying to come on up, any time, don't even bother to call. If she's not there, she leaves the key inside a faux rock she ordered from a garden catalog and now keeps by a post near a side door, with the word "serendipity" boiler-plated into the stone. When she told Norman this, he wondered just who it was she expected to fool, advertising her hiding places like that. Might as well get one with the word "key" on it. "Help Yourself." "Back at Noon." But then he thought, you know, it's not like she's in New York or anything. It's fucking New Hampshire. Folks are a little slower, a little more trusting.

Serendipity, he thinks, driving. Serendipity-do-dah. Do-be-do-be-do.

———

Pimletz is moving now. At last. At least. He's pointed toward the Bar Harbor Public Library, determined to source his dried-up flow of e-mailings, certain he is onto something. He hasn't thought things enough of the way through even to guess what he's on to, but he figures this is enough of a first step, this going forward. No sense tilting the machinery with theories.

Pet said to take the cell phone with him in case she thought of something she needed. She was thinking, maybe one of them lobster roll things they do up there, but then Axel would have to pick up one of those cooler-thingies so the mayonnaise didn't go bad on the drive home, so that would be, like, two things she needed: the sandwich and the cooler. Two things, one call, no biggie. Anyway, Pimletz has got the phone set to Roam now that he's left its home area. He's also got a map and a hardly used reporter's notebook with the *Record-Transcript* banner stamped on the cover all stuffed haphazardly into a black leather shoulder bag he'd taken to carrying back and forth to the paper. He never had any work to take home with him (or, resultingly, to bring back to his desk the next morning), but he liked the way the bag made him look, that the other guys all carried them too.

The sun, setting behind him, seems to light Pimletz's way like what's left of a fire. It's too bright for headlights and too soon for streetlamps, and yet the road is bathed in the kind of dulled orange you might get if you left a handful of candy corns to soak in hot water for a couple hours and then spilled the residue out in the sink. Jesus, this book has got him thinking in descriptive terms. Trying, anyway. He's thinking, burnt sienna. He remembers the name from those super-sized Crayola boxes as a kid, but he can't recall the color. It's not a color he normally encounters, and yet he's guessing maybe this was what they had in mind. This color here, this muted orange in the graying sky. If it doesn't already have a name, this is something that should be called burnt sienna. Or ember. Even better. He's wondering if this is a good name for a crayon color, if anyone's ever thought of it, if there's any money in marketing new names for new colors to the Crayola people. Ember.

Ah, here it is, easy enough to find. The public library. Not one of those strange-to-fathom, mostly concrete structures he's used to seeing in the new-monied suburbs of Boston, in the city itself. No new money here, judging from the library, just a basic clapboard building with a couple not-quite-thought-out extensions grafted to each end. Basic. Looks like it was once somebody's house; there's probably a tub in the bathroom. He leans into the latch-bar on the heavy front door and wonders how it is such a simple-looking library in such a simple-looking town is even wired to send out the kind of e-mailings he's been getting.

Leave it to technology to root itself in the unlikeliest places; but then, leave it to convention to hold fast. Library has still got a card catalog file along the side wall, he notices, stepping inside. Pimletz can't remember the last time he saw one of these. Shit, even the Roxbury branch back home has had its catalog on computer since forever. He wonders what all those libraries did with their files when they switched to computers. As furniture, you know, it's a pretty interesting piece. Lot you can do with it, all those tiny, deep drawers, those hook-down brass pulls. Make for a kick-ass sewing kit. (An elaborate utensil drawer?) He wonders if maybe there's some kind of after-market for such a thing, but then he thinks probably the antique dealers have already picked up on this. Probably all the good card catalog files are already gone, and out there, and refinished, and occupying space in some of the finer homes in North America. The conversation piece to end all conversation pieces or, if restored to their intended use, to end all conversation.

He steps in the direction of a slender, plain-looking woman at the desk facing the front door. She's sitting where he expects to find a librarian, in the manner he expects to find on one, except she's wearing a Patagonia fleece pullover and sipping from a bottle of manufactured water—altogether, not librarian material. Plus, she looks like she's twenty. Pimletz runs a reckless inventory of all the librarians he's ever seen, in all the libraries he's ever been, and he can't come up with another this young, this casual. Oh, there are the students manning the desks at the university libraries he is sometimes made to visit, but those shouldn't count. This one's even got on black nail polish, he sees now, stepping closer, and this strikes him as another first.

He wishes he had a card to give her to help explain himself. He must've asked Volpe about a million times for a box of business cards, but the conversation never went the way Pimletz planned. "What," Volpe usually railed, "you're expecting to hear back from the dead?"

"Excuse me," he says, attempting eye contact and conversation at roughly the same time, a combustible bit of social interaction for which he has never demonstrated tremendous facility. "This the public library?" As soon as he says it, he wants it back. Of course this is the public library. Says so right out front. There are, like, a shitload of books piled high and all around. That card catalog thing. Jesus.

"Last I checked."

Pimletz all but sighs. At least she has the courtesy not to rip into him for being such an ass. "Good," he says. "Thought so."

She smiles. "Something I can help you with?"

He doesn't know where to start, so he finds a spot in the middle of what he has to say. "There's probably a log or something," he says. "Right? The people who use your computer. They sign in?"

She's not sure what he means, but she means to help. "There's a sign-up sheet," she explains, "if there's a wait or something. We only have two terminals. I don't know if that helps."

Pimletz doesn't know either. "And if there's no wait?" he tries. "If there's no wait, what happens, you just sit down and start typing?"

"Basically. We're pretty loose about it."

He considers this, wonders what good it does him, flits back to the beginning. "So if I wanted to go back a couple weeks, see who was using the computers at a given time, you know, six o'clock on a Thursday night, there wouldn't necessarily be any record?"

She shakes her head no. "Even if there was," she says, "I'm not sure I could give that out. I'd have to check."

"Could you?" he asks.

"Check?"

"Or see if there's a record. Whichever you have to do first."

"Six o'clock which Thursday night?"

"No," he says, reaching into his bag for his reporter's notebook and flipping it open to one of the few blemished pages. "That was just an example. These are the times and dates I'm looking for." He shows her.

"You a cop?" she says, taking the notebook.

Pimletz wants to laugh, but catches himself. "Nothing like that."

"A reporter?"

Nothing like that, either, is what he should say, but what comes out is, "You might say that." You know, she might. She did. What the hell.

Her eyes take on another shade. "Well," she says, conspiratorially, "let's see what we can dig up for our friend, Mr. Woodward."

Pimletz doesn't catch the reference. "Pimletz," he corrects.

"No, I meant, as in Bob. Woodward and Bernstein." Beat. "Watergate." Beat. "Hello?"

"Oh," he says. "Right." Jesusfuckingchristalmighty. "Them."

"We're studying them in school," she explains. "Journalism class I'm taking. "*All the President's Men.* The right to know versus the right to privacy." She shrugs. "Pretty basic stuff."

"I guess," he says, wanting to enlighten this black-nailed student librarian or, at least, to move her along.

She disappears for an adjacent room without any help from Pimletz, presumably to look for the computer log, although, just as likely, he suspects, to get away from this would-be journalist who can't organize his thoughts for shit. She returns a couple beats later with one of those marble-covered notebooks he remembers from grade school, open to one of the first few pages. "How far back we going?" she asks.

═══

"It's not even dark," observes Nils Veerhoven, home from two cleanings and an installation, expecting dinner. He twists open a shut window blind. "Who watches television, middle of the day?"

Anita Tollander Wood Veerhoven, for one, and if this comes as a surprise to Nils then perhaps the man is still a few hints short of a fucking clue, as Norman so neatly put it last time he called. Who doesn't watch television in the middle of the day? This is America. This is what people do in America. Plus, the day's all but shot, and it's not like Anita's twiddling her thumbs over some talk show or rehashed sitcom or *Jeopardy!* It's not like she tapes the soaps to watch later. No, she's got a movie going. One of Wood's, one she hasn't seen in who knows how long.

Elemenopee, with Judy Garland as a small-town teacher to his superintendent of schools. Alongside the predictable love story, there's a bit of racial tension regarding a black janitor wanting to send his son to Judy Garland's class, believing he'll find a better education there than the one that's finding him at the mostly black school across town. The picture sank when it came out and since has fallen into disfavor among African-American groups for its outdated depiction of white middle-class values concerning blacks. Even the title—meant, simply, to indicate the middle letters of the alphabet, singsong—was a source of controversy. It stood, for a time, as a pejorative phrase for blacks wanting to pass in white schools, all of which goes to explain why *Elemenopee* is one of the few Terence Wood movies not available on video. None of the cable movie channels will touch it, still, but it turns up here and there, edited for broadcast. Here it is on TV38 out of Boston, shot through with commercials, in the late afternoon, as if no one will notice. Or, more likely, as if no one has. Probably, the guy they've got programming this day part has no idea of the original friction surrounding the picture; probably, he just saw Wood and Judy Garland in the credits and figured, hey, this is something we can put on.

The picture came and went on its first run before Anita even met Terence Wood, and, for years, she's known it only as a regrettable footnote to an otherwise not-regrettable career. Wood himself didn't even own a print, and he kept a copy of almost every picture he made. She did see it once, however, back when it first came out, at the old Trylon movie house in Rego Park on Queens Boulevard with some girlfriends. That's how it is with Anita and the movies. She remembers where she saw them, and with whom, and what was going on in her life at the time. *Some Like It Hot. The Half Shell. Suddenly, Last Summer.* They came with her own story attached and everything else, but that's not how it is anymore. How it is—now, after Wood—is completely different, and it's not just because she was married to all that picture-making and it became a part of her. It's mostly because of the disease of multiplexes and the killing off of great old movie houses like the Trylon. Who could remember they saw *Klute* at the downtown Cineplex Odeon on screen number six? Who could care?

And so, coming across the listing in the newspaper, Anita was too happy to drop what she was supposed to be doing (bills, answering the business phone, dinner). She let the picture take her back: to a time of poodle skirts and unvarnished dreams, to holding hands with Lester Tankoos in the balcony and thinking about kissing, to walking with her friends across the parkway overpass to watch the installation of the great globe on the World's Fair grounds, to when movie stars like Terence Wood soared bigger than life and the holes in her heart were small enough to fill.

Nils takes one look at the small screen and knows enough to wait for a commercial before saying anything more. He doesn't have to wait long. "Any calls?" he says.

"On the machine." She doesn't turn from the screen when she says this. She's working to keep the illusion of what's happening in the picture, to push her reality from her mind, to remember her Wood as he was before, to be astonished all over again just how much Norman looks like his father, to lose herself in what she's already lost.

"Dinner?" Nils says. He doesn't know the rest of what's going on in his wife's head, not even a small piece of it, but the picture comes back on before Anita can say anything. She shushes at him and waves him away, and he is left thinking, how about that? The great Wood, he is here even when he is not.

===

Sound system fucking kills. For a full-size sedan. (Shit, for a rental!) Norman has got the radio cranked full, heavy bass, classic rock, and he makes room to wonder what kind of middle-aged Riviera-driving gnome would even need such a killer car stereo. It's overkill. What, Simon and Garfunkel sound better cranked? Bread? "Baby, I'm a Want You." Baby I'm-a little hard of hearing, so could you just turn up the volume, thank you very much?

There is something incongruous, he thinks, about tooling around in a barge built for tedious old people with Eddie Veder howling through the speakers at full decibel. He makes himself a camera, pulls back from the scene, frames it just right, imagines how it must look to someone else. This last is key, how it looks. Always, last couple months, he's pulling back from whatever he's doing, panning, taking it in from some other perspective. He's outside himself, beside himself. Anywhere but inside. He moves about like he's being watched, only it's Norman doing his own watching, and now he gets to thinking this Buick wouldn't be so much for shit if the top came down. There's a sun roof, but he can't figure the controls, and anyway a sliver of wind curling down from up top just wouldn't do it for him like a full gust of speed-limit air. That's what this scene needs. He wants to listen to his Pearl Jam and have his face and hair slapped around in the significant breeze and have it look like a shot from some road movie. It's a transition scene underneath some frenetic road music. He's on the run. He's happening. He's the young generation, and he's got something to say.

He fishes on the seat next to him for another bottle, but he's sipped through the peach, the black cherry, the citrus. He doesn't get why they even bother with the flavors, these Smirnoff people. They all taste the same, like medicine he can just barely tolerate, sugar-coated as if for a child, and he takes his pulls thinking they must be good for him. The vodka goes down like something he needs, and, with each swallow, he's thinking he needs another.

White. He's thinking, maybe if this Buick were white with chrome runners, top down, it wouldn't be so bad. Or maybe white is too pimp-ish, too overdone. Okay, not white. Red. Cherry red. Or a deep blue. Anything but the mucus green he's driving, and, anyway, the chrome is what's central to the shot. There's no chrome, but he's thinking chrome. He's thinking he could set up the shot so the fading sun bounces off the chrome in such a way that it reflects the landscape going by. He's tight on the car, but there's enough light and shine to pick up all the trees and foothills and crap. There, in the chrome, he'd get the reflected scenery, hard to make out until the eyes adjust and pick up on it, maybe slow the scene down a bit to help the audience focus, but it's distinctly there. Man against nature. Progress over permanence. Like that.

You know, with the right music—hard-driving, no real melody, loud—the shot could do a lot of exposition for him. It could sell what he's about, where he's going, what he's been. It's all right here, the whole of his experience, enlarged for the screen. Or, reduced is more like it. He'd have to leave a few things out to fit it all in.

'Course, there's always the problem with how to move off a connecting shot like this without leaving the audience feeling taken. You can't be too transparent. Norman's always hated those movies where the passage of time is montaged together. The easy cliché is the pages flipping on a calendar; that's the textbook DON'T from his advanced storytelling class. But it's more than that. It's romance blooming. People drifting apart. Seasons changing. They always seem a cheat, a perversion of the way things usually go, so, in his own work, he looks for less conventional paths to the same idea, to move his story without putting his characters through any false paces. Like here, with this driving shot, the thing to do is take the story with it, set it up so the driving goes to state of mind—confusion, loss, disorientation, whatever—and to set it up that the guy's been drinking. You establish it before that he drinks, and you reinforce it here. He's just driving, is all, doesn't care or even think much where he's headed, and then you show him drinking, lost in thought. But then you layer in some unexpected turn. Maybe he pulls up in a supermarket parking lot and climbs out and starts dancing to no music. Maybe he's nailed for speeding and winds up facing drunk driving charges. Maybe he turns around and starts heading back in the other direction. Something. Some kind of kicker to turn the scene around.

He closes his eyes to picture the scene. He has to see it first before he can write it, but what he can't see, with his eyes momentarily closed, is that he's all over the road. He can feel the swerve in the big car, the loss of control, but he's too caught up in his own movie to do anything about it. He feels it, but he can't react to it. Or won't. He wants to see how the scene plays out, but what he can't see is the flatbed truck coming toward him from around the bend, carrying two treated-wood playground sets and leaning into its own blind curve just up ahead. He hears it—the scrapescreach of tires going the wrong way, the loud blare of horn, the stillness in the air all around—but he can't open his eyes to it, not for the longest time.

=====

Well, this just isn't happening. Not in this epoch. It's been a while, and Pimletz has turned up nothing. The computer logs the too-young librarian made available held no leads and no hope that he was even close. Turns out, they weren't even logs, just a couple dozen sign-in sheets, and Pimletz could make no sense of the names. Turns out her name was Evelyn, the librarian, although she went by Evie, telling Pimletz that when you name a child Evelyn, you pretty much consign her to a career in library services. "And you?" she asked, wanting to put this professional association on a first-name basis.

Pimletz doesn't make the leap with her. "And me, what?" he says.

"Your name. What'd your parents pin on you?"

"Axel. Axel Pimletz." He wants to throw in how it wasn't his parents, just his mother, but it seems like more information than she needs.

"Axel's wide open," she says. "You could be anything you want."

"Yeah, well, tell that to Volpe," he says, "my boss at the paper," but then he catches himself, thinking this is more information than he wants her to have. He ha-hems this throat, turns back to the marble notebook. "So, then, this is it?" he says. "This is the extent of your records?"

"Pretty much."

He considers this a moment. He drives all this way, and there's nothing to go on but a couple dozen names he can't place, some he can't even read, and he looks over the entries again to see if there's anything he missed. He wonders what he was thinking in the first place, what he was hoping to find, why he didn't think to call ahead, save himself the trip. It's not like he didn't have a phone, like the roaming charges would have killed him. Then he notices the clock on the wall— 6:45—and thinks back to the time stamps on most of his e-mail transmissions. Most of them were sent around eight, nine o'clock at night, and most of them seemed long enough to have taken at least an hour or so to write (longer, for him!), so he's got time of day working for him. Okay, so if there's a pattern here, a routine, maybe whoever he's looking for is about to walk in the library door and head for one of the computer terminals. Could happen. Could be this person is a creature of habit. That's how you solve a puzzle, right? You look for patterns, routines, and it absolutely could be that this is somebody's window for electronic blustering.

"Be okay to wait for a while?" he asks Evie. "See who comes in?"

"We close at seven on Tuesdays."

Pimletz figures this means it's a Tuesday. He's given up on the days of the week at the cabin. Each day is just another one beyond deadline.

Evie sees he looks confused and offers an explanation. "I know," she says, "like, why Tuesday? What's so special about Tuesday?"

He nods. He's not really listening. He's thinking his next move.

"Well, see, no one was really coming in Tuesday nights, back when they were showing *Roseanne* at eight. Remember, she was on at eight for a while? And the folks up here were big into that show, and the place kept clearing out around seven, and, you know, a lot of the staff wanted to get home to watch it too, maybe have a chance to make dinner beforehand, so we voted to make it an early night." She pauses, to see how this is registering, doesn't notice that it's not. "A regular little democracy we've got going. Now *Roseanne*'s not on anymore, but we've kept it. Breaks up the week, saves some money in the budget. Heat, in the winter. You know."

Pimletz smiles like he was paying attention. "Even just the fifteen minutes," he says. "I'll just sit over there by the door, see if anyone comes in."

She shrugs, puts her hands up palms out as in surrender, as if she's all but helpless in the face of such illogic. She's thinking, we close in fifteen minutes. Who's gonna come in to use the computer when we close in fifteen minutes? It makes no sense, the way this Axel person goes about his business. And with his name, everything should be so wide open.

Pimletz, waiting, wonders at the trip he's made, the extra effort. It's good that he's out, he thinks, that he's taken a proactive approach to his predicament, but then he's back on how it hasn't helped, how he's no further along than when he started out. He could have spent the time sitting down and actually writing, but to do that he'd have to come up with something to say, and to do that he'd have to call on reserves of ability he is not certain he has. It appears, suddenly, a fool's errand, his going out and looking for some phantom e-mailer like this. It seemed like a plan, but, really, it was no plan at all, just a putting off of a plan, and yet he won't move himself off the bench by the library door until seven o'clock. It was a bad idea, but he won't give up on it. True, it was no more foolish than agreeing to do the book in the first place, but he's not backing down on that one just yet either.

"Ding, ding, ding," Evie finally says, like an alarm clock. She's waiting on him just so she can close up and get home.

Pimletz looks up and sees he still has six or seven minutes until closing. "Clock slow?" he asks.

"Something like that."

He gets it. "So that's it?"

"Pretty much. You can watch me shut the lights and lock the door, but the show's basically over."

He is resigned, at last, to his own muddle, and underneath his resignation, he feels hungry. "There a place to get something to eat?" he asks. He hasn't had any nourishment since breakfast. "Something quick?"

"There's a coffee shop down the street, shouldn't kill you."

"You on the payroll?" he says. "High praise like that, should be tough to get a table." He amuses himself with his ability to sally. He's a regular Hamlin.

"You asking me out?" Evie wonders.

He hadn't thought of it, hadn't meant to, but it doesn't seem such a bad idea. Why not? He doesn't mind the black nail polish, the difference in their ages. "This is something you'd consider, having dinner with me?" he asks. He wonders if this counts as her asking him out or him making the first move, in case anyone's keeping score.

"Not really," Evie says. "It's just, I couldn't get a good read. You know, you asking about dinner. I didn't want you to think I was rude."

Oh.

In truth, Pimletz would have thought no such thing, but now that this Evie has put it out there, he's brooding over his inadequacies. He smiles nervously, plays with his hair, worries what he smells like. Must be his breath, done him in. His out-of-shapedness. His uncertainty. The general loserly air around him. He's bottom-heavy with despair, certain he'll never get his shit together in this department. He can't even get it together for a one-shot deal. Last time he went on a date, he wore a new pair of pants and left the apartment with a clear length of tape running down his leg advertising his inseam. The thing he's got going with Pet is something else. He knows enough to realize it's got nothing to do with him. He's just there for her. A distraction. On his own, for real, he's had about no luck.

Down the street is which way? Pimletz thinks, there's left and there's right, but which way is down? South, presumably, but he's too turned around to even guess at south. He starts out anyway, thinking he'll double back if he doesn't find it quickly, but then his eyes are sucked in the direction of an odd-colored light a couple blocks away, a soft green. Actually, it's more of a coolwet, minty green, brightening its section of street like a cigarette commercial. He's not sure his powers of description are at full strength on this one, but he remembers a series of cigarette ads a couple years back using roughly the same color. Newports, he thinks. Anyway, he's never seen colors like this glowing from a storefront sign, and, as he approaches, he sees it's some kind of wet neon. The letters are fairly flowing with this odd shade of green, and soon he is on top of it enough to make out the message: Grace.

The name doesn't tell you what it is—restaurant, New Age clothing store, palm reader—but the storefront itself, with its big picture windows, Good Food awning, and generic Menu dipped into the sill, gives it away just fine. Pimletz is guessing this must be the coffee shop his librarian friend had in mind. He can't see another possibility.

Grace.

Pimletz steps in and finds a run-down coffee shop with missing counter stools and mismatched tables and chairs, and his first thought is the place has almost nothing to do with the hot sign out front. A sign like that, you'd expect less-than-florescent lighting, an espresso machine, fresh flowers on the tables. And then there's this giant piece of astonishment: he steps across the threshold and is met by cheers and applause. Genuine full-throated cheers and full-bodied applause. The people inside are strangely delighted to see him. There are about a dozen customers, most of them crowding around the biggest table (actually, three small tables pushed together), most of them with at least one swatch of red-and-black plaid on at least one item of clothing, and it's as if they were waiting for him. He thinks maybe he's stumbled onto a surprise party meant for someone else. It's a peculiar recurring dream, played out for real. No, no, no, he wants to say. It's not who you think it is. It's just me. No one special. He doesn't know how to respond except to half-smile queerly and move tentatively for an open table and hope these people stop looking at him.

Then, from a back door, there emerges a man dressed in a lobster suit attempting to sing a song Pimletz can't recognize and the lobster himself can't remember. "Be our guest," the suit sings, in a deep, cartoony voice. "Be our guest, be our guest, and I don't know the goddamn words. Da-da-dum, da-da-dum, da-da-da-da-da-dum." The applause from the moment before turns into a kind of rhythmic accompaniment, but these people can't keep the beat beyond a couple measures. It all falls away beneath great, rolling laughter and affinity and the clapping of hands against tables.

"You'll have to excuse my friends," he hears, sweetly. The voice, also strangely, comes from the perfect mouth of an overweight waitress who has somehow managed to arrive at Pimletz's table without his knowing. "They had a bet going, how long it would take someone new to come in. On account of the sign."

Pimletz doesn't have any idea what she's talking about, and his face gives him away.

"The sign," she explains. "They just put it up today. Flipped the switch 'bout a half-hour ago, just after dark." Then, as if it follows: "We don't do much business here beyond our regulars."

When she talks, Pimletz is fixed on the perfect way her lips fit together, on the just-enough wetness she's got going on, the way she pauses her teeth at the edge of her tongue between thoughts. "It's some sign," he allows. It's all he can manage. "What color is that, exactly?"

"You're asking me?" she laughs. "Ask lobster boy over there. Harlan. He's the one made the arrangements." She calls over to him, "Hey, Harlan, tell him what color that is you picked for out front."

Terence Wood winds through the small gathering, struggling out of his lobster head on the way, thinking he might have called his old friend Angela Lansbury for some help with those lyrics. "Some kinda lime green," he says, taking off his mask to reveal a thinning head of long gray hair and a full gray beard; his face, from the costume, is red with overheating. "They had a name for it in the catalog."

"That's okay," Pimletz says. "It's just it's not exactly a color you find in nature."

"Well, Gracie here," Wood says, "she's not someone you're likely to find anywhere else either." He puts his big, red-suited arm around the too-large waitress, and Pimletz gets she's the Grace from the sign and that there's something going on between her and this lobster fellow. (The easy puzzles he has no trouble solving.) So much for him and those perfect lips.

Wood: "The deal is, you're the first one we pulled in off the street, so dinner's on us." He hands Pimletz a menu with his left claw and sticks out his right in introduction. "Harlan Trask."

Pimletz reaches for the cloth pincer and feels ridiculous. "Axel Pimletz," he says, shaking, wondering if the detail that he was sent down the street looking for the coffee shop should be factored in to the situation.

"Think I'll join you," Wood says, not quite asking. He throws his head in the direction of the large table. "Those assholes back there, they ran out of interesting conversation a couple months back."

"Hey, I heard that," Lem hollers over. Then, to Pimletz: "Don't let Harlan fool you. It's him run out of things to say."

The others laugh.

"Watch he don't get started on *General Hospital*," Jimmy Salamander contributes. "You'll be here all night."

Another laugh. Wood thinks, they'll laugh at anything, these guys. Be nice to have to work for it once in a while. "Don't mind them," he says to Pimletz.

Pimletz nods to indicate he doesn't.

"Coffee?"

It's the big waitress, Grace, with a ready cup, and these people have all been so oddly agreeable, Pimletz doesn't have it in him to decline. In truth, he can't drink coffee. It gives him the shits, fierce, but he can nurse at it until the food comes.

"So, Axel Pimletz," Wood starts in, pulling up a chair, "what brings you into town?"

This is conversation, Pimletz tells himself. Guy's just being friendly. He doesn't really want to know, not the whole story. No one ever wants the whole story. He takes a sip of Grace's coffee. "Just some research," he says. "For a book." He says it like it's nothing to be working on a book, sipping coffee, talking to strangers.

"You a writer?" Wood asks.

"You might say that." (There's that line again.)

"Anything I've read?"

Shit, in just a few seconds, Pimletz has left himself exposed, and he wants to rewrite his way from the hole he's now in. "Technical stuff," he tries. "Highway commission. Road usage. Traffic patterns." There, he thinks. That should buy him some time, redirect the discussion. Then he thinks, road usage? He looks over at this Harlan person to measure the man's hoped-for disinterest, but what he gets back is an eery connection. Something in his eyes, his voice. Something familiar. He studies Harlan's face, but he can't get past the beard and the long hair. The eyes, though, they're what bring him in. They're a deep blue, and certain, and locked onto Pimletz like they don't want to miss a move. And the voice, if he could just hear a bit more of it, uninterrupted, he's guessing maybe he'll pick up on something there too.

"There a story goes with that lobster outfit?" he asks, hoping to get Trask talking.

"Is there a story?" Wood bellows, a little too largely. He leans back on his chair, turns his head for Grace. "He wants to know what the deal is with me and this lobster suit."

"Tell him how I caught you in one of my traps and now we just let you out for feedings," Chester suggests, with unusual wit. "Tell him how we're just fattenin' you up for the tourists."

"That's basically it," Wood says.

"What can I get for you, Axel Pimletz?" Ah, here's that Grace again with those lips. She seems to want to sneak up on him.

Wood reaches for the menu with his exposed hand and sets it down on the table. "Just fix us up with something special," he says. Then, turning to Pimletz: "That okay with you? You're not on any kind of restrictive diet?"

Pimletz wonders what the appropriate head movements are to indicate yes and then no, sequentially, but the surprising Grace is off to the kitchen before he can comment either way. He is flustered, briefly, by the exchange, and, in a more sustained way, by the exchanges of the past several minutes. He fills his uncertainty with a sip of coffee. He doesn't know what to do with himself, what's expected, and the coffee is something to bridge the spaces between. Been forever since he last had coffee, he thinks, sipping. He'd forgotten what it tastes like, how it always seemed more satisfying in the smell than in the swallow. He'd forgotten, also, what the caffeine can do to him, and how quickly. Jesus, it cuts right through him. Or maybe it's not the caffeine as much as the thought of the caffeine. Maybe it's all in his head, but now that it's in his head it's also everywhere else. "There a bathroom?" he asks this Harlan Trask person across the table, not wanting to let on any urgency in his voice.

"In the back," Wood says, pointing.

"I'll just be a minute," Pimletz says, standing, reaching for his shoulder bag. "I can leave this here?" he says.

"You don't trust a man dressed like a lobster?"

"It's never come up."

Wood smiles and removes his other claw. Then he unzips the top of his costume and lets it fall to his waist. "There," he says, himself again, just about. He means to be accommodating. "Now it's just a man who was recently dressed as a lobster."

"Half-dressed," Chester adds.

Wood has had about enough of his geek chorus. "Thank you, Chet," he says, "for clearing that up."

Pimletz grimaces urgently and hopes it looks like a smile. He hangs his bag on his seat-back and moves swiftly for the rest room, and as soon as he closes the door behind him, his bag starts ringing, like it was waiting for him to leave. Two Stools doesn't pull much in the way of cell phone activity, so the sound is, at first, hard to source. The ringing is faint, muffled, and it takes several peals for Grace and her regulars to figure where it's coming from.

"That guy sittin' with Mr. Trask," one of the Lennys finally says, from behind the counter, pointing. "His bag."

Wood hears this and wonders if maybe his transformation is complete. Used to be, he'd hear a cell phone and everyone'd reach for their belts or their vest pockets, see if it was them. Him too. Now he hears this ringing, and he doesn't think to move. It's not as if it occurs to him and he has to stifle the impulse. He doesn't think of it. He finally leans in for a better listen, only by this time, the ringing has stopped. Six or seven rings, then nothing. "You sure?" he says, back at Lenny.

Lenny nods. This Lenny doesn't say much; the other one, he's another story.

Mike: "You think someone should go in there, tell him he's got a call? Could be important."

"It's important, they'll call back," Acky offers. "That call return feature the phone company's got out now? I don't understand it. There's answering machines. There's trying again. It's not likely you'll be missin' too many important calls."

Lem tells how he dialed a wrong number once, couple weeks back, hung up after realizing, and a couple minutes later got a call back from an irate invalid who said he had some goddamn nerve making him fight his way across the room to answer the phone and then to hang up. "If you're askin' me," he says, "that call return is for beans. I get a wrong number, all of a sudden I'm an asshole."

Just then, the bag starts ringing again, and before the chowderheads can debate what to do about it, Wood reaches in for the phone. He's not about to hear it discussed into the ground. "Axel's line," he answers, large enough for the others to hear. "Highway commissioner to the stars."

Pet, at the other end, is thrown to her chair by the voice. She's standing, and then she's forced to sit, that's how hard it hits her. She's thinking, after what she just heard on the local news about Norman, maybe she has cut cellularly into some other dimension, maybe what's happened has somehow obliterated the lines between the here and gone. Shit, she doesn't know what to think. "Wood?" she says.

"Pet?"

You Say You Want an Evolution

Hospital. Nashua. Next afternoon. No one saying the word "coma," but each of them thinking it. Wood. Pet. Anita. Nils. Grace and Pimletz, off to the side, wanting to be let in. It's out there and obvious and foremost in their heads, but what comes out is how lucky he was, Norman, the way his car looked, the way the truck driver gave his report of what happened. People talking just to hear themselves, to avoid dwelling on how things are. The swing sets were mostly fine, the talking goes, except for a stretch of snapped rungs on one of the ladders and a bent plastic slide, but the Buick apparently spun and hit in such a way that it seemed to want to swallow the truck. It collapsed in on itself, around the truck nose, making room.

Pet went out to the scene with Nils on the way to the hospital to see for herself. She came away astonished there was even any air left in the Buick after the impact, forget poor Norman's smushed body, but the rest were able to get the same impression from the pictures—that is, all but Anita, who couldn't bring herself to look.

It was Nils noticed the broken glass from Norman's flavored vodka bottles, and, when he pointed it out to Pet, she turned on him. "Say anything and I'll kill you," she threatened. "I mean it."

"What?" he said, knowing what, and that she probably could.

"I mean it, Nils. This gets cleaned up. That's what you do, right?" She looked at him, her eyes mad. "You're in the clean-up business. Clean it the fuck up." She knew she was being stupid, crazyridiculous, that the police already had been to inspect the crash, that the fact of Norman's drinking was already a matter of record, but she wanted to give Anita a chance at some perspective. She wanted her friend to deal with whatever she had to deal with before dealing with everything else. There should be at least that.

Nils stepped back to his van and took out a vacuum and a loose duster. He knew not to mess with one of these Woodwomen when they got going with one of their ideas. They want what they want.

What's also out there and obvious and not being talked about is Wood resurfacing in this way after so long. A tragic accident, a chance encounter, a misdirected phone call, and he is sucked back into how he was, alongside the same subset of people who drove him to what he did or, at least, didn't keep him from it.

Funny, the way things happen. Ironic, funny, one of those. The doctor says there's a good prospect Norman will come out of this okay, the next twenty-four hours will be the tell, so Wood thinks in terms of his own circumstance. He'll have time to get his mind around what happened and, for now, supposes he's been looking for a way back in, a reconnect with his kid, a chance to undo some of the pieces of the new life he'd made and remake pieces of the old. If he's honest with himself (and this seems a good place to start), he can see that lately he'd been thinking it was too sudden, his checking out the way he did. Too extreme. The deeper he got into it, the further removed, the harder it was to reach back out to Norman, to reclaim the parts of his old life worth having. He's never placed his thinking in just these terms, but here it is. It wasn't like the old Wood to squelch an impulse, so he can't exactly fault himself for making his sudden and not entirely thought-out exit, but he can at least listen to the new impulses finding him in this room. He can remain open to his own remaking. After all, they remake pictures all the time out there in L.A., so the notion is essentially innate to his species; it's what you do, when there's nothing else. *The Tall Blonde Man with One Red Shoe. Cape Fear. The Absent-Minded Professor.* Even *The Sons of Simon Pettigrew*—one of his, a western, updated as a vehicle for Angela Basset, Whoopi Goldberg, and Halle Berry, with Cicely Tyson in his gender-bowed title role. Even the ones opened to not very much business are up for remaking.

It's like a do-over, he thinks, a second serve, and he wonders if this isn't where Norman has taken them all right here. Another chance to get it right. An editor's mark—STET—on an unfinished manuscript: *this whole section right here . . . take it out . . . no, wait, never mind, leave it the fuck in . . . what the fuck was I thinking?* It's out and then it's in, right and then not right, and then (somehow!) right again. It can't make up its mind.

He looks over at Grace, not knowing what to do with herself, surprised to be included in this unfolding. He marvels at the places he's made for her in the middle of his uncertainty. He works to understand his feelings. No, she's nothing like the women he'd been with before, and it's not just the way she looks that sets her apart. It's not her delightful lack of education. (In the past, if he went with someone who'd never gone to college, it was because she hadn't yet finished high school.) It's where she comes from, what she's done, how she manages. She works fourteen-hour days, mostly on her feet, makes just enough to keep going, send a little bit down to Florida for her father. He wonders what her dreams were when she was young, what she wanted, if she's even come close. He wonders why they've never talked about this, why he could never share with her the truth about himself, and, underneath the wondering, he recognizes the thing between them was mostly about comfort. Was, is, whatever. There was an easiness to how they were together, once it got going.

And then she went and shocked the shit out of him when the news of what happened to Norman began to filter through the coffee shop last night. He all but dropped this Axel Pimletz's phone. He let out a low, almost guttural moan and scrambled to Grace's rabbit-eared black-and-white, desperate for confirmation. When it found him a few minutes later from the mouth of Tom Brokaw on NBC, there she was, and now everything between them is subject to change.

"A sad footnote tonight to the legacy of actor Terence Wood," Brokaw began, and by the time they popped a years-ago photo of father and son onto the small screen, Grace was at Wood's side, her arms around him in a slanted bear hug, his nose thick with the grease and sweat and trouble of her working. Man, it threw him to have to hear about his kid like that, and, at that point, they didn't have this doctor's good prospect to hold onto. They didn't know shit, and, on top of that, to have to process that the charade of the past months had been revealed, and somewhere in the middle to have to take in the up-close dew of perspiration on Grace's upper lip and not bite it off and have it be a part of him. It was a condemnation of the life he'd quit and the one he'd replaced it with, and an anchor holding him to the new place he'd made, all at once and mixed together. He couldn't think where to put his regretting.

"So, what?" he said, turning up from Grace's compassion, leaving her lips alone. "Everyone knows?"

"No," she said, brushing back his hair, dabbing at the slather of quickly gathered nose run from his moustache. She covered his brow with downy-wet kisses. "Just me."

He thought about this and considered it a good thing not to have to make a serious scene in front of Gracie's regulars; it was enough of a scene to be crying like this, collecting the softsweet kisses of his great bear of a woman. The rest of it would come, he realized, but he didn't want to have to explain his crying just yet, his behavior since he pitched into town. He wanted to keep it to himself. And to dear Grace, bless her big-bottomed, bear-hugging soul.

Then, it followed, there was the matter of how his estranged and nearly widowed wife came to find him on a left-behind cellular phone, and Wood didn't leave it to Pet to explain. He was too flustered to think of it straightaway, and it didn't occur to him in any kind of focus until after he'd pressed the End button on the device, scrambled over to the television, and started wondering if these latest turns weren't being taken by some other group of luckless people, if maybe there wasn't some other plane of existence he might tap into where the choices of the past months had not been made. It was a long processing of information, the inverse of how it was last fall. Then, in the first weeks after his checking out, he had to remind himself each morning of his new circumstance until, finally, the things he had going with Grace and Maine and Larry Lobster and his being out from under had taken hold. When he heard Pet at the other end, it wasn't enough to erase his new situation. It opened a door, but it didn't pull him through.

Pimletz, emerging from the bathroom after just these few moments, picked up that something was happening. His nose for news began to flare, the way it did when he walked in on someone else's breaking story in the newsroom. It wasn't quite a sixth sense, but it was a fifth and change. "Hey," he said, returning to his table, trying to guess at how the attention of the room had shifted, "what gives?" He said this to no one in particular, not really knowing anyone in particular, and not fully realizing it had been about a decade since people said things like "what gives?"

Wood slipped from Grace's comforting and stepped to the table. "Your phone," he said, holding it out to Pimletz. "It rang."

"Really?" He'd forgotten about the phone. It didn't explain the attention of the room, but it was something to think about.

"Look at me," Wood insisted, pulling close, the juice of his various lives by now coursing through him like never before. "You know who I am, or you fucking with me?" His voice had turned since Pimletz first came through the front door. It was hard, flat.

"Harlan Trask," Pimletz said quietly. He paused to see how this registered on the face up against his. "Did I get it right?"

Wood inched closer still. "Look again," he said.

Pimletz looked again, but he had no idea what he was looking for. The other man's face was wet, perhaps from crying. It wasn't raining outside that Pimletz could remember. He looked up, inexplicably, to see if the sprinkler system had been activated, if they even had one in a place like this. He couldn't think what he'd missed.

"You've never seen me?" Wood tried. "You don't know who I am?"

Pimletz shook his head.

"You're sure?"

"Pretty sure."

"And now you've seen me it's not a face you can place?"

He looked again, making certain. "No. Never seen you before." For a beat, Pimletz thought this Harlan

Trask was getting ready to do a card trick with the flowery show he was making of the fact they'd never met.

Just then, Wood made the connection himself. It knitted itself together and came clear. If he had to wait on Pimletz it would never have happened, and he led the asshole his publisher hired to finish his book (it was in the papers!) to a back table to sort through the mess of these last hours. It took a while explaining, and when he was finally out with it Wood felt a tremendous weight lifting from him. First there was the weight that had lifted when he disappeared six months ago, and now there was this new weight in its place, and alongside his thoughts of Norman, he kept thinking, okay, it's done. I've said it. Now I can breathe.

Pimletz, as the situation gradually emerged, couldn't move off thinking what this meant for his book. That was the first thing on his mind. First, last, only. He wanted to flip ahead, see how it would all turn out, where it would leave him. He wanted to summon Hamlin on the cell phone, get the fucker's help in figuring the puzzle. He wanted to call Volpe, tell him to hold the first edition, he had a scoop he wouldn't believe. (But then he thought, well, maybe this isn't one for the paper just yet; maybe we can make more of a splash with the book if we time it to coincide with publication; he was thinking like a business man, as if he had a real piece of the back end, when really all he cared about was being counted in.) He wanted to ask Terence Wood how it happened that he was not, in fact, dead, and what his plans were regarding his autobiography. He wanted to ask about Norman, how he was, what his chances were. In all, he wanted to say the right things, but his skills in this area were never much to begin with, and here they were further eroded by concern for his stalled book project. He didn't have it in him to think what it all might mean for the man who suddenly appeared before him as alive as he had ever been on screen, the man who's left-behind life Pimletz had all but taken up. He couldn't think what it meant for Norman, laid up in a hospital down in Nashua, or Pet, waiting on Pimletz back at the cabin. No, all that floated to the surface was what this meant for Axel Pimletz, his going-nowhere career, the twenty-five thousand dollars that had been waiting for him at the other end, and the thought that, probably, with Wood back in the picture, he wouldn't be getting any more of whatever it was he'd been getting from the man's wife.

=

Pet, on the other side of the cut cell transmission, was left to draw her own take on the same situation. First, there was Norman to consider, but, on top of that, now there was Wood. What the fuck was that? Him picking up Axel's phone? Him not being dead? What? She wondered, is this some end-around, him wanting to get out of a picture? Or not paying alimony? It made no sense, it wasn't like him, but it was all she could think.

She'd gotten used to Wood's being dead, the memory of what they had, the way his star had lifted to where it was. First, it was waking up every day and having to remind herself what had happened. Then it was processing what had happened, and then it was a part of her. One morning, she woke up and it just *was*, and it colored the memory of everything that had come before. Just as the motion picture industry had found a way to set aside the shit work Wood had been doing at the end of his career and celebrate the good work he did at the front, Pet had found a place to put his shitty treatment of her and not have it infect the rest. There was that time, early on, when he brought back some kind of venereal disease from his sleeping around, and Wood slinked into bed, thinking Pet was asleep, and applied some topical antibiotic to her pussy beneath the covers. He was too chickenshit to come clean about it, and she was too much of another kind of coward to confront him, and they moved about in this kind of mutual deceit until they could no longer look away from it. It wasn't just this one thing. It was all fine on the surface, but there were layers and layers of betrayal underneath, to where the surface finally fell through. But now, with Wood gone, Pet had at last been able to shore up those betrayals and return the surface to the top, where everything between them was fine once more. Now, at last, she could look back on his under-the-covers deception and think it was just Wood, you know. It was just how he was.

And now this. Out of nowhere, he was back, and she didn't know what to think. She simply told him her news about Norman as if it was the most natural thing in the world, his answering the phone. *Oh, it's you. Wood. Hey. Long time.* Her thoughts were all over the place, her head a collage of how things were—early on, late, just last week—and how they were just then, and how they'd be the week after next. It was all bundled together, but all that came out was about Norman. She delivered her news, and Wood was gone, leaving Pet to wonder if Wood was so much a part of what she was feeling about Norman that she couldn't separate the two. She had no instincts for a transformation like this, no place to look for help. She wanted to call Anita, see if she couldn't get her to look at things more clearly, but she stopped herself before dialing because, ultimately, you know, this whole revelation flowed from what happened to Norman. As confused and alone and spooked as Pet was, she still couldn't tell Anita about her son over the telephone. She'd have to drive down, tell her in person, but then she realized—shit!—Anita'd likely bump into the news on the television or hear it from someone else, and she couldn't think which was worse, to have to hear it from her on the telephone laced with the news of the born-again Wood, or to have to hear it from a stranger.

As it happened, it was Nils who brought the news home to Anita, and he did so lovingly and with great care. At least he meant to. He didn't know the part about Wood, so he just went with the straight accident account, which he collected from the portable radio in the carport, where he'd been organizing his tools and equipment. He went about it systematically, the way he would a major carpet job after a flood. He wrote out a little script in his head and hoped he could follow it. Then he went back into the house through the kitchen, where he found Anita tidying up from dinner, making sandwiches for tomorrow's lunch.

"Sweets," he said tenderly, "there's some news about Norman, just over the radio."

Anita turned away to steel herself against what she might hear.

"He's been in an accident," Nils continued, like he planned. "He's okay, they said. In the hospital in Nashua." He threw in the part about his being okay. They said no such thing, just that he was taken to the hospital. If he was dead, they would have said he was dead.

"When?" Anita said. "Where? What?" Her head filled with knowing and with images of Norman as a little boy, crushed inside his Big Wheels plastic riding toy. It wasn't her full-grown Norman being pulled from some full-blown wreckage, it was her baby being pulled from a heap of primary-colored plastic. Then she tried to think what Norman was doing in Nashua without telling her, thought maybe Nils had heard it wrong. She didn't question the part about Norman, just Nashua, as if it mattered whether he was hit by a flatbed truck in New Hampshire or someplace else. Either way, it was like she always feared. Since she gave birth, she walked about expecting some great tragedy. She didn't know how other people sent their children off into the world when she was so consumed by worry. Even now, with Norman living on his own in New York, it hasn't gotten any better. She noticed, in among her racing thoughts, that she was thinking still in the present tense, as if nothing had happened. He's living on his own in New York. He's got his own place. He's fine.

"We can call," Nils said, his hand on her shoulder from behind.

"Yes," Anita said, still turned away, looking down at the sandwiches.

And they did.

Cut to Norman's bed in the critical care unit, all of them not saying anything, making room for what's changed.

Wood, finally: "So, like, what the fuck am I doing here, right?"

His wives flash him looks that, between them, could mean a hundred things, but there is no good place to begin.

Nils moves to fill the silence. "Frankly, yes," he says, "now that you mention it."

"And, frankly, who the fuck is she?" Pet says acidly, indicating Grace in the corner of the room. "Your personal trainer?"

Wood's not about to let Pet crack about Grace's weight or the fact of her being here, but he's stripped himself of any authority he might have had over the situation. He's up for grabs, and so is Grace. "How 'bout we just leave Gracie out of it," he announces, as firmly as his position will allow.

"Say goodnight, Gracie," Pet straightlines.

"Pet," Pimletz interjects, surprising himself with his attempt at forcefulness. The others look at him as if he's just brushed his teeth with dog vomit, and he slinks back to his place on the wall. He doesn't know how he fits into this scene, if he fits at all, and he tries to look at his situation objectively. Here he is in the raw middle of these movie people, people he reads about in magazines, and they're all about as fucked up and fucked over as any group of people he's ever met. He's connected in only the most tenuous way, and yet, when he thinks about it, he realizes he is more deeply rooted to what's going on than anyone else in the room will likely acknowledge. They may not be larger than life, these people, but they are life itself—Pimletz's life, at last!—and he sets this out in his head as if it makes sense.

Also, he's back onto *The Wizard of Oz*, the one movie he knows well enough to reference. He's trying to think like these people, connecting his life experience with a scene from a movie. What he comes up with is everyone hovering around Dorothy's bed, waiting in black and white for her to wake from her dream, only here it's not a dream, and he's no Auntie Em or Uncle Henry or whoever the hell else they had crammed into the shot. About the best he can do for himself is the guy who eventually turned out to be the wizard, the carnival humbug on a breeze through town who, for some reason, stops by to check on the little girl hit her head in the storm. He's like the farm hands, too—no ability to feel each moment, to think for himself, to stand up for his convictions—but, mostly, he's like the guy who doesn't belong. He doesn't even get to come in the room, he has to lean in through the window. That's the parallel. He's got no role beyond circumstantial, and he leans himself more firmly against the back wall of the small room, waiting for the others to realize he's got no reason to be here and start asking him to leave. It's only a matter of time.

Grace, too, is wondering how she fits and waiting for it to come up in strained conversation. She doesn't want to press too close to Wood, waits for him to come to her, if that's what he wants. Whatever he wants if fine. Let him play it how it works because, eventually, she knows it'll be just the two of them back in her apartment above the coffee shop or maybe someplace else. His son will be okay, she's sure of it, and his wives will crawl back into the lives he left behind, and it will be just them, back up in Maine, somewhere. She believes this deeply, and, in the places where believing doesn't reach, she prays for it.

"How 'bout I get us something to eat?" she suggests, wanting to get out of the small room, leave these people to themselves.

"I hear you're good at that," Pet stings. "That's why he hired you."

No one moves in Grace's defense, not even Wood, but he does turn and ask if she wants company. She shakes her head no, but he goes anyway. It's like she's got her own gravitational field, this hold she has on him. He hadn't realized it until now, out in the real world, and now that it's hit him, he gives himself over to it.

Yielding, he flashes back to a time in Cannes, a side trip to Monaco, whooping it up with some of the drivers there, and then getting back to his hotel and turning on CNN and hearing one of his new drunken, fearless friends had wrapped his car around a light pole and suffered massive head and spinal injuries. He had a press breakfast the next morning to blow smoke up the ass of whatever picture he was there to promote, but, after that, he hired a car and driver to take him to a hospital in Nice, where his drunken, fearless friend had been taken. In his boarding school French, he managed to determine that the guy was on the reanimation unit. It was the same setup they've got here in critical care for Norman—same basic machinery, but over there it was called reanimation. He considers the difference in out-look. It didn't even strike him, then, but now, in con-trast, it seems such a pleasant, joyful outlook on what it is. Reanimation. He says it in his head in a French accent so that it sounds like something he might order off a menu, and, in saying it over and over, he loses what's happened to Norman and fixes on himself. As he steps outside the unit with Grace, he notices for the first time the stares of the nursing staff. They know who he is. They know there are reporters camped in the park-ing lot waiting on word of Norman. They've made sense of the whispering on Wood's arrival. It's the first time in months he's been on the receiving end of these stares, and he doesn't know whether to relish in them or look away. He's been unmasked, revealed.

Reanimated.

He leans back in to Norman's room and catches Pimletz's attention. The man is wallpapered to the cor-ner. "You coming?" he says.

Pimletz lets his eyes answer for him: *Me? Where? Now? You mean right now?*

"My Boswell," Wood declares, holding the heavy hospital door for the man who might as well help him sort through what's happened, set a few thoughts down on paper, long as he's here. "What, they picked you out of a hat? That how you got the job?"

Pimletz doesn't get the reference or the joke. "Fuck if I know," he says.

About the Author

Daniel Paisner is one of the busiest collaborators in publishing. He has helped to write dozens of bestselling and headline-making books with prominent entertainers, athletes, business leaders, and politicians, including Whoopi Goldberg, Anthony Quinn, Geraldo Rivera, New York governor George Pataki, former New York mayor Ed Koch, and FDNY battalion commander Richard Picciotto, whose account of his epic tour of duty on September 11, 2001, *Last Man Down,* became an international bestseller. On his own, he has written nonfiction books on baseball, television, small-town America, and other national pastimes. *Mourning Wood* is his *second* first novel.